Also by Shirley Hazzard

FICTION

The Transit of Venus
The Bay of Noon
People in Glass Houses
The Evening of the Holiday
Cliffs of Fall

NONFICTION

Greene on Capri
Countenance of Truth
Defeat of an Ideal

The Great Fire

Shirley Hazzard

The

Great Fire

Farrar, Straus and Giroux ❦ New York

Farrar, Straus and Giroux
19 Union Square West, New York 10003

Some portions of this book originally appeared, in slightly different form,
in The New Yorker and in Antaeus.

The characters in this novel bear no reference to any living person.

Library of Congress Cataloging-in-Publication Data
Hazzard, Shirley, 1931–
    The great fire / Shirley Hazzard.— 1st ed.
    p. cm.
    ISBN 0-374-16644-7
    1. World War, 1939–1945—Influence—Fiction.   2. Reconstruction (1939–1951)—Fiction.
3. Hong Kong (China)—Fiction.   4. England—Fiction.   5. Japan—Fiction.   I. Title.

PR9619.3.H369G74 2003
823'.914—dc21

                                                                    2003049189

Designed by Abby Kagan

www.fsgbooks.com

1 3 5 7 9 10 8 6 4 2

FOR F.S.

Parce que j'ai voulu te redire Je t'aime
Et que ce mot fait mal quand il est dit sans toi

—LOUIS ARAGON

The author wishes particularly to thank—
in long affection, and for patient encouragement
with this work—the following friends:

    Christopher Cooper, colleague of Chinese days
    Morton N. Cohen
    Jonathan Galassi
    Donald Keene

                              S.H.

Part One

1

NOW THEY WERE STARTING. Finality ran through the train, an exhalation. There were thuds, hoots, whistles, and the shrieks of late arrivals. From a megaphone, announcements were incomprehensible in American and Japanese. Before the train had moved at all, the platform faces receded into the expression of those who remain.

Leith sat by a window, his body submissively chugging as they got under way. He would presently see that rain continued to fall on the charred suburbs of Tokyo, raising, even within the train, a spectral odour of cinders. Meanwhile, he was examining a photograph of his father. Aldred Leith was holding a book in his right hand—not reading, but looking at a likeness of his father on the back cover.

It was one of those pictures, the author at his desk. In an enactment of momentary interruption, the man was half-turned to the camera, left elbow on blotter, right hand splayed over knee. Features fine and lined, light eyes, one eyelid drooping. A taut mouth. Forehead full, full crop of longish white hair. The torso broad but spare; the clothes unaffected, old and good. As a boy, Leith had wondered how his father could always have good clothes so seldom renewed—a seeming impossibility, like having a perpetual two days' growth of beard.

The expression, not calm but contained, was unrevealing. Siding with the man, the furniture supplied few clues: a secretary of dark wood was fitted in its top section with pigeonholes and small closed drawers. This desk had been so much part of the climate of family life, indivisible from his father's moods—and even appearing, to the child, to generate them—that the son had never until now inspected it with adult eyes. For that measure of detachment, a global conflict had been required, a wartime absence, a voyage across the world, a long walk through Asia; a wet morning and strange train.

There was no telephone on the desk, no clock or calendar. A bowl of blown roses, implausibly prominent, had perhaps been borrowed, by the photographer, from another room. On the blotter, two handwritten pages were shielded by the tweedy sleeve. Pens and pencils fanned from a holder alongside new books whose titles, just legible, were those of Oliver Leith's novels in postwar translations. There were bills on a spike, a glass dish of clips, a paperweight in onyx. No imaginable colours, other than those of the foisted flowers; no object that invited, by its form or material, the pressure of a hand. No photograph. Nothing to suggest familiarity or attachment.

The adult son thought the picture loveless. The father who had famously written about love—love of self, of places, of women and men—was renowned for a private detachment. His life, and that of his wife, his child, was a tale of dislocation: there were novels of love from Manchuria to Madagascar. The book newly to hand, outcome of a grim postwar winter in Greece, could be no exception. And was called *Parthenon Freeze.*

If the man had stood up and walked from the picture, the strong torso would have been seen to dwindle into the stockiness of shortish legs. The son's greater height, not immoderate, came through his mother; his dark eyes also.

All this time, Leith's body had been gathering speed. Putting the book aside, he interested himself in the world at the window: wet town giving way to fields, fields soggily surrendering to landscape. The whole truncated from time to time by an abrupt tunnel or the lash of an incoming train. Body went on ahead; thought hung back. The body could give a good account of itself—so many cities, villages, countries; so many encounters, such privation and exertion should, in anyone's eyes, constitute achievement. Leith's father had himself flourished the trick of mobility, fretting himself into receptivity and fresh impression. The son was inclined to recall the platform farewells.

He had the shabby little compartment to himself. It was locked, and he had been given a key. It was clean, and the window had been washed. Other sections of the train were crammed with famished, threadbare Japanese. But the victors travelled at their ease, inviolable in their alien uniforms. Ahead and behind, the vanquished overflowed hard benches and soiled corridors: men, women, infants, in the miasma of endurance. In the steam of humanity and the stench from an appalling latrine. Deploring, Aldred Leith was nevertheless grateful for solitude, and spread his belongings on the opposite seat. Having looked awhile at Asia from his window, he brought out a different, heavier book from his canvas bag.

IN THAT SPRING OF 1947, Leith was thirty-two years old. He did not consider himself young. Like others of his generation, had perhaps never quite done so, being born into knowledge of the Great War. In the thoughtful child, as in the imaginative and travelled schoolboy, the desire had been for growth: to be up and away. From the university where he did well and made friends, he had strolled forth distinctive. Then came the forced march of resumed war. After that, there was no doubling back to recover one's youth or take up the slack. In the wake of so much death, the necessity to assemble life became both urgent and oppressive.

Where traceable, his paternal ancestors had been, while solidly professional, enlivened by oddity. His grandfather, derided by relatives as an impecunious dilettante, had spiked all guns by inventing, at an advanced age, a simple mechanical process that made his fortune. Aldred's father, starting out as a geologist whose youthful surveys in high places—

Bhutan, the Caucasus—produced, first, lucid articles, had soon followed these with lucid harsh short stories. The subsequent novels, astringently romantic, brought him autonomy and fame. Renouncing geology, he had kept a finger, even so, on the pulse of that first profession, introducing it with authority here and there in his varied narratives: the Jurassic rocks of East Greenland, the lavatic strata of far islands; these played their parts in the plot. In Oliver Leith's house in Norfolk there hung a painting of the youthful geologist prowling the moraines on his shortish legs. A picture consequential yet inept, like a portrait by Benjamin Robert Haydon.

Leith's mother, by birth a Londoner, was of Scots descent. There were red-cheeked relatives, well connected. A fine tall stone house, freezing away near Inverness, had been a place of cousinly convergence in summers before the Second World War. Aldred had not been an only child: a younger sister had died in childhood from diphtheria. It was then that his mother had begun to accompany, or follow, her husband on his journeys, taking their son with her.

And on the move ever since, the son thought, looking from his window at the stricken coasts of Japan. Two years ago, as war was ending, he had intended to create for himself a fixed point, some centre from which departures might be made—the decision seeming, at the time, entirely his to make. Instead, at an immense distance from anything resembling home, he wondered with unconcern what circumstance would next transform the story.

From a habit of self-reliance, he was used to his own moods and did not mind an occasional touch of fatalism. He had, himself, some fame, quite unlike his father's and quite unsought.

IT WAS NEAR EVENING when he arrived. The train was very late, but an Australian soldier sent to meet him was waiting on the improvised platform: "Major Leith?"

"You had a long wait."

"That's all right." They went down ill-lit wooden stairs. A jeep was parked on gravel. "I had a book."

They swung the kit aboard, and climbed in. On an unrepaired road, where pedestrians wheeled bicycles in the dusk, they skirted large craters and dipped prudently into small ones. They were breathing dust and, through it, smells of the sea.

Leith asked, "What were you reading?"

The soldier groped with free hand to the floor. "My girl sent it."

The same photograph: Oliver Leith at his desk. On the front cover, the white title, cobalt sky, and snowbound Acropolis.

Leith brought out his own copy from a trenchcoat pocket.

"I'll be damned."

They laughed, coming alive out of khaki drab. The driver was possibly twenty: staunch body, plain pleasant face. Grey eyes, wide apart, wide awake. "You related?"

"My father."

"I'm damned."

They were near the waterfront now, following the bed of some derelict subsidiary railway. The joltings might have smashed a rib cage. You could just see an arc of coastal shapes, far out from ruined docks: hills with rare lights and a black calligraphy of trees fringing the silhouettes of steep islands. The foreground reality, a wartime shambles of a harbour with its capsized shipping, was visible enough, and could, in that year, have been almost anywhere on earth.

The driver was peering along the track. "Write yourself?"

"Not in that way."

"Never too late."

The boy plainly considered his passenger past the stage of revelations. A dozen years apart in age, they were conclusively divided by war. The young soldier, called to arms as guns fell silent, was at peace with this superior—civil and comradely, scarcely saluting or saying Sir, formalities no longer justified. Intuitively, too, they shared the unease of conquerors: the unseemliness of finding themselves few miles from Hiroshima.

"How do you manage here?" The man had a deep, low voice. If one had to put a colour to it, it would have been dark blue; or what people in costly shops call burgundy.

"Can't complain. Not much to do when you knock off, except booze. No girls, not that you'd want. Too many people doing things for us, and then we're not let out that much. Lot of idleness in this Occupation game."

Night fell, crudely splashed along the piers with bright official lights. Reaching a sentry post, they were directed to a wooden jetty. When they got down from the jeep, a sharp wind billowed the officer's open coat. Now he heard and smelt the sea, glimpsing its black motion beneath splintered planks. Saw, through the doorway of a shed, a metal table and field telephone, and tea in a tin mug: the drear and dented interior that, in military matters, passed for home. Two sailors of the Australian Navy looked at his papers. There was the indifference and slight hostility of indolence disturbed. They glanced at coloured ribbons on his uniform. A small electric generator gave off, in addition to din, a whiff of scorching. Someone said, "Mind the cord."

At the end of the jetty, a launch tipped her riding lights in reflecting waves while these men took their time and the water slid about below rough timbers, charged with the oils and tar and detritus of overturned ships, as well as with more recent victorious trash. Beyond this inland—though not landlocked—sea, there was the ocean. In China, throughout two years, Leith had been in boats, ferries, barges, and sampans, on rivers, lakes, canals. The ocean had not much come his way.

"Yair, well. I suppose you can go over. He's not there, but, the Brigadier. Gone to Kobe."

"And when will he get back?"

"Yair, well, should be tonight. I reckon he'll go straight home. Up in the hills, that's where he lives. Not on the island."

"On the island, can they put me up for the night?"

"All the room in the bloody world. Buckingham Palace on Abdication Day."

Leith went out with the driver. "I'll need you tomorrow. I don't know your name."

"Name's Talbot. First name Brian. Sir."

Together they lowered Leith's gear into the launch, where a sailor stood silent at the helm. Leith, dropping down beside his kit, called, "Goodbye then," and Talbot raised his hand. They were cast off, rocking on a swift sea, breeze rising and salt spray; a night sky starry above marching columns of cloud. The harbour lights drew away, and dim lights of the town. On hills and islands there was an ancient darkness, whose few lamps—of kerosene or tallow—were single, tremulous, yellow: frugal and needful.

"No fishing lights?"

The helmsman said, "Minesweeping." He added a comment that blew away, so that the soldier heard only "Weeping."

Behind them on the pier, Talbot would be showing the book—"His father"—with a slight sense of betrayal. But it matters to have something to tell. Remarks would be made about the row of ribbons: "The medal." In the boat, Leith was silent as if alone. Solitude, flowing cold from the sea, fairly streamed, also, from his companion's back. Ahead, the island grew electrically present in a grid of lights.

In the pattern of disruption that had been Aldred Leith's life for years, arrival had kept its interest. Excitement dwindling, curiosity had increased. Occasion revived an illusion of discovery, as if one woke in a strange room to wonder afresh not only where but who one was; to shed assumptions, even certainties. On the sea that evening, such expectation was negligible. Earlier in the day, in the swaying train, Leith had written to a wartime comrade: "Peace forces us to invent our future selves." Fatuity, he thought now, and in his mind tore the letter up. There was enough introspection to go round, whole systems of inwardness. The deficiency didn't lie there. To deny the external and unpredictable made self-possession hardly worth the price. Like settling for a future without coincidence or luck.

He thought, How mood changes all, like an accident.

Cascades of bitter drops came across the boat. Leith's coat unfurled like a jib. The little riding lights, rocking emerald and ruby, would have shown the man smiling—as a man may privately smile at almost anything: over the memory of a girl or the prospect of a good dinner; at the discomfiture of an enemy, or a friend. As a woman smiles over a compliment or a new dress. With Leith at that moment it was the shared incident of the book that pleased him, the young soldier turning up at Kure with the same book in hand—a long shot, yet familiar.

The engine subsided. They were settling into the lee of the island, which was coming to meet them on a branch of white lights. At the mole, a uniformed sailor waited with a boat hook. The launch paused, plunged, sidled, drawing raucous breath. There was a paved quay dashed by foam and stained by tides—a stage from which a grandiose stair mounted to a portico of angled columns: a travesty of Venice, owing much to Musso. The naval academy of the defeated had become a hospital for victors.

And when, he wondered, saluting the antipodean sailor, shall I mingle at large with the defeated themselves?—what I've come for. For that, and Hiroshima.

He heaved his kit bag out on the flagstones, sprang to the wet ledge, and waved off the boat. Stood a moment on the paved brink, scarcely thinking; only breathing the night and its black lappings.

Indoors, a foyer whose beams and architraves might bring down the house was floored with gritty terrazzo and seared with light. Another, huger stair resounded with Occidental boots and voices, and with the high speech, soft or yelping, of young Western women, astonishing because unheard in many months. Men and women in uniform, all Westerners, were going up and down: active yet not quite purposeful, unprepared for peace. They glanced at the new arrival climbing among them, and women noted a durable man.

When he had registered his arrival, he was shown to a high narrow room with an army cot, a blanket, and one infirm chair. The little room had an unconvinced Westernism: dimensions, door, window taken on faith by untravelled Japanese draughtsmen. The high window looked on a shaft. One lightbulb dangled. Leith's sole familiar was the heavy canvas bag that, resting by his feet as he sat on the bed, took on, with its worn and weighted fellowship, the speckled contour of an old dog: barrel-bodied, obedient.

Having flung a few things on the chair and closed a louvre on the cold shaft, Leith went out again. He found, in an office, an Australian woman in her shapeless forties, talkative; good-natured as her brown wool dress. He enquired for Professor Gardiner.

"He's gone to rest." As if Gardiner were a roosting bird, or had died. "He's been with the doctors, and gone to take a nap. He's not that young, you know, and then he's been through the fire."

"Can I leave a note?" Leith took a slip, wrote, and folded. Asked, fatally, "Are you with the army, then?"

"Oh, an army wife, just helping out." Becoming arch with the heroic male. "Husband's with the Signal Corps. I only came here last week. We were a hundred wives in a little ship, all the way from Sydney to Kure, five weeks without stopping. Well, we did put in at New Guinea, but just for water, not to go ashore . . . Oh, wonderful, my first holiday ever. Morning tea in our cabins, the Chinese stewards, the laundry done. Oh the tiny islands, the ocean. No worries, just to stop the kiddies from falling overboard." She chatted on, five weeks without stopping. "Some of the women hadn't seen their man in four years. Got married as hubby went to war. On the ship, the officers took to us. There was one lass—"

Leith handed over his note.

"So you're the major, then, Major Leith. He's been expecting you a couple of days. Been quite on edge." Her glance went to the red inch of braid. "He'll be down to dinner. They want you to stop by the main office." She thought his eyes, well, beautiful.

A handmade arrow directed him to Administration. In poor light, a khaki soldier of his own age was tapping with index fingers on an antique typewriter and did not soon turn round.

Staff Sergeant Wells, from Ballarat, said, "You never took your key," handing this over on a string. "We never saw your papers."

Documents were examined. "Yair, they told us to look out for you. A room to yourself." The antipodean note was peevishly struck: None of your Pom airs here.

"It doesn't matter, I'm only here overnight."

"Ar, the room's there, you're in it, aren't you." Leafing through credentials, some of which were in Chinese characters. "How're we supposed to make sense of this?"

"The translation's attached."

"What is it, Japanese?"

"No. I've been two years in China."

"Welcome back to civilisation. You've got to sign for the key. You've got to turn it in when you leave. The mess is on the second floor, you'll hear the gong. Meanwhiles, you get a drink in the lounge."

Going downstairs, Leith encountered on a landing the smell of hospital—of military hospitals behind the lines, to which regulation antiseptic soups and soaps were common. Field hospitals, by contrast, smelt thickly of mortality: reek of spilt intestines and festered blood, of agony, fear, decay. His own terrible wound, of which a long broad welt, down all his left side, was fading, had come in the last autumn of war, a year after the episode of the medal. On the earlier occasion, in Tunisia, he had been hit on the same side, heart and lung missed by a filament. "You lucky bugger," said the medical officer who dressed the wound; as if grumbling. The patient said, "Fuck lucky." And the doctor, saturnine: "You're alive, aren't you. You can't have everything."

A war was over, and he had been, he supposed, lucky. Having had much, though not, as yet, everything.

Long and narrow, the lounge had possibly been a dormitory. Furnished now by a scattering of vermilion chairs in false leather, and by an improvised bar, on trestles at the far end of the room, where a score of servicemen and a dozen nurses stood talking and laughing and flirting under a canopy of tobacco smoke; dropping ash from fingers and spilling drink from paper cups. The table was ranged with bottles and scattered with dropped nuts and flaked potatoes. The men were, in varying degrees, drunk. The younger women had unrolled their regulation hair for the evening. Some of them were pretty, and had exchanged their uniforms for coloured dresses; and wore, on slim wrists, the linked bracelets of gunmetal, black and gilt, improvised by Japanese peddlers from the fallen scraps of war and sold to conquerors on the streets of ruined cities. Two or three of the girls trilled and twirled to imaginary music while a soldier, who knelt at their feet, was setting up a gramophone from a ganglion of wires.

That was the scene, for those who might later recall it, on a spring night of 1947 on the island of Ita Jima in the Inland Sea of Japan.

Leith, entering, pausing, was struck again by the presence and voices of young Western women, and by the naturalness of it.

A lone elderly man in a pale suit, cast adrift in an armchair, had clearly never belonged to anything other than civil life: frail, gaunt, small, he looked civility. A crumpled linen man, a crumbled cast of a man.

A young officer nearby gave up his seat to Leith. "I'm just off anyway."

They thanked him. Gardiner shook Leith's hand. "I saw you go up the stair this evening. I recognised you from your letters."

Words, Leith thought, that a woman might have used. "I was afraid I wouldn't get here. Been delayed everywhere."

"I sail in the morning. We have the evening, the night." These words, too, incongruously lover-like. They sat, silenced by all they might say.

Gardiner's pallor announced the cruel imprisonment of three years and nine months. His handclasp was a bone-china claw. Aquamarine eyes were overbright for his condition. Leith had been told, He can't last more than a few months, everything's giving up. Old beyond age, he was only in his sixty-first year.

Men and girls glanced out at them from the twirling end of the room. Gardiner said, "You're awaited here with interest."

"A curiosity."

"A celebrity." Gardiner used the word indulgently: an expression that had come to power during his absence from the world. "Well, we've both weathered it all somehow. I've got tuberculosis, it turns out, on top of everything else. They're giving me a new drug from America, which plays merry hell. Side effects, they say. Side effects, after-effects. Sending me back to Britain like this. Repatriation. *In patria*. But my territory has always been here."

His parents, Orientalists, had settled in Japan long since. Born in Bremen, the father had taught at British universities, become a British subject. During the Great War, the name had been Anglicised, from Gaërtner. On the shortest day of the year 1941, the Japanese government had offered this only son the protection of the Axis, proposing that he reclaim his German paternity. He had chosen the prison instead.

"You call me Ginger. We don't have time for gradations. Ginger. I had hair once, and it was red."

The gramophone broke out:

A hubba-hubba-hubba, hello, Jack—
A hubba-hubba-hubba, just got back—
Well, a hubba-hubba-hubba,
Let's shoot some breeze,
Say whatever happened to the Japanese?
A hubba-hubba-hubba, ain't you heard?
A hubba-hubba-hubba, got the word
I got it from a guy who's in the know,
It was mighty smoky over Tokyo.

Men and girls were clapping and chanting along with the music.

A friend of mine in a B-29
Dropped another load for luck.
As he flew away he was heard to say,
A hubba-hubba-hubba, Yuk! yuk!

Professor Gardiner was making a low humming sound that was not the tune of any song. "We might go down to dinner. One floor. Food's unappetising. My table manners are bad. I've got this tremor—you've noticed, no doubt. Had it since the first war, but more pronounced now. Effects, after-effects. You won't mind if we go at a stately pace, stairs are the devil for me."

Leith helped him up, coaxing the bones together.

A tinned meal was served, by Japanese, at a long table where there was shouting and smoking, like a students' hall, and beer and hard liquor set out in bottles. Gardiner was greeted by doctors and nurses, and by patients in dressing gowns.

"Decent people, but the place is laconic. Surprised by peace."

"I should see the director tomorrow. I have to move into his establishment—a set of houses, is it, in the hills? I've been billetted there."

Gardiner was struggling. "My teeth are the devil, these new snappers they gave me. My own were all knocked in or gave out in the prison camp. Try not to mind me. In the hills, yes. The central house is pure, you know, not like this. The place itself, in woods, is quite beautiful. There's a small valley, deep like a fell, with a falling stream and a temple. The property was a retreat for an admiral when the academy, this building here, was created in the thirties. Now, yes, it's Driscoll and his crew. They've flung up a lot of prefabs, Nissen huts, that sort of thing, you'll probably get something of the sort."

"I need to spread my papers about."

But Gardiner was pondering the Japanese house. "Yes, a fine place. It's under some protection or other. They only use it to dine in. Now it's Driscoll and his lot. Brigadier Driscoll."

"He's a medical man?"

"An administrator of hospitals. I believe he qualified as a doctor."

"And as a man?"

Slight gesture. "They're not liked, Driscoll and his wife. Driscoll's an angry man. Hurt, you know, unsure. Drinks a good bit, blusters. Offensive. People don't like it, of course. Visitors are sent there, distinguished visitors, that sort of thing. Not so much Americans, Americans have their base at Kure, and all Japan to play in. British, rather, like yourself, or Australians like the Driscolls—scientists, historians, journalists. It's Hiroshima that draws them. They come to inspect the sites, spend a few days, sleep up there in the hills. Damp, I can tell you."

A slight Japanese was collecting plates and replacing them with clean ones: pastel plastic plates from the new world, whose very colours—pink, yellow, powder blue—clicked as they were carefully distributed. The man serving was mute, with lowered eyes.

Leith sighed: "Weeks in such a household." Now, he thought, they would talk in earnest. And Gardiner himself put on a pair of steel-rimmed glasses, in readiness.

"You'll be travelling. Be warned, though. The wife looms. A married daughter has just left for Honolulu—you've been lucky there. Two younger children have arrived, a strange little pair—a boy who's seriously ill, apparently, and a quaint little mermaid of a girl. I saw them laughing together, the only laughter in the place. As for Driscoll himself—such people hold the positions for the time being. In Japan, they have power."

Leith wondered at this dwelling on irrelevant Driscolls. "What power, after all, can they have over me?"

"Yes." Gardiner smiled. "I expect you can take care of yourself."

Leith flushed, afraid of being misunderstood as having alluded to the medal.

They leaned back, too polite to be caught taking stock of one another. Gardiner saw an experienced man in his thirties, notable as to build, brow, mouth, and hands: all the things that are said to matter. Pride, or reticence, might be due simply to solitude. He saw a man who had been alone too long.

He continued, "Yes, you're in the clear. Certified as brave."

"Many have been braver. Yourself."

With celluloid spoon, the professor probed a slack pudding.

"You have the certificate to prove it. Though I suppose you get sick of the medal."

Leith nodded. "Nevertheless, I think that valour of the kind will lose its spell. Young people are turning away from martial exploits. If we live long enough, such medals may be seen as incrimination."

"Don't deprecate. You're young yourself." Gardiner said, "This is disgusting," indicating the pudding. "Somebody had to fight Hitler. I wanted to go back myself, in 1940, when I saw they would make a fight of it. However, a secret chap from London came to see me, said I'd be more use to them here. Well, you see what came of that. But you, you're inaugurating your ninth life."

"In some countries, cats are allowed only seven." Leith said, abruptly, "I have so much to ask and am afraid of tiring you. First, I need a tutor."

Gardiner fumbled at a linen slit, produced a folded paper. "This seems a possibility. He's been a librarian, seems sound. He's licensed by the Americans. One can do nothing without that."

"So I've found. I hadn't expected, in Tokyo, to find—"

"A dictatorship?"

"And myself among the defeated. At headquarters I was received by a little martinet, hysterical with importance. He told me that the last foreign visitor to cross his path had been sent packing. He said, 'We lifted his passport.' "

"For a while there, you were in the court of Haroun-al-Rashid." Gardiner asked, "Are you married?"

"Divorced, from a wartime marriage." After a pause, he went on, "We were married in Cairo. Then I was off in the desert and she was posted to Colombo. Time went by, we could scarcely meet. She found someone else. So, for a while, did I. We assumed we'd grown apart—a usual thing. She wanted to remarry. When we met in London, the spring of '45, to arrange the divorce, it seemed for a moment that we might have managed it after all. Too late then, peace was sweeping us away." He had scarcely thought of these things in two years. It was vivid, however, that single final day spent in London seeing lawyers, walking away together in the wet park, and at last making love in a hired room. The hotel, small and decent, had made no difficulty: their passports were those, still, of husband and wife. Oh, Moira, he'd said, our sad story. And she had shed silent tears not intended to change things. Her arched throat and spread hair, and the day dying in the wet window. The marriage was dissolved, evaporating along with its memories and meetings, and the partings of war; the letters increasingly laboured, the thoughts, kisses, regrets. The lawyers were paid. The true marriage, indissoluble, was simply the moment when they sat on the rented bed and grieved for a fatality older than love.

Gardiner said, "You know about my wife?"

Leith nodded. "I've had no such loss as yours."

"I didn't know for a year. Not until they taunted me in the camp."

His Japanese wife, having tried to join him in prison, had been declared destitute by the authorities, and renounced by her parents. In 1943, she committed suicide. Gardiner said, "On the day of her death, she tried to send into safekeeping some copies of my early books, from the time when we first knew one another. All she had left, my poor girl." He said, "You keep returning to these things. You can't close them down, as one closes down the compartment of a damaged ship, just to keep the vessel going, or at least afloat." He said, "This difficulty of being."

"One reason men go on fighting is that it seems to simplify."

"You've done that, and know better. And are young yet. Experience will reclaim you through the personal, much more will happen for you. After much death, living may come as a surprise."

He means love, thought Leith forbearingly. He sometimes thought the same thing himself, and with the same forbearance. The evening was seeping away, Gardiner was dwindling. The proposed discussions of the night, the shared accident of Asia, receded, and he could not revive the importance he had given them.

Gardiner said, "My room's got two chairs. We'd be private there." When they had climbed back to the lounge, however, he said, "Better sit a moment."

It was the long room again, and the gramophone bawling. The remaining drinkers sprawled, morose, on red chairs; and one floral woman continued to twirl, slowly, alone, a top winding down.

Sweetheart, if you should stray
A million miles away
I'll always be in love with you . . .

Leith drew up a bamboo divan and helped Gardiner into it. Gardiner said, "It was the stairs."

"I'll get you a shot of something."

He came back with brandy. The professor was listing in his bamboo chair: an old pallid man who said, "Be right in a minute," whose fingers could not hold the paper cup. Whose colour and texture were that of old bread. Aldred Leith took his hand, saying "Ginger."

Ginger said, "Sorry. Regrets, many . . ." and "Thanks for all."

Leith was crouching by the sofa. An officer wearing red tabs came up and knelt, too. Someone lifted the needle off the raucous record, making it squeal.

2

IN THE CRYSTAL MORNING, Leith was driving with Talbot into green hills: discarding the exploded dockland, winding around ledges of emerald rice. They stopped the jeep on a spur, jumping down among tough grasses to look out at sea and islands and to watch, some moments, the small white departing ship, elderly, simple, and shapely, that would have carried Gardiner to Hong Kong on the first leg of his deleted journey. Men and women are said to grow young again in death, but Gardiner, his snappers removed, his slack jaw bound up forever, had appeared immeasurably withered on the night of his death. The little ship, sailing to its appointments, passed among islands all glorious with morning, on a blue course channelled by minesweepers. The man watching was aware of Japanese grasses beneath his boots—of earth and gravel and of stunted shrubbery trembling nearby. There were tufted wildflowers and specks of red and purple that might be speedwell or some odder saxifrage. He was aware of the reprieve.

From a distance, on an outer ledge of terraced rice, his fellow man looked back at him: a single figure wearing a hat of conical straw and a red shift that came to his knees.

The young driver, profiting from the hiatus, had meanwhile peed behind bushes. When they resumed the ride, with Leith at the wheel, Talbot remarked, "I don't suppose you got much sleep."

"A couple of hours. Not that there was much to do for him, poor chap."

"Rough on you, starting out with that."

"With a death, you mean—a bad augury? Well, one was there. No one else really knew who he was. It was another war death, deferred." Side effects, after-effects. This time yesterday I hadn't met him. Today he's dead, and I'm his only mourner.

They had churned into wooded country.

"Pines, are they?" asked the boy, indifferent.

"These are cedars, these tall ones. Pines are up there, on the right."

"We weren't taught about trees. At Sydney it was gum trees and Moreton Bays." Bushes of wattle, bottlebrush. "Soil's sandy." Then, "We heard more about British trees, from the songs and books: Hearts of Oak, beeches, birches. How green and wet they are, and how they play for dead in winter. Seemed more spectacular than the gums and the Bush."

Leith said, "My home, if I have one, is near the North Sea. Bleak country in winter, the wind sweeping over, and the sleet. Bitter, solitary. Where I am, it's not forested, although there are stands of trees, nurtured. It has its beauty."

"How's that?"

"Oh—changing lights and skies, and the low land. Sense of separation, almost from terra firma." He laughed. "Away from it, as I've mostly been, I can become sentimental." He noticed how often he qualified the reference to home: If I have one; I'm mostly away.

Brian Talbot said, "I'd like to see places before I settle down." The settling taken for granted. Down, down. The wife and kiddies, the house and mortgage, the lawn and lawnmower, the car. "I suppose being here is a start." He was not really convinced that these uncongenial scenes, and these impenetrable people—tireless, humorless, reclusive—could meet the case.

Thought made him vulnerable. That was the Australian way: say anything out of the ordinary and there was the laugh—the good laugh, not having much to do with goodness. You had to watch yourself. But you got curious, all the same. And then, Leith was not likely to take advantage.

"You won't need war now, Talbot, to see the world—hardship, maybe, but not slaughter. Until this, war has been the way out, for most men." Soldiering, or seamanship. Young recruits with their dreams of transformation: of conquest, plunder, fornication. Even, in some, the dream of knowledge. Inconceivable, in advance, the red mess and shallow grave.

Women's yearnings had scarcely featured, being presumably of mating and giving birth. Their purpose had been supplied to them from the first: *their lot*. A woman who broke ranks was ostracised by other women. Rocking the boat instead of the cradle.

The wheels threw up dirt and noisy gravel. Labourers passed them in pairs and foursomes, all moving downhill, all bearing burdens; each falling silent as the car approached, not meeting glances from these invulnerable strangers in their well-fed uniforms. Wrapped in shabby darkness, women came shuffling, one with a great bundle of kindling on her back, another hooped under a strapped child.

The man thought, Their *lot*. A brute word.

He said, "It's the devil, Talbot."

Talbot looked at the roadside. He hadn't expected this contest, continual, between a decreed strength and the nagging humanity of things. Any show of softness would bring, from his companions, the good laugh—to shut him up, perhaps, they being baffled as he. Yet the man at the wheel felt it, too—who, with his coloured ribbons and great medal, couldn't be accused. Talbot had been told that this warrior, though wounded and captured, had escaped his prison and fought again in the last winter of the European war. So the story went, anyway, and some of it plainly true. Straightforward matters you could understand.

"You speak the lingo. Sir."

"I've made a beginning. My languages are from China, where I was a schoolboy. Here, I need a teacher." That morning, at Kure, he had called on the tutor recommended by Gardiner.

Talbot looked at his own hands, which were spread on his knees. Young hands, seemingly unveined, broad, supple, modestly capable, and with decent nails. He compared them with his companion's, resting on the wheel: brown, definite, broad in the palm, and long-fingered; like the man, experienced. By extension of impressions, Brian would have liked to ask, Do you have a wife, a girl? But refrained.

Leith said, "The teacher, this morning. You saw him, elderly, respectable. If I were to get up a small class with him—depending on what I find here—would you care to join in? A few hours a week; I'd square it with your outfit, I think I could do that."

It was too much like having your bluff called. Brian, hedging, said, "But you—you're already halfway there. You know a lot of it."

"I'll be seeing him more often, he'll probably come to me up here. In your case it would be separate, with a few of your chaps if they care to join. That would be down in Kure, near your quarters." Leith said, "Think it over."

The boy's impulse was to withdraw. It was too outlandish, and too much trouble. You despised Japs, you ridiculed and killed them. They'd behaved like animals. You didn't learn their lingo. You didn't study any language, even your own. He'd done a bit of French at school, compulsory: *Je m'appelle Brian, donnez-moi à manger, je suis né en Australie. Donnez-moi à boire.* Arriving at Kure, he'd been given a Japanese phrase book got up for Occupation forces; but had no use for it. "Well, thanks. Well, yair, I'll see about it. Let you know."

He could imagine the hoots of his mates. Yet knew that, to them, he would defend the idea.

He asked, "Ar—what would this . . . ?"

"I'll take care of that, it won't be much." Leith thought of the teacher, on his beam ends.

"Your shout, then?"

"My shout."

They drove on, less contented. Another mile or two and they'd arrive.

BRIGADIER DRISCOLL was coming from the pond. In youth an athlete, Driscoll continued to hold himself in past tension, barrelled against every challenge. Wet and near naked, his body was corded by evidence of past exploits, muscles and sinews pushing up through tissue, as roots of an old tree might displace a pavement—the impression confirmed by a trunkish neck, seared by pale creases. On head, chest, limbs, the curled hair was grey.

Driscoll cried out, "Dench"—loudly, although the uniformed subordinate was by his side. Dench, a small man, had already registered the approach of Aldred Leith. Mumbling at Driscoll's ear, Dench let his glance wander on the stones and beaten earth of the path, among clustered azaleas, on a Nissen hut in the trees. Throughout the coming months of their acquaintance, Captain Dench never did look Major Leith in the eye.

Driscoll stood. The expression "stock-still" might have originated with him. Driscoll said, "Fresh water," and, as Leith came up, began to towel himself, currying with circular vigour the matted hair of chest and head. "Never drank it. Never thought I'd swim in it." Blew out his cheeks and spat. Under fizzing brows, the splenetic stare. "Beats their flaming bathhouse, at any rate." He told Leith, "In Australia, we have the ocean."

Leith agreed. "Very lucky."

"Too right there." Buried his face in the rough stripes of the towel, hands pressed to eyes. "Luckiest in the world." The two men walked on. Dench, a sallow phantom, followed, coughing. "You're Leith, are you. You just made it for lunch." He said, "We don't wait."

Leith was looking at a house among trees: the house, clearly, that Gardiner had praised. He had nearly forgotten the Driscolls, to whom Gardiner had attached a sense of struggle and whose impulse to resentment he did not understand. It would be pleasant, now, to see the house and, as he discovered, its enclosed garden, coming into view: a small plane of pebbles, into which a man in black was working concentric patterns with a long-handled brush.

They stood at the negligible threshold.

"You've seen your quarters."

"Yes."

"We had those plywood jobs put up right off. Bit of a walk down there, but you've got your comforts. We use this place once in a while as a mess. A bit of local colour. We like to be congenial." Driscoll broke off to shout, "Melb! Over here."

In red rayon, his wife was arriving.

Mrs. Driscoll was of middling height only, an illusory tallness being created by her large forcible head and martial shoulders, and by fluffed white hair that, upswept, made its contribution. Behind spectacles, at the centre of a thick lens, the eye shone, small, animate, and marble. To Leith, who went forward putting out his hand, she said, "I'm sorry for you." A piping voice, active with falsity. "Arriving on such a humid day. We're just going to table. We put in a proper table, we don't eat off the floor. But I suppose you like things to be Japanese."

"I have no preference."

"I'm a decisive person myself."

As yet immune to her, Leith waited to perceive her effect. Driscoll himself, while maintaining drilled belligerence, showed some loss of patina. A partnership, but not an equal one.

Dench had come back, carrying military clothing on a coat hanger.

Melba was saying, "We don't wait. We don't stand on ceremony here, no matter who. The parliamentary delegation left on Friday, now it's the university lot. To us, they're just people."

With Dench's help, Driscoll was struggling into his clothes.

Leith was weighing the possibility of rooms in the town.

The woman said, "We don't go in for conversation here: we like plain talk. We Australians are easygoing."

Driscoll put in, "We're a good-natured lot. Have our faults, like the rest of you. But the old heart's in the right place."

Beyond its partitions, the house opened on the garden of placed rocks and stunted trees. There was no view, or sense, of woods, hills, or far-off sea: distance had been conjured, and enclosed.

"Their awful gardens."

He'd forgotten her.

There was a small commotion of greeting, and Western men were seating themselves at a table. Finding a place on the long bench, Leith was relieved at the sight of a burly scholar he had met in Nanking, a historian named Calder—who, changing place, came to sit beside him, perhaps with a similar sense of deliverance. A short taste of Driscolls engendered solidarity.

Calder said, "So you got here."

"And just in time, I'm told."

Someone murmured, "We don't wait," and there was clandestine laughter, like school. At each end of the longish table, a Driscoll kept watch. Barry Driscoll was telling that he preferred dogs to cats any day, read real books rather than novels, and thought opera a joke. As Gardiner had said, the Driscolls were disquieting as a symptom of new power: that Melba and Barry should be in the ascendant was not what one had hoped from peace. It did not even seem a cessation of hostilities.

They had grasped, eagerly enough, at a future as yet unrevealed to Leith and to what they would have called his kind.

There was beer, and sake in tiny cups. Dishes had been set out, tea was poured, and flowers floated in a bowl. Two women in kimono, possibly mother and daughter, slipped about, providing and removing. The girl was extremely slight, in body nearly a child; her unobtrusiveness so notable that one watched to see how it was done. The older woman's face was a tissue of wrinkles, expressionless. There was also a young man in dark Japanese dress, who came and went and was seemingly in charge.

Calder told Leith that the youth had been partly educated in England, son of an ambassador or a minister of legation. Brought here to act as interpreter, he had become a sort of *maggiordomo*: "God knows what he's thinking."

Opposite, there had arrived a boy of indeterminate youth, a Westerner to whom the serving women gave soft attentions—he in turn addressing them in unpractised words of their language, little beak aloft; then looking around the company with bright dispassionate eyes. Beneath a rick of fair hair, the face was triangular. In sunless skin, the lips, unexpectedly full, made strokes of mobility and colour. There was special food for him, and difficulty in eating it. The boy, hunched and angular, was afflicted by some abnormality. On this theme, too, Leith recalled the words of Gardiner.

Gardiner who, yesterday at that hour, had been alive, awaiting him. Who was proving indispensable.

Down the table, a civil engineer from Bradford was recounting an experience at Kagoshima—one of those tales in which the traveller is the clever one, the indigenous inhabitant venal or infantile. He said, "I'm just giving facts," mistrustful of anything that might be called a story. Leith, half-turned, half-listening, was looking along the reddish flowers and red lacquer, the ceramic cups and Western cutlery. He could see a hand at rest. It was extended on the tabletop, where it lay like silence. He waited for the other hand to appear, as a watcher of birds awaits the arrival of the mate, the pairing. And soon the right hand came, shifting a disc of sauce before settling alongside its fellow, while the soldier looked with pleasure.

"Mr. Leith."

Across the table, the boy, smiling, might have seen it all.

"Is it true . . ." Voice neither fully broken nor childish. Except for bright eyes, the lifted face was mask-like: apertures—of eyes and nostrils—so precise and close as to recall the little muzzle of a cat. As with a cat, too, some charm of clairvoyance.

The boy stretched his hand. Leith had to rise, in order to clasp it.

"Benedict Driscoll."

So this was the son of those.

"Why did you walk across China?"

"I wanted to do it, and it was proposed to me." To answer candidly, with no indulgent smile, was to exorcise the gratuitous suspicion that stood sentinel at either end of the table. "But I can't say that I walked across. I had to bear south, due to the civil war. I'd hoped to take the northern route of an Italian traveller of long ago, but it wasn't workable." What had been possible for the monk Carpini in 1245, in heroic old age, was no go in 1946 for a modern man in prime of life. "And I wasn't always on foot. In trains, often, or waggons, or carts, or on a mule. Or by river."

"It was the large idea, though." The boy looked down, shy about what moved him.

"Which is perhaps necessarily formless, except in the traveller's mind. I mean that it can't be comprehensive, like a single objective, or done conclusively."

Benedict said, "There might be a danger in doing one thing well. People get waylaid into the single segment of knowledge."

Calder said, "And why not?" Was a don again, snubbing a cheeky freshman. "If one has given, devoted, a life, one's energies. Easy to talk of erudition as if it were limiting, pass judgement out of sheer ignorance. I myself would not judge people by their knowledge of Erasmus; but have possibly earned the right to do so."

"Erasmus?" The boy's bright eyes resting on Calder. People were listening. "Erasmus of Rotterdam was born in 1466, not at Rotterdam as one might suppose, but at Gouda. Real name possibly Geert. Studied at Paris, and entered the priesthood with reluctance in the momentous year 1492. In 1499, was welcomed at Oxford. Taught Greek at Cambridge, but wrote mainly in Latin. Died at Basel in 1536, unattended by any priest. Is paradoxically remembered for his translation of the New Testament."

Calder grinned. "Fair enough." Leith was laughing outright. Benedict, satisfied, was fatigued by his little performance. The young manservant came to stoop over him, and helped him away. The table was disbanding.

Calder said, "Well, I'll be blowed." He would have liked a smoke, a chat. But Leith told him, "I've been hoping for an hour to look into the garden."

Mrs. Driscoll, materialising, said, "We lock up here now. The staff has to clear away."

"Closing time in the gardens of the East," said Calder.

LEITH STARTED ON THE PATH that led down to his quarters, a walk overhung by low, knotty pines angled by weather—for this slope was ultimately exposed, beyond some undulations, to the sea. He saw that

Benedict was being helped along ahead of him, and hung back in order not to interfere.

Melba Driscoll had come after him. "You've seen our tragedy."

Leith said, "You have a remarkable son."

"It's been diagnosed. We've never been sure, but now a specialist in London . . ." She said, "We've been through so much."

He said, "A cruel disease." He could not hold out against her, but felt disloyal to the boy. Aware of it, the mother nevertheless led with the trump card of her son's affliction.

"People have no idea. And so hard on his father, who was a champion." She came close to him, lowering her voice. "A mother can stand it better. Women are given special strength. We are very strong, Aldred."

He disliked, of course, his name on her lips; and she knew it.

Driscoll came to her side. "We have to take our medicine. He's seen the best bloke. No stone unturned." Solemnity was directed at Leith, as people will speak to foreigners with affected formality. "No expense spared."

Conscious of another presence, Leith turned his head in hope of release.

Melba said, "Our little girl. Helen, say how-do." She told Leith, "You've missed our eldest."

Ginger had mentioned, You've been lucky there.

The girl was quiet, shaking hands.

He said, "I was wondering to whom it belonged, this hand."

Withdrawing it, and smiling, she touched her bodice.

Melba would not stand for it. "You see the likeness. Everyone does." She meant, To herself.

"I do, yes. Remarkable." It might be less surprising that this youngest Driscoll should so resemble her brother than that she should share his unlikeness to the parents. Most striking was the girl's well-being. It was as if, in this child, Benedict had been re-created in radiant health, the hair made glossy, the skin vital, the form sound. With a second try, Nature had pulled it off. The eyes were of the same uncommon clarity, and rounder.

She fingered the blue buttons.

He said, "Like a caricature of a beautiful hand."

She might have liked, now, to look at her hand, in order to see it in that light. But the pleasure would keep, and was best enjoyed alone.

She said, "I should go. Ben and I are going to read."

Barry deplored. "When I was her age, try to keep me indoors."

"Thank you," she said. The words must have been for Leith. Her voice had that lightness, not quite of childhood, that precedes female experience. Since love, like influenza, leaves a huskiness. She walked off composedly enough, but, as the man saw, ran the last steps to her brother's side.

Melba said, "They're never apart. Not since Helen could crawl."

"Not a good life for a kiddie." This was Barry, with complacency.

"But they're company for one another. There's nothing here for young people." With a gesture, Melba implicated the entire archipelago as far as the Kuriles. "Even if my poor boy was able."

Brother and sister had been abroad since Christmas, in the custody of a British friend. A diagnosis had been made. There had then been the long voyage out. Their apprehension of the imminent landfall might be imagined: reunion, curtailment. Leith saw that the Driscolls used the daughter for the care of their son. And saw also that this abuse was as yet her sole salvation.

In his room, he found letters on the table and sat on the bed to read them. He forgot the Driscolls, in favour of other discoveries of the day: the ascent coiled around green-combed terraces, and the last white sight of Ginger's ship; and his good, pleasant, irresolute driver.

There was a brief letter from his father, which he put aside for reply. A notice from his bank was on excellent paper, ivory-coloured and headed by raised lettering in coal-black cursives: the first fine stationery he had handled in years. A scattering of postcards was a signal of dwindling correspondence—he had, for some people, been away too long. A good letter had been posted from Bombay by an army friend now sailing towards Hong Kong. A single sheet, from a woman who would soon join the postcard category, enclosed photographs: "I was in Szechuan at the beginning of spring." The snows blotched above, the blossoming below, and the steep village stepping to the river's edge. The quilted men and women at their work, smiling at the photographer with resigned surprise.

If he were minded to feel homesick, it would have been for that.

Leith's greatest preoccupation at this time was his work, the medium through which he conceived a future life. He had set himself to render consequences of war within an ancient and vanishing society. That visionary or preposterous undertaking had engrossed him for two years, and would in some degree influence the remainder of his days. His theme—of loss and disruption—was pervasive now throughout the world. With the sombre choice, there had come much happiness in far communities. There had been the singular, transcendent encounters. He had no wish to explicate or control. The collective scramble of soldiering had confirmed a need of solitude—a measure of which could be created at will, even among others. From events of war he had wrested the lonely elements of maturity. He wanted, now, discoveries to which he sensed himself accessible; that would alter him, as one is altered, involuntarily, by a great work of art or an effusion of silent knowledge.

Aldred Leith had developed stoicism that might have been a temporary condition of his war, of his task and travels. He knew, however, that the capacity for affection must be kept current if it is not to diminish into postcards. And that responsiveness in youth is no guarantee against later dispassion. His father, in this, was something of a caution. In Oliver Leith, an intense, original lode of high feeling had been depleted: he was working, now, from a keen memory of authentic emotion. The son knew himself more resilient and less egotistical than the father—even if possessed, as he had always been given to understand, of less genius.

WHEN HE HAD REPLIED to everything but the good letter from Bombay, he went out and walked up the path to a shed that had been pointed out as a common room from which mail might be despatched. From that rise, one could look up to the original house on its screened plateau. He saw that it was by no means closed, and that one or two figures moved, in the late light, across its partitions. Aware that persistence would lead to nothing good, Leith nevertheless branched off uphill, sighting, beyond a mass of iris, the little lake, a catchment area, in which the Brigadier had that morning taken the waters. With his back to the raw cottages and unsightly common room, Leith again remembered Ginger, who had said, Quite beautiful. It was true: the place itself, had it been de-Driscolled, was a paradise. But that, of course, applied to all the world.

At first, he did not connect the voice with the house. Someone was screaming, not for help, but in a paroxysm, a seizure. Not with a woman's voice, although it might seem so, but in a high keening recognisable from scenes of other violence. A man, hysterical. The man was Barry Driscoll, who was shrieking into the face of the young Japanese who had been described, at table, as his *maggiordomo*. Though menaced by Driscoll's body, the youth did not flinch or retreat, except perhaps from a shower of saliva that, visible in a shaft of light, appeared as punctuation. Nor could it be said that he was impassive. The word, rather, would have been "incalculable."

Leith, entering, stood at a distance from Driscoll's back. The youth of course saw him, but made no sign, his eyes remaining fixed on Driscoll's. Leith began to understand that the young man had taken the key and come back to the locked house at an unauthorised hour. That was his offence. Driscoll's imprecations were all that the worst could desire; and Leith already looked to a future in which he might forget them.

He supposed that the young man had come up here with a purpose graver but similar to his own: to be, for an hour, alone and ageless.

Realisation had taken seconds, before Driscoll whipped round shouting, with no change of tone, "And what in hell are you doing here?"—as if outrage had been compounded. Like a boxer or dancer, he rocked from one foot to another, almost stamping. The disengagement of the two men watching both maddened and cooled him: the presence of a witness generally has this twofold effect. Shrewdness returned, and a heavy sweat, and the instinct for vindication.

He and Leith stared at and, in that moment, detested one another.

To gain time, Driscoll repeated, "Why are you here?"

There was no responding to this, or to anything that Driscoll might later have to say. In his mind's eye, Leith saw the three of them standing in the slit sunlight, in disparate versions of manliness. After some moments, he stared to where, across the long table, the Japanese youth stood, exactly as before—except that they looked, now, into one another's eyes.

Leith turned and left the house. Driscoll had in his fist a bunch of sharp new keys, which would have made a savage weapon if dashed in someone's face; but he was no longer dangerous in that way, and had set to thinking how to cover the exposure. There might be other incidents, recorded or obscured, beside which the present outbreak would not look well.

When Leith reached the common room and looked back, he saw that the young Japanese had also come away and was walking in a different direction: a thin figure soon screened by trees and seeking, no doubt, other forms of shelter.

LEITH WAS AT THE DOOR of his own cottage when it occurred to him that the grassed verge on which he stood must be the rim of the valley of which Gardiner had spoken. (He was getting used to these promptings from Ginger, and found them comforting.) There would be, here below, the temple, the spring, the little cataract; and somewhere nearby, in tangled growth, an access to the path that led to them. Following the scene with Driscoll, he didn't fancy the excursion, nor did he want to infringe on it for some better occasion. Thinking only that he would scout out the track, he skirted the rim of the descent. Looking into the sunset, he was shading his eyes with his hand.

He was full of the incident up at the Japanese house, not quite going over it but seeing it, as before, in his mind's eye: the three men standing in their silent geometry. At this hour, all three of them, dispersed about these hills, were reviewing it also, in some weird and dissimilar communion. He recalled Calder's words about the ascetic

Japanese: "God knows what he thinks of us," and wondered what he might do for this youth beyond the look exchanged.

He had scarcely gone fifty yards when he again heard voices. They were speaking in English, and he realized that he was near the last cottage and that the speakers were known to him. Moving forward, he could see through shrubbery the crude exterior of this larger house and an undraped window framing brother and sister: the girl, intent, and turned away from his view; the boy's head and shoulders quite plainly resting on the tall back of an invalid's chair. Absorbed as lovers, and paired, too, in the attitudes of giving and receiving.

Having evidently exchanged some words, they both laughed—a subdued, simultaneous laugh, like an audible smile. (Here was Ginger again: "The only laughter in the place.") All were quiet then: the girl and boy, and the man on the path who feared to disturb them. Within moments, the girl's voice was heard again—and on a note of resumption, for she was reading: "The funeral of the late emperor was decently performed, the capital was silent and submissive." She was accustomed to reading aloud, and did so with no faltering or false effects. Recounting the last delusions of Byzantium, she paused. But the brother made no comment, and she completed the ancient story.

3

HE WORKED LATE at his notes, and at midnight looked over a Japanese lesson, repeating new sounds in undertones. At this stage, competence appeared an exciting improbability, which he went to sleep pondering.

He woke at sunrise—from habit, since the little room remained dim—in the wake of an oppressive but irrecoverable dream. From habit, too, knew that the dark sensation would linger through the morning, whose first light he at once let in through door and window. Revisiting the events of yesterday, he thought again that he would look for rooms in the town, though that would involve the American base. He recalled the brother and sister in the window, and the girl with the book, reading.

In his malodorous small bathroom, he doused water over his face and head, shaking himself dry like a wet animal. Then, without shaving, dressed at once, choosing his boots for the scramble down to the temple.

The sun was well up now, drawing humidity out of the valley. ("Damp, I can tell you"—that was Ginger.) Leith walked carefully behind the larger house, not choosing to repeat the adventure of the previous evening, when, thinking back on it, he fancied that Benedict had seen him. The secluded path was a mere trampled indentation of spikes and nettles and harsh stems tufted like thistles.

He found himself passing by a square window, open but netted with fine wire. Its meagre sill was level with his waist. The room into which he glanced was mostly occupied by a wide bed, leaving space for a chair and tiny table and a chest of brownish drawers. The table, by the bed, held a book, a lamp, and a bottle of pinkish liquid. Underclothes were spilt on top of the chest, and a pair of small shoes aligned below—sparse details filmed over by the fine wire netting that gave them the significance of a composition, a context for the girl on the bed.

Who lay on her side, sheet pushed back over raised hip, body reaching forward as if to follow her free arm, extended beyond the mattress. A thin shift disclosed her shoulder. Innocence, of youth and sleep, were entire and defenceless, but involuntarily prefigured knowledge. So would she lie, one morning in some imminent year, in the abandon now simulated here.

The man had not slowed his step. But, striding on, envisioned the tableau more precisely, retrieving the profile nearly effaced in the bunched pillow and the fall of uncombed hair. That the sight had pleased him was natural; natural, perhaps, some sadness also.

He found the path at once and made the first descent, through low scrub that must lead into a glade, visible below. It surprised him that there was no birdsong. The sun was well up. Fungus shone like blisters on the trunks of trees. His foot slid on toadstools—digital, clothy, yellowed as fingers stained with nicotine. The track appeared to peter out, though one might sense its direction readily enough, into the little valley. The stream, or its cataract, became audible, and there was a suggestion of ancient roofing, tiled, glinting farther down.

That was his goal, though he would not reach it this day.

The body lay in the centre of the glade in a welter of blood and innards partly contained by a coloured robe and loosened obi. The slippered feet projected, inviolate. The soldier was familiar with this phenomenon of the unscathed feet, blameless, irrelevant.

Of course. He probably said it aloud.

Before dawn, as he slept, there had gushed out this emanation of an extreme. The man understood, now, his presentiment of the morning.

The head had not been severed: the youth had acted alone.

Flies and ants were at work, and the hot smell of immediate decay. The blood was beginning to congeal. The body was warm yet, as Leith turned it slightly by its raised left shoulder—the right arm remaining beneath, still involved with the bloodied weapon. The head fell back: the young face ghastly, the eyes in their last distress. Eyes that had exchanged with him, hours since, their pained humanity. Straightening up, Leith realised that from here, through trees, you could see the sea. The site had been chosen, perhaps long considered.

In Germany, near the end of the war, a woman standing over another such shattering had looked up at him: "*Mein Mann*." He had thought her old and bent; then saw that she was no more than twenty.

He remembered the young people sleeping above, who must not see.

WHEN HE WALKED UP the slope to report the suicide, he learnt that Driscoll was away, on the island. He found Dench, who brought the men down with their equipment. Leith stayed with them awhile, then went to his own rooms to wash. Dench had been resentful, as if Leith were somehow to blame. Driscoll would find it hateful—that Leith, having witnessed the preliminaries, should have been the one to come upon the consequences. He himself felt secretly culpable—as if, with that look of acknowledgement, he'd conspired in the act.

He must write his account of the morning, and sat at once to the task—which was his way when most reluctant. He had not spoken with the deceased, nor seen him for more than moments on the day of his own arrival. An impression of reserve, possibly vulnerable to conditions of defeat. He might have been unfamiliar with military practice. (This was the closest he could come to suggesting Driscoll—who would pick it up right away.) He knew nothing of the private life of the deceased, or the position of his immediate family, which might enlarge understanding.

It was there if anyone chose to ask. But nobody would, it would remain obscure. If something of the kind recurred, Driscoll might be in trouble. But things do not recur exactly, and the sole result would be that Driscoll would hate Leith's guts.

He sat on the bed and removed his stained shoes. There was a knock at the door, and he got up in his stockinged feet to answer it. It was the girl, Helen, with a pint bottle of brandy in her hand.

"We thought you might want this."

"Come in. That's kind." He had not eaten, and did not want the brandy, but went into the minuscule kitchen to fetch a glass. They sat side by side on the bed, she in her flowered dress, he, unshod, in the shirt and trousers he had not yet changed. He believed that he did not want her there; but was pleased by her restraint, and her thought of him. He remembered how he had seen her in her bed.

She said, "Aki is making our breakfast. Ben thought you might like to eat with us."

Again, he believed that he did not want to do this, but said, "With pleasure." He swallowed brandy, to please, but felt better for it. "I have to clean myself up first. Is half an hour all right?"

She said, "Oh yes," and prepared to leave.

He astonished himself with an impulse to take her in his arms, which of course he did not do. Yet some tenderness passed between them, in reaction to the horror of the morning. The entire world, he thought, needs comforting.

When she had gone, he shaved and took a shower in the cramped bathroom, combed his hair before the steaming mirror, and noted the effect of the experience on his face, not simply as an opening of old wounds. He put on civilian clothes—a clean white shirt and the linen jacket he kept for civil occasions. The jacket, long crumpled back to its vegetable origins, had been ironed and rehung. And he registered the fact that presences, helpful or otherwise, could enter his room at will. He put the draft of his statement away.

There was the depression in the bed where he and the girl had sat. He thought how long it was since he had been alone in a room with a girl, and had made himself presentable in consequence: a cat washing itself after a needed meal. Looking for something to take as an offering, he came up with a paper volume, blue and white, of *The Centuries' Po-*

etry: Bridges to the Present Day, with a photograph on the back cover of the young editor gripping his chin amid thoughts too deep for tears. Work on the bloodied ground might have been completed, since he heard no sound of it. The door to the larger cottage was unlatched.

Below a window, the brother was lying on a daybed, propped by a bolster and striped cushions, his feet slightly raised on a rubber wedge evidently cut for the purpose. He was wearing a plain dark cotton gown like an unbelted kimono, over which his hands were folded. On his belly, over the dark cloth, an upturned book shifted with his breathing. He watched, as it seemed, a facing wall: the flimsy wall of the room in which he might well die.

Leith wondered at all this death pursuing him.

Beside the boy, Helen was sitting in a low chair, level with the divan. The same morning that touched her brother's scanty hair gleamed on her own full head and down her healthy arms. They were aware of Leith instantly, girl quickly rising, boy making a gesture to excuse immobility. They were so pleased to see him, and said so. They did not speak of the tragedy. Helen thanked him for the book, smiling with all her clear eyes. Her enthusiasm shamed him for having chosen the volume he could most easily dispense with.

She set up a collapsible table. He sat in a military-looking chair. Helen held out his cup and saucer with a hand that shook enough to rattle the china—so that Leith, taking it from her, could say, "This morning makes you tremble."

"It happens sometimes. Since I was"—she would have said, "young," but thought better of it—"quite small."

Benedict smiled. "Two years ago."

They must wonder if the tremor was a portent of her brother's affliction. The girl added, "When I'm excited."

"We're both excited," said Benedict, "at having you here."

Leith could see that this might be true. But said, also with truth, "You are kind to me," and took a twisted bun from a tin. He said, "You're reading Gibbon."

"Are we loud, then?"

"No. I loved hearing it. The best thing in a long while."

They told him that they had read the entire work, on the ship from England, and were now going over favourite passages. They were also reading Carlyle, which he might overhear—"For that's a loud book, in its way."

"An excited book, rather."

Helen said, "But the excitement is magisterial."

Leith said, "I think—"

"What?"

"That about large subjects there can be many kinds of books, playing on our sympathies or alienating them. Truth can be a synthesis, or an impression."

It was new to him to speak this way with a child. But then, a girl of perhaps fifteen—who knows history and says "magisterial"—a girl already embarked on her secret biological life, has taken leave of childhood. He had looked discreetly, as men and boys will do with girls, for the slight shape of her breasts in the pretty dress.

She wanted to ask about the large events of his own life, but could not bring herself to it. However, there might be time, and one day he would tell her of his own accord.

Benedict understood that his sister had for the moment left him to be with this man. Soon, or at last, their own long pairing would be sundered; but not just today. Being in company was, that morning, a solace to all three of them, in each of whom the thought rose and fell: Had we done differently, the man might be alive.

Benedict said, "There might have been mass suicides in Japan, with the surrender. Why didn't it happen? Is it because the Emperor decided not to die?"

"I wonder. A member of the imperial family did commit *seppuku*, but it was hushed up. There may have been more suicides than we imagine, in the days of the defeat. Not something that would be explored or divulged." He said, "I thought I might learn about this, travelling the country. Instead, here, at once, it reveals itself."

The boy said, "It comes to us from the war."

Leith would not say, The second such death, for me, in a matter of hours. To speak of death with this sick boy, and with the girl, was disturbing. He put down his cup, leant back, and crossed one foot over his knee. He must write up the sworn statement involving the father of these children. There would be an enquiry, however perfunctory. The deceased—Leith had not yet asked his name—had he been brutalised, or in any way provoked to take his life? He had been, not a prisoner, but a recent enemy in custodial care. His degradation had been brought home to him. Leith had seen him for few moments. Had heard him cursed. They had exchanged that last glance of fellowship.

If he were to write such things, there would be no staying here. But then, had he not already intended to leave?

His light-coloured socks were flecked with blood. These young people would have noticed. He got up, saying, "You'll let me come again?"

Benedict said, "It would be wonderful."

When they parted, the death flowed back into each of them. The tray being cleared away, Benedict lay down with his arms over his chest, in isolation. And there was Helen in her chair, separately and equivocally stirred.

At length she slipped down on her knees by the daybed and clasped her brother closely and laid her head on his folded hands. Except for the movement of his fingers on her hair, it was as if they slept together.

He said, "You are thinking of what is to come."

HE WROTE OUT, with formalities, the statement as already drafted, making an exact copy for Driscoll. (A typewriter, eventual and portable, had been promised, and sheets of carbon paper.) His glance fell on the letter earlier set aside, to his army friend, who, now concerned with war crimes, was sailing East. In his mind, he had framed a reply—"My dear Peter"—but the narrative, of Tokyo, the Inland Sea, the death of Gardiner, had become, and literally was, yesterday. He would have to begin again.

It was noon. He would walk up the path and leave the copy of his statement for Driscoll, having seen the original safely deposited. He had kept his draft. For the time being, he sat on there, elbow on table, chin on palm, like the poet on the back of the anthology; recalling Benedict's scant hair, and the girl's tremulous hand.

Dear Peter—

This should greet you at Hong Kong, a place for which I keep affection. In my Shanghai boyhood, Hong Kong played second fiddle as the great port of the China trade, and will now be in the ascendant. My Japanese venture, in its second month, begins to take shape. The role of conqueror remains alien and distasteful. There is something equivocal about having prevailed so completely over one's fellow man—I don't speak of systems or regimes, but of individuals. Quite different, to my mind, from the extempore impersonations of victor and vanquished that successively fell to your lot and mine in the war. I'm glad—aren't you?—that our military lives are ending.

Needing to work in this region, I've established myself in hills overlooking Kure—that is to say, near Hiroshima, where I've begun my enquiries. I continue to be, as in China, a *franc tireur*, assisted not at all by official sources. Secrecy as to the catastrophe and its consequences is controlled here by the American Bomb Survey; and is such, in the case of non-Americans, that I've been sending my meagre notes away to safety. Even this far from conspiratorial letter goes by safe hand. A contrast with my China wanderings, where I walked, through chaos, as my own man.

Up here in the hills, the officer in charge is a medical administrator from the Antipodes. He and his consort make a formidable pair. They have a frail and remarkable young son, and a little girl who is a changeling. Seeing these young people, I am thinking that a child can be born fastidious into cruelty and can hold to reason and a sense of justice. There is, thank God, no explaining this.

When you're settled, I would like to come in your direction. T. V. Soong is taking over in Kwangtung, bringing his private army with him. Soongs and Chiangs, and credulous Washington, will cost us all dear in the end, which is so soon to come. We'll see the Deluge: archaic iniquity swept away by the new Juggernaut of the doctrinaire. Meantime, I've a mind to see Canton again, and to cast an eye on Soong and his Salt Troops. Or perhaps it's simply that I miss China. Missing China is my habit of years. I was even homesick for China while I was there, a paradox emblematic of that enigmatic land. At all events, it will be fine to see you again, and in this hemisphere.

Having signed and folded the letter and sealed it, Leith then wrote, in his notebook:

I have learned that Benedict Driscoll is twenty. He suffers from a disease called Friedreich's Ataxia, which disables and will ultimately kill him. This was diagnosed three months ago in London, when he was still relatively mobile. Since then the condition has accelerated, as if released by its identification. The family, coming from Sydney, had been living a year in Bengal, where Driscoll, the father, held some administrative post in hygiene under the governor, Richard Casey, an Australian. In London, these two waifs were left by their mother in the protection of their former tutor, an Englishman who had known them in Australia. They are wonderfully well-read, a poetic pair who live in literature and make free with it. They are right to cling to it: it has delivered them.

Helen's age, not yet disclosed. Possibly fourteen? Fifteen? Wanting to be thought older, she doesn't let on. Within ten years will be dissembling in the opposite direction. Women are soon obliged to appear young beyond their years.

Since the night of Gardiner's death, the night of the twirling girls on Ita Jima, I rediscover memories distinct from war. Often of women, of my youthful loves—Aurora, Gigliola. Not so much Moira, perhaps because our story achieved, in London, that nearly ritual fulfillment. It is incompleteness that haunts us.

Having written this, he put the notebook away, in a small gimcrack safe that he'd acquired, along with other documents and a box of lead pencils called Venus.

4

UNFIT FOR SCHOOL LIFE at Sydney, Benedict had been taught at home. The Driscolls had found a tutor: an Englishman impoverished and under a cloud, like many another emigrant to Australia. His name was Bertram Perowne. It was said that Bertram came from a grand family, and in his fine-drawn and diffident way he certainly looked and spoke the part. However, he laid no claim to the connection, and it was plain that the family, grand or not, did nothing for him. He worked in a shop in the morning and came to the Driscolls after lunch. Helen, returning from school at three, had shared her brother's lessons.

Getting himself back to England in mid-war, Bertram had purportedly been recruited for some cerebral task to do with coding. This again was hearsay, to which Bertram, in letters, made no allusion.

Benedict said of him, "For us, he was Adam, naming the world."

Helen said, "He is our good angel."

Leith thought that Bertram had been both Robinson Crusoe and Man Friday.

It was Bertram who had cared for them in England, where he now appeared to have some means. Their mother had brought them to

Britain from India, astonishingly—for the Driscolls in late war had seen something of the world and had spent that unexpected year in Bengal. The post in imperial India had been another of Barry's stepping-stones, leading to Kure. In order to be on hand for the move to Japan, the mother had left the children in London with Bertram. It was Bertram who had seen Benedict through the medical tests, and had taken the brother and sister as far as Naples for their sailing to the East.

Leith thought that it would be interesting to hear Bertram's view.

He felt himself in some measure to be Bertram's successor. This sequestered pair wanted the history of the world. They also wanted his own story. They asked him, How was this, Where was that. They questioned him about his youth, his travels, his walk through China. But rarely, as he noticed, asked about the war—from shyness, and possibly from a sense that the conflagration must flare forth of its own accord.

It did not displease him, after long silence, to tell them something of his tale.

They asked him about his name, which they had never heard before.

"No one has. When I was a child, I was told that it denoted a sage. Later, I found that it was a venerable sage, an old geezer: the elder. It was my grandfather's name, and seemed right enough for him. But he, too, had borne with it since infancy." Leith remembered his grandfather, a rangy old chap, very tall, with white hair on top like high cumulous cloud. Once in a while, that elder Aldred had given him, from a box on the mantel, a gold sovereign with the effigy of Queen Victoria. He had told the boy, "I never cared for the name, but one gets used to it."

They asked him, "How did you learn Chinese?"

"I was nine, and it was due to a little girl of five."

Aldred, in his tenth year and living with his mother in a hotel suite in Shanghai, was attending a school for foreign children from the International Concessions. His father was, at the time, engrossed by Russian exiles in Harbin. In the lobby of the hotel in Shanghai, the boy observed the comings and goings, across marble floors, of taipans from the princely hongs—those merchant princes, British, American, French, Dutch, Danish, with interests along the coasts of China and Siam. Mr. Seth, the banker, had once invited him for an ice cream in the café.

There was the young Moller, with a fortune in shipping and a string of horses that the boy longed to see; and S. T. Williamson, high and bulky, who had a trading house of his own in Hong Kong—not as grand as Jardine's or Butterfield's, but to be reckoned with. There were wives, pale and ailing, who could not withstand the climate. There were women, European and Eurasian, of a worldly attractiveness. There were the White Russians, with their historic loss. Tourists came off the great liners, strolled the Bund under parasols, and were beset by beggars. From time to time, from Europe, there was Royalty with its entourage. There was the Tiger Heat. There was sharp cold, and the rains. There was, from the interior, the Yellow Wind.

In lobby and lift, Aldred often saw the English child with her amah: a keen little pink-and-white creature whose name was Charlotte.

Charlotte's carroty curls were bound with coloured ribbon. Her pretty frocks were smocked over her diminutive chest. On occasion, she had in tow her demure and distant mother; or was with her parents together—the father being distant, also, and more discreetly auburn. Vitality, withheld in the parents, had been released in the child. Charlotte was to be seen most usually with the black-clad amah, who loved her, and with whom the busy little girl carried on swift conversations in the dialect of Shanghai.

One noon, during a fierce season of typhoons, Aldred was going up in the lift with his mother, while the Chinese operator by rote announced the floors—*sam lau, sei lau*—at each stop drawing back the folding inner gate with his gloved hand so that it would not unsuitably clang. Aboard, too, were Charlotte, her amah, and her father. The child was interpreting some mild dispute between parent and nurse; and doing this so rapidly and efficiently, and quite without bravado, that even the discreet lift boy smiled. Aldred's mother stood, an attentive presence, against the panelling, her green silk dress fluttered by an overhead fan that stirred, also, her hat of woven straw from Bali, fine as gauze. Her name was Iris. Her willowy figure complemented the white-suited column of the British father, pillar of the establishment, and the short, staunch amah in black tunic and trousers with her black hair coiled and varnished and her smooth face the colour of teak.

Aldred noted his mother sizing up, as was her habit, the situation—a process that usually touched on social standing but might take subtler forms.

Turning the key in their door, releasing hat pin and laying hat on sofa, his mother had rung for lemon squash and taken money from a purse to tip the floor boy who would bring the tray. Having done these things, remarked: "And why, Aldred, should you not also learn Chinese?" To which the boy had, in effect, replied, "Why not, indeed."

Leith told them, "So it was Charlotte who began it. Oh, Charlotte, where are you now? And where did events sweep you away, before I could greet you in the dialect of Shanghai?"

"I think," said Helen, "that your mother deserves some credit."

"It's true. I'm often slow to pay tribute to her. But Charlotte was the catalyst."

Slanting his difficult head, Ben looked round at Helen. "I grow envious of this red child with powers beyond our own."

Helen, with satisfaction: "Who is now a matron of thirty, whereabouts unknown."

It occurred to Leith for the first time that the red child, then, was the age of his own dead sister; that this had been his mother's thought as she listened that day in the ascending lift, and had moved her to consider the future of her small surviving son—whose life had been, thereafter, shaped by the moment.

EVERY OTHER DAY Leith drove down, with Brian Talbot, to Hiroshima. The outskirts of the town were being re-created in thousands of plywood houses, recklessly close, it seemed, to the site of the disaster. Taking his interpreter, and using his own increasing knowledge of the language, he was able to talk to men and women working on the new constructions—people of the region, some of whom spoke openly, most of whom were reticent or refused entirely. In order to speak with injured survivors, or with spokesmen of the community, permission was required from the American Bomb Survey, and the foreign applicant was accompanied by an appointed officer. On several of these occasions, Leith and Talbot had been in the company of the same Lieutenant Carroll—courteous, cautious, impersonal.

One morning, Carroll told them that his term of duty was almost finished: he would be returning Stateside. These were his words, with a slight relaxing of formality. In Talbot's jeep, they had crossed the tramline and were approaching the momentous scene—where the main force of the explosion had been received. These again were Carroll's words, and he never did say The Bomb. To Aldred Leith's questions, he responded with practised and sometimes technical expressions, and with a suggestion of relief, as if more usually accustomed to inanities. Talbot asked one question only, to which Carroll had his prompt and measured reply: Yes, the scientists examining the site and the survivors were inclined to think that there remained some danger in the atmosphere, though not for so brief a visit as our own.

The girders of the dome had been examined for their unaccountable resilience. Why yes, the casualties were estimated at a quarter-million, that being a tentative figure only. Why the explosion had not been directed initially to an uninhabited zone, or why the first exercise had been followed by the raid on Nagasaki, he had no idea, those decisions having been made in the closed and no doubt wise councils of our leaders. However, he did ask Leith if he could suggest a strategic reason. He had never sought an opinion before. Aldred, turning to him from the front seat where he sat beside Talbot, remarked, "I doubt there was logic, other than that shaped to the predestined act. By then, neither side was interested in sparing anyone, even themselves."

Carroll said, "Yes"—for him, a daring intervention. After a hesitation, added, "I was on Okinawa that year, through June."

At the American nucleus near the port, they had beers tasting of tin and wrote addresses on unlikely scraps of paper. Driving back to the compound, Talbot mumbled, "I suppose, a decent bloke." They left it at that until the driver said, "He has a different voice, for a Yank."

"Not a Yank at all. He's from the Deep South. That's their accent. He's from Georgia."

Talbot laughed. "Well, I'm from the Deep South myself, as far south as you can go. And with the accent, too, to prove it."

BENEDICT ASKED HIM, "What will you do with it all?"

"I'll write it, and it will be published. The account of China, which was proposed to me. Japan has been my own addition." He said, "It has all come upon me by chance."

Late in the war, he had been asked, by persons in power, to write in confidence about the town of Caen, all but destroyed in the first days of June 1944. In those times there was no lingering and his work was completed quickly. But he had spoken with many persons grieved and embittered by ruin, and by the gross ambiguities of their liberation; and had related these matters with simplicity and truth. The report, in French and in English, had been presented in good time, and he had never expected to hear of it again.

In Paris, on a cold morning of April 1945, he was sent for. Dark grey, diminished, chipped, and soiled, the city seemed a scale model of its former self; a wintry film in black-and-white. In the offices to which he was directed, dinginess gave place to splendour. Paintings, rugs of stitched roses, fine furniture signed by the *ébéniste* were less of a luxury than the warmth, which even pervaded corridors. Senior officers came and went, apparently without the pinched signs of suffering: immune, as they would have had you believe, not so much to glorious death as to the squalor of chilblains, boils, and empty bellies in the surrounding streets. The man who had sent for him was unexpectedly young, not tall, but with a clever face and elegant limbs. Logs were burning in a marble fireplace, to which they drew up velvet chairs.

"My paper on Caen had reached his desk. He had informed himself, and knew about my youth in the East, the languages, the war. He'd grown up in China and Indochina, and knew that these places were evaporating, transforming. The last days of all their centuries should be witnessed and recounted by someone who was not a spy, not a sociologist, beholden to no one." All this very concise from the young general aslope in his chair, stretching crossed feet to the fire. "He offered me two years in China, and a free hand. I should keep my military rank, which, as he said, would sometimes help me if it did not otherwise provoke my death. A contract would be drawn up protecting my right to publish. Official circles should not be drawn in. I accepted at once. I was younger then. Presumption was immense. I suppose I had been in an arrested state with the war. One aged rapidly enough at the end of it. We shook hands and had a drink on it."

"What did you drink?"

"*Champagne nature.* A fine lunch was wheeled in." He had asked to look at paintings, and walked a bit about the room. On the desk, there was an old red folder tooled in gold and a silver box for cigarettes. There was a photograph of a beautiful youth in naval uniform, who was not a son.

"Did you see him again?"

"We met repeatedly in the following days. I went to his house, which was grand with books." Leith said, "He told me he was ill, which I'd perhaps begun to realise."

Leith would not speak to Benedict of yet another death. At their parting, the Frenchman had said, "However, I hope to live to read your book."

"I'm sure you have better reasons than that for living."

"None."

WHEN HE GOT UP to leave them, he said, "I'm having this teacher come, you know, an elderly Japanese, three times a week. He could come to you, before or after seeing me, as you'd like."

Ben said, "Do you mean it?"

"Of course."

THEY ASKED HIM, Had he crossed the lines of the civil war? Since the Nationalists had removed the capital to Nanking, how had he entered Peiping, the city about which they were most curious? Leith explained that the road to Peiping was cut, and the railway. The city was besieged by the Communists, but one could fly in almost daily. Mao would move, but not quite yet. Mao need only wait. Leith had crossed the lines, at times by accident, but also by finding someone to speak for him in advance. He had regularly deposited his possessions—his notes and books and letters of credit—with friends, at a British or French enclave or consulate.

"Did you have books, to read on the way?"

"That was hard. Books are heavy, as is water. I carried one indispensable book, and a couple of Chinese lexicons in tiny print. One becomes starved to see one's own language—even on a discarded label whirled by a dust storm, or among the detritus of stolen UNRRA supplies."

"Did you talk to yourself out loud?"

"Like Billy-Oh. Recited, too, when alone, and even sang arias."

"Did you ever get lost?"

"Often. Of course, since I had no precise route, everything was grist. But sometimes I'd find that I'd gone in a circle."

"Did you ever think that you might—"

"What?"

"Stay forever in some place?" Helen meant, Love someone, and remain, and make a Chinese family. She was glad that he had not.

"Yes. Once, in particular."

He was in Yunnan, on foot and leading a mule rented in a village near Chaotung. "I was going from Kunming towards Chungking, where I'd left my tackle with a friend." It was May, he had slept in the open. After sunrise, came through steep bushy hills into a valley floored with green cultivation—less alluvial than the land preceding it, for now he was moving away from the great river. By a stream, there was a line of low, close houses, each bowed under its scalloped roof. The hill above the tiny town was gravid in the way of that landscape, its grassy garment stretched like soft cloth over an imagined anatomy of ancient, unremembered walls, graves, and ditches: a tumid rise, over which you might mentally pass your hand. On a nearer slope, feebly scattered with ash and poplar, a pair of pale, horned cattle were grazing. A woodpile was deftly stacked; a basket hung from a branch, and there was a small shrine, arched and tended.

On a third, sharp peak, the stripped remains of a Halifax bomber: the Ark on Mount Ararat, or the ribbed cradle of a stranded quadrireme.

Leith tethered the mule under a tree. Two men in the valley had already left their work and were climbing up to him as he came down. A third man followed slowly. A woman in black tunic and trousers came from a doorway and shouted, voice ringing harshly out in that still place, which was differently awhirr with the murmurous season.

He explained himself. The third man, who came on slowly and was deferred to, was the village elder, and spoke some careful Chinese, while the others used dialect. This older man, lightly built, had possibly been tall until reduced by toil and time. Good face, hairless; slight smile, courteous and unsurprised. A blue cotton gown—faded to a chalky mauve and draped from a latch at one shoulder—cleared his ankles. The high soft circular collar was unfastened. A darker cloth had been wound about his head in a flat turban. Wide sleeves almost covered the clasped fingers. A saffron face with the Tibetan look common in that region, and the clear light eyes.

Summoning this figure, one year later, Leith was aware of the convex brow with its traceries of experience that had infinitesimally evoked the veined hill above them, and only now found its place in his mind.

Helen asked, "What was the one book?"

And Benedict: "The book comes later. What next?"

"The bomber had been there since 1942, off course in torrential rain. That is Yunnan, it is named for that: the low clouds and fog, the cloudy south. There was an explosion after the crash, then a great fire that, despite the rains, smouldered on overnight. The villagers struggled up in the wet, but explosions kept them off." He did not tell that they could hear cries throughout the night. Later, they had stripped the wreck of whatever had not burned. "They took away some salvage and what they found in the cockpit. There were fifteen bodies, and they buried them farther down, under a cairn of stones."

These had to be disinterred. Dismantling the cairn was rough work in the sun, but that was not the trouble. The remains had to be extracted and handled. The men worked in the sun, nearly naked, with cloths over their mouths. All were sick. They urged Leith to leave them: "We're more accustomed." He said, "I may be more used to it than you." There were identity discs, and scraps of writing like scorched papyrus. They sluiced water on their hands, bundles of camphor leaves were brought. When the work was done, they reburied the bodies and closed the cairn. He went downstream to bathe and wash his clothes. The smell would be weeks in his nostrils. The men came up as he was climbing from the water. When they pointed to the purple scar down all his side, he said, "It was the war." The war among his own people that had waited, even here, on its perch.

In one of the dark houses, the elder showed him a heap of scraps: part of the flight manual intact in an asbestos box, some instruments of mangled metal. Leith wrote out the names, as far as he could decipher, and directions for finding the valley. He added underneath: "Halifax bomber with complement of 15 RAF crash-landed in low cloud on flight from Calcutta to Kunming, June 1942. Thirteen RAF noncommissioned officers and two pilots, one of them acting navigator. Graves of all fifteen at this spot, recovered by villagers from wreckage farther up the mountain."

He told the elder, "When I reach Chungking, I can send a message. After a time, people will come, Englishmen. The bodies will be taken away."

"To their families?"

"Yes."

"To their tombs?"

"Yes."

THERE WAS THE MATTER OF PETER EXLEY, whom Leith might visit at Hong Kong.

"Is he your best friend?"

Leith considered the schooldays question. "Of surviving friends, he's one of those who've stayed in touch and write regularly. Inevitably, the intervals lengthen. We share a sort of bond. He believes that I saved his life."

Benedict's whisper: "And did you?"

"Not impossible. The event rushes at you, you act without reflecting." He said, "The Chinese hold that if you save a man's life you become responsible for him. Something of the kind has come about between Exley and me. He's impressionable, a dreamer for whom, yes, one's inclined to feel responsible."

Ben said, "We like the sound of that."

"But then—he isn't lucky." Unsuitability of saying this to that unlucky boy. "Of all my friends from the war, Peter has least impetus to remake his life. We all hang back, one way or another, but he more than most.

"We had odd, early connections. Found that we'd been students in Florence at the same time, before the war. Must have passed each other often in those streets. And then, when we first met, in Cairo in 1942, each of us was carrying the same book." He laughed. "It was in the dark, a room in a seedy hotel where we'd been billetted. The lights had failed, as they often did. Coming into the room, I could just make him out, by the window. At sunrise, we found that we had the same book."

Helen, almost shouting, "What was the book?"

But he interrupted her: "My God, something of the kind happened here, when I got off the Tokyo train. But then it was my father's new novel." A lesser matter. "Peter's a bit older than I. Seems younger, without seeming young. In any case, a dear man. Knows he's unfortunate, but doesn't see it as a card to play."

"He can't," said Helen, "be so very unlucky. If you saved his life."

Part Two

5

IN HARBOUR ON THE FIRST MORNING, Exley saw the pastel villas on the mountainside, here and there among vegetation: looted, unroofed, their marzipan interiors lined with rot; some of them rebuilding under bamboo scaffolding. Looking out from shipboard, he realised that from those airy slopes there would be a grand view over the straits to the mainland. Obviously, the place to be.

That same noon he stood by windows up at MacGregor Road, in the officers' quarters, while a sceptical soldier searched through papers for his name. While the soldier riffled coloured pages, Peter Exley looked down the green mountain to the town scribbled along the shore: noting the cathedral, the post office, the governor's villa; and the bank, which was higher than all these. It was much as he had supposed. Beyond the narrow harbour and the shipping there were small bleached mountains at the verge of Asia.

He was aware of some consequential element that he had not identified. And with indifference realised it was beauty.

There was no place for him at MacGregor Road, no record of his request. It would have been quiet up there and relatively cool; just below the fog line—damp, of course, with the green smell that Exley at first mistook for freshness and soon recognised as decay. But there had been a mistake and every room was taken.

Redirected to the barracks, he went down unsurprised on the cable car in the afternoon heat. The July air was a blanket, summer weight. The barracks looked like Scutari. Presenting himself, he was led along a creaking verandah and up a soiled stair. Everywhere, the breath of mould.

A corporal unlocked the door. There was a second, inner door, slatted and latched. Pledges of another presence were distributed about the room. At the centre of things, marooned on wooden floor, a tin box was stencilled with name and number. The better bed, by the window, was heaped with dirty laundry and overhung by a dingy clump of mosquito net. There was the quiescent menace of a gramophone.

"Can't I get a room to myself, at least?"

"Put you down, sir, soons we got one. Bit of a wait, I'd say." There was a fair-sized garrison in the colony—Buffs, Inniskillings, Ghurkas. In any event, no one would offer preference to Exley, who had no flair for attracting favours.

The corporal told him the mess hours. Exley asked, "Is there something like a library here?"

"Any books get left, they put em on a shelf near the stairs. Mostly duds, I'd say."

It was 1947, mid-July. His pocket diary said "Saint Swithin." Exley took off his tunic and sat on the inferior bunk. His shirt stuck like a khaki skin. Overhead, there was the croak of a slow, ineffectual fan. Rails of light, red as electric elements, striped the shutters. Walls were distempered sallow. There were marks where heads had greasily rested, where furniture and kit had been stored, where hands had sweated around knobs and switches. There were smudges of squashed insects, with adhering particles. Damp had got at the quicksilver of a long mirror on a mahogany stand. On the wall by the other bed, pinups were pinkly askew and lettered signs carried insults, facetiously obscene.

Gloom without coolness. The mirror, unreflecting, was like the draped pelt of some desiccated leopard.

There was a century here of obscure imperial dejection: a room of listless fevers. Of cafard, ennui, and other French diseases. The encrusted underside of glory.

Exley, later, had no clear memory of seeing Roy Rysom for the first time—though sharply recalling that first sight of Rysom's dented tin box, its stencilled legend WAR GRAVES COMMISSION suggestive of the decomposing contents. He remembered that he was reading when Rysom came in and set the jazz belting, dragged off his boots, flopped on his bed, and began twitching to the music. Rysom's foot in its dank sock stuck out from the military blanket, toes curling and uncurling erotically to the music; his fingers convulsively beat on his chest, like hands of the dying. Peter Exley had watched men clutch themselves and die, and be covered up by regulation blankets. Men shot to bits in the desert, blown in half by land mines, festered with infected wounds: the whole scarlet mess covered by the military blanket.

Your feets too big.
Don't wantcha cause your feets too big.
Mad at you, cause your feets too big.
Hate you, cause your feets too big.

Rysom's records were mostly jazz. Life with Rysom was suffused with noise: the mess boy calling him to the telephone—"Mistah Rai-sam, Captain Rai-sam." Rysom yelling for cold beer, as trams rattled in the road below and the dockyard siren hooted or the gun boomed noon. Rysom said it was funny they should both be Australians, he and Exley, and on loan to the British Army. He said, "You War Crimes lot," and hooted like the siren. Rysom could introduce disbelief into anything, unmasking was his vocation. With suspicion he turned over Exley's Chinese and Japanese textbooks, his volumes on international law: "A beaut racket." Spreading a double page of Japanese characters, he uttered a stream of mad, paralaliac sounds, his comic rendering of Japanese.

Rysom was forever doing imitations: of a language, an accent, a personality; a man.

Rysom had dreams from which he woke shouting: dreams, like Exley's own, of men dismembered and sheets of flame. Each, in the night, now fought alone the war that neither could survive.

On his cot at the barracks Exley realised how much of his soldiering had been spent flat on his back, waiting for war. War had provided a semblance of purpose, reinforced by danger. Danger had been switched off like a stage light, leaving the drab scenery. And there they were at the barracks, he and Rysom, two years into peace and bored to death by it. Each must scratch around now for some kind of compromise and call it destiny.

ON HIS FIRST MORNINGS in the colony, Exley set out early. The short walk to his office led past the cricket ground, the club, the blotched statue of Queen and Empress restored to its pedestal: a decorous few hundred yards where Europeans were walking to their work in the trading companies and government offices—the sun-dried men, sometimes accompanied by pale seemly wife or daughter in starched flowers or well-pressed pleats. At that hour, too, the tourists were coming ashore from the President Lines, headed for tablecloths, carved ivory, and cloudy jade. A surge of early purpose seemed to be leading to something more than the chronic anticlimax of nightfall.

The harbour was an old photograph, a resumption: grey ships of war, shabby freighters, and the stout passenger ships with banded funnels. And the swarming sampans and lighters, the junks with tan sails boned like fans and the tan-coloured bony man at the stern working the yuloh; the greater junks, like galleons; and the coastal steamers off the Praya, arriving from Amoy or Swatow, or from green Saigon.

The office was in the bank building, the best building, the white block formed like a cenotaph that had been pointed out to Exley at the time of his arrival: the highest building, and the only one air-conditioned. The bank had thrown over the historic slow rotations of the ceiling fan in favour of the new climate, man-made. This building of thirteen storeys was, one was told, the tallest between San Francisco and Cairo. Exley, however, had a cubicle on a low floor, in a set of rooms occupied by fellow officers. A group of translators in an inner room were local staff. There was an Admiralty clerk, on loan, who did the legal drafting, and a naval messenger had a chair near the door.

Three servicewomen worked in a room next to Exley's own: none of them pretty, none really young. One of them, Miss Brenda Mills, showed signs of ill nature. Of the other two, Exley could not be sure which was Monica and which Norah, and left it too long to ask. All three lived at the Helena May Hostel above the town. Each had been taken out in turn by the British officers on the floor, who had nothing favourable to report. One other woman in the office was Eurasian, of Portuguese descent. This was the typist, Miss Rita Xavier. There were, also, two Cantonese amahs, who brought tea thickened with condensed milk, cleaned the rooms, and in their tiny antechamber laughed with gold teeth at the pidgin jokes of the Admiralty clerk, who puffed his pipe at them in passing.

Here, through mornings and long afternoons, Peter Exley explored a heap of files and despaired of justice. His office had access to a terrace paved in big red tiles, undulated by the rains. The terrace, rarely used, looked towards the harbour. Seagulls wheeled there, and a cormorant at times alighted. On fair days, Exley would go out and lean awhile on the wide ledge. Would look at the war memorial on its patch of lawn, and at the parked cars and parked palm trees, and the sea beyond. The heat soon drove him indoors. Even so, he got a name for mooning.

That first summer, in the steaming evenings, he would leave the barracks and walk east or west until the long streets became entirely, incontrovertibly Chinese. He would stroll past the hundred thousand stalls and tiny shops of food, of clothes, of soap and pots and bamboo baskets; past the minuscule dens hung with lanterns and braying out harsh music, where the soft smell of opium exuded into fumes of the street. From what would once have enthralled him he would bring away only a flare of alien colour and raucous sound, a stench of crowds and cooking; and that scent, sickly as boredom.

Having walked in this way an hour or two, he would then return by some divergent route, perhaps along the docks—ignoring appeals from vendors or beggars and the offers from women whose negligible bodies seemed weighted with gold teeth and platform shoes. It was difficult to invest those meagre frames with sensuality, or to covet the lean shanks displayed by the flowered dress slit to the thigh. In these districts, Roy Rysom claimed to cut his swath almost nightly. Yet at the end of his own excursions Exley would often discover Rysom having dinner tamely enough—tame hardly describing Rysom's way with chopsticks—at the King Fu in Des Voeux Road, where a scattering of officers was always to be found. Sometimes Exley sat down with Rysom's group, giving himself over to the uproar of loud companions, the clamour of Chinese diners and of waiters yelling to the kitchen. From the gallery above there was the incessant clack and crash of the mah-jongg pieces, the spitting and shouting of the players.

His fellow soldiers repeated the stale anecdotes of lonely men. If anyone told a joke against himself, Rysom laughed too loud—his need for advantage vigilant as fear. If they walked back together to the barracks, Rysom, turning oracular, would caution Exley against his expeditions in the Chinese town: "Filth."

Filth was in fact on Peter Exley's mind in those first weeks: the accretion filming the Orient, the shimmer of sweat or excrement. A railing or handle one's fingers would not willingly grasp; walls and objects grimed with existence; the limp, soiled colonial money, little notes curled and withered, like shavings from some discoloured central lode. Ammoniac reek, or worse, in paved alleys and under stuccoed arcades. Shaved heads of children, blotched with sores; grey polls of infants lolling from the swag that bound them to the mother's back. And the great clots and blobs of tubercular spittle shot with blood, unavoidable underfoot: what Rysom called "poached eggs." In such uncleanness, nothing could appear innocent, not the infants themselves or even diseased chow dogs roaming the Chinese streets, or scrawny chickens pecking at street dirt.

What had not harrowed Exley as a soldier in Egypt or South Italy now brought revulsion. He longed for a measure of cleanliness with which he had somehow associated peace. Returning to the barracks with Rysom, he said, "I realise now that I came out here to be well fed and housed and to have people wait on me. I see now that was in my mind."

Rysom kicked open the door of their room. "Well, this is it, mate—the life of luxury."

The greater thing was heat. In North Africa, the sun had been neutral, an impartial horror of war. Now, with cessation of hostilities, heat came out in its true colours as the enemy. The privileged of the colony clung to the mountainside. The rest took refuge in any merciful shadow or flutter of the humid air. The town never cooled: streets and street stalls broiled all night in the glare of naked electricity or paraffin lamps. A dry skin was an ultimate luxury, even for the privileged, even on a soft white body. Lust, if there was energy for it, must be consummated in a lather of sweat. And it was the same thing, no doubt, with love.

EXLEY'S TYPIST, the Portuguese Miss Xavier, was thin and possibly thirty. Skin like an apricot, with an apricot's minute brown flecks; straight black hair, not abundant, curved on shoulders. At her throat, in the soft hollow disclosed by a Western dress, a small gold crucifix quivered like a heart. Convent schooldays lingered about remote Miss Xavier. Someone—Brenda or Monica—told Exley that her four sisters were nuns.

"Eurasians," Brenda told him, "maintain a caste system of their own. It's no good mixing up in that."

It would have been pleasant to refute dogmatic Brenda. But in truth Miss Xavier of good family held aloof from Mr. da Silva, chief of the translators. Da Silva in turn condescended to his colleagues. All dealt brusquely with the Chinese.

Peter Exley wrote in his notebook: "There is a community of mixed races here claiming Portuguese descent through the Jesuit settlements at Macao. They interpret the British to the Chinese, and vice versa. I don't refer only to language, though that is their essential service. I mean that they form a bridge by which business is rationally done and power exercised. Disdained by both factions, ill paid, indispensable, and far too obliging." If he wrote this to his parents in Sydney, his mother would write back, "So interesting, pet," and put his letter with all the others in a cardboard box. She would tell some crony, "Peter always feels for the underdog."

She could not quite suggest, but pervasively implied, that some cheerful young woman would redeem her son's restlessness—not perceiving that the son, whose wanderings were far from wayward, was in some respects overredeemed already. Her husband, if appealed to, would turn another page of *The Sun*, remarking, "She'll be right"—habitual invocation of Destiny whereby the Australian male quelled speculation. He had given up expecting sense from this eldest son, whose bookishness led nowhere and who frittered the last of his youth scrambling round crammed little countries and learning dead inimical languages like Italian and Japanese.

Peter's unaffected impressions were meanwhile sent to Leith, whose letters at this time comforted him, supplying a companionable measure of intelligence, and testifying, within Exley's isolation, to a previous sharing. He saw how Leith, more reticent than he, nevertheless responded to new circumstances as to fresh existence, experiencing antipathy or charm as the essential matter of finite days; accessible, even so, to dreams engendered. Out of their mutual reprieve, Leith had salvaged immediacy; had kept faith with the fugitive vow of every man in battle: If I get through this, the hours will be made to count.

Leith now hoped to pass through Hong Kong in the autumn. With cautious warmth, Exley looked to the exchange they then might have, not all at once, but over gradual days. He wondered about women in Leith's life. He had noted the little girl who was a changeling—aware that men will display love when they cannot help themselves.

IN AUGUST, Peter Exley was assigned to the interrogation of a Japanese officer charged with atrocities to prisoners of war. He had already noticed the man in the exercise cages behind the barracks, on a private road that led through trees to the general's house. The prisoner was listless, slight, still young; short limbs, cropped dark head. Sometimes the inexpressive eyes met Exley's. It was difficult to say, then, who was the accused.

Among those who gave evidence was the skipper of a Dutch merchantman on the Surabaya–Kobe run. Exley's letter reached this Dutch captain on his way north, at Singapore or Penang, and ten days later, landing in the colony, he came to make his deposition. He was something over fifty, Hendriks by name: dark eyes unmoist in dry face, soft knob of nose. His body itself, short and tough, announced taciturnity. He gave his evidence in brief, competent assertions, and in correct, peremptory English.

He had been taken prisoner at Tanjungpriok, the port of Jakarta, early in 1942.

In Exley's little office at the Bank, Hendriks told his appalling story with detachment. When the documents had been prepared and signed, the Dutchman said, "We are in port some days. You shall lunch on board."

On a Sunday of inhuman heat, Exley found himself on the Kowloon docks, following the shadow of the godowns until forced out on an asphalt wasteland where coolies hauled cargo for hoisting. The Dutch ship, squat and shabby white, had a short white superstructure cramped amidships. With driblets of rust on her hull and at the outlet of the anchor cable, she recalled the smirched bathtub of some old hotel. Exley was shown to a dim saloon, well enough kept up in its dark old way, with panelling and polished brasses and heavy chairs that had defied typhoons. On a long table, a snow-white cloth was set with the dishes of the *rijsttafel*.

Hendriks came in at once, his seamed flesh emerging, at collar and cuffs, from a uniform white as the table.

Bols was brought in a crock of ice, along with the circular baked patties that, according to Roy Rysom, contained dog. As the indoor contrast passed off, the heat in the saloon became terrific. Condensation slid from cold glasses and formed a puddle of white starch around the ice bucket.

At table they were served, in silence, by a Malay and two Chinese.

The elaborate ordeal of drink, heavy food, and blazing sauces slowly consumed the afternoon. It seemed easier to loll there than to cut the thing short, Hendriks being clearly unprepared for any abrupt departure. Exley disliked his blunt manner with the servants, the orders rapped without a glance; and his unquestioning assumption of a right to bore. Drink settled in at eyes and temples, pulsating in purple rings. There were extended silences into which the ice collapsed with sharp sounds in crock and glasses and both men softly mopped at eyes and jowls as if quietly weeping.

Exley realised that Hendriks was getting ready to talk.

Hot towels were brought, scented with sandalwood. Hendriks offered cigars from Havana and maraschino in a pudgy bottle: "You shall have a glass." His hair, mouse-brown perhaps on a cool day, was dark with sweat and from some shiny unguent.

He said, "This Jap," pronouncing it "chap"—"This Jap of ours looks normal enough, would you say? Yes. Has been a cadet, privileged. So he goes to war, he ties prisoners to trees for bayonet practice, he eats human flesh, by preference the liver. Touch a nerve, the primitive is there." Hendriks chose a cigar and, with a small blade, clipped the tip. "You've been at war yourself, you've seen that."

Exley said, "I make a distinction between combat and perversion. Between soldiering and sadism. You may think that naïf."

"No, of course, I too wish to do so. There is cruelty beyond even that of battle. You look the man in the eye, then coolly kill him. You drop a bomb and dissociate yourself from the consequences. Is it murder or is it war? Is war in any case murder? That is what your commission pretends to decide."

"You think it mere pretence, then?"

"Excuse me, I use the word *prétendre*, 'to claim.'" The Dutchman sucked on his cigar, crossed foot over knee. "Yes. I was in a freighter, off the coast of France, when Holland was overrun. Mid-May, that was, of 1940. We were unarmed. Our captain was a small man, smaller than I, bow-legged. Ugly. We were bound for Rotterdam, when we had the news on our radio." Long wheeze of cigar. "The next morning, a U-boat surfaced across our bows.

"The captain of the U-boat—they are young in the submarines— the young captain stood out on deck with the megaphone. Two sailors at his side with the machine gun. We would be taken prisoner. This was the decent German, young man but old school. Unless we resisted, we would not be sunk. No. He would force us to an occupied port—

perhaps to Rotterdam itself—turn us over, and take our ship and cargo as his prize."

Hendriks pressed the towel to mouth, to eyes, and sighed.

"Well, we had our lives to save, we had families. Our skipper had four children. He stood on the bridge talking terms, reasonable, while the U-boat drifted closer. When she was right under our bows, he suddenly gave the order: Full speed ahead. And we ploughed through the U-boat, we ripped her in two, the submarine and the young man, and all the rest of them. They went down like skittles—you know how that is. We kept going, we didn't look back for survivors, we didn't stop until we reached Plymouth with the gash in our bow. At Plymouth we drank up, we laughed, we were proud." From his chair, Hendriks turned his soft-nosed profile towards Exley. "I suppose that's all right?"

"Not all right, how could it be? But it was war, you defended yourselves."

"So we said, exactly. And our Jap—would he not also produce his justification: reprisal for horrors witnessed or undergone? You say he took pleasure in the cruelty. And we too, we rejoiced in it, I assure you. Never so happy, perhaps, before or again. That mild, pious, ugly man of ours turned murderer in a second, and was overjoyed with the result. Of course we were happy that our skins were saved, and happy with our victory. But we were happy those men were dead and that we had killed them."

Hendriks knocked away a block of ash. "In any case, I took ship again, got to Portland, went on to Jakarta, and ended up in prison all the same. Prisoner of war—that was a Western concept Japan wished to follow. In their emulation of the West, they allowed some of us to survive. Had they known my parentage, they might have despatched me at the start." Peering into Peter Exley's eyes. "I'm part Javanese. You realised it?"

Exley stared.

"Yes. Grandmother East Indian. You didn't guess it? The tiny feet, the hands, the nose." Dispassionately indicating these, gesturing to the white shoe cocked on his knee as if it were disembodied. "In Holland they know it, or in Java. With us it was not as with the British. We Dutch—you notice I say that—we Dutch bred with the *indigènes*, we sometimes married them. And there are many such as I." Relapsed in his chair, presenting the undulant profile. "One day it will all mean nothing."

"I don't know that it means anything now."

"Ah—caste remains a useful advantage. To defy it, one still must suffer. Tolerance, the relaxation—that is far off. Too remote for you and me."

The revelation had made it impossible to get up and go. Some interlude was required in tribute, there could be no hastening away. Hendriks, having ceased pronouncing, fell into a silence in its own way oracular. Exley hung on half an hour, the ship melting round him. The two men took leave of one another at last, with assurances of a reunion when Hendriks next came to port. It was evident to both that this would not occur.

IN SEPTEMBER there were cooler evenings and, at the barracks, an issue of winter-weight blankets. At a Chinese tailor in Queen's Road, Peter Exley was measured for a suit in grey worsted. The tailor's shop, upstairs, was called Old Bond's Treat. The tailor himself, dreaming with open eyes, continually deferred the fittings.

Rysom said, "The bugger takes opium."

At the bank, refrigerated vapours mingled visibly with pipe tobacco. Miss Rita Xavier now draped a linen jacket on her shoulders as she typed and filed, and wore nylon stockings on her slender legs. With autumn, her virginal aspect was on the turn for spinsterhood.

In the adjoining room, hefty Norah thumped her thighs and shouted, "God, I'm getting porkers." And shaggy dark Brenda scowled with unplucked brows—as she had scowled one evening at a shipboard dance while returning Peter Exley's tipsy kiss. Rita Xavier's face, by contrast, was very nearly impassive. If Westerners had contributed shades of expression to the human face, Peter wondered, were they to be praised or blamed? Was responsiveness in itself something to be proud of?

In his notebook, Exley wrote: "Miss Xavier dislikes speaking Chinese in front of us 'Europeans.' I hear her at it, directing the office cleaners—a pastiche of Mandarin, Cantonese, and even Hakka, learned in childhood from her amahs. She has good French, taught by the nuns. Some Portuguese, presumably. English excellent, cultivated—a better enunciation than my own. A fine vocabulary, curiously unrelated to any literary knowledge whatever: she chooses good words as they do in Latin countries, from having no alternative. Tells me she had an English governess, a young woman married to a non-commissioned officer stationed in Hong Kong between the wars."

Exley closed his notebook on the governess. Some educated girl of good family, condemned by injudicious love to isolation in the colonial lower ranks. The colony was a backwater then, overshadowed by Shanghai. Shanghai was the place to be. The loneliness of such a life, the unfairness. The wilting pink-and-white, the ailments, the wretched economies. The unforgiving good family: "She has made her bed and must lie in it." And the bed itself losing its magic. Some Amanda or Cassandra, fallen between two stools, between two wars.

The everlasting question of women, the absence of women, of pink-and-white women. Even the glowering Brendas were in demand, let alone the pretty Camillas, the English roses. In this respect, the racial lines were quietly and implacably drawn. Hendriks, the oracle in his rusted bathtub, was perfectly right: to flout the agreement, you could not be casual; for you would be made, by both sides, to suffer.

"How terrible," said Monica or Norah, "when there are children of mixed race."

When Monica, Brenda, or Norah said this, Peter Exley was walking with all three of them on a late afternoon to the Helena May Hostel. He had been invited to tea, for his birthday. They had gone up through the park and passed above the barracks. It was cool as they climbed. Simply to cease sweating was an inducement to thought, and Exley had forgotten his companions.

Monica gave him his cue: "Tragic, don't you think?"

They suspected Exley of harbouring large ideas which he would not have the gumption to assert.

He said, "Well, it happens."

Giggles, as if at something audacious. There are women, he thought, who can paralyse a man's best instincts.

He said, "As I see it, the mixed races seem indispensable here."

Brenda said, "Like the Virgin Rita." The three women laughed, pausing to do so with vehemence.

"That nun."

"A nun, like her sisters."

"Sister Rita."

"Santa Rita."

"Pretty prickly for a saint."

"Santa Claws."

He could not walk ahead or fall behind. An overhang of trees shadowed his face. There was the smell of green decay that he had once mistaken for health.

At the hostel, in the lofty lounge, balancing his cup on the arm of a wicker settee, Peter watched these disputations, thick-bodied women stumping off to fetch cake and a bowl of sugar with silver tongs; plumping down on the chintz roses of plumped down cushions and fondling with near abandon the shamefaced, slavering Labrador belonging to the maiden directress. The airy room, the light of Asia, and strange red lilies in a vase could do nothing for them.

Brenda sat facing him, hair shoved back from ears, jowl distorted by a bad mosquito bite; flushed from nuzzling the salivating dog. While imploring Exley's advances, plainly summed him up as a poor thing. The low estimate had nothing to do with her yearning to be chosen and thus brought into existence. Judging him a poor thing, she would yet have married him and given him a devoted form of hell. Exley knew it. They had mutely agreed on the elements, if not the outcome.

As ever, his thoughts drawn by pathos; his imagination captured, when it might have been fired.

6

BENEDICT WAS UP, sitting in Helen's chair. An American doctor interested in his case had sent a new medicine from Tokyo, which had brought him better mornings. Leith found the boy finishing his breakfast, a sheaf of crossword puzzles at his side. Puzzles from *The Times* were sent by Bertram.

Helen was up at the house.

Benedict, if his respite lasted, would be interested to see Hiroshima. Leith said, "Of course we could do that."

"Helen might come. If I can't manage it, Helen could go without me." He said, "She needs to do things on her own."

"Does she say so?"

"No." Benedict said, "This is a new degree of seclusion. Even in India, where we were out of the city, she could go about and see things. She had friends. And I was better then."

"Hiroshima isn't a joyride. We could take her elsewhere." Leith doubted that the parents would let him make a habit of that.

"We had that grand journey, halfway round the world. Even then, she was expected to stay close." Benedict said, "I will tell you about Marseilles.

"At Marseilles, we set foot on Europe. We'd sailed from Bombay and called at Aden, did the Red Sea, surfaced at Port Said. My mother, along with the two of us. Helen and I sat up on deck all night in moonlight to see the coast of Crete, to pass Messina, sight Stromboli at dawn. The ship's engines went on the blink, and we lolled awhile in the Strait of Bonifacio, within ecstatic sight of Corsica and Sardinia. Helen remembered that John Henry Newman had composed his hymn there in similar circumstances, and she and I furtively sang 'Lead, Kindly Light,' and cried.

"At Marseilles, the port had been destroyed in the war. We walked from the dock straight into the heart of the city."

"Along the Canebière."

"You know everything. There was a market that day—serious stalls of tools and farm implements. Then, tables of much rubbish. My mother wanted a comb, and gave her change purse to Helen, who went and bought the thing. We had bitter coffee standing at a tiny café on wheels. My mother said, Undrinkable. We'd never seen espaliered trees, and thought they must be blitzed or dead. At the end of the avenue there was a tiered monument to the dead of all wars. We thought it looked very fine. People were kind. We were two creatures from the colonies. At least, however, and thanks to Bertram, speaking French.

"My sister wanted to walk to the monument. But I was tiring, and from the look of it, climbing would have been involved. Then she and I would have liked to lunch at one of the little restaurants around the market. But my mother wouldn't hear of it: we should return to the ship for lunch."

"Why?"

Benedict laughed. "Why, because on board we need not pay. In such matters, as in much else, we are helpless. Like Royalty, I carry no money. Unlike them, I have none. In any case, there was also the impulse to resist our pleasures. So we trailed back to the ship, Helen lagging behind. Near the dock there were ramshackle blue buses—for regional people, I daresay, going home from the market. One was marked CASSIS and another AIX, on cardboard signs stuck in the window. To think that such names were within our reach. As we boarded the ship, one of the buses could be heard starting up. A fellow passenger from the ship came to us breathless to say that Helen wanted us to know that she'd gone to Aix-en-Provence by bus and would be back for dinner.

"My mother was, as Australians say, ropable. And I—I was dumbfounded with admiration and love."

The man was picturing the girl in outgrown coat, setting off alone for Cythera in the blue rattletrap.

Ben said, "You will understand it. Not just that she'd thrown our mother over, in full knowledge of the fearful consequences—the Mad Scene in which our mother would play Ophelia, Gertrude, and Claudius all together. What was marvellous was that she had also thrown *me* over, breached our agreement, acted entirely for herself. Saved her soul. I even enjoyed my own pang of resentment, which showed the necessity for her gesture."

Less enjoyable had been the long afternoon. The mother shrieking: "Anything can happen to her. ANYTHING."

Ben, from a deck chair, had disbelieved that the white slave trade was centred on Aix.

"She knows nothing, can't you understand, she knows NOTHING."

"And whose fault is that?"

Helen had come back punctually for dinner. "I had felt for her as the day declined, but she was beyond our reach. There is no arguing with exultation. My mother tried everything in her arsenal, but Helen was immune for the evening. She was beautiful. The last straw was that she had brought back a packet of some sweets they make at Aix, further violating the matriarchal purse. Having had something over from the bus fare and after a *café crème* outdoors in the Cours Mirabeau, and the purchase of a postcard. An English couple for whom she translated the menu had ordered her a *croque monsieur*, possibly sizing up the situation. Hallowed be their names. She was hungry on return and had a hearty dinner, our mother all the while declaring that she herself could touch nothing."

Ben said, "Later, in the first-class lounge, she ate them, though. My mother. I mean, the Calissons d'Aix."

Sunday, grisaille. Suspension. Even the cataract in the gully below hangs in midair, awaiting Monday. This afternoon I finished a draft of my first section on China, and have been reading it over. It strikes me that, in the interest of coherence, an infinity of impressions have been sacrificed and, along with them, some experienced truth. So it must be reworked. In the meantime, the thing emerges as worth doing.

Damp English day, in which I've thought persistently of Aurora. My recurrent images of women appear less like memories than a means of restoring life to what has mattered and was passingly eclipsed by war. It is ten years now since she and I first met and were lovers; six years since I last saw her. I realise, too, that I now have a substantial past—which means that I am no longer young but have become more interesting to myself. I used to think that our story, hers and mine, was far-fetched, even freakish; but see now that the experiment of love is itself aberrant, more often than not, and doesn't lend itself to classification. A letter this week from Aurora, funny and charming, put me in mind of all that, and prompted a dream of her, with predictable result.

Recollection is also aroused by questions put to me by my two young people, with whom I indulge myself in orgies of answering. Retrievals not free of pain. For two such cloistered beings, their own adventures are bizarre enough. I learn that on the last leg of their voyage to Japan they were obliged to spend time in Hong Kong, due to the seizure of the cruise ship Van Heutz, *boarded by Chinese pirates at Mirs Bay two months past. Helen and Ben were to have taken the ship from Hong Kong to Kobe, and had to wait in a Hong Kong hotel while the shipping company sorted out their case. They seem to have enjoyed it as another reprieve. Helen thought it would have been exciting to be aboard when the ship was commandeered. Ben and I said nothing.*

The parents have allowed these children, one of them mortally ill, to

*wander the world alone. Given the context, I return to the conclusion
that worse might have happened.*

Leith thought that, if he replied at once to Aurora, he would write
a love letter, which was out of the question. All the same, it would have
pleased him, that Sunday evening, to write such a letter; even if not to
her.

He would not walk over to Helen and her brother. Aurora's tale was
not for them. They were taken up with Carlyle, and had reached the
atrocious farewells. He had heard the girl, that day, read out the word
"NEVER!" They had enough on their hands, and in their future.

He sat thinking of the name: Aurora. First heard when he was seventeen or so.

On a Saturday of the 1930s, he had gone to the ballet with a friend
called Jason Searle. They had got to know each other in their last weeks
of school, having shed adolescence in advance of their peers and made
friends as men rather than boys: Jason was the elder, not only for having turned eighteen, but for having already undergone the metamor-
phosis. Remaining friends, they would soon go to different universities.
On that Saturday afternoon, they had seen, in a suburban hall, a trio
of duets from great ballets, well performed. As they walked towards
Soho, where they were to dine, Aldred Leith had said that the classical
ballets would be more poignant if their stories were less defined: "That
is, no facts or names. Who ever heard, for instance, of anyone called
Aurora?"

"My mother's name."

"I beg your pardon."

"It suits her, actually." The youth Jason then said, "I'm rather in love
with my mother."

Jason was an only child. His mother had been deserted—as it appeared, on expensive terms—by Jason's father, who decamped to Kenya
when the boy was four. Jason had been "out" to Kenya three times,
finding animals and landscape revelatory; but oppressed by the colonial
life ("Boozing can be a bore, you know") and, it might be guessed, by
father and stepmother. Jason thought that he might eventually want to

live away from Britain, but not in the colonies. At university he became known as both precocious and mature. There was the brilliance, also, of a temperament that generated expectations. As it was, he left the university without taking a degree and travelled at once to Spain, where he died of wounds fighting for the Loyalists in a minor skirmish of the Civil War.

Some months after the event, Aldred Leith received a note signed "Aurora Searle," thanking him for a letter of sympathy, informing him that Jason had wished him to have certain books and a picture; and proposing an afternoon on which he might call.

At the agreed hour, on a day of bitter cold, Aldred had gone to the house near Regent's Park. He knew the flat, which occupied a floor in a rather grand building; but had never met Searle's mother. Her brief letter, simple and civil, had offered no clue.

He rang at double doors—expecting to be ushered, by solemn servant, to a darkened person in darkened room. She answered the door herself: Aurora, in palish, pinkish tweed and a silk blouse. Fair hair, falling over shoulders. She said, "How cold your hand is. You came without gloves." They went into a room that he had never previously seen, smaller than the living room, where walls were covered in moiré and chairs in chintz. There were freesias in a vase, and a fire burning. Above the mantel, on which stood a pair of old china figures of John Bull and Britannia, there was a mossy painting of women by a river.

She said, "Shall we have a nip of something? What do you like?" Speaking low, with a slight inflection that recalled the voice of Jason. Leith saw, however, that Jason's colouring had come from the father. The mother was blue-eyed, and gold.

She put wood on the fire. Body and gestures were lithe and unaffected. Looking for a bottle in a low cabinet, she did not bend but sank swiftly to her haunches, with straight back. She poured, handed, sat down. "You wrote a grown-up letter. Something few people can ever do."

"He helped me grow up. He was adult before I was."

She held her little glass, looking at the fire. "Whereas he kept me young. I was eighteen when he was born. My youth was spent with him."

So she is forty. Aldred Leith, who had turned twenty, saw the small foot and pretty shoe, the slim calf, the fold of soft material at the knee. Her clothes were loose on her, from loss of weight. On a wrist incredibly slender, a little watch slipped about with her movements. She wore no ring.

He saw that she was too young to have died with her son.

She asked about his plans, his interests; and they spoke of the threatened war. Once or twice she quoted Jason—"Jason thought," "Jason felt"—and appeared to do this naturally enough. But the young man understood that she had schooled herself to it, so that the son should not become a closed subject.

He said, "Jason once told me that he was in love with you."

He could not have imagined, beforehand, that he would say this quiet, bold, familiar thing, which put them on sexual ground. Callous in his own ears, the words were involuntary; but an approach. And, had she not then lifted dispassionate eyes, he might have added, "How beautiful you are."

She was practised in turning imprudence aside. She said, "The things he wanted you to have are on the table behind you. Won't you look through them?" When Aldred got up, she went on, "He left a page, it was in his desk here, asking that books and objects go to friends. There were other requests." The man, with his back to her, a heavy book in his hand, listened to this new, lowered voice. "And a letter was brought to me, afterwards." She had meant to say more, but did not or could not.

There were perhaps thirty books, and a small picture in gouache of the Roman Campagna seen beyond angled roofs: the date, 1780, the painter's name French and unknown to him.

Aurora said, "How shall I get them to you?"

It was agreed that he would take some things then and there, and return another day. Aurora fetched a bag of canvas twill. Having packed some of the books and wrapped the picture, Leith remained—hesitant, graceless. Aurora lit a lamp. For an instant, above the glow, her face showed discomposed and tragic, and the strands of hair became a splintering. As he hoisted the bag, the phone rang.

The receiver in her right hand, she held out her left in a gesture of goodbye. She was saying, "Hello . . . Oh . . . Yes, as you like." He understood from the tone that she was speaking to a man. Releasing her fingers, he went away disconsolate.

BEGUN THAT WINTER, their affair lasted through the spring. It was not Leith's first passion, but his first engagement with lion grief and its transformations. Aurora, in an episode that she never afterwards minimised, pursued this evidence of her continued existence. She had a habit of crying in her sleep, which he could scarcely bear for her. A habit, also, of calling Aldred by her son's name, which he did not mind, seeing it as central to their entire connection.

Love could never be, for her, a calculated act. But she observed and understood herself, and soon withdrew. Leith was to study, that summer, in Italy; and she said, "Italy will soften the blow." She told him, "We will see each other always." But these two were no longer lovers when, the following September, they ran into Aldred's father lunching in a restaurant near Covent Garden.

The son remembered the charming restaurant, charming father; the discreet liveliness around them, some red velveteen luxury, and their own soft talk. How his father, coming up, joining them, was at his best—the elder Leith having only a polarised best or worst, with no intervening tropic of moderation. Rising to the occasion, all three assumed their parts. Aldred was the son; but, sitting slightly back from the other two, perceived what was happening and what would ensue. In those moments, he possessed the event, while his father, with all his seasoned subtlety, was trapped in it, predestined.

Oliver Leith could be, and that day was, most amusing. And then he was handsome, and well known. (They were hardly seated when another diner, unknown to them, came to their table: "I think you're Oliver Leith? Just want to say, I love your books.") His long face did sometimes, even then, show unkindness. But it was unkindness of the suffering, needful, consequential sort, avid for women's love. He did not so much want a safe haven as the stimulus, rather, of disturbing another's peace. And then, Aurora's femininity was of the kind that seeks, ultimately, to devote itself: in her, as in many women of her time, there was something of the victim. Reading all this, the father drew her on, suspending the ritual show of disbelief that, as far as his son was concerned, had all but annihilated communion.

This, with Aurora, was the most enduring of Oliver Leith's liaisons. And of hers.

Aldred, in Japan, thought judiciously of his father, who had never cheaply courted fame, yet could not live without it; who, despising sycophancy, exacted submission from those about him. Not a great man, but interesting and singular. Not loving, but seized, even grandly, with the phenomenon of love.

"I WATCH MY SISTER learning Japanese. Our old roles are reversed: I now sit in on her lessons. Concentration fails me. I take in something, but I tire. Meantime, I love to listen. You perhaps foresaw this." If I had lived, I should have liked to learn all languages, read all books. And be the sensualist I might have been.

Such were the speculations, desolate, voluptuous, that Benedict Driscoll could not forgo.

Helen asked Aldred Leith, "When you learned Italian, were girls involved there, too?" From diffidence, she rarely used his name.

"They were." He said, "Should I be more alarmed by your curiosity or my own compliance? The idea was that I should sit the Foreign Office exams, a stiff proposition then. Romance languages were required, that was the least of it. There was a villa above Florence where one could study with a teacher but live *en famille*: the place an enchantment, the owners uniquely lovable, my fellow students few and agreeable. In an hour, one walked into Florence.

"There was also fascism, rife in city and countryside. At night, young men held the gladiatorial battles of an unequal civil war. Up at the house, the head of that family, a lawyer and well known, had lost his livelihood by declining to enter himself in the fascist listings. That was their reason for taking students as paying guests. No doubt we were watched and reported, but English oddities at Florence were still an old habit, hard to simplify. I went there three times in the course of two years, a strong factor being, yes, the daughters."

"How many, and what names?"

"Two. The elder, Raimonda; the younger, Gigliola. Yes, they were beautiful. Also, three sons, one of them already conscripted for Mussolini's army in Africa. That was Dario, later to die in Greece." Leith said, "This story does not end as well as Charlotte's."

"We don't know how things went with Charlotte."

"Benedict, let me keep Charlotte. Let Charlotte be safe and happy."

And Helen: "Yes, yes. Charlotte lives happily. Wherever she is. Which of the sisters did you love?"

"We were all in love with both of them. At first I was mad for Raimonda, the more reflective of the two." Gentle, good, and tender creature. "Raimonda was, however, spoken for. At weekends, her suitor would arrive, handsome, from Pisa, where he was becoming learned at the university. From Monday to Friday, I was free to yearn after Raimonda." And to imagine that she, in her maidenly way, felt something in return. "She was my elder by a year. As summer progressed, my case seeming hopeless, I turned my attentions to Gigliola."

A laughing, quicksilver girl, with high breasts and sun-streaked hair. "Gigliola played the flute, and played fast and loose with the lot of us. That first year, I was the last of the foreign students to leave and so had some advantage. Nothing spectacular, unfortunately. Still, she came to the station to see me off." In a white dress and red sandals. And put her brown arms round my neck and her cheek to my shoulder so that I kissed her ear as the train was leaving and her hair came to my mouth. In a desperation of helplessness and desire, he had felt that impulsive pressure all the way to Domodossola; and sporadically on, across frontiers, throughout an autumn and winter in which his studies drew praise and he continued his friendship with Jason Searle, who was very soon to die; he too, in war.

Having extra money at Easter, Aldred Leith made, with extravagant excuses, an extravagant journey, reaching Florence by train at sunrise. Across from the station, pavements were being hosed, a café was opening up. Workmen were taking their coffee, and coughing and stamping against the cold. At the counter, Leith ordered *caffè corretto*, not because he needed the fillip of cognac but by way of celebration. Through the miraculous dun-coloured streets, shabby, odorous, malodorous, and rumbling with early carts, he crossed the river and walked out, euphoric, to the Scopeti—where, by an ancient causeway, he turned off for his destination and his dear. The chill watery morning grew fine and mild, a countryside glimmered celestial. Entire hillsides of iris, pergolas of wistaria, overhanging fronds of lilac breathed out drops and petals as he passed. In a stone village, by the high historic house where descendants of Machiavelli were stirring, two yoked white cows lumbered past him drawing an empty tumbril and dropping, in unison, their steaming dung.

I wear the clothes that are seemly, I take the nourishment for which I was intended and which is mine alone: I converse with the great minds of an ancient world. And from these discussions have distilled a little pamphlet entitled On Princedoms.

The country people smiled, seeing bliss; aware that his own smile was not exclusively for them on that morning when he loved the world.

He approached the house by a path through fields. On the last slope, where vines, scarcely budding, were interspersed with olives, he heard the flute. The house, on its rise, was a splendid ship to which he was being piped aboard. On the carriage drive, pebbles spilled under his boots. In the cold waxy hall, he swung down his knapsack, scarcely felt on the walk. Music ceased, and the girl came running down the stairs while her mother from above called a caution: "*Adagio. Adagio.*"

She had the flute in her hand. She was not Gigliola, she was Raimonda. Gigliola had gone into Florence to meet the wrong train.

Impetus was irreducible. He took Raimonda in his arms and gave her the outright kiss intended, all winter, for her sister.

When Gigliola came, agitated, in a small calèche that she drove herself, he ran down the drive to meet her, scattering more gravel. She flung down the reins and sprang—she too—into his arms. They, also, kissed; again, unchastely—the man registering the same desire experienced, moments past, for Raimonda.

As he came back to the house leading the girl and the little horse, the mother remarked to her amused husband, "Where expectation is high, ambiguities generally enter."

Raimonda, flushed but calm, appeared with coffee on a brass tray. She handed the flute back to her sister.

Near evening, alone in his room and leaning out to close shutters on scenes where fruit blossom flared in twilight and a walnut tree was leafless, Leith could relive his arrival. The youth, which he as yet was, being proud, elated, undecided. The adult, already present, smiled.

Years later, he merely recounted, "I arrived."

Helen said, "I imagine it."

If anyone could, it would be she.

At the villa, circumstances were restricted. The family was becoming dangerous to know, and would soon be isolated. The affianced scholar from Pisa had withdrawn in tears at his parents' insistence. A cousin had gone, with the Italian Brigade, to fight for Franco in Spain. Other relatives accused them of putting their kindred at risk, which was true enough. The teacher, Lionello, was distraught in expectation of conscription. Italian lessons were suspended. "He came to see me and wept, poor Lionello."

Leith said, "The girls took on my education."

Helen imagined it.

A columned loggia one morning, and Gigliola telling him, "*Pátina*, not pateena. *Cándido*, not candeedo. *Fáscino*, not fasheeno."

Gigliola, not Raimonda.

"*Ótranto*," she said, "Not Otránto. Bríndisi, not Brindeesi. Arístide, not Aristeedis." And, sharply, "*Smèttila*," pushing away his hand.

Or it was evening and they were in a garden.

"*La luna calante.*"

"We call it waning, the waning moon." He laid his palm on her breast. "Gigliola, I—"

She put her own palm to his lips. "*Attenzione.*" Laughed.

There were so few days. There were scruples. Gigliola, despite bravado, was eighteen, and virgin. Gigliola had been handled; but, as yet, with care. When he came back in the summer it would arrange itself. So he thought, when not at her side.

And there was Raimonda, whose very forbearance galled him. On the other hand, when he saw her, tall and slender, laughing in the kitchen with the rosy cook, he regretted the impossibility, as it was by now, of renewing that particular kiss.

Kissing them all, he returned to England, in time for his birthday.

When summer came, all was in ruins. From a fellow student who had come from Florence, he heard that the father, Emilio, had been briefly arrested and beaten. Had been given the choice of receiving fifty lashes in public or being given, privately, a litre of castor oil. Having chosen the latter, he staggered up ten days later from his bed and suffered a stroke. The family had been served with a fine, impossible to pay, and were faced with confiscation of their property and dispersal.

Having this news, Aldred Leith went from Cambridge to Norfolk, to see his father.

"To ask my father. Who only said, 'It'll have to be worked out, how to send the money.' I'd kept calm telling the story, it was the only way with him. When he said that, however, I went to pieces." Put his head in his hands, while Oliver Leith put through a call to his agent in London. "After childhood, we become prepared for coldness. It's generosity that disarms us."

Helen was in tears, precisely for that reason.

"Oliver was capable of that. Still is, no doubt. So I went again to Italy. My father had money from translations, deposited with his agent in Milan. The agent, Englishman married to an Italian, warned me against speaking in his office, and we did our transaction in the cathedral, with a show of piety in a back pew. The money I carried to Florence was more than the fine. My father had given me a note for them—one line, typical: 'I hope to meet you when the war is over.' The war that had not yet begun."

When Emilio was dying, he said, "And I haven't done it." Hadn't signed.

They were almost isolated. No more fine suitors for the girls. For Leith, the gift of money had placed Gigliola out of bounds: he could not solicit what she might now yield from gratitude or obligation. She herself was intimidated by horrors, and by the charmlessness of existence. The local chief of police, a fox-faced widower with whiskers dyed ginger, sought Gigliola's hand. The girl was frightened, but pretended to laugh: "*Quel vecchio* Volpone." Mother and daughters were much indoors, and together. Two older servants stoically remained, and the gardener.

From the countryside, there rose the hot smell of crops drying, fruit ripening, old walls discarding their moss. At evening, the scent of petunias. By day, the big kitchen was cooled, through an open trapdoor, by a current of frigid air rising from the cellars. Into the igloo of that *cantina*, Aldred would descend, bringing up butter for lunch or the veal for dinner, and demijohns of dusty red. In earliest morning, would gather salad and ripe tomatoes from the cutting garden, and flowers that the girls arranged in vases. In an atmosphere of unreality and disaster, he was touched and happy.

One noon, he sat with Raimonda and her mother, shelling peas. The cook, Agata, was at the stove. He was the man now, in a household of women.

The mother said, "Aldred has a tender heart."

The youth blushed. "Not tender enough, perhaps."

Raimonda pushed a fugitive pea in his direction. "Tender enough. But reluctant to show."

And this was a girl he had kissed with abandon.

"One was raised that way. Schools strict. Parents not demonstrative." He hoped to end the discussion by eating a whole handful of peas.

Raimonda said, "That was their affair. Now it's up to you." The tone in which she said this, without rigour or rancour; almost in reverie.

He had come as their deliverer, bearing human solidarity. He was aware of a greater, putative rescue: that he could marry one of these girls and carry her to safety, or whatever passed for safety in the year 1938. No one, of course, alluded to this possibility.

In the year 1947, Leith could speak of it in Japan. "I was too young. Not simply because of my age. I was unformed. Had Gigliola been much older, and less attractive, I might have done it. There would have been the understanding—a marriage of emergency, the prompt separation. But to marry the actual Gigliola, take her away and perhaps cast her adrift—I wasn't ready for that."

Benedict shook his head. "You can't reproach yourself."

Leith stood up. "If I'd done it, she'd be alive." He said, in a voice they had not heard, "She was shot." It was as if he himself had not expected this end to the story.

They could not think what to do—unless to embrace him, which as yet they did not dare.

Helen brought green tea, her hand inevitably trembling. She and her brother were quiet, but excited by the story and by his having confided it. They talked a little between themselves. Seeing him moved, they did not want to stare. The girl thought, How close we are, this instant.

Helen looks at me as no one has for years. Perhaps, no one ever. I am telling these things for her. Not just to cut a figure, but to share my life. It's she who rouses Aurora, Gigliola; the death of Gigliola precipitating realisation. And if I know it, so must she.

He joined in their talk. He was calm as before—and greatly disturbed by what was indubitable and unreasonable, and would not give ground.

He told them that he had been, several times, to the temple. The custodian was always there, not readily visible: "He materialises." He had also climbed to a hilltop beyond the Japanese house, from which there was, to be seen, a world of bays and islands.

He told Helen, "We'll do these things some day."

When he went away, he knew that there was no possibility of it. If he brought her into the valley, or to the far hill, he would take her in his arms. His very happiness distressed him. He wrote to Peter Exley and set a date for his Chinese journey, which would remove him, for some weeks, to a great distance.

LEITH ARRANGED TO TRAVEL, first, in northern Japan, and from there to Harbin and Shanghai. He would then fly south and visit his friend in Hong Kong—from there sailing back to Kure; for he had a fancy to enter the Inland Sea from the west and see the islands. He expected to be away two months.

At the compound in the hills, no one could imagine his absence; even those who wished him away. He had brought substance to that counterfeit place. Of those who loved him, Ben feared to die before his return. As did also Helen, if differently.

On the morning of his farewell, Helen herself departed. There was a cultural expedition, to Kyoto and Nara, for dependents from Commonwealth forces. Helen had been asked, but could not be spared. She expressed no resentment, though Benedict wept in the night on her behalf and for his helplessness. There had then come a casual remark to their father from some person of standing. ("Dignitary," Ben believed, "is a one-word oxymoron.") A general whose own womenfolk had left by a repaired bus route had wondered, "Why didn't your girl go?" And Helen, hastily equipped, would now travel alone, by train. Her mother would see her aboard, she would be met on arrival.

"They are taking no chances," said Benedict, "of a second Marseilles." When Ben conjured up Marseilles, it was as if Napoleon invoked Toulon, or Montgomery El Alamein.

In the echoing shed used as common room, Aldred Leith sat to breakfast with the sister and brother. His own imminent departure deepened the mood of separation and change. He had left so many places in recent years, but partings had rarely counted: he had forgotten that partings could create this involuntary pathos. When the others came, he was sitting at a round table in the empty hangar, considering the distances that he, and she, must travel.

Benedict had been driven up the path for the occasion. Aki, who cared for him, helped him to table. Then Helen came, in her dress of small flowers; bright hair brushed back behind black ribbon; thin hands turned, by nervousness, to starfish. Feet hasty in pale shoes. Aldred got up. Seeing her agitation, Ben croaked, "Come on, it's only for five days," and she, smiling, walked her fingers over the top of his head as she passed. It was the larger parting, naturally, that weighed.

The men had left a place for her between them at the Formica table; but she, not realising, seated herself opposite, where teabags and powdered coffee, and cardboard novelties, had been set out with a thermos of boiling water. She made coffee and took a bleak Nordic biscuit. She said, "I wish you were coming."

Ben asked, "Which of us?"

"Both."

Leith pushed back his chair and crossed his foot on his knee. Watched her bite the penitential biscuit and wipe her mouth with a flap of coloured paper. A child, excited. A woman, and beautiful.

He said, "I envy whoever sits opposite you today in that train."

She held her cup steady. A couple of pinecones rattled onto the tin roof.

To his reproving self, the man acknowledged: I know. But could not help it. It was the alacrity of her saying "Both." Her freedom, and his own thrift. How prodigal, in these matters, are many women. And the occasion was producing some transparency. It was the man in the train whom he envied, the man who next year, if not today, would sit opposite and reach out for her, and take her.

He was right to be going, but not glad.

8

ON THE MORNING OF LEITH'S ARRIVAL at Hong Kong, Exley went to Kai Tak to meet the flight from Shanghai. The makeshift airfield—a scarred runway and provisional buildings on reclaimed land—resembled other settings in which these men had known each other, even to the overhang of scraped hills and dry mountains in whose shadow life was being improvised anew, if not afresh. Exley was thinking that he would say this to Leith. The sun was barely up, the sea breeze clean. It was the first day of autumn.

He parked his borrowed car between a pair of Quonset huts in the military segment of the field. From those wings walked onto a stage where all activity was in that instant precipitated, as by magnetic force, far off at the water's edge—concentrated there in a black swirl seared by flame and in a frantic convergence of vehicles and men. Havoc first broke loose in silence and slow motion. But then the sound came in, of sirens, motors, and the low explosive roar. And a pandemonium of men running and shouting. And Exley himself started to shout and run, and heard the same cries, of "God Almighty" and "Jesus Christ," from his own throat; until waved back by an airman in overalls, painfully sunburned, with an antiquated red flag in his hand.

"Enough trouble without you."

An older man was halted beside him, in RAF khaki. "Came in too low, hit the pile of rubble. The usual. The field's a death trap." The smashed plane was blazing into a cloud of particles, the black reek, and the ash, now reaching them. They all streamed with sweat.

Peter Exley asked, "Is it the plane from Shanghai?"

The older man, heavyset, said, "Must be."

Peter Exley heard himself say "No," like an obstinate infant.

The boy of the flag was also saying "No," brushing iridescent fragments from face and hair with his forearm. "No." He extended his flag arm, pointing it beyond Exley's head: "There."

Peter could make it out, the painted shape against the mountain: the machine coming in, silver, first descending, then rising abruptly, tilting, circling. Again, an illusory silence before the volume returned in a normal roar, with the red boy saying, "That's it, there, the Shanghai plane."

And the khaki man asking, "What's the one, then, that bought it?"

"Morning plane from Canton, second time since May."

Leith came from the Shanghai plane with a string of passengers: grave, sunburned, saved. Smiled as he found Exley in a gathering at the gate. When they had shaken hands and were walking to the car, Peter said, "You saw the crash."

"Poor devils."

"I thought it was you." Angry, aggrieved. "They told me you were dead."

"Heraclitus."

"I was furious." At the event, at his own hysteria, and Leith trying to get him through it with banter.

They trundled to Nathan Road, heading for the car ferry. He said, "I mean it. You'd run out on me."

Kowloon ran out at the end of their road in a display of spars and funnels. Across the strait, the green romantic mountain. Leith was staying at the Gloucester. He told Exley, "I gave your address to one or two people."

"Two letters came, I should have brought them. We can stop off at the barracks on our way."

Aboard the ferry, they stood on deck, watching the island arrive over the water, above junks, sampans, and lighters, and an American warship called *Valley Forge*. The villas, repaired, stood out from green declivities; there was the long, low, discoloured litter of the town at the shore. Sunstruck names of old companies could be made out on façades along the Praya: LaPraik, Dodwell, McKinnon Mackenzie; and a forest of Chinese signs. Beyond these, there were the ranked godowns.

Leith said, "I always liked it."

"I like it well enough." Exley seemed committed, now, to this measure of approval, even as he felt pleasure; even as he felt responsible for the occasion and the scene.

"I see the cathedral, the club, all the icons. Government House has acquired a Japanese tower."

"They decided not to pull it down. In fact, it doesn't look bad."

"The tall building is new since my time. The bank, is it?"

"I work in there, as it happens. The man-made high point—a primeval fact that ever excites attention."

"One of my early memories is being taken to the highest point in London by my godmother, a far from primeval figure in toque, dust coat, and lavender spats. My cousin and I climbed a spiral of three hundred and something steps. The monument to the Great Fire. It was worth it, though, at the top."

At the barracks, Leith sat on a trunk while Exley looked out his letters.

"Thanks." Glancing, pocketing, pleased.

The trunk was marked FARELF.

"Far East Land Forces. It's what I'm attached to. Not sentimentally, you understand."

Leith was looking round the room. "Peter, this is bad. You can't stay here." Noting the encroachment of Rysom's chaos. "Who's the chap you share with?"

Exley sketched in Rysom. He agreed: "I've let it drag on. They said there was no choice, but I should have kept after them."

Rysom irrupted as they were leaving. Exley made introductions.

There was the slight tension, on their part, of having just criticised this man—who, with his adverse quickness, picked it up, saying, "Speak of the devil, eh?" And turning to Aldred Leith: "He talks about you all the time."

"Mentioned you exactly twice."

"Got up at dawn to meet you. Excited as a child."

Peter said, "That's true enough."

Dissatisfied, they went their ways.

At the hotel, Leith had a large corner room with a terrace and an oblique view of the sea. The two men stood out in the breeze, leaning on an iron balustrade, while the world was exclaiming in the street below. In Des Voeux Road, the rattling trams, the new Studebakers, and the bells from pedicabs; in Pedder Street, the rickshaw coolies clearing space for their tawny stride with shouts of *Hai-yahh*, while a row of their fellows, squatting at the curb under Jardine's arcade, took their noon meal, the bowl in thick fingers, the other hand rapid with motions of the sticks. The scholars passed, slippered and gowned, the sun-coloured Buddhists, and the French nuns in sky blue under the white and mediaeval headdress. And the tourists, with wallets rashly displayed, filing into the Swatow Lace Company.

As they watched, a Chinese funeral came from Queen's Road in an outburst of colours and costumes and percussion instruments, the bowed mourners walking behind. Banners, lettered and fringed, proclaimed the virtues of the defunct—or so Peter Exley had been told. Leith said, "What I see is an advertisement for the band." The procession passed on, in a great collision of cymbals.

Reverberations of the crash were subsiding. By now, misery would have circulated: the dead would be named, the relatives informed; existences derailed. With the onlookers pursuing what had seemed, for the first grateful hour or so, their own charmed lives.

Leith unpacked, turned over a pile of mail, and sent for their late breakfast. There were still, of course, the two letters untouched in his pocket. And Peter, going to wash the morning off in the bathroom, thought that Leith would now be free to open these alone.

In the bathroom mirror, Exley's face was grimed, his eyes reddish. When he doused his head, flinty grit circled the basin, yellow pellets dissolved. His sweated tunic, pristine that morning and now slung on a peg, was similarly coated. The balustrade had added its own sooty touch at elbows.

When he came back, the room was full of light, the shutters open, the fan rotating. Breakfast stood on a wheeled tray. It was clear that the two letters had been read, though nowhere to be seen. Leith was sitting back in a familiar attitude, foot cocked on knee, hands clasped behind his head: abstracted, well pleased.

BENEDICT'S LETTER WAS SHORT, in an irregular hand:

Dear Aldred,
The way we miss you. Two American officials came looking for you. One nice, one not. I think they may be spies. They will come back. So will you, and in your case we'll exult. I am in a better phase just today. Helen will tell you how we speak of you, and love you—

Ben

Both envelopes were in Helen's hand. Also the following:

Dear Aldred,
When you were at Harbin, we looked at Harbin on the map; at Shanhaikwan, the same. When you get to Kwangchowwan, think of us with the atlas open. Still—

Maps are of place, not time, nor can they say
The surprising height and colour of a building
Nor where the groups of people bar the way.

These lines are about Verona, where we went with Bertram and where I put a rose on Juliet's tomb. Sad Newman, in the Strait of Bonifacio, smuggled a line from Romeo and Juliet into his hymn. Did you realise?

Looking up Shanhaikwan, I learn that it "is situated" where the Great Wall descends to the sea. Describe this, please, when you come.

Tomorrow, Ben is being taken to Tokyo, having a place in an ambulance plane, to see the American doctor who keeps track of his condition. He will be away a week. I am not to go. I am always afraid of their keeping him. This must occur to him, too. We don't speak of it.

Kyoto and Nara, now a month ago, seem a hallucination. Of this, too, when you come. The nice American, of the pair who came for you, took us out in a launch for my birthday, making all arrangements, miraculous, for Ben. His name is Tad. He is kind. He speaks some Japanese, but is subordinate to the other man, who is civilian. I can't ask him why they are here, as it might sound sarcastic.

We fear to weary you with our high feelings, but they don't change.

Helen

When he was alone, Leith closed off the noise of the street. He took off his boots and jacket. He drew the letters from his pocket and lay down on the sofa to reread them. He might have liked to speak to Peter Exley of these letters, but not to violate the immediate pleasure. In coming days, he might talk about Helen and Ben. About Helen. That release must find its moment.

You will come back. When you come. It was years since anyone had longed for his return.

As they sat at breakfast, Peter had said, "You look young, Aldred, for someone who just walked a thousand miles. When you came from the plane, I thought you older. But not now."

Leith took hotel stationery from a drawer and found his pen.

Dear Ben,
I think you will long since be back from Tokyo. What I hope, naturally, is that you've been helped by those days. In three weeks, I'll learn more, and perhaps recount something of these places where my travels appear to me as a farewell.

Please imagine, dear Ben, how pleasant it was for me, coming here this morning from Shanghai, to have your letter and Helen's safely delivered by my friend. Thank you for this, and for your words, which I hope to deserve. I'm writing now to Helen. You know my affection for you both.

Aldred

My dear Helen,

The letters, yours and Ben's, were so welcome this morning. Throughout my time in the north, I was busy, and seldom alone. But no one was reading Carlyle in the next room, or bringing me John Clare with tremulous hand. I have a volume of Chinese verse for your birthday—as I think, well translated. I have worked out that you are seventeen.

I remember the Verona poem, which you will say for me soon.

I know nothing of the two men who alarmingly "came for me." It's in fact quite possible that they are investigators. Washington is busy around the world these days, rooting out subversion. That I am not subversive would not help me in the least. If Thaddeus is kind, as you say, he should not be mingling in that Judas racket.

Seeing Peter again seems very natural. I think he is lonely here, and glad of my company, as I of his. The arrival this morning was unnerving, coinciding with the cruel crash of a local plane. We both, Peter and I, feel pursued by evocations of wartime violence, unexorcised. In my case, I think these now recede.

When I think of what has recently been, I'm incredulous that the world is preparing for more war. When I think of Hiroshima, I'm aghast, and helpless.

I still mean to come by the small ship from Hong Kong to Kure, though it adds three days. I'd like to enter from the west, by the narrow passage. In Japanese, the Inland Sea is called a strait. How do your lessons go?

May our high feelings never diminish.

Aldred

He put his two letters in a single envelope, addressed with both names. Holding this on his palm as if to weigh it, he felt it to be reckless. Reassured himself; but left it unsealed, one letter to be reread before sending.

He wondered what Tad's age might be.

He was to lunch at Government House, and walked along Queen's Road, then uphill through the park. All as it had been, as if never harrowed. In the vestibule, a fellow guest murmured, "We won't get a square meal here. It's iron rations, to show solidarity with Home." At table, Leith sat on the right of Lady Grantham, whose conversation was dispensed in iron rations. Indoor light was shrouded by elderly curtains. A youngish woman of good breeding sat on his other side, plump and sociable: handsome Miss Fellowes, wearing a hat of white silk flowers. She was unmarried, in her late twenties: a fair face, and kind. Her eyes and hair were indistinct, scarcely hazel. They found that they were staying in the same hotel, she for much longer. However, this mild gauntlet, laid gently down between them, languished along with bottled peas and beetroot and finger bowls. And they spoke of Yokohama, where Audrey Fellowes intended to visit her brother, who had lost an arm in Burma late in the war. A guest, who was her cousin, told him, "Audrey rallies to the afflicted. She is maternal."

Before leaving the table, they exchanged addresses in Japan, and in remote Britain, with ironic consciousness that they were not to meet at the Gloucester Hotel. Her good hands had a commonsensical way of bringing pen from handbag, of writing address in green notebook; aligning fork and knife. How women, he thought, develop capability, out of their hundred thousand rehearsals. As yet, Helen's hold on things was tentative, unless with a book.

Even so, I want her to grow older, to enter her nineteenth, her twentieth year. It's only that the circumspection comes in, and the charmless good sense.

Although he was meeting Exley later at the barracks across the way, he accompanied Miss Fellowes down to Queen's Road; and there shook hands most cordially. They understood, also cordially, that it was the least he could do.

That evening, he posted his letters, remembering that he'd considered the content injudicious. Remembering that his word had not been "injudicious" but "reckless." He wrote up his notes, and attended to the rest of his mail. At midnight, he reflected on the crash. It could easily, as Peter had assumed, have been himself. After wartime escapes, he'd expected better from peace. Putting out the light, he fell asleep a saved man.

HE WOKE with the early din of Pedder Street. A thin newspaper appeared under the door. In the bathroom mirror he looked unslept, but had his breakfast and read the paper. The crash at Kai Tak was on the front page, outclassed by a headline announcing, from Canton, Soong's arrival as governor of Kwangtung. On an inner page, the *South China Morning Post* carried a column of provincial cast about new visitors to the colony, where his own name was included, along with that of C. V. Starr, a big player in America's China game.

At eight, having bathed and dressed, and left a message for Peter Exley, Leith went out. In civilian clothes, he was a man in white and grey like many another, part of the illusory continuity. Almost everything he saw and smelt was recognisable, yet had been through the great convulsion. The resumption was an exercise in conviction, which has its own reality. Since childhood, Aldred Leith had been suspicious of reality, the word—having seen that every man had his version.

He walked along the Praya in the sun, pleased by his clean body and clean unsoldierly clothes. The port was in early ferment. He was nudged by a pack of beggars, mostly children, one of whom insistently thrust into his face the undulant head of a paper snake. He spoke to them, and gave some money; there was a squabble, and he walked on. To elude pursuit, turned into Chater Road, where a Chinese usher from the bookshop was taking down long shutters. The universal odour of bookshop, closed all night on the mildews of its ranked treasures, brought a past life before him—as is said to happen in drowning. But how, he wondered, entering and taking up a book, and even breathing it in to sustain remembrance, could one ever verify or explode the myth, except by drowning.

Helen Driscoll is in her eighteenth year.

Seeing him shrug, and smile, the young man in charge came forward: "Help you, sir?" The educated English youth to be found in such an outpost: dark lock of hair, damp dark eyes, pale complexion. We are never quite well, or pleased, in these places. (Yet Aldred Leith did feel well, that morning, and pleased.) The boyish, prewar sensibility, anachronistic, recalled the pensive photograph on the back of *The Centuries' Poetry*. Leith had long since given the entire set of volumes to Helen and Ben; to Helen.

He bought a new novel by a rising author, about wartime love in West Africa. He already had a military map of the island, but found another—better, because more personal, with old villas and monuments marked: of time as well as place. He recalled that Helen needed a chart of the northern heavens—which the bookshop did not have. On his way back to the hotel, he stopped at Watson's for toothpaste and shaving cream. The same staid premises; but shelves abloom with perfumes from France, lacquer for nails, and pretty concoctions of creams and powders—frivolities unseen for years in Britain, which had much need of a spree. Around the world, survivors were dabbing behind their ears and colouring their eyelids and brushing powder from their bosoms, without apology. They did not need to prove themselves. History, implacable, had done that for them.

In scorched cities, girls were twirling and trilling, and giving velvet glances, in spite of all they knew. They were laying roses on the tombs of lovers.

At the hotel, Peter was waiting. As they took the lift, he said, "Look, Aldred, it's damnable, but I'm duty officer for the afternoon."

In the room, Leith put down his packages and showed the map. "I'm thinking of a long walk. I remember the path. You leave from the Magazine Gap Road and wind over these hills, ten miles or so. It comes down somewhere near Repulse Bay." With a finger, he traced pale dots. "It has a name, Sir Cecil's Ride. Sir Cec having been an early excellency, I suppose."

"You'll be doing it without the horse." Exley said, "If we leave now, I can put you on your road. I still have the car." They would meet in the evening. Peter saw the package from Kelly and Walsh. "Can I see what you've got? I could have let you have my copy. The best novel since the war."

Leith had changed his boots and was filling a flask from the bottle of boiled water on the table. "So we still carry the same books, Peter."

Exley was touched. It usually fell to him to be the one who remembered.

THEY GOT DOWN FROM THE CAR on the gravel margin. The track was clear enough, leading through a damp socket of the hillside, and marked by reeds. Of these stalks and fronds, Leith said, "I think it's sedge."

"I've never known what it looked like. Aldred, if you're carrying money, better give it to me, and your watch. This is a lonely walk."

The man said, "I've made a lot of lonely walks," smiling to extenuate.

Peter was concerned, as at Kai Tak. "And keep an eye out for grenades, which are peppered through these hills." He said, "I wish I were coming along."

But Leith, he saw, was glad to go alone; and was, with patience, waiting for him to leave. Exley watched him start out, treading among tangles and brambles on a path littered with small stones and shafts of granite. It would not be a good place to break a foot or an ankle.

Leith amused himself thinking that Peter Exley was the only person in the world who knew his whereabouts; who, having cautioned him about grenades and hatchet men, would in the event have to come and find him. To save his life, in fact. Then they would be quits: a relief to both.

He was aware that he had willed Peter's departure, so that he could walk by himself and need not speak further. There was no irritation in this; only a need for perspective.

9

FOR THAT AFTERNOON, Peter presided over a set of military offices, largely empty. The personnel had developed, along with the heat, a rash of excuses—errands, illness, emergencies—during those heavy hours, when it might be imagined that little was taking place through all the somnolent East. The room was unusual in having a shelf of novels; and a shortwave radio, screwed in, as a precaution, to a bracket on the wall. It belonged to a Spitfire pilot, rarely present, who perhaps felt that he had already done his bit, and whose phone calls were exclusively from women, often anxious about the evening.

Exley attended to the few matters brought to him. Those who came and went were easy, civil, passingly companionable. They were able to maintain decorum by knowing nothing of one another.

Peter had brought his Chinese lexicon and a textbook of phrases set by his teacher. As the long orange afternoon drew on, he thought, as he often did, about the rest of his life. A particular cause of this was the proximity of Aldred Leith, with whom he was to dine; and who, knowing his past, might help him read his future.

Long ago, on an evening in Cairo, Exley had told the story of an only child in the genteel suburb of a remote harbour at whose outer escarpments the Pacific surged and pounded. Of Father at his law office and Mother laying the table for his return. Of the uninspired good school where bully boys and mild ones alike prepared for the same timid adulthood. A well-behaved boy, clever in class, brown at the beach—if lacking, in games, the flair of coordination. A fair assortment of friends, and no convinced enemies. Some early sense, ominous, of strength unexercised.

Aged eleven, at a friend's house after school, lolling on a back verandah amid the smells of banked lantana and baked eucalyptus, he flipped pages of the friend's album of secret pictures turned up in a toolshed trunk. There were coloured plates, full page, torn raggedly from magazines or cut painfully from good books. There were undraped women, reclining, and men with them; and a good deal of pale flesh. Something was wrong: nothing was furtive or complicit. He said, "These are paintings." He felt they had been presumptuous.

"Beautiful" had been a housewife's word, innocuous: his mother's word for the show of local handiwork at Mosman town hall. Now, in soft countryside, a radiant woman was turned in a dance by a near-naked man, her fine hair and garment all drifting light as air.

"Can I have this one?"

The chum, name of Kevin, feared some unauthorised indecency. "You'd better not."

Still, a beginning had been made. After that, there were books, alarming to his parents and teachers. He could not pronounce the names, at first, that roused his father's hilarity and the neighbours' solemnity: "Something not right there." As time passed, the derision of his little circle cooled to sceptical awe. There was apprehension that it might all be leading somewhere.

His parents enlisted a teacher of art, as they might have sought out a neurologist or other specialist in aberration. The man was impressed, but unnerved by the boy's single-mindedness. He thought it would pass with adolescence.

Loneliness grew on him with his relegation to the statelessness of art. There was Europe, remote as Paradise and more convincing. There was France, there was Italy. In the lending library at the junction, the two women in charge—a brawny pair, with cropped hair and tailored shirts—had attached a russet poster to the wall: ROMA. Peter's mother found the atmosphere unwholesome and the spelling affected.

There was the Law. His father had it out with him. Peter was eighteen, they had come unscathed through the Depression. "I don't begrudge your schooling. We can afford the Uni. But not for the art stuff, son. We don't go in for that in Australia, you'd have to leave the country. Break your mother's heart. I'm counting on you to do Law and join the firm. You can keep the art up, on the side."

Mother, in weak tears, could feel for him as long as he did not prevail.

He sent away for fine photographs, financed by menial odd jobs embarrassing to his parents. The packages took four or five months to arrive from London or Florence: the fastest mail by fastest ship was two months on the way. Alinari in particular did not have the habit of prompt reply.

He had learned some French at school: *Je m'appelle Pierre, je suis né en Australie.* He bought an Italian grammar. He was studying the Law. Was reading Homer, Hardy, and Tolstoy. He had been for the first time somewhat in love—with minuscule Pattie, who played the viola, and whose fine fairish hair hung, rather than swung, when released, well below her hips. She could sit on it, as the ultimate proof of maidenliness. Pattie had the bones of a sparrow, one might see the heart flutter under feathery clothes. Fragile shoulders scarcely bore the tentative weight of Peter Exley's arm.

Peter brought Pattie home to tea, and she arrived smaller than ever, her beige hair in two long plaits. Afterwards, his mother said, "All her strength's gone into that hair." His father, on the other hand, favoured the girl—having feared, from art history, abominations.

Pattie's birdlike pulsations were reproduced in a self-approving timidity and a voice that barely reached his ear. Like the rest, Pattie assumed that he would outgrow the Great Masters and sought to speed the process with an occasional impertinence, averting unsullied eyes from

Titian's *Danae*. The viola was to the good, of course, and the reciprocated attachment. And the hair played its part, though that, too, was colourless.

Pattie, becoming nebulous, evaporated.

The university gave companionship. There were evening classes in art appreciation. Among fellow students, Peter found some literary feeling, some political curiosity. He earned a little money with weekend tutoring; had a stealthy brief affair with a professor's wife called Norma, who laughed a lot; and a protracted misunderstanding with a student named Hazel, who often cried.

His dread now was to be trapped at the Antipodes. War had broken out in Spain, Mussolini had massacred Abyssinia, Hitler had set his sights on Czechoslovakia. Peter was in his twenties. If all Europe was to be dismantled, he must see it first. In a war, if he stayed, he would be called up, shipped out to some marshy ground, and blown to bits. Once abroad, he would at least have seen something beforehand. In the week following his Bar examinations, in which he had done well, he took cabin passage in the ship *Strathnaver*, leaving for Tilbury in one month's time.

His mother cried every night. "We'll give it a year, then."

His father, grim, said, "All right, but let's call it a day next Christmas. Your mother's gone out on a limb for you." Peter could see his mother twittering on the branch, like feathered Pattie.

The day of sailing was ecstasy no anguish could mar. There were, first, the Australian ports to be got through: Melbourne, Adelaide, and tin-roofed Fremantle, with letters from home at each of them. Only when the Equator had been crossed did he feel safe. There was Colombo now, and Bombay, Aden, Port Said: all the sacred places of pilgrimage, the stations of the Australian cross. Aboard, he learned from a British traveller that an exhibition concerning Giotto would shortly close at Florence. Leaving the ship at Messina, Peter Exley set foot on Italy.

He reached Florence three weeks later, having passed through whole stages of growth. If he slept, did not recall it; but remembered dawns when he was already active in ancient towns; and an evening when he left the sooty little train at Cisterna in order to enter Rome on foot, sending his luggage ahead. There had been dark walls at Viterbo, blond palisades at Orvieto. And, one evening at dusk, the station in Florence, and a church glimpsed through a steaming glass door.

He found a room in Borgo Pinti, in a house where students took lodgings. To conserve money, survived on errands performed for an elderly Englishman, elephantine Mr. Crindle, heavy breathing and heavy drinking, veteran of war and wives, who lumbered out each day with the support of Peter Exley and a blackthorn stick, to buy a thing or two and take his coffee in any sun going: who spoke rapid Italian in pure English pronunciation, and had, between wheezes, a fund of anecdotes and an endearing bark of a laugh.

In Cairo, in 1943, Exley had told Leith: "I learned from Crindle. It was from him that I first heard of tolerance, and where tolerance ends. He was good at sorting things out. I'd grown up in a country where sameness was a central virtue. Crindle made variety legitimate." He said, "That spring, in Tuscany, was my first in a deciduous land. The first spring in the world, as far as I was concerned." Then there were women, who all seemed to have lived before: their graces, innate as dreaming.

Then there was fascism, at Florence in vilest forms. "Again, it was from Crindle that I learned about that."

Crindle told him, "Mussolini is as bad as Hitler, and has taught Hitler a lot. You're just in time, here, for the onset of the Racial Laws."

"We've had racial laws in Australia for generations."

Crindle looked astonished; but said, "By now, nothing surprises me."

Exley, in the Cairo night, went on: "In his offhand way, Crindle knew a great deal. One of the British students told me that Crindle was said to be sending information to London. When I spoke to him about this, he laughed." Archie Crindle, majestically slumped in his wicker chair at the Giubbe Rosse, brownish tweed drawn back from striped shirtfront like the shed skin of an overfed reptile—an effect intensified by the texture of threadbare tweed and by Crindle's heavy eyelids.

Crindle saying, "Demmed elusive, what?"

"On the face of it, a preposterous choice for a spy. But after his death I thought it might be true. He liked to winkle out hidden things."

"So he died."

"Died in the new year of '39, in a spell of bitter cold." Exley said, "He left me two thousand pounds." His unlooked-for sorrow over Crindle's death; and the astounding two thousand. Peter, then studying at the Accademia, was earning little more than his bread by giving English lessons and translating the correspondence of a small importer of jams, teas, and shortbread. The letter from Crindle's solicitors brought his gratitude, and a long reprieve. And quelled his parents, impressing them for the first time with the merits of great art.

"The money was in England. In any case, I knew that I'd have to leave Italy, even if war was delayed. I mean that the game was up, for me as well as for the world. I would never be an art historian. In Australia, I'd had no basis for comparison. When I got to Europe, I wasn't even at the beginning, among those younger than I who'd spent their lives in full awareness. Isolation had made me arrogant, too. I wasn't prepared for the quality of thought in others. Spiritually, the Law had taught me nothing. Most painful of all was to recognise, once in a while, a passion greater than my own. The excuse of war enabled me to withdraw."

He said, "I've always given in easily."

"That's waffle. You'd done a lot."

"I'd come from the land of the single hope attained. One thing didn't lead to another, but was the sole consummation. People longed for a house and garden, or they pitched it all on a sight of the cliffs of Dover. The women longed to be married, come what might. The evidence achieved, you could die happy. In my childhood there were many such walking about, who had died happy and could leave it at that. And they were the enterprising ones. The effort of my exotic interest, of getting myself abroad and discovering ten thousand paintings, learning a language—all that my fellow students took for granted as preliminary, that was the immense feat on which I'd expended my en-

ergies. When the train took me out of Florence that summer, I was escaping under cover of war." He said, "All the same, I cried."

THE HONG KONG EVENING, with air like broth, was charged with Asia's
unapologetic smells. Leith walked with Exley to a low-roofed tavern on
the docks. Peter had discovered the place on his wanderings: the entry,
open to the street, gave on the waterfront. There was the hot, stark
electric bulb, supplemented by spirit lamps whose mild reek was agreeable. The plain front room just held the two men, the couple who
served them, and the furnishings—quite as if it had been composed
around them. They sat at a low square table, on bamboo stools. There
was a frequent passage of Chinese patrons into a back room, evidently
larger, from which fast emphatic talk was heard, and high laughter, and
some heroic clearing of lungs.

Hot wine was brought, and small delicacies. Having sketched in
their separate afternoons, these two might attempt to touch other experience.

"Aldred. If I can ask, has your divorce gone through?"

"Yes. Contrived after the barbaric laws of my country and yours.
The decree was issued some months past. I learnt of it at Chungking.
Moira has remarried."

"Anyone we know?"

Leith shook his head. "I never saw him. A decent chap, I gather,
who handles high-flown insurance, connected with Lloyd's. I can't—
God help me, I can't remember his name." He said, "I saw Moira before I left London. We met to sign papers."

"And how was that?"

"It was quite affecting." Revelations that need not be shared. "Quite
all right." Curious, in this place, to think that Peter had memories of
Moira. He thought that Peter would soon say, I liked Moira.

Exley said, "She was a darling."

A fish—garoupa, as it was called—was brought to them, cooked in
a sweet crust. Peter went on, "I recall her as capable, even efficient, but
suddenly funny and lively. Principled. Pretty. I'm saying this badly."

"No, exactly right." Moira is now near thirty, and perhaps with child. Charlotte also.

"I have a photograph of your wedding."

"I too." Everyone in uniform, the hectic handsome faces, the buxom matron of honour with shining eyes. Gardenias. The commanding officer gave away the bride. Aldred recalled Peter at the wedding, rather drunk. Peter had not been best man.

"Dick Summers was best man."

"Yes. Who was killed a couple of months later."

Peter said, "You too will remarry." Plucked a bone from his mouth. "I would like to marry."

"A good thing that would be, Peter, if I may say. Someone in mind?"

"No one. However, the idea—or ideal, at any rate—attracts me these days. Obviously, in practice, more difficult. But then, so is the single life difficult—drinking, lusting, languishing. Vacancy, loneliness."

They agreed that the fish was excellent. A young woman came from the back room, in shift and trousers, smiling. Received compliments, bowed, and withdrew. Down her dark blue spine, the thick, glossy, lacquered pigtail flopped heavily in a life of its own; evoking, in Exley, by vigorous contrast, the inanition of far-off Pattie's pusillanimous plait. Well out of that beige existence, at any rate.

He said, "Even if there were the choice, one needs the time. In these places, we are always facing some date of departure. And who knows if a desirable woman would want me."

"I should think it likely, you know."

They smiled—at the dismantled fish, it could have been, and the discarded chopsticks. People came and went, bringing hot scented napkins, hot scented tea. Peter said, "Earlier, one was careful not to commit oneself, lose one's head. I'll soon be thirty-six. There seems to have been a penalty on all that caution."

"The price of vigilance is eternal liberty." Leith did not consider that he himself had been vigilant with women. In the case of Gigliola, there had been immaturity but no calculation. It was only now that the necessity came home to him that he must weigh his words with a woman—weigh them, as he had done last evening, the envelope balanced on his hand.

Impossibility, which had appeared a safeguard, now seemed illusory.

His scruples. Scruple was a tiny measure, used perhaps by a jeweller or chemist. He had never dealt, in love or otherwise, in such minute quantities.

Along Sir Cecil's Ride, he had dwelt on the letters received, which had given him pleasure so simple and apparently pure that he could not feel some die had been fatefully cast. What struck him, on the contrary, was just the rarity of such charm in his days. The adventure of China, his engrossment in his drafted book, were not in question. But the context of his travels had been, as he had written to Benedict, a sustained farewell. All had occurred in an inward solitude, without intimacy, without the exposures of tenderness.

Following his marriage and its wartime dispersal, women had intersected his life in episodes unexamined, never entirely casual. The commitment to prodigious months of nomadic existence had itself been an engagement for near-celibacy. A need of women, even for their mere congenial presence, was for the most part ironically subdued. War, and peace, had separated him from closest friends, male and female. There had been the maleness, and boredom, of comradeship, the solidarity of combat; the relief—as it sometimes was, despite all the talk—of being free of the provocations and perplexities of women.

There was the word he had summoned for his father's photograph: "loveless." His mother's letters were attentively framed to avoid any late offering that her son might find, by now, an infringement. His father had, at most, tinkered with the parental role, taking it up sporadically like a neglected hobby and allowing it to lapse. Meanwhile, the son had cultivated independence—and valued it highly, observing the wrangles of his contemporaries with their parents. Exasperated by unsolicited emotion, as yesterday, when Peter's distress at the airfield had threatened him with undisguised affection.

To live for, there was his new work, and the great works of others. As to more poignant reasons left to him for living, there had been, in Paris, the response of the French officer: *Aucune.*

Now Peter was saying, "And you?" After this wandering, Aldred, are there women in your life?

It was clear that Leith would reply. Nor did the question trouble him. He was silent so long that anyone but Peter Exley might again have spoken.

"A girl has become dear to me. Something unsought, and impossible."

"Is it the changeling?"

"Of course." He said, "Her name is Helen, and she is roughly half my age."

"The name can't be bettered. And the rest will alter."

"Over years. So much is wrong. She, from the romance of it, imagines herself in love—or so I believe. I, at this age and stage, have grown serious. She is in these respects ignorant, having been allowed no life of her own. I can't envision myself as—what used to be called—her seducer. Still, I'm not a monk, and we live in proximity." Bleak words—which were a comfort to utter.

"Has this been said?" Peter meant, Do you make love to her? He feared to be misinterpreted, or intrusive.

"Only in the undeniable silence that can be denied at any cruel future time. My apparent role is avuncular, though she and I, and her brother, know better."

"And the brother?"

"He, in this, is the uncle to us. The parents, two hurt and irreparable figures who hate too readily, have decided to dislike me. They are much away, but have a deputy, a sad sort of Caliban, who keeps track. Nothing might please these three more than to discover me in some indefensible violation: I should thus, in their view, be brought to my knees." He said, "The letters, yesterday, from sister and brother, gave some happiness it would be hard to renounce. Discreet, as were my replies."

A dish of kumquats had been put on the table, and four small coloured cakes dusted with sugar. Leith said, "This is very good." He did not mean the kumquats, though the fruit were luminous in their blue dish. It was the quiet speech, and their shared lives.

When they left, Peter said, "It's pleasant, having you here. I'll miss this when you go."

"You might come and see me in Japan. Think about it."

"I could meet Helen and Ben. Or would they feel that I was sizing them up?"

"They, and I, would be pleased. Things must change for you now, Peter." Then Leith called to mind Audrey Fellowes—who had an air, herself, of seeking change.

ON A MORNING OVERCAST AND GUSTY, they drove out to the prison at Stanley, where the colonials had been interned by the Japanese. "Desolate," Peter remarked, as they crossed the island. "Looted since then, and abandoned." There was a plan to construct houses. But no one wanted, as yet, to live with spectral sufferings. "They were marched out here on Christmas Day, 1941, with what they could carry—men, women, children—and here they stayed, for close on four years. Beatings, starvation, diseases, death: the usual. After Hiroshima, after the surrender, they walked back into town, the survivors. Took up where they'd left off. As you've seen."

Peter had been taking depositions in the trading houses and banks, and in the colonial administration. Had called on taipans and clerks, and on their wives. Had stood in lofty offices, where looted furniture had yet to be replaced. Strolled on the arcaded upper terrace at Jardine Matheson's to talk with white-clad Number One; ascended in an ancient lift at Gilman's, or Butterfield & Swire, to hear the evidence of Numbers Two and Three. Sat in thin cubicles with juniors of the Green Point Cement Company; or waited in airless outer offices among the Chinese clerks and indispensable Portuguese, listening to the clatter of the abacus and the excruciated cough, the random languages. There was the Englishman appearing in a doorway: "Well, come in." The plain office, the pile of tedious, lucrative papers stirred by ceiling fan, the harbour fluted through slatted blinds. Blackwood table, creaking chairs. Unlikely setting in which to make an eventual fortune.

He told Leith, "Scenes from Conrad. Men from Conrad, passing the port around and relating adventures. Not all were phlegmatic, though most were. Not all were impressive, though some were. No one went to pieces in the narration. Generally indifferent as to the fate of their captors and tormentors, certain of whom were remembered as being far worse than others. Disdainful, however, of compatriots who'd behaved meanly in the camp or—if left at large through some technicality—had collaborated on the outside.

"Polite with me, pleasant enough." They would see him out to the expiring lift, or down the cracked linoleum stairs: "You must come for a meal, I'll get the wife to ring you."

If the wife rang, he went. Sat under an awning at Deep Water Bay or Shek-O before Sunday lunch: gin again, and the excellent prawns; hot sun, green sea. The indistinguishable small servants coming and going, the expatriate terrier underfoot. The colonial women, limp or hearty, filmed with perspiration. The houseguest out from Britain— some boy like a lily, or the strapping daughter of a retired colonel. Lace mats on mahogany, Georgian silver. Hunting prints, foxed, on humid walls. The starched servant holding the platter. The colonel's daughter remarking, "They all have those marvellous teeth, it must be the rice."

These were their days, seamlessly renewed. What their nights were, or their abhorrent dreams, they never did let on. Peter said, "I wasn't the journalist, or the social worker. Wasn't there to interrogate or pronounce. I needed their experience more than they needed to recount it. These were people who'd had to invent privacy in conditions where there was none. I wasn't there to dismantle that." He pointed. "That's where we're headed, towards that bay." He said, "One received an impression, that's all. As they would have had their impression of me."

The wind that shook the car was fierce enough to be blowing islands along a steel horizon, or clouds across rough water.

"With the women, yes, it was different, particularly if they'd had children with them in the camp. Absurdities recalled, and small gestures, and petty feuding, and the nervous inroads of hunger and climate. Grief over separations. Terror of the guards, terror at the deaths, and the hopelessness of years passing. And the grievances that women nurture differently from men. Some dark humour, some contrived pleasures.

The few books, read aloud, read and reread. Little concerts were got up, when allowed, and those who had a voice sang—arias, hymns, shanties, Gracie Fields. Poems were remembered, poems were composed. One heard these things from the women.

"The men invented illusions of order, coherence, authority. The senior civil servant among them set up a miniature tribunal to hear complaints, quarrels among the prisoners. This little court would regularly meet to adjudicate, dressed in its rags, showing its sores and scars. When I asked one of the women what penalties were meted out, she laughed. She said, 'That was the difficulty—how to punish us, who were so punished already.' It was the sense of form, I suppose; of remaining answerable to what had been one's standards."

He said, "One is always wondering, how would one have borne up, oneself, in the course of years. I met a couple who were married in the prison. They told me about it, all smiles. Brave." They had reached the sea. He said, "Well, here we are," and turned off the engine.

THAT DAY, Leith was lunching with the General. Near the barracks, Flagstaff House was white, colonial, comfortable in its own small park on a private road. The wind had dropped, the day had cooled, the lunch was ample. There was no other guest. These two had known one another in war.

With the changing season, both wore the short jacket, with latched canvas belt, called battle dress, and serge trousers rather too warm. The General, with white hair fluffed about his ears and face more florid, had lost some flesh with peace. His benign, enquiring face, well suited to growing older, had been paternal even in the field.

At table, a lobster was prepared to give up its flesh without struggle. The General said, "We feed you here, not like His Excellency. In the colony they say, 'So you lunched at Government House? Where did you go for tiffin?' We're all on a short rein now, but why mortify yourself over an extra mouthful? Britain's bankrupt, an extra round of drinks won't tip the scale. I don't apologise for giving you a good Bordeaux, instead of that dandelion wine or elderberry juice from Kent, served by

H.E. Since we've come out of it alive, Aldred, we should value our pleasures."

Our pleasures. He and I have killed, hand to hand, and have absorbed it. Can recall it, incredulous. Our pleasures were never taken that way, as by some in battle. Once, after a skirmish in the desert, a fellow officer whom he had never considered vicious had remarked, "A man who hasn't killed is incomplete, analogous to a woman who has never given birth." Embracing the primitive; even gratified.

If I were to speak of this now, here with the lobster and Bordeaux, facing the portrait of the shy King, this man would respond better than most: no pat answers; appalled by the unexampled horrors—the concentration camps, the Bomb itself. Yet not about to break down either. In the car that morning, Peter had said, "No one went to pieces." Well, they did and do, and one has seen it. But it's like the phenomenon of suicide in all our lives—the wonder is that more don't commit it.

There had been the ritual death in Japan, and Helen coming to his room.

Leaving table, the General said, "I see you've recovered from that bad business." Seeing no effect of his wound.

They went into a larger room, less upholstered, where a detailed map of China, occupying one wall, was studded with the progress of the civil war. Invited to trace the route of his travels, Leith was relieved when attention strayed. When they spoke of the Chinese war, the General flopped down on a striped settee. "Being handled as badly as possible by our side, you know. We're in the hands of the absolutists now, Aldred, Britain has no say. No influence." He said, "I can't quite believe that means no responsibility."

Later, walking in the garden, he told Leith, "When the change comes, and the capital returns to Peiping, we'll try to keep some formal tie, even if it's only a *chargé*. We'll get hell from Washington, but they'll be glad in the end. Anything else is infantile, the stakes being so high."

He asked, "I suppose you'll be leaving the army now, Aldred."

"Not for a while. However, yes. I'll want to change things."

Seeing him smile, the General thought, Some girl, no doubt. And smiled himself. When they parted, he told Leith, "Come again, while you're here. I like to see you. Keep well, my dear chap." Returning to the house, he said, "That's one, at least, who came through it"; and asked that a cup of tea be brought to him. His staff thought him in a good mood—which, to do him justice, was not unusual.

Leith, crossing the road near the barracks, at once ran into Peter Exley.

"Look, Peter, here's the name and number of the bloke you call to get new quarters."

"God, Aldred, you've never gone and asked the General."

"Of course not, what do you take me for; I asked the ADC. We'd more or less recognised one another. I didn't mention you, but you can call if you like and say he suggested. If you get new rooms while I'm here, I'll help you move. Protect you from your cellmate." He said, "But that would be after I get back from Canton. Tomorrow I start out on that excursion."

Walking back to the hotel, he thought that by tomorrow Helen might have his letter.

THE ENVELOPE addressed to both was brought to Helen by Aki, who helped Benedict in the mornings. She carried it, since Ben should now be given breakfast, into Leith's own room, using a key he had given. In the shuttered light and faint clothy smell of the absent male, with the dim books and objects that had enjoyed his company, she fingered the embossed insignia of the Gloucester, and even the plain, rather large handwriting on the envelope: glad that she could picture the very place where she had stayed with her brother during their days of hiatus at Hong Kong.

With a knife from the blotter, she slit the envelope; and lay on the bed to read, pulling out both letters and setting Ben's aside. There was no one to see that she lay there with her life changing, glad to be alone and on his bed. She held the letter up and read it, then let it lie on her body and covered it with her hand. And thought of his comings and goings at the hotel, where the lobby was an arcade of pale green marble.

In the marble, which was repeated on each floor, the afternoon light, touching green, inspired a seeming watermark. On the top floor also; where, with fine view of the strait, there was a bar with small wicker tables, a serious but not solemn restaurant, and a dance floor at which, on weekends, a band from Manila in pastel zoot suits played foxtrots for shuffling couples, and a crooner, also Filipino, delivered Crosby or Sinatra into a cupped microphone:

I love you for sentimental reasons.
I hope you do believe me,
I've given you my heart—

or sang out to the night sky of South China about the Atchison, Topeka and the Santa Fe, or the Chattanooga Choo-choo as if these were human and close to his heart. On the dance floor, the colonial men accelerated and reversed, in lightweight evening clothes. Their women wore silk. The Chinese couples were all slim and young, the girls wearing, without exception, the cheongsam. Eurasians came, worldly, in Western dress. The lights, colours, leisure, the music and food were of peacetime. As was a paucity of uniforms, and the predominance of smiling youth.

One noon in late winter, Helen Driscoll had been sitting by the windows in the bar, lunching with the master of the passenger ship that had brought her and Benedict this far, on their voyage to Japan. As they sat at table, she could see herself in the glass, lunching with this man, with the extraordinary scene spread beyond and below, and wearing a new white dress, from a fine shop, that had been a present. She hadn't been so exotically, ecstatically independent since Aix.

They ordered cheese omelettes and disinfected salads, which came with brittle, noisy triangles of toast. The skipper had a fine Scots profile: sharp nose and firm jaw. His eyes, blue, not old at all. Meeting her by chance in Chater Road, and inviting her, he had asked about Benedict, who was feverish, and about their departure for Japan. Now, as they sat at table, he spoke of the death, in the previous year, of his wife, and the unsettled state of his young daughter. When Helen asked about his war service in the Merchant Marine, he smiled: "Better not to speak of it, my dear." His manner with her was compassionate, and tacitly indignant on her behalf—something she had experienced once in a while with Bertram Perowne, but which came from this older man unexpectedly and with enigmatic shading.

He was sailing almost at once, for the Conradian ports. She asked if he might one day come to Kure; and he, still smiling, said, "If you are there." When they left, she went down with him to the lobby to say goodbye. Standing over her, he put back her hair with his sunburnt hands. So close, he smelt of starch and tobacco, and of the whiteness of his uniform touched with gold. When he left her, she watched him cross to Watson's corner and disappear, forever, towards the waterfront. Having had a fine morning, and wearing her new dress from Pâquerette, she was surprised by desolation.

There was another thing. An English family, generational landowners at Hong Kong, had been enlisted to entertain the stranded boy and girl; and liberally did so. The introduction had come about through Bertram, who, putting them aboard the ship at Naples, had been hailed by the owner of the shipping line, with whom he had gone to school: "Hullo there, Bertie. Long time." If this fortyish lord, himself sailing to the East, recalled that Bertie had shipped out to Australia, before the war, to avoid an indecency charge, indecencies since then had apparently cast Bertie's version in the shade. The shipowner and his wife were solicitous with the young people on the voyage and, reaching port, saw to it that they were befriended.

In this way, Helen and Ben had been invited to a villa at Shek-O, on a promontory overlooking the water. There was Sunday lunch, you swam in the sea, tennis was played, and after supper, the fishing fleet shone with acetylene stars. Benedict—still, then, in intermittently fair health—was appreciated, tended. The family had tall, clever sons. There were young people who all seemed lightheartedly in love—with whom, after dinner, one drove back into town, squeezed together in an open car, singing to the night about the Foggy Dew, and the Nut-Brown Maiden. For brother and sister, it was as if, as a treat, they visited the natural condition of youth.

On the third such occasion, Benedict was not able to come. At evening, the young people proving too many for their one returning car, a grave and rather separate man—perhaps near forty—offered Helen a lift in his car, which waited with a Chinese driver. This man, too, was staying at the Gloucester.

Ben and Helen had already noticed him in the hotel: lean, tall, reserved. A thoughtful face, and a schoolboy head of flopped hair, prematurely grey. Grey eyes. He wore easy poplin suits in tones of sand or pearl, and immaculate shirts striped blue; but was not dandified. All told, a distinctive addition to the teeming streets. He was an heir to one of the grand merchant houses of the East, whose name he bore, and had come out from Britain, avoiding the winter, to learn the postwar ropes. A young wife had stayed at home with their newborn child. After two months in the colony, he was at the eve of departure; and in the car told Helen that he was flying to Singapore the following morning on the first leg of his journey home.

At first they spoke about the lights of fisherfolk out past Ly-ee-mun—nor was this banal, since he told her about the Tankas, who had traditionally fished these waters and had a language of their own. By now, it was completely dark. The girl, in her corner, enjoyed her sense of the far, dramatic place; the adult, mannerly companion; and the circumstances, always congenial because interesting.

The car, powerful and new from England, climbed the unlit Shek-O hill and swung down for the city. There was no high-hearted singing about the Foggy Dew, or the Nut-Brown Maid, or Ye Banks and Braes—only the gentlemanly gravity of her companion, who asked with circumspection about herself and her brother, and how they passed their days. He did not condescend. Her low responses were matched to his mood.

When they came into the hot lights and smells and clamour of Wanchai—the driver navigating children, chickens, and chow dogs—the two passengers fell silent, Helen conscious of some constraint, now, between them and wondering, as one does, whether it had arisen from anything she'd said.

They reached the hotel. The driver handed her out of the Jaguar, for which she thanked him. And the merchant princeling, having given quiet instructions for the morning, followed her into the arcade.

The lift boy took them up: *sam-lau*, *sei-lau*. The man, Matheson, who would get out first, stood with his back to the Chinese boy and the exit: an intent, almost suffering face, and his eyes on hers, questioning. When his floor came, he leant forward and took her small breasts tightly in his hands, a moment only, and went away without a word.

In Japan, six months later, Helen lay on Aldred Leith's bed, holding his letter and considering these overtures of the Gloucester Hotel, which she had pondered and never confided to a soul.

SHE SHOULD GET UP AND GO. Tad Hill, who was again at Kure, should drop in on them at that hour. Ben should receive his letter, still folded by Leith's envelope. Eventually she would show Ben the letter lying under her hand, anything else being unnatural. Besides, most people might think the letter inconsequential. Not Ben, however; or, for that matter, Tad.

10

AT CANTON, Leith had been asked to stay in the British Consulate, on the small island of Shamien, which, devised out of reclaimed land, was attached to the city by a causeway. He told Peter Exley, "However, I feel I've done my imperial bit for a while. I liked seeing the General; and even at Government House there was a pleasant woman at table." Amused by his own deviousness in preparing the ground for Audrey. "But Shamien is in miniature, you've seen it, the foreign life is bottled up there—consulates, banks, merchants. I'll stay in the town, with a scholar from my father's China past who's been teaching at Lingnan."

Peter, visiting Canton weeks earlier, had seen Lingnan: the university in decay. Students and teachers had shown him the classrooms and dormitories of broken windows and cracked walls, the ransacked library. Like China itself, stricken, fatalistic, with nothing to hope for in the present, and trepidation of what would come.

Peter's trip to Canton belonged to his early weeks at Hong Kong, in the time of his recoil from the accretions of the Orient. Canton was his first experience of the land of China. He'd found the city squalid, and indistinct with chaos. The river supplied an alluvial consistency and colour closer to that of flowing land than of water. Before reaching the sea, the Pearl River would pass through a banked channel; but at Canton one might imagine that it had completed its course, so strong was the sense of estuary. On that illusory harbour, suburbs of sampans, aligned, rose and fell with the river—as if, swarming ashore, they had mingled with the dun habitations on dry land. Refugees from the civil war had created teetering settlements even on the groups of logs floated together at the docks of timber yards. The city appeared to sway on its own silt. At its periphery, the disintegrating shrines and statuary, each in isolation, rose up out of sediment damply packed or, in summer, hard-baked. And always, on some rise, the Chinese tombs usurped the soil.

Exley did not tell Leith that he had found Shamien a relief—having felt guilty for it even at the time. Trees, gardens, smooth buildings, an airy cleanliness, and a pink baby in a pram. He realised that the city would be different to him had he gone there, now, with Leith. They would have walked the overwhelming streets; would have traced the ancient walls and pagodas, and the Buddhist temples in the western quarter, of which Peter had discovered only a flickering shadow or derelict crust. But Leith had not suggested it; and, in those days, certain of Exley's war crimes cases were about to go to trial.

Mulling this, Peter was stowing his possessions in cool new quarters up at MacGregor Road. This, too—space, privacy, view of sea and hills—was owed to Leith. Inevitably, Roy Rysom had remarked on it: "So Our Hero fixed you up in style."

"You yourself get more room this way." Accounting for himself to the end.

That was on his last day at the barracks. It was evening, and Peter was putting books in a box. Rysom was on his bunk by the window, his arm overhanging the bed with drupes of hairy fingers. Though thick, the fingers were not stumpy but tapered off in oddly arrested tips. As if a potentially good hand had chosen to go no further. When wielding fork or pencil, Rysom grasped the implement far down the stem.

If we two weren't Australians, this would be Russian literature: I brooding over my books, Rysom by the window singing Lensky's aria. But literary Russia was no place for Australians. Reverie by the open window in the sweet futility of a mild evening was yet to strike the Australian male as a requirement. (There would be the question of fly screens, for one thing.) And Exley felt his existence stirring in its coma—scarcely Destiny, but a tremor of change. He could not take up again where he'd left off. Some things were as well left off. Nevertheless, in a previous life, he had acted: he had boarded a ship and sailed. Had landed in what was, with all difficulties, a chosen life. He might still choose. Life with Rysom had nurtured lassitude—dragging Peter down to the bottom, their joint passivity seen in the absolving perspective of outrageous history.

Rysom was turning pages of macabre photographs. "Take a dekko at the Graves album, mate?—cheer you up a bit." He said, "Bloody peace put me at a loose end, same as you. Then the Graves job turned up. Just shows you should never say die."

A panic-stricken ribaldry passed off as virility, authenticity. Passed off as truth.

He and Rysom had been raised on the Australian myths of desecration—on tales of fabulous vomiting into glove compartments or punch bowls, of silence ruptured by obscene sound: the legends of forlorn men avenging themselves on an empty continent, which, in its vast removal, did not hear or judge them.

These things Peter Exley knew, who had been born and raised to it all, and endangered by it. Who had released himself into the lavish hospitality of art. Because of his own hairbreadth escape, the condition did not excite his compassion: the attack on whatever withheld itself in mystery—a woman, a culture, a work of art; the sense of private self. All could be exorcised with a beer and a jeer; the mockery, like the drink, being passing assuagement only, of the wound that would not heal.

He thought it an interesting expression: to excite compassion.

Rysom folded his arms under his head. A huge yawn made a grotto of his face, stalactites of stained teeth. "I heard you were on the town with a mulatto."

"That's right." This would have been an hour at a teashop with Rita Xavier.

Rysom dragged at his blanket with calloused toes. "Next time you can tell her about the White Australia Policy."

LEITH CAME BACK with the morning plane from Canton. Exley could not go to Kai Tak to meet him. Before he could muster apprehensions, Aldred rang from the hotel, where he had the same room and where they would meet that evening and go to dinner nearby.

Darkness came earlier now. As they left the hotel in the dusk, Audrey Fellowes was arriving. Leith, making the introductions, invited her to join them—aware that Exley might be disappointed, but thinking that he might equally and ultimately be glad. Miss Fellowes accepted with just the right amount of pleasure. Immediately, however, the feminine minutiae came in: she must go first to her room and, as she put it, "tart myself up a bit," after a day spent with the Kadoories out on the New Territories. The two men sat down in the lobby to wait.

"Peter, I hope you don't mind. She's a fine girl. I'm pleased to see her again."

"Not at all. I can see she's nice. Pretty, too."

She surprised them by reappearing within moments in a fresh dress, with sleek hair and new colour on her fair and smiling face. She had, yes, dabbed scent behind her ears; hoped it wasn't overdone: "It's called Bond Street. Made by Yardley, the same who make that lavender water that we were allowed to splash around on outings from school." It was easy to see her as a spirited schoolgirl. Too easy, thought Leith, who divined some controlled shyness.

Dinner went more than well. It was pleasant to the men to have a woman's company. She was observant, intelligent, amusing, and asked questions that were acute without being assertive. As to the colonials, she thought they had a nice life, if they would allow themselves to enjoy it.

"They keep discounting it as artificial. A kind of disclaimer, I suppose. For myself, I don't object to a little artifice for a while, after what we've all been through and with what seems to be in store."

Both men wondered about her war: there was her age, perhaps twenty-seven, twenty-eight. Very probable, the lost fiancé, bereavement, anguish. The bombardment, and possibly the women's army. When she mentioned the brother in Japan, she withdrew very slightly into another shade of self. She would certainly visit him at Yokohama, but not quite yet. A second brother was in India.

Relatives were strong in her story. In Hong Kong she had the cousins living in May Road.

Her dress was exactly suited to her age and nature, and for the simple but citified place where they dined. Voice pleasing, manner animate but serene. She was clearly aware that her two companions took stock of these things, as of her soft round arms and bosom: she was used to that experience—although "resigned," Leith thought, would not be the word. All the time, she no doubt formed her own impressions. When she goes back to her room and takes off her earrings and shoes, and her dress, and looks in the mirror, what will she recall of these moments and, for worse or better, smile about?

She and Peter were talking of the old Walled City of Kowloon, a remnant of pre-colonial Hong Kong in dispute between the Chinese and Britain. Their encounter had fallen out very well, without show of contrivance.

Having seen Miss Fellowes back to the hotel, the two men turned away for a stroll along the Praya. Peter said, "I enjoyed being with her. Thank you for that." He made no attempt, as another man might have done, to hedge his approval with some knowing criticism—only adding, "Nice woman."

Now it's up to them. He and Peter would, for a last time, spend the following evening together. Leith was near departure, and engrossed by the fact. Alone in his room, it occurred to him that, in different circumstances, Audrey being in the same hotel, he and she might have spent the night together: such things had happened in his life. This came to him because he had missed Helen crucially all day.

A similar idea, less starkly identified, crossed the mind of Audrey Fellowes as she closed her shutters on a last glimpse of the new moon and climbed into her bed. However, and for some time now, she had not regarded a telephone with high hopes, or expected illumination from the moon.

"EUROPE WON'T HAVE ME on the old terms." Peter, considering his future. "In Australia, it would be the partnership in the law firm, in the cards ever since I can remember." Momentous childhood excursions to his father's gloomed office in Castlereagh Street—tinkering with a stapling machine, clattering the keys of a mastodontic black Remington Rand: All this will be yours. "In a few years, my father will retire. Naturally, I feel it for them, too." They'd been right when they told him, a dozen years ago, You'll break our hearts. "When I leave here, I'll go and spend time with them. But I'll have to know, by then, what I mean to do. Otherwise, it's putting my head in a noose."

When we're indecisive, yes, the wishes of others gain. If that had never drastically been the case in Leith's life, he'd felt the lash of it in small things. There can be danger in supplying what people say they want: they may have got used to the inaccessibility of long desires, shaped their lives otherwise, even want the grievance of being thwarted. On the other hand, a gesture might give great happiness. He did not say this to Peter Exley, who was already beset by equivocations. "Could you practise law in Britain and have your parents visit you?"

"I suppose it will come to that." Give them the trip: cliffs of Dover, Stratford-upon-Avon, Stonehenge. He still had most of Crindle's legacy, accreting over years of war. He saw himself patient and kind with them, enjoying their pleasures.

He also saw the idea as crude and heartless. If they declined to be bought off so cheaply, he'd admire them.

Wooden boards rose and fell under his feet. He and Leith were on a tilting boat, offshore at Aberdeen, where people now drove out from the town to dine. The fishing port was tiny, picturesque, as yet genuine. An evening liveliness of lights and voices was set against small dark lightless hills. Hygiene was uncertain, electricity often lacking, mosquitoes rife. Even so, candles smoking with insecticide could not blight the

taste of deep-sea fish, or the improvised enchantment of the scene—
which, seen from surrounding slopes, was a faery place of coloured
lanterns etched with spars of the long flat fishing boats; its calm seas
stippled with acetylene galaxies.

Leith said, "The world is transforming. Australia may change."

"Over years." It was the answer that Leith himself had given about
Helen's advancing age. They were harsh, now, about time, and could
not afford philosophy.

An explosion of Chinese music brayed out from one or another of
the floating taverns. They laughed, and Peter said, "Even so, there's
quiet out here."

"The illusory quiet of the world": small flaring hubbub of humanity, and the encompassing night. That ancient balance had tipped long
since.

"Aldred, I've been thinking about you and your girl."

"I thought it was your amatory affairs that we were considering, Peter." But Leith would be glad, now, to speak of what most concerned
him. "Her age is the devil."

"And partly the attraction."

"If she were even a couple of years older, it would simplify."

"But she would be differently lovable."

"Had this tale been told to me of some other man, I'd have condemned him."

"There's been nothing to condemn."

"I wish there were." Leith said, "To incite love, then dismiss it—I
don't see that. Or to marry her, over the parents' convulsions, at an age
when, whatever else she knows, she doesn't know herself—another
wrong. Even reasonable parents might be right to object."

"To wait a year or two?"

"I think of it a great deal. A time is coming when we'll be at separate ends of earth, unable to meet or speak, with time passing. If it
could be arranged for her to come to Britain while I complete this
work and publish it, we'd learn to know each other. She could stay
with my mother. I could propose this to the parents, who will be
fiendish whatever the outcome."

The Driscolls. Clairvoyant Ginger had spent his last hour of life warning him about the Driscolls. And he had tolerantly smiled: "What harm could they do to me?"

He told Exley, "And there is her brother, whom she will not abandon while he lives. Here again, my years are passing."

"It doesn't appear insuperable. As you say, all things now transform themselves. Exposed as you are to change, circumstances will force the issue." It was new for Peter to represent, with Leith, the sagacious side of things. "In the interim, you're in love with this mermaid, for which anyone might envy you. As I do."

They paid, and were taken to shore, standing in a cockleshell that slid, a living thing, among the junks. On land, a taxi materialised. Exley said that there was a fine walk back from here, over hills to the town. They should do it by daylight, if Aldred returned. Leith thought, more likely that they would soon see each other in Japan. Neither of these things would happen.

AT THAT SAME HOUR, Audrey Fellowes was spiralling down from the Peak in an official car, reflecting on her evening at the Admiral's. Not resisting its formalities, but finding nothing memorable other than the chocolate soufflé and her own brocade dress, worn for the first time and, she felt, wasted on two stiff men of gold-laced middle age who had been her companions at table. One of these, an expert on ocean currents, had improved late in the dinner, telling her about the Kuro Siwo (she had written it into the little green book extracted from her velvet bag), a blue salt stream to be encountered off Yokohama. He had, however, overdone things with an excursus on the North Atlantic Oscillation. By then, with the soufflé demolished, the Admiral himself had raised a small gavel and smacked it down trimly on a wooden circlet near his wineglass, saying, "Gentlemen, you may now smoke"—which was the signal for the ladies to withdraw.

The men got to their feet as the women, trailing long skirts, filed off to the drawing room, where Lady Boyd offered coffee or tisane, and crème de menthe; and, by euphemism, suggested a bathroom—which, from delicacy, all declined. She mentioned that Aldred Leith, such an odd name, had been invited for the evening but could not come.

Miss Fellowes said, "What a pity." And meant it.

At MacGregor Road, Peter Exley thought that he might ring up Audrey Fellowes in a day or two.

At midnight, in his hotel room, Leith put down a novel of war in Burma. He understood, not altogether calmly, how serious his dreams had become—and how explicit, when Peter could use those words to him: "love" and "envy." And he himself had said "Marry." And what if it is all hallucination?

Nevertheless, he went to bed rather happy, with nothing resolved.

11

"BIT OF BAD LUCK, EH?"

Leith smiled, but saw no reason to reply. The ship's purser, expertly rocking with the vessel, stood over him as he read. The islands being all but invisible in rain, a score of other passengers were distributed around the saloon, reading also, or talking in low voices; at one table, playing cards. The ship had entered the strait and would dock within the hour. Talbot would meet him, they would reach the compound by two.

He looked at his watch.

After broaching, with Exley, the story of Helen, he had been revisited by its impossibility. Had revolved the mystery so often, and to no purpose—except that it was pleasurable—that he could awaken, on successive mornings, to what he supposed was a sense of proportion. The thing was charming, and might remain so: it could not be allowed to develop.

He didn't much fancy the process of making this plain.

He found himself again consulting his watch, while the ship rose steeply, and fell into a trough where it lay shuddering. This grey exercise was repeated, propellors grinding, while an ashen lady was helped away, groping at a handrail, to be sick.

Within days of arrival at Kure, he should leave again, very briefly, for Tokyo, where part of his lost baggage had been discovered: books and winter clothes. Intermittent absences would help them both—in the end, wherever that was to be.

In the recovered luggage, there were books that Helen might like to have.

His watch was not a new contrivance such as visitors to Japan now acquired but an old one, Swiss and good and gold, from his godmother on his twentieth birthday.

He was not the first man to wonder, Is she the plaything, or am I?

HELEN HAD WASHED HER HAIR. In order not to disturb her brother, who slept after breakfast, she used Leith's bathroom, which she afterwards set to rights, drawing out from the basin a tangle of her own hair entwined with that of others. Before the rain, she had gathered wintry flowers from the hillside and put them on Leith's table in a vase brought from Kyoto. Helen stood by the table, a comb in her hand.

The little safe was latched but empty. They had kept Leith's papers in a locked box beneath Ben's bed. It did not surprise or scandalise them that these peaceable pages were being safeguarded from the interference of their own father.

It was past noon, but the ship was not expected to dock on time.

Helen went back to their cottage, where Ben was sleeping in his room. She looked in the mirror, running her fingers through her hair so that it stood out all round her head. With the cool weather, she dressed in a dark skirt that came, in the new way, well below the knee; and today in a blouse of silky colours, the gift of a friend in Bengal. She had left the mirror, when her mother came in with the storm and stood in the open doorway, subduing a tartan umbrella.

Helen shut the door and propped the umbrella on a newspaper. Melba Driscoll had a list of tasks, which her daughter took note of.

And Helen should change out of those good shoes, she must be mad. When Melba removed her raincoat, it was to be seen that she, too, was dressed for an occasion.

The girl was always quiet with the mother. Not passive, not sullen. Today, radiant.

The mother said, "You look a sight, I must say."

If the daughter had spoken, she would have said, "You are cruel."

"As if you'd been pulled backwards through a hedge."

Neither would forget.

Helen made a motion for quiet. "Ben's sleeping." She agreed that she would come up, soon, to the house for lunch.

When she was alone, Helen dried the floor and went to the room where Ben was stirring. As she stood at the end of his bed, he opened his eyes.

"You are a sight," he said, "for sore eyes."

She sat on the bed and took his hand.

"Why are you crying?"

"Not crying, really."

"Aldred comes today."

"Yes."

"We're glad." He lifted their joined hands and held them to her cheek. "We love him."

"Yes."

Benedict disengaged his hand. "Can I touch your hair? Do you remember, in the bank in Hong Kong, the two men talking about your hair?"

"I'd forgotten. Yes."

They had been to the shipping office in the bank building, together with a Portuguese assistant deputed to help them arrange their deferred passage to Japan. At that time, with the long voyage out and afternoons at Shek-O, Helen's hair was tinselled, oceanic. They waited in a little press of people, in front of two young Chinese who evidently discussed the frail boy and his sister; and who, as the line shuffled forward, broke into an exchange, one of them sketching, by cropped circular gesture, the girl's head and shoulder.

Later, in the street, Helen asked their escort, "They were talking about me?"—having heard *Fan Kwei* and *Kuniang*, among the few words known to her and in the tone, unmistakeable, concerned with oneself.

And Miss Prata had laughed and nodded: "They were marvelling, yes, at the Foreign Devil's hair."

In Japan, Benedict said, "He'll find you changed."

"In what way, changed?"

"With thinking of him."

LEAVING BRIAN TALBOT to his lunch in the common room, Leith loped across the spongy upward ground into which the weightless house seemed, that day, to be scarcely set. When he came in shrugging the storm from his shoulders like any Westerner, and slapping his cap against his leg, his coat was at once removed by light hands: a gesture seeming to relieve coat as much as owner. But the house itself would not enclose him, or identify. Translucent structures are not welcoming in cold rain.

The day had been unfortunate, all omens adverse; and the man himself at odds with the eagerness that quickened his step.

It was now, however, that his luck—if that's what it was—turned.

As Helen was the first to realise that he had come, their instantaneous glance was not observed. Her parents had left the table for confabulations elsewhere. Beside her, Benedict's empty chair was the sole place vacant. As if this were not enough, just as Leith reached her side, a great fireball cracked over the house with such force that one of the fragile women serving fell to her knees, keeping hold of the dish she had been handing; and stayed so, a stunned supplicant, while guests rose from table to help her, unclear whether the explosion itself, or fear of it, had struck her down.

The man therefore walked through detonation and striped darkness, past a kneeling woman and scrambling guests, to the only figure who remained seated. How desolate, had she not been there.

He sat down, took her left hand, which was nearest, and released it.

That morning, in a past life, he'd imagined saying, "And how have you been, my dear?"—something of the benevolent and neutral kind. And now did say exactly that; which came forth to them as the most exalted question in all the articulate world.

A new table, of Occidental height and material, was glazed in wipable grey. On this, dishes and implements, and feathery amber flowers, had been placed with such accuracy as to confer, by mere transforming human intention, some opaque beauty. Or it was their own fresh vision of Formica.

They should now say something, for, though thunder persisted, the room was coming out of its swoon. The kneeling woman had been helped away (and where to, in those prismatic spaces?). The diners recomposed themselves. Leith was greeted, he was introduced. The historian Calder, himself back from a journey, came round the table to ask questions about besieged Peiping. And doing this, thoughtlessly propped himself between man and woman, providing tweedy shelter. From happiness, Helen scarcely ate; while Leith went hungrily through a coiled sea creature, fixed in seaweed, that he might otherwise have found inedible.

When they got up, he asked her about Benedict. "I must see to my stuff. Then shall I come round?" Outdoors, in the squelching world, rain had drawn off into purpled sky; green smells were sharp, chilly, wet, delicious.

He collected his belongings and the waiting mail—regretting that there could be no envelope now that moved him. In his own room, he stowed things rapidly away, as if overdue in the very place where he had just arrived. When he then stood still, his hands resting on the blotter of his table, he could feel again the motion of the ship in the morning's storm.

When he reached their little parlour, Benedict was standing near the door, supporting himself with one hand on the lintel and with a cane held in the other. There was the small shock of finding the boy on his feet, and the expected pang at his deterioration.

"Takes you aback, to find me upright. A sense of imposture. If one thing improves, another worsens." Ben's speech was growing difficult to understand. He said, "There are so many things to go wrong with the human body. When people are well, it's a miracle of coordination."

Leith said, "If men had devised it, it would never have worked at all."

Ben was wearing, over one of his dark gowns, a grey woollen wrapper.

"You've become a sage, Ben."

"It's just the shawl." There was a play of light and shadow, and Helen coming from her room.

"Helen has grown."

Ben said, "It's true."

And Helen, joyful: "I'm five feet three and a half."

"And I, five ten and a half. Five eleven, if I stand straight."

"You always stand straight."

"That comes from having been a sergeant. I never had such power as when I was a sergeant."

He'd meant something more: her new tension, new dimension.

He produced a book, and she went to fetch a knife to prise apart the coloured paper.

Ben teased him: "What about me?"

"Any book of poems is for both of you."

"No, no. All is now for Helen."

They sat, Helen in the low-cushioned chair with a blue book in her lap.

"It's for your birthday, which I wasn't aware of. Next time, I'll know better." By then, it might seem paramount. They felt so kindly for him that he said, "I should go away more often, in order to have such a welcome." He would be gone a day or two, in Tokyo. "They've recovered some of my stuff, which I must identify."

Happiness spilt from her eyes, like the glance exchanged under the storm. It was fresh and strange to him, that by merely arriving in that obscure place he could create such pleasure, in two others and in himself. In her. What I came back for, to be loved like this.

Aki made tea for them, Helen bringing biscuits. Leith had a folder, which would go in the box beneath Ben's bed. Along with his notes from China, there was an envelope of photographs, which brother and sister asked to see. The lamp was on, the room was cold.

"How fine they are." Benedict was turning pearly matte surfaces of Asian scenes: trees inclining from promontories, a great junk spreading her slatted sails, tiled roofs accepting a sandstorm.

"It's the Yellow Wind. In Italy, there's the red wind from Africa; in Greece, a brown wind brings mud from the Levant." The world's colours, streaming away in the gale.

Huge sculptures stood free from tombs: winged lion, maned horse, gigantic ram.

Ben asked, "Are there any of you?"

"Two or three, there somewhere. One, touristic, on the Great Wall. An old school friend took it, who came with me from Shanghai."

"What were you like, as a schoolboy?"

"Hellish, I suppose. Well, there was a lot of dreaming."

"Can we have it—this one?"

"If you give me one in exchange."

Helen read out, from the envelope, "Hedda M. Morrison, Peiping."

"I took the negatives there, it's a serious place. Otherwise, one hears of rolls of film that don't come back from the developers. You're told that they didn't come out. I took few, and didn't want to lose them to censorship. There are some of Hong Kong."

Helen held up Peter Exley. "Is this your friend? You didn't say he was good-looking."

"He might come here for a bit. He'd like to meet you."

Benedict told Helen, "So we've been discussed."

"Don't grudge me the pleasure—being so far off—of speaking your names." He got up, saying, "I must tear myself away." Which was what it felt like.

When he'd gone, they were still: Helen reading her new book, Ben dozing or, as it seemed now, lapsing into a trance. When he next looked for her, she was sitting upright with the book half-closed over her hand—looking, but not at him.

"What is it?"

"The book." She went on, without focussing. "Oh, the vast distances, forlorn partings, terrible journeys. The loneliness."

Ben said, "The helplessness, and longing."

She said, "The Never."

NEAR EVENING, Aldred walked up to the common room to make his arrangements for Tokyo. In the fuggish room, a man straddled a chair that was turned backwards. He was on the phone, deploring: "You were notified, I fully indicated . . ." A man in his late forties, just the age of the century, with a fleshed and nearly featureless face that paradoxically represented a type.

Leith was aware that this was the man from Washington, come to find him. When he was not laying down the law, the man's lips were twitching. Leith thought that men go to pieces differently in peacetime, outside their borders.

An associate stood by, impassive: a loose-limbed young officer in American uniform, with hair so closely cut that colour was indeterminate. He introduced himself: "Thaddeus Hill."

Who had been kind, and whose good face was not more than twenty-five years old.

"Helen wrote of you. Ben, also. You befriended them." Leith did not want to seem to stake a prior claim, even while doing so.

"It's a privilege to be friends with them. Fun, too." Tad said, "They're on their own"—meaning in their singularity or their isolation, or both. "Great kids. They think the world of you."

"And I of them." Aldred felt that, had Thaddeus Hill been present at table to witness his arrival, no thunderbolt would have deflected his attention.

They would have liked each other entirely, had it not been for the contest.

Tad said, "I'll look in on them tomorrow. We just got back, Mr. Slater and I, from Formosa. We're down in Kure."

Noting their connection, Mr. Slater was fast concluding at the telephone. He could not be everywhere at once.

What Leith could not put together was the role of Thaddeus, with his good manners and face. He supposed it would reveal itself. He said, "I myself am just back, and already making plans for departure."

Slater said that he would welcome an opportunity. "We think the world of your record." Possibly had not expected quite this man, or so deep a voice. "We have the greatest interest in your work."

Which was safe enough under Benedict's bed.

"Thank you."

"You're welcome." Slater said, "Well, fix it up with Tad here. I'll be away a day or two myself. Have to go to Osaka."

Ósaka, not Osáka.

Leith might have said, My work is of no interest to you, being in its way a meditation. But reflectiveness is hateful to men mobilising grievance.

Something sordid.

Slater was meeting Driscoll and went out, removing Tad also. Leith, having made his phone calls, walked downhill under a tigerish sunset. He did not intend to talk to such a man; but lightness of heart had been shaded. And he did not care to think that, calling on Helen and her brother, he might find Thaddeus Hill there—especially since Tad had proved likeable. "One is nice," Ben had written. "The other not."

AFTER DINNER, while she was reading to Benedict, Tad came in, bringing a small heater for their low-wattage room and a bottle of aquavit, of which he accepted a glass. He told them that a box would come from Tokyo. At a store of imported goods, he had bought two loden coats in different shades of olive green.

"I hope the size is right. If not, you'll grow into them." He said this, doubting that Ben would ever need the coat, or grow.

They were highly pleased, and said that he should never have done it. (Brother and sister meanwhile having identical presentiment of their mother's comments.) Helen said that it was an American present: generous, needful, and fun.

"I guess you mean cheeky," he said—a gift of serious clothes being presumptuous. However, they needed coats. Let the terrible parents take umbrage; they could blame it on American crassness. And—though this was no consolation—he would soon be gone.

She said that, in England, she'd had a warm coat but had outgrown it. "We left for the tropics just in time."

Tad asked, "Can I look at this?"—the book, which was on their table.

Ben said, "Aldred brought it."

"I meant to say that I ran into him." Tad was turning pages. "Impressive," he remarked. "The man, I mean." He put down the book. "The book also, as I can see."

"Helen has been reading it."

Tad said, "Quite a salon you kids are running here." Pronouncing it *salonne*, he was being American for them to the top of his bent. Sprawling a bit, so far as their rickety chair would allow. Laughing, they were grateful for long-limbed, self-deprecating goodness. And childish enough, too, to be excited about their new green coats.

"I'd like to take you two to the movies." He told them that the American base had set up a picture house that on certain evenings showed, with crackling and lapsing, films that could cause no offence—"to our tender American sensibilities, kids." At any rate, Occupation families were welcome, and he'd look into it.

Ben said, "Late in the day, I'm not much good. Or early, for that matter."

Helen suggested that he might sleep in preparation. He said, "We'll see. I'd like to go"—which was true. It was equally true that he had begun to fear departures from the talismanic routine of his stark survival. Helen saw it, that he dared not break the remnant of a spell.

Tad said, "I'll fill you in." When he had gone, with a wave like a heron's, Helen stood at the open door. "Benny, you must see it, the full moon." Her life, and even his, in the little prison of their rooms, had also rounded and ripened, grown luminous.

THREE DAYS LATER, coming from Tokyo, Leith was met by Brian Talbot, who said, "Home again."

A transient room in a military compound had become his destination. For the time being, he didn't mind.

There was a heavy, historic-looking box with his printed name, and a strapped suitcase, which the two men heaved aboard the jeep. "My books," said Leith. "Or what's left of them." For there had been losses, thefts; and water had got in. "And some winter gear." They set off in the mild afternoon. Their route was being patched and threw up black gravel splotched with tar. Talbot told him that a new coast road was planned: "Scenic stuff." At the port, mines had been conclusively swept. The sunken ships were all raised now, and taken for salvage.

"Getting to be quite a beauty spot," he said, and squawked a laugh.

Sea and islands had always been beautiful. It was the blunderings of men that made the idea laughable. Leith smiled, though not for that reason.

Brian Talbot followed the direction of his companion's thoughts, having seen Leith at times with Helen, and being nudged by other soldiers who frequented the common room. There had been nothing to report, except what is invisible and irrefutable.

It would not have troubled Leith if Talbot, who probably wished him well, was aware of that attachment.

Brian told him, "You won't be seeing me much longer. Marching orders. Back to Aussie in a month or so."

"Good God. I can't be glad, but I suppose you are."

"Yair, oh well. Time to move on. I won't be sorry to leave the army."

"Would you like—I don't know—some document? A letter of recommendation?"

"Thanks, I hadn't thought about it—but yair, thanks, she'd be good."

Some friendly word should be ventured. But they were careful with one another, and there was still time.

"I suppose I should've done more with my stretch here. Never took you up on your offer, the lessons."

"Later on, the experience will count, perhaps."

"When I'm old and grey, eh? Something to tell the grandchildren. Who won't want to listen."

The settlement of Occupation families having expanded, a traffic light had been planted at its centre, where the PX created convergence. In that miniature, denatured suburbia, Talbot was an appreciated point of reference, greeted by housewives to whom he raised a cheerful hand: "Ar there, Mrs. Wells"; "Be seeing you, Miss Geary."

"Quite a following you've got, Brian."

The driver grinned: "You get the whole story, in the end."

At the compound, they stacked the baggage in the common room. Leith left Brian having beer with a pal, and went out in the last of the light. He had extracted his greatcoat from the unloaded suitcase and had it over his shoulders.

Halfway down the path, in a small clearing where jeeps were allowed to turn, Helen was standing with Tad Hill. It was clear that they were setting out together. Helen was wearing a long greenish coat that Aldred had never seen, and pale stockings; and her shoes, while too summery, were for city use. A purse dangled from her arm. And Tad had a tailored uniform, not khaki but fawn, such as American officers wore for civil occasions, and in which he looked well. Helen had seen Aldred. And Tad, turning in the direction of her expression, came to what might have been attention.

Reaching them, Leith smiled and spoke. Tad, who, on a slight rise, appeared tall, smiled too: "I'm taking this lady to the movies." He explained about the American shed at the port.

Helen's immemorial feminine look: regret, accountability, resistance, and a plea for indulgence.

"What are you seeing?"

She told him, "*Meet Me in St. Louis.*"

Tad said, "It's Louis, not Louie. In real life, if not in song. Saint Louis, Missouri. Hell, what do I know, I'm from Cincinnati."

Aldred laughed. "I hope to hear about it."

"We might get a bite down there. Along with the movie house, they've set up a place with hot dogs, Cokes, all amenities of high civilisation." Tad remarked, "We'd better get going."

"Ben couldn't come." She should have prevented herself from saying this.

Aldred said, "How nice you look." With her flushed cheeks and a wisp of pink silk at her throat—in the collar of the new coat that something warned him not to mention.

His room, put in order as before, had lost its sense of destiny. He hung his coat near the door, unpacked his small bag. Might have liked hot tea, but settled for whisky. An ineffectual heater had been placed near the table. He switched on the lamp and lay on the bed, turning over his notebook from Tokyo—where he had written about reconstruction, about the vexed question of the Japanese theatres, about the education of Japanese women and the hygienic official brothels for American troops.

Tad would take her hand in the dark. And what would she do? In the overlong coat, she had seemed fully grown—embarking on the years in which men would contend for notice, locking antlers. He would have liked to say this to her, so that they might laugh together. He wished he had never seen her.

He went on writing about Tokyo: about places of worship, and the monks.

It was all absurd. Without the coat, she was a child.

In this way, the evening advanced—he writing on a lined pad, or at times reading in one of the books he'd kept by him. At last, half-asleep, he was aware that Helen had come back with Thaddeus. Heard voices on the path, the opening and closing of a door, and the young steps of a man going up under the trees. A flashlight glimmered past his windows. She would recount the evening to her brother. The three men in her immediate life.

He had not eaten and was hungry. He got up, reaching for his boots, and went out to find his dinner. By now, half an hour had passed since her return. There was no light in her rooms, except for the gleam left on, always, for Benedict.

In the common room, Tad was sitting at table reading a newspaper, with a plastic tumbler in his fist. Made a motion to get up when he saw Aldred Leith—who raised his hand and went to the rusted refrigerator to fetch a tuna sandwich and a wedge of cheese. They were alone there and sat down together, and Tad poured him a glass of quinine water. Neither said what they might have: Get some work done? or How was Judy Garland? Affability must dissolve and be re-created.

Thaddeus Hill said, "You've never kissed her." There was no particular emphasis; and when Leith did not reply, he went on, "She doesn't—didn't—know how to kiss."

"She's sixteen." Lopping off a year to make his point.

"She's seventeen, and in love."

Leith had won. Would not have chosen the word, but there was no other, for the moment. He said, "She'll be eighteen, and nineteen."

"My guess is, she'll still be in love."

Since generosity was in the air, Leith said, "Much more has to happen."

"Yes. I don't plan to forget her. I'll stay in touch." Tad said, "She's somebody. They both are." Tad might now have added, "Great kids," but refrained.

Leith said, "That's the first thing that will happen."

"The boy's death."

"Yes. In Tokyo I went to see the doctor, the American doctor who interests himself in Ben's condition. I was able to do that without showing my hand—to the parents, that is."

Tad said, "The Parents."

"Exactly. The doctor's all right, a bit callous. More attuned to disease than to boy. Hopes to make a discovery. The disease is little understood. But then, so is the quality of this boy."

"Doctor could use a little humility?"

"Yes. One fears experimentation—Ben to be kept going as a lab case. The assumption is that Benedict will live some months, even a year. But with such deterioration that he could not stay at home."

"Wherever home is by then."

"Home is with Helen." It was his own discovery. "One can try to be helpful when that happens."

"We'll all be split up soon. Four corners of a square world."

"The doctor has a clinic in mind, in California. Where he would study what they call the progress of the disease. Helen could not go there." He said, "The doctor has a grant to write about this. It may help someone in the end, but not Ben."

Tad thumped his fist three times against the table's edge. "Fuck. Fuck. Fuck. I should tell you a couple of things. I've asked to be relieved of this Slater assignment. I'll soon be going home. They fingered me for it because I knew some Japanese. For me, it was a chance to come here. I didn't know what I was getting into—which is exactly what you think it is, but worse. Dumb, I guess. In any case, I want out of the army now. Go back to college on the G.I. Bill, get my doctorate, see what comes next. Slater'll give me a black mark—a black mark from these guys being better than the Congressional Medal, from my standpoint." It occurred to him that this was tactless, but Leith laughed.

"Meantime, there's this. You, I take it, are a British subject. Okay. Then you don't have to talk to Slater, he has no jurisdiction, and I say, Don't do it. It's all in bad faith, whatever you say will be misrepresented, they have their knife into you."

"Why?"

"Oh—because it's you, because it's China, because you shortcircuited the bureaucracy, because you were favoured by that gutsy French guy who died in Paris—yeah, that's the name—whom they call E-Feet, their way of saying Queer. Most of all, because you're clever and decent, and go your own way." Tad examined the rim of the pounded table: "I guess I broke this a bit. Or maybe I broke my hand. Slater and Driscoll get together, if that means anything to you."

"You mean, because of Helen."

"It would be their way to fault you. She's under age. On the other hand, the Driscolls will soon leave here, taking Helen with them. The boy will be shipped out to California. Driscoll has his eye on a post in New Zealand. He was born there, did you know that?—was taken to Australia as an infant. The post is medical but political, you have to be born in the country to deserve it. These are Driscoll's steppingstones—Bengal, Kure, New Zealand. One day I reckon he'll just step right off the goddamn planet. Come to think of it, there've been worse ideas than that."

They got up and shook hands. He said, "I'll see you. Maybe tomorrow."

"Thanks for all of this. How was the movie?"

"Don't bother. So goddamn cheerful." Laughed, waved. "Lotsa luck."

TAD HAD BROUGHT HER TO HER DOOR: "This is where I kiss you." Afterwards had held her by the shoulders, as if to shake her, wake her. Amiable, exasperated. When he went away, she heard and pictured him loping uphill with his lean Taddish demeanour: musing, bemused. She did touch her lips with the side of her hand—not disgusted or derisive, but distant.

This, then, was the flourished reality: a brute fact, to which lovingkindness was simply, or not even, a preliminary. There had been a screen between her and this. Reality was a wet thick thing alive in her mouth.

It seemed to her something that dogs might do.

She came indoors. Ben slept. Now there would be unshared thoughts, more and more of them—divined, perhaps, but undefined.

Tad had looked at her with the expression of the man Matheson in the lift in Hong Kong: a secret that he was willing her to share, and which should now be disclosed.

Helen undressed, lay down, and slept.

In the night, she got out of her bed and, without lighting the lamp, fetched her new coat and went and sat on the low step, in the setting of the moon. There were cold planets and a cold quiescence. She put the coat around her shoulders and sat, hands clasped over her knees and her chin resting there. She could smell the Pacific, churned up by the storm. Thought how in childhood she had watched the eight-metres and the smaller boats, even the Vee-Jays, sailing Sydney Harbour—whitely, soundlessly, as if unmanned. Only when the regatta veered near shore and the wind blew from that direction, there came, with swish of hull on water, the shouts and curses, the bellowing and bullying about the boom and the cleat and the sheet, and the billowing jib: all the hysteria of manliness. A rush of copper limbs, a thudding of bare feet; and the whipshot thwack of a slackened jib that should have been taut.

Because of the kiss, she might have liked to consider the evening a turning point, momentous. But, with the ill-timed precision of women in such matters, only felt what was lacking. Something that either of them could have put a name to.

WITHOUT UNDRESSING, Aldred Leith had also slept. He had dreamed of Gigliola, or of a confused Gigliola who was sometimes Raimonda, together with a third woman who was identified but speechless—as the dead are, not always truly, said to be in dreams. Even as he slept, he supposed that he had raised the ghost of Gigliola by telling her story, and as part of his renewed turning to women. From this, he was awakened by desire. The moon was in the room, and he lay contemplating his dream, his body, his intentions: all at that hour unmanageable.

There was Tad's concession, something better than surrender. Tad had kept his possibility in reserve. Aldred himself had said, Much more will happen. Or was it Ginger who'd said that? He remembered how Ginger had said, of his dead wife, "My poor girl."

He hadn't told all of Gigliola's story. At the end of the war, he had learnt how she had been shot down in the country road, climbing over a wall in violation of the German curfew: going to meet a boy, younger than she, who'd been shot, also, in consequence. She had dragged herself, dying, to a ditch by the road. At this recollection he exclaimed, and sat bolt upright in his bed.

Raimonda had married a British officer and gone with him to Africa.

In his first days with Helen and Benedict, the girl had started on some verses by the tragic Italian from the Adriatic, loved by Ben. Halfway, her voice had broken. After a pause, she told them, quite collectedly, "I'll take it up again later. When I've hardened my heart."

He got up in his crumpled clothes, in which he was used to working at all hours, never understanding why he didn't first undress.

She was standing, straightening her spine against the frame of her door. So nothing need be said, except his name and hers.

"Your second kiss of the day."

"You saw Tad."

"He's been our go-between."

"Why should he tell you?"

"It was in a good spirit. Even sacrificial." Though not quite. They arranged themselves on the step. "There should be words."

"Say them."

"We must find them out." He said, "If I quoted, you would only finish the line."

"We need nothing."

"For my part, untrue." He passed his arms under her coat, Tad's coat, beneath her upraised arms. "Does that trouble you?"

"Yes. No. It seems—"

"What?"

"Like the night. I can't explain." Then she said, "If the moon came up only once in a hundred years, the whole world would stand watching."

Leith said, "*La luna calante*," and fell silent. He withdrew his arms and took her head in his hands.

"Why go?"

"Because you're fourteen and I'm one hundred."

"Seventeen, and thirty-three."

"I give you, for the moment, the best answer." The truth being that you are seventeen and I am not one hundred.

The strain of fatalism had seen him through involuntary horrors. In this matter that had from the start depended exclusively on his own judgement, it was new to him that it could not have been otherwise.

The abrupt parting made her childish. They might have stayed all night on the cold step together. She wanted to say, You won't pretend, tomorrow, that it has not been? Abject—but she had observed the cold process of what men call coming to their senses.

———

ON THE FOLLOWING MORNING, there was a letter from his father.

My dear Aldred,

I was very glad to have your description of Peiping (if that's how
they're spelling it these days). Although I've never been in a city
under siege, most cities give that impression now, so hard to get
in and out of. Aerial bombardment is putting an end to sieges,
as to much else. But in Mao's case he need only wait. I'm glad
that my Athens book reached you. Thank you for your good
words. It's had a fine press, providing an excuse for moralising
in the Sunday papers, who warm to their perennial theme of
my frigidity. It's selling well in Greece, where it has been
banned. A Greek journalist says that I'm trying to drive their
(teutonic) royal family into exile. Well, exile is their country.
Greece was in bad shape, strenuous. Every road "kakos dromos,"
so one travelled on foot or by donkey; and, at my age, suffering.
I'm invited to Belgrade by Broz Tito, and am provisionally
accepting for September, if he hasn't been swallowed by the Soviets
by then.

What I should like best would be to come in your direction,
alas quite impossible. If any chapter is closed for me, it is that of
Asia. I follow your own Eastern adventure keenly, and look
forward to its fruits. You do right, I think, to brood on that
astounding scene before it is recast—before it gathers planetary
momentum and loses arcane fascination. However, the
consciousness of a last time, in the sighting of places or persons,
can be a sombre business, which pierces even in youth, and
multiplies with age.

At risk of growing maudlin, I might add that I look forward to
your return. Iris tells me that you should arrive before spring.
Meantime, I'm curious as to how you flesh out this new stage of
your life, and hope to hear more—as do Iris and Aurora, who by
the way have at last, and amicably, met. A curious coming round of
things.

My love ever—

This, which was signed "Oliver," was far and away the most feeling letter that the adult Aldred had received from his father. It was written in a sprawling but legible hand that showed no sign of age. Oliver Leith's letters were usually dictated to a machine. Typed up, on a special size of small stationery, by a secretary with whom he had long since ceased to have an affair, they were signed and despatched each day. Indirection of process favoured the writer's desire to thwart a posterity seeking evidence, beneath the aloof public figure, of the presumably tormented artist who wrote love into books and dissembled it in private life. Such letters—of set brevity, controlled egotism, and laboured goodwill—were seldom of lasting interest. That a covering of tracks might itself be seized on as revelation, the author naturally foresaw; and, once in a while, signing some particularly innocuous batch, would mutter, "Let them work it out," as he dropped the pile into a waiting tray. A sense of opposition gave stimulus.

The son's impulse, to reply warmly—before scepticism protectively returned—arose from the letter's portent of death, and even from its seeming acknowledgement of long indifference. A son had not thought to be so easily disarmed.

Dear Oliver,
Your letter touched me.

He sat some minutes with the pen in his hand, before realising that this might be enough.

Of course, the words might strike his father as merciless.

The pen rolled away. Having got up to retrieve it, Aldred Leith walked about the room, vaguely setting things to rights and weighing some conversational addition to his reply; treading softly, for his father's overture was a rare bird that might flap away screeching.

The word "flesh" characteristically went to the centre of things.

At last he shook his clothes together and went next door.

Benedict was alone. Helen had gone to use a sewing machine in the parents' house. The two men were pleased to be by themselves, knowing she would come.

"Ben, was there ever a time when you felt close to your father?"

Benedict put the crumpled frame of his fingers together. "You see, my illness came on me early, but not enough to be convincing. My father thought, wanted to think, that I was malingering. There was threatening and shouting, and dragging; and on my part writhing, resisting, and screaming. He was set on my becoming a champion swimmer, took me to Balmoral Baths at sunrise, all seasons, and plunged me in. Derelict wooden piles slimed with green and cruelly barnacled. Fear, humiliation, agony in an ear. I shrieked, he shouted, once or twice it came to blows. Neighbours complained. Finally, mastoid trouble was discovered; there was an operation, also awful. By then, something was irrefutably wrong with me, and he couldn't bear our joint failure—my failure and his; we were saddled with it, one way or another."

"Your part was involuntary, given the circumstances."

"His too, given his nature."

"No. We owe ourselves more disbelief than that."

"The Australian male is not good at self-doubt. Someone else must always be to blame. Otherwise, Aldred, a nation on its knees."

Leith held up a tumbler that stood at the bedside and helped the boy to drink through a straw.

Benedict went on. "However, to answer your question. Yes. When I was very small, before all that at the baths, he was proud of my alertness. He'd do little tricks for me, and we'd laugh together. He'd sit me at the kitchen table while he peeled me an apple, peeled it with a bone-handled blade, all in one go, and we'd laugh and twirl the spiral of apple skin between us till it snapped. Fun, funny. He seemed like God, naturally, but I also realised that he was wounded, weak, untruthful, and I felt the more tenderly towards him for that. We were a bit in league. Against my mother. Even later, when I was already culpable, a liability, he used to do his tricks for Helen, she'd have been tiny then. There was a brown, shaggy glove, form of a half-monkey, and he would wiggle it for her and swoop it at her, and she would squeal with delight. And we'd laugh, all three of us. But he and I, the males, were for that moment again complicit. I don't remember where my elder sister was—off somewhere with my mother, or at school. Then I deteriorated. And Bertram mercifully came; Helen and I grew clever and close. And there was war. Meantime, there had been, in my father, some conclusive submission to my mother, embitterment towards me. By the time we went to Bengal, things were fixed, and there was his public ambition, his avarice. Helen and I pretty much went to the wall—she being useful to my uselessness." He said, "I'm tiring now."

"Shall I leave?"

"No. Wait till she comes. Just this. I used to hope I'd last long enough to see her independent. Not going to happen. Bertram would help her, he loves her, and has come into some means. Affinity, her great necessity. I hoped I'd see her—not safe, exactly, but released. Now, perhaps—"

"You need not fear for her."

Helen arrived in a dark woollen dress, with two pieces—bodice and unshirred skirt—of a basted dress over her arm. Leith got up and found another chair for himself. There was the smell of freshly cut cotton. He asked, "Can I see the dress?" and stood at her side as she spread it on the table. She told him that the material came from a cache of Liberty cotton in Bombay and was sent to her by a friend.

Benedict looked up: "Frida. Elfrida Ladd."

Leith said, "Your adventures. This is the first I hear of Frida Ladd."

"I was rather in love with her."

And Helen: "And she with you."

"No. You say that, but she was only kind." But he was flushed, and glad.

Helen told Leith, "She was a war widow. She was Lady Ladd. Her husband was on General Wavell's staff. Flying back to India from Cairo, his plane was shot down, in mistake for Wavell's." Hesitation. "They had already lost a boy, their only child. He was sunk in a ship of evacuees from Britain." Looking at Leith apologetically, as if to say, There is no end to it. "She had pattern books; and a wicker box, all in order, of shears and scissors and thimbles. Coloured silks, threads, tape measures, and a little cushion full of needles. She taught me to sew."

The girl had thus eluded the taste of Melba Driscoll. Leith now knew of Frida Ladd, who was good and brave, and had lost her child in the sinking of the ship called *City of Benares*.

"I only got as far as two patterns. I can vary the colours and the prints, but the dresses are what you've seen—round neck with long sleeves; scooped neck with short sleeves." She laughed.

"And where is she now, Lady Ladd?"

"Still in India, but in Delhi. She remarried. Now, with Partition, they're leaving India, going back to England. She sent us a photograph of the wedding. She'd be thirty."

Ben said, "Thirty-two."

"Is she beautiful?"

Ben said, "As an angel."

They wanted to know, Had he been in India?

"Once, for just three weeks. Sailing East, I broke the journey at Bombay—to cast a glance, at least, on India before Partition. There was somebody I wanted to meet, whose ideas for India seemed, then, to touch the predicament of China." Ten improbable days spent on cracked verandahs and in steaming rooms with Acharya Vinoba Bhave, talking of the Land Gift movement. "Whose ideals, I should say. I'd gone to him for ideals, I think, but the saintliness undid me, and I began to talk practicalities out of self-preservation. He dismissed me, and so civilly." Leith laughed. "What a fool one makes of oneself, and knowing it all the while."

Benedict said, "You're an odd coot, Aldred. A man who actually likes to laugh at himself."

"Not enough, I daresay."

Helen was making buttonholes—almost businesslike, as she sat narrowing her eyes to the needle. And she also laughed—at herself, and from the thrill of living, which had come without her having to compel or devise it. And in these thin rooms that scarcely admitted light, let alone deliverance.

He said, "I should get back to my China puzzle."

"Why?" asked Ben. "When nothing will ever be nicer than this."

So Aldred Leith sat in the extra chair, and was pleased, like most men, to see a woman sewing—or knitting, or winding wool, shelling peas. Serviceable, soothing, seated. Stilled, for the moment, to little more than an occasional murmur or useful click. Benedict fell into the half-sleep in which he softly twitched or mumbled—much as a domestic animal might do, but without an animal's health. When he abruptly woke, Helen put down her work.

"Do you need anything?"

"Yes. Something to be said, or read."

They spoke of the anthology that Leith had brought from China, and Helen asked him if he had read the poems in Chinese.

"Some of them, yes. Not for a long while now."

She asked, "Why did you enlist as a soldier? Knowing many things, you might have been useful differently."

"That August, I was staying on a property in the south of England, waiting, as I thought, for the Foreign Office to decide my fate, after I'd sat their examinations. To pass time, I worked on the land there, hard work, and I liked it and liked the men of the place, more or less my age, with whom I reaped and dug ditches and handled muck." And in the evening cleaned up, and went in the village looking for girls. "The ploughing was done with horses, the countryside was poverty-stricken, we milked by hand and took the milk to a station by horse and cart, so that it could go by rail to London. The older men spoke dialect—'thee bist'—I suppose, the last of that. The war came with September, and during the autumn most of the young men joined up. Something fresh for them, a different drudgery, chances, change. They wouldn't believe the reality, though their fathers had fought in the Great War. They weren't jingoistic, and couldn't work up a generalised hate—nor for that matter could I. The war had begun tamely, the Blitz was yet to come."

He said, "It was the closest I could come to classlessness. There had always been the division—my speech, my means, my education. Enlisting put an end to all that. I felt that any one of them could despise me for doing otherwise. I was young, but not all that young. And perhaps wrong, but not all that wrong."

"Too diffident," said Ben.

"Or too proud." His mother had been appalled. "Later, with the Pacific war, I did feel I had a card to play. But by then I'd been commissioned in the field, I'd had special training, they wouldn't let me go."

Helen asked, "Would you sit the examination again now? Or is it too late? I mean, the Foreign Office."

"The examination—you see, I passed it. I got the notice of it that October. By then, I was in camp, waiting on the cliffs for the invasion that never came. No, no, those ambitions long since evaporated, I can't believe I ever had them."

THEY WERE CURIOUS ABOUT THE MEDALS. Benedict said, "You can't wear that rainbow and then not tell."

"I'm obliged to wear it, in uniform. You can't think I wandered through China dressed like this."

"This one, for instance." Helen was pointing at a scrap of blue.

"That was truly undeserved. The only good hour I had, in the last battle." In the dark, in the rain and mud. "On the last night, the division got separated, the communications were down. The enemy were shelling the dead ground between our two groups, waiting for daybreak to finish us off. The last chance was to fall back through the wood and get down to the river before the sun came up. We had no means of telling the rest of the men, who were disastrously trying to join us in our trap. The sergeant, Mackie was his name, and I were crouching under bushes in the rain, and the shelling went on, ceasing awhile, then starting up again, and ceasing. I was timing the intervals. We made it regular intervals of fourteen minutes: fourteen of firing, fourteen of silence. I went to the officer in charge, Bates, holed up near the supplies with a straggle of our men—the others being deployed in the wood behind, along with our wounded and dead. Bates was a good chap, young—though he didn't look it that night. We had to stand close to see and hear one another, the din was terrific. I told him I could carry a line to our people who were cut off downriver. Meanwhile, the barrage was going on. I said I could get through with the line during the next silence."

He remembered Bates's eyeballs, shining in a face ritually blackened for action.

"I can't allow that."

"I used to be a sprinter."

"I don't believe you."

"Would I lie?"

"Yes. And nobody's ever broken four minutes on the mile that I know of."

"It's not even half a mile."

He said, "Broken ground, wet, dark, and you encumbered."

"While we were at it, a chap from the signal corps brought the line in a frame, showed me how they pay it out. While I was gone, they would set it up at this end."

All that had taken seconds. Bates was hesitating, seeing the frame: "I don't believe you can do it." When it got to twelve minutes, Leith had started out for the edge of the open ground. Bates, quietly: "Good luck."

He told them now, "It was more like an hour, all things considered, but went off all right. The men were pleased, too—a fractional victory saved from the fiasco."

"They might have changed the timing."

"But they didn't." He said, "The following day, all went to hell. Much later, in the prison camp, I learned about this." The ribbon. "It meant that Bates or Mackie or the signalman had survived." When he got back from his run, the signalman had said, "If I'd laid odds on you, I'd have made me fortune."

Helen, with clasped hands: "What did you think of, while you were running?"

"I've never felt more free." It was true, he had often relived it; more than once, had dreamt it. Thudding and slithering in the dark, under the rain, no longer filthy or afraid or doomed. Not cowering under cover, but up and running. For an hour, he disposed of his own life.

Had he died then, his ghost might have run on, exultant. Even now he thought, Could have been worse than go like that.

Ben said, "Helen looks as if she's had a narrow escape." He asked, "For the other medal, the great medal, did you go to the palace?"

"Certainly. That was just before I came East. Yes, yes, the King, Queen, princesses, and a few of their old, old relatives, Guelphs and Ghibellines, whom one had seen in the press in group photographs of grand occasions. The George Cross people were there, too, looking infinitely real in civilian clothes, and including some women. Not a large gathering—a number of potential guests had died qualifying. It went better than one liked to admit. At first we stood around looking sheepish, but after drinks circulated people cheered up and talked. There was a chap from the Irish Guards who'd been in the same action with me, in Tunisia. An adventurer who'd falsified his credentials to join up, and would have been court-martialled if he hadn't turned out heroic." Wheelchairs, crutches, false limbs, eye patches, and some shocking disfigurement. The rooms, bleak, grandiose, run-down. The great works of art were not yet retrieved from their wartime caverns in Wales.

"Did your parents come?"

"In fact, they did." It surprised him to remember. It was like prizegiving day at school: his mother and father dressed up, Iris actually shedding tears. His father thought that the palace had watered the wine in order to forestall any heroic drunkenness. In the last half-hour—again like a children's occasion—there was overexcitement, high voices, laughter, petulance: expertly dealt with, for they were all soon dispersing under what seemed to be their own steam.

TAD WAS LEAVING JAPAN. He came one cold morning to say goodbye, knocking and entering, but finding no one. Aki appeared, to tell him that Benedict was sleeping and Helen would soon return. Tad sat awhile on the rickety chair to wait, taking note of the characterless room that he and others would remember. When Helen did not arrive, he went out to meet her on the path, and immediately saw her coming down, wearing the green coat that was fetchingly too large for her and too long. Her head was lowered, but she saw him and came up eagerly as if to embrace him. They walked back to the cottage together, he with his arm about her shoulders. From that, she knew that he had come to say goodbye.

Both, for different reasons, were glad that Aldred was out.

In the cottage, he sat on Ben's divan. "Come sit by Tad."

Taking off her coat, she did so. She said, "Today you look less like Tad. More like Thaddeus Hill."

"And feel more like him, too. Whoever he is." He said, "Eyes like a huskie." He could not understand her eyes, except to imagine a future in which she would look appreciatively, regretfully, less and less shyly, at men whom she could not entirely feel for. If things went badly, might at last take one or another of those imperfect possibilities, as women did. In that drab instant, he could almost wish that Aldred Leith should now have her.

He said, "Perhaps I've overdone the hayseed." He held her kind hand, as he had done at the movies: a hand too polite to say no. "I've been unlucky here. The old incurable untimeliness. I learnt that at school. Not that I understood it then. I guess that's what school's for, to give you something to fall back on, later, when times get tough." He pulled out a handkerchief and touched her eyes. "Hey, stop that. If anyone's going to cry round here, it'll be Thaddeus Hill." From another pocket, a scrap of paper. "This is my address, I'll need your news. Things will happen, you'll let me know."

"Things will happen for you, too." Girls with white smiles and long legs; girls known as Blondes, and called Baby.

"For now, this will hold up, one way or another." He would have been preferred by the parents, welcomed as a relief: a simple American matter, at least as presented: Boy meets Girl. He could not picture Helen in Cincinnati; or, by now, see himself there.

He released her hand. "Will you kiss me, Helen?"

She did so. And he thought, with bitterness, that she had learnt her lesson.

AUDREY FELLOWES SET SAIL for Yokohama in a ship of the American President Lines. Peter Exley saw her off, sharing champagne in her cabin with her cousins from May Road, and a handful of colonial well-wishers, pleasant enough, who had brought flowers, chocolates, oranges, books, and who took stock of Peter as a possible match—some of them feeling that Audrey might do better, others that it was high time.

It was time, at any rate, for visitors to go ashore. Briefly alone, she and he kissed, with kindness if without passion. Peter might very well come to Japan, where she would now stay at length. They would keep in touch. He gave her Leith's address, should she get to Kure. Each wondered if they would really become lovers, or even meet again. Each awaited, from the other, something more. Her eyes were untroubled, nearly indulgent, as if she were his elder. But women are often that way, after twenty-five; and he could see how they might become guarded.

She was less handsome but prettier, in a soft wool dress with flowered scarf. A small circular cameo was pinned near her shoulder. The moment touched them, and they said that they would miss each other; which was painlessly true.

From his windows at MacGregor Road, he watched the *President Polk* leave the harbour. He knew nothing of President Polk, but assumed that the shipping company would have checked the record, beforehand, for anything scandalous. Then he did miss Audrey, with whom he could have spoken of such things.

IN THE COLONY, mornings were now crystalline, the mountain majestic. News from Europe was dark and pinched. They feared another winter like the last, no fuel, little food. A friend at Swindon wrote to thank Exley for a food package: "The corned beef saved us, actually." England was living out of tins.

In late October, there was the wedding of the chief translator, Mr. da Silva. In silver script, Peter was invited to attend the marriage of Mercedes Prata and Jeronymo da Silva at the Catholic church near Happy Valley, on a Saturday afternoon. A similar envelope was propped on Miss Xavier's desk. The head of the office, Colonel Glazebrook, had also been asked. Just these three.

Peter left his written acceptance with da Silva, and shook da Silva's hand, at the same moment that Glazebrook brought his regrets—appearing in the doorway cap in hand, for he was off to the airfield to meet a brigadier: "My best to your good lady."

The day before the wedding, Peter said to Rita Xavier, "If you're going to da Silva's wedding—"

"I don't think so."

"I was going to say, we might go together." When she didn't reply, he added earnestly, "Miss Xavier—forgive me—I hope you'll go."

"Captain Exley," said Rita Xavier, "I have no need to condescend to Jeronymo da Silva."

"You mean that I do. That I do condescend."

"You intend to be kind. But just—so far." Small, delicate chopping gesture. Hands reclasped.

She was on to him. He had never sought da Silva's company; strongly suspected that da Silva might be boring. But he would go to the wedding and count himself a decent chap for giving up an hour of his far from precious Saturday. And was eager to enlist others in his un-demanding humanity.

He would have said, "You're right," but the realisation might seem too swift.

She said, "Since you mind, then, I'll come."

Monica told him, "There'll be tears before bedtime."

On Saturday, Peter took Rita Xavier to Happy Valley in a down-pour. Rain rocked the cab, and drenched them as they ran for the church. They were shown to a forward pew, where Rita sank at once to her knees and Exley took short breaths of church air languid with in-cense and tuberoses, and with emanations from the mould that streaked the apse. In the half-dark, Asian women under hats of Western tulle turned to see them. Da Silva, pin-striped and trembling, stood by the altar. A pin-striped brother was best man.

Lights went up to the sound of an organ, and the congregation stood. A priest appealed to God in the tone of a cabaret crooner. The Latin seemed bizarre, but Latin has many nationalities.

In front of Peter Exley, a heavy woman was showing fear of thunder.

The bride's veil was being lifted. Her hand, inert, was linked with da Silva's. In the curio shops of Queen's Road, there were armies of just such ivory Madonnas: an impassivity not quite Christian.

The priest resumed the Latin service, in which the congregation joined. Peter Exley, from Australia, was the solitary European.

After the ceremony, the bride and groom stood in the portico. The bride's free hand, in white glove, repeatedly touched her throat. There were depressions below her eyes. Above her head, the veil was bunched like mosquito net. Her father was crying. Exley hardly knew, in the cir-cumstances, how to congratulate da Silva. But did so heartily, and was introduced all round.

How often one could be both moved and bored at the same time.

When the rain let up, the guests stood in a soggy enclosure beside the church, dodging drops from trees. Photographs were taken, the women dabbing away raindrops and tears. Da Silva thanked him too much for coming. They would all have a better time when he was gone.

Crunching on sodden gravel towards a taxi, Exley invited Rita for a drink.

THEY SAT in the upstairs gallery of a small café in Wellington Street. Below them, in the pit, there was a smoky crowd. Youth and uniforms recalled the time of war, but nothing of war's suspense. In wartime, in such a place, there would have been the hopeful songs—"When the Lights Go On Again" or "There's a Great Day Dawning." When that dawn came, it seemed that all Europe had died in the night.

Rita put back her hair, and it fell behind her shoulders. The crown of her head was spangled with rain. Her silk dress was patterned with small roses, and the gold cross hung at her throat.

She said, "This is pleasant."

He thought so himself, and hoped she wasn't being appreciative.

Coffee came in a white crock. Peter had a glass of whisky. In the pit below, the officers sat in twos and threes, mostly without women. Other ranks were nonexistent. There was a wet-weather Saturday crowd of Chinese couples, but no families.

"What happened to you in the war?" It hadn't occurred to him before to ask this off-duty question.

"We moved to my uncle's place at Macao. People left Hong Kong, if they could, when the Japanese came. We thought there would be air raids, another bombardment."

She would have been in her early twenties: a family of pious girls, hiding from soldiers.

"Many Chinese left, too, for the countryside." She was nursing her cup in both hands, a wintry gesture unfamiliar in that climate. "This island was never empty, but when there's fear, there's a kind of emptiness . . ." She looked in the cup, seeking her right to a complex notion.

"I know," said Peter. "Silence falls."

"So—we were at Macao. Portugal being neutral, Macao had many refugees." She was younger, speaking of her youth, her hair about her shoulders; her good silk dress and silky skin. "We were crowded into my uncle's house. We missed our home. Loneliness, but no privacy—a small thing to complain of in a war."

The five girls—and the male presence in which they ate, washed, dressed, undressed. "You have four sisters, if I'm right?" So Brenda or Monica had told him.

"Only two." Surprised.

"And both are nuns?"

"One is a nun. The other is married and has children."

Below the balcony where they sat, the pianist was taking his seat. Rita, looking over the railing, remarked, "He's Russian." She ate a little dod of cake, Chinese translation of the scone. "His parents live in Shanghai. When Mao takes over, what will become of them? They fled once, where can they go now, having no passport?" She said, "Stateless people cannot even become refugees."

The pianist was playing Chopin. Rita said, "He himself has a French wife." After hesitation, continued. "She's old, an invalid. Some say mad."

"So he married a nationality."

Slight smile. "Such people must pick up any nationality going." They could not expect to enjoy national pride, or other dangerous perquisites of birthright.

Now, from the piano, it was Cole Porter. The piano was quietude itself, as he recalled the blare of Rysom's gramophone. He said this to Rita, adding a few words about his months at the barracks: the incautious relief of telling about oneself, not indulged for a long time. With Audrey, he had been reticent.

"I've just moved to 'D' Mess, uphill, a great improvement."

"Couldn't you have done that earlier?"

She was right, of course, but disappointing. Woman's sympathy should be complete, untainted by the reproach of common sense.

The pianist had come round again to his first number.

"What's that song?"

"It's an étude by Chopin."

"I thought there was a song."

"You're right, someone put words to it. 'Deep in the Night,' something like that."

" 'So Deep Is the Night.' " In a low, tuneful voice she sang some phrases: " 'No moon tonight, no friendly star to guide me with its light . . .' " The occasion had gone to her head, tingeing her cheekbones a tipsy pink. " 'Be still my heart . . .' "

The pianist was on to Rachmaninoff: "Floods of Spring."

"I should leave soon." She felt that she had shown excitement.

He saw that their mild goodwill now appeared to her as a source of possible trouble. However, fairness soon rolled over him again, like fog. Evasion, after all, took many forms: in her, this repressiveness; and, in himself, the general amnesty for humankind.

He said, "I suppose da Silva's reception is in full spate." The wedding was already a damp memory.

"Oh yes. There are two or three places where those things are held, Kowloon-side. The families expect it. It wouldn't be possible to do differently."

He supposed her married sister had toed the line; the other, also, in a way, by entering the convent. He realised how few choices she had—intermarriage in the small community, or the nunnery. Or the marginal position in the ill-paid office. He thought, incorrigibly, of all the girls, affectionate and aware, who had shed their bloom.

As they went out, Peter was greeted here and there from the crowd. In a smoky mirror saw himself—tall, with conventional good looks; slightly stooping, with khaki strokes of uniform and hair. And Rita beside him, subsumed in the noisy but decorous scene. He wished for the unequivocal company of Aldred Leith, or—unexpectedly—of Archie Crindle, for whom endless allowances need not be made. He thought that, when his cases had all come up for sentencing, he would sail for Yokohama.

THE NEXT WEDDING INVITATION was from the Glazebrooks, who were giving, in gilt letters, cocktails at the Hong Kong Club on the occasion of the royal marriage. Colonel Glazebrook's good lady, ethereally fair and interestingly young, was said to have been an actress or a model. Exley had sometimes seen the Glazebrooks in the street, arm in arm. A previous good lady had been bettered.

Before the party, Peter had to go to the parade ground, where guns were fired for the far-off princess—whose photograph in that morning's newspaper had shown her buxom, bridal, smiling: bedecked for lineal procreation.

It was November, but summer flared that day for the last time. On beaten sand the men marched in the heat, saffron kilts swirling, blue bonnets undulant. Complex formations intersected, to a barbaric skirl of pipes. "Flowers of the Forest" was played and, by the Royal Marines, "Hearts of Oak." The climactic anthem brought collective rigidity, followed by slow dispersal.

There was one misadventure. During the parade, a huge soldier fainted, left in the sun on the maidan until taken up with other debris when all was over. The incident enlivened the hot watching—the show of precision having created, in onlookers, a desire for some conspicuous error. The image of the collapsed soldier—pleats rucked over raised belly, pale knees awry—lingered with Peter as he walked down to the Club. A discarded man, like the bole of an uprooted tree. By disowning and dishonouring the failure, authority had transformed it to an assertion.

The Glazebrooks' party was held in an upstairs room at the annex. There were flowers, long windows, and a floor of polished teak. Mrs. G., in fragile dress, stood near the door. As Peter arrived she drew him aside: "Do something about that potted palm and I'm your slave." He slid a ficus in its brass cachepot over glossy boards, and looked back for her approval. She blew him a kiss, lifting a lacy sleeve. She was called Hermione: fair curls, a red laughing mouth, and the loose pale dress with lavender ribbons.

When people were spontaneous, Peter Exley was ready to love them.

Monica and Brenda stationed themselves each side of Peter, a brace of female warders. Planning escape, he got a boy to bring gimlets. He knew the women would refer to his afternoon with Rita; and, when they did so, remarked, "Don't be daft."

The Colonel came up. "Who are you daft over now, girls?"

"Peter's potty about Miss Xavier."

"Miss Xavier. Ah. Miss Xavier is serious. There would be no trifling with Miss Xavier."

The women howled, as was their way when nothing was funny. As their sputtering subsided, Glazebrook went on: "And now I must tear myself from you charmers." As he and Exley drew away, he made a low, sighing sound. "Poor clots. Can't stand 'em, frankly."

The room filled up with older officers and their wives, and with the young unwed. There were also the merchants and bankers, the Bishop, the harbourmaster. The Colonial Secretary would look in, on his way to a grand dinner. All the blotched statues, restored to their pedestals. The French consul, known to be the Sûreté man, arrived with pretty daughter, accompanied by the director of the Banque d'Indochîne. The actors doubled their parts—villain in one scene, bystander in another. The same few players represented a crowd, the same sparse voices called for Caesar.

After the solemn and joyful toast, Peter took his leave of blond Hermione: "That's a pretty dress."

"Thank God you like it. My husband says it looks like underwear."

"Then you must have lovely underwear."

"Famous for it." Laughing into his eyes.

Exley, at her side, basked in the little flirtation. As he admired the dress, however, it struck him that she might be pregnant; and the idea, with its utter exclusion, drained his good spirits. He had already turned away when Glazebrook himself came to ask his wife if she would like something fetched for her, food or drink. At her refusal, the husband murmured, in the amused undertone of love, "You're supposed to have cravings. Don't you crave anything?"

And her smiling soft reply: "Only your indulgence."

When he left the party, Peter walked along in the night, thinking of Hermione—imagining some Hermione, animated, charming, and quite without pathos, who might be his own. And why, he wondered, should she merely be without pathos? Since she was in any case a figment, let her be downright lucky. He laughed unhappily, sounding drunker than he was.

He thought of Audrey, who needed some gesture from him—which might, in the first instance, be his journey to Japan. He had never been prompt with gestures, one must be born to that. It was long since he had given affection or received it. He seemed to have dribbled away a lot of feeling in a kind of running sensibility, like a bad cold.

He had told Aldred Leith, "I envy you." He sometimes had dreams of tenderness in love, as others might dream its eroticism.

He passed through the marble arcade that led to the best hotels, remembering how he had come here with Leith on the morning of the plane crash. There was a fashionable dance floor called the Gripps, up red-carpeted stairs. And there he found a table, ordered a Tom Collins, and sat watching the dancers and tapping his foot abstractedly. It seemed an age since the military scene at the parade ground. He made an effort to recall, now, the huge soldier collapsed among his marching comrades.

In the emotional befuddlement of a third drink, he suddenly spotted Rysom among the dancers. Rysom in civilian clothes—orange jacket, clean white shirt, and a tie forked with emerald lightning—was trundling a stout woman round the floor, while the band played "La Vie en Rose" and the lights turned pink. It was Rysom all right, even if his expression—earnest to the point of urgency—was unfamiliar. Nothing in Rysom's account of himself had suggested that he might at last be found in this established and expensive place, intently circulating in the dance.

The emergence of Roy Rysom at the centre of the very vortex that Rysom himself derided was disquieting. In taking Rysom more literally, or more sincerely, than Rysom took himself, Peter Exley might have been left behind yet again in the general stampede to safety. Exley had imagined that he knew at least what Rysom was. Now it appeared that Rysom had stolen a march on him by unabashedly having it both ways. He and Rysom had agreed, it had seemed, on one another's debility. Now Rysom had broken faith.

He walked back to his rooms, which took him half an hour, and scrounged a late dinner from the mess boy. It occurred to him that the *President Polk* would by now have reached Yokohama, and he wrote, before turning in, a brief letter to Audrey Fellowes at her brother's address. As he hadn't intended to write so soon, and the tone was a little warmer than required, he might look the letter over in the morning. Yet it was a means of conversing—of which, on that soft night, he felt the need.

13

ON NEW YEAR'S DAY, they walked into the valley. After a wet night, a brilliant morning. Aldred had by then been repeatedly to the temple, always finding the custodian—shadowy, grave, nearly wordless; but never meeting worshippers or other visitors. The shrine was possibly off-limits. The custodian might have returned unbidden, like the gardener at the house uphill who had reappeared with peace to resume his raking of the pale *koichi* into whorls.

However that might be, it was the first day of the year, quite mild, and the first time that Helen had come with him, passing through the small clearing where a man had died. He handed her down over a last wet carpet of slithered leaves into the brief ground near the entrance, at which they removed their shoes. The guardian was not visible, though possibly nearby—perhaps deterred by the presence of a Western woman or by this show of implicit weakness in the hitherto solitary male.

Or he might have been indoors, indistinguishable among the effigies in burnished rows. Drier leaves had scuttled through the entrance; and shifted in a patch of sunlight. The smells of camphor, incense, sandalwood, enclosure were not churchly. He and she did not speak or stalk about, or otherwise lord it over the unresisting place. In the formal effect of silence, the waterfall played, without paradox, its part.

Returning, they separated to climb the path in single file, he reaching back to take her hand. In the fair weather, they were without coats. In those days, their bodies were taking reciprocal shape, tentative, delectable. He had never yet said Love: the Rubicon word, with its transforming powers.

Helen was to go alone to her parents' rooms, where Benedict would also be brought and lunch would be prepared. The Driscolls, man and wife, were leaving for some commemorative occasion—there was often an event of the kind, which they unfailingly attended, leaving Dench in charge. Thus, at the top of the path, Helen walked on by herself, straight into that other existence where she had less and less place. As she walked, she put her hand to her mouth to hold his kiss, and to her breast to enclose his touch.

The man, instead, went to his own room and to his table—to those papers where the ruined continents and cultures and existences that had consumed his mind and body for years had given place to her story and his. He could not consider this a reduction—the one theme having embroiled the century and the world, and the other recasting his single fleeting miraculous life. Having expected, repeatedly, to die from the great fires into which his times had pitched him, he had discovered a desire to live completely; by which he meant, with her.

BENEDICT now had someone to care for him in the night, an older Japanese with medical training. Aki himself stayed longer hours, even when Helen was present, for she did not have the strength to move her brother or help him rise, and such things were increasingly required. At Ben's request, she still read to him, although more and more he drifted into half-sleep, looking for her as he woke; at once recalling, even so, what they had read and where they'd left off. His speech was indistinct, except to her, who understood and interpreted. Benedict continued to do the British puzzles sent to him by Bertram, but now she told him the questions and inscribed his answers, his hand being ineffectual.

Aldred, coming in one morning and finding them laughing—Helen with the crossword puzzle in her hand—was told of their new method: "His idea was that I should read out the number of letters, and then the clue. But he's taken to giving me the answers before he hears the question.

"I told him: three-three-three-two-three-three. And he said, 'The Old Man of the Sea. What's the question?' " Leith sat beside her, and they were, all three, for the moment, amused and healed. Benedict said, "Like old times"—meaning, a matter of weeks ago. Pleasures did not exhaust him. He said, suddenly and distinctly, "You must manage it, somehow."

In the short daylight he and she would walk on the farther slopes, from which you saw the sea. It was January, but they invented warmth outdoors in secluded places. He knew that if they were to meet in his room, he would take her to his bed. He knew that, however many times they walked about the hills and dales, this would ultimately occur.

It appeared to him that, in his scruples and forebodings, he was assuming the role of apprehensive maiden; while the girl became the embodiment of loving impulse. She was on a dangerous margin where she would do whatever he asked, because he asked it. Meantime, among the groves and saplings and angled trees, he had touched and seen her body.

He must speak to her as he had not yet spoken. He would talk to her parents. Concealment galled them. Unready for scenes and accusations, he and she might end by precipitating these in order to be open.

One morning, among the hills, Leith said, "Discovery by Dench would be too bad."

"We'd hear his cough beforehand." She had thought it out.

"I think he fancies you."

She nodded.

It is hard to surprise women in these matters.

"Has he bothered you?"

"No. Just creepy."

"Everything underhand. The new power in the world. Like that man Slater."

"Who came with Tad." She said, "Tad is halfway round the world." Tad had sent a card from Cairo. Helen said, "This raincoat smells like the earth"—because they were lying on his old coat from the war.

"Yes. And, like the earth, old and dirty. I got it back in a box of 'effects,' as they call it, when I was in England in '45. They'd been stored in Lincolnshire, in a barn near Branston where we spent the nights before the battle." He said, "Getting the box, opening it, I myself as next of kin receiving the pitiful leavings of the deceased. Living the experience that my mother would have otherwise endured. This coat was the first thing, folded on top: like a body. A book, a few letters, socks, handkerchiefs, my good watch, a shaving kit—irrelevant overnight stuff. Through an oversight, I was alive to take charge of these relics, only lacking the letter from the colonel commending my valour. The colonel, who in fact had died alongside me in the action. *Things*, Helen, the sad silly evidence of things." He said, "We're told that possessions are ephemeral, yet my God how they outlast us—the clock on the bedside table, the cough drops, the diary with appointments for that very day." And the meaning ebbing out of them, visibly.

"I'd expected to die in that expedition. I suppose I thought of that when I bundled those things into the box and tied it up and wrote my name and number on it and got a receipt. I've no memory of that. When the box came back to me, the owner of those oddments was dead, I was my own survivor. It's only lately that I'm reunited with the young man who lived before. During those postwar weeks in England, I rode a motorcycle, raced it round a track in all weathers—wearing this coat, I suppose. Exorcising immobility—the wound, the prison, the waiting."

"The war itself."

"Yes. The impotence of the defeat, that September. Battling in the mire, more like 1915 than 1944. More like Agincourt: rain, mud, the freezing cold. The enemy's proximity, their faces, the shared intimacy with fear and death. Explosions, slaughter. With the wound, I was captured on the last day. I'd been all night in the forest, dying."

She was lying in his arm. He could see her adult tears.

"In a lull, we had tried to get down to the river, but they got wise to us, we came under their fire, there was no going back or forward. They'd got close and were throwing grenades." There was a splash, and the colonel's head had been blown away. Himself, spattered with that bloody matter—thinking at first, unsurprised, that it was his. Then came his own wound, blowing off clothes and flesh, ribs to ankle.

"Near dawn they came through the trees and captured me. The battle was over. There were stretchers, lorries full of their own wounded, other trucks for their dead and ours. Screaming, moaning, delirium, carnage."

He asked, "Why do I tell you this?"

"You're telling yourself."

"They stacked us, the wounded prisoners, into a disused barracks behind the lines. The bunks were in tiers, three tiers or four. Our medical officers were few and exhausted. The German doctors took care of their own people first, thousands of wounded on both sides. Our walking wounded did what they could. Before the battle we'd been issued with little packets of morphine, sulfanilamide; ominous supplies. Our medical men had crawled around among the dead, retrieving this stuff where possible, and we were glad of it. The wounded who'd been heaved into the upper bunks were hard to reach. They couldn't get down to relieve themselves. Shambles."

"Could you think? What were you thinking?"

"At first it seemed easiest to go on dying. Then one imagined tetanus, gangrene, amputation. There's a gap I can't fill. After some hours, a German doctor came, a surgeon—another one, old with fatigue, who later became young. Told me I'd been lucky. They'd always told me that, and now I see that it's true." He said, "I took his name, he was decent, humane. God knows what became of him."

"They put you in prison."

"A prison hospital. Later, the camp. Then the interminable winter, recovering, shivering, hungering, learning German. Waiting for letters and books. Waiting for the war to end, which it showed no mind to. We got news, when other prisoners were brought in. Some of our lot would go out to the wire to greet the arrivals, cracking bitter jokes at them. Once in a while, there would come some chap one knew. One day, Peter Exley turned up, the damnedest thing. It was then, really, that we got close. One talked. There was time for it, God knows."

"And you escaped."

"No credit whatever for that. Things were on the move, we were preparing. Bombs fell, and in the pandemonium a few of us got away. Even so, it was slow going, and two weeks before I reached our lines. Where by luck I was taken under an influential wing. They had a job for me, and I was sent to Paris, then to Caen. In Europe, war was ending terribly; in Asia, terribly continuing. We knew nothing of the Bomb. The concentration camps were opened, taking the lid off hell."

He held her close in her coat, saying, "I've never had generalised feelings about any of it. One is compelled to act collectively, yet revulsion, compassion will be felt privately, reciprocally. Can you understand me, Helen? In England, in that spring of 1945, I saw my people, saw my friends—what was left of them—and rode the motorcycle round the track. The first renewal was coming East. China drives all else to a periphery, for a time."

When they got to their feet, he kissed her, and gave his hand as they walked downhill. He said, "All that came out of unpacking the box from Branston."

"It came from your earthy coat."

"Which has now been exorcised and blessed, and must be cleaned." The stained coat, once boxed as his shroud.

She had to go to her brother, and it seemed that they might not exchange another word. However, when they reached his door, he said, "Helen, come in for a moment," in the most sombre way in the world. She sat on his bed, and he beside her, as they had on the day of the suicide. He was mindful of how she'd seemed to him then, a child; mindful of his impulse to embrace her. He held her hands and said, "I make you old, with telling you grim things. When I should only have said that all my past has been displaced, now, by this love."

Her expression—considerate, apprehensive—remained unchanged, so that he was nearly moved to specify: our love, yours and mine. As if there could be some mistake. But she, finding nothing incomprehensible, lifted her hands to his face and actually laughed, saying "Love" in return, before exchanging their grave, preoccupied kiss. She said, "We are being so serious."

He said, "As this has happened to us, we should talk of what's to come. Not just of our difficulties, darling, but of our selves, our happiness, our adventure." He could not bring himself, then, to speak of her brother's crisis, but told her, "If you agree, we should first tell Ben."

"Who knows already, and is glad."

"We must think, too, how best to approach your parents." Who loomed, in that moment.

When she got up to go, he said that he would come that evening. They parted as at some long separation. She said again, "We are so solemn."

"I must get used to gladness," he said.

14

WHEN THE COLD WEATHER CAME to Hong Kong, after Christmas, it surprised less by severity than by its effect of clearing the air. Looking across the strait, you now saw, as if from a great height, the interior life of the mainland: grouped habitations, laborious paddies, serpentine paths, and the smoke of small necessary fires. There was the detailed foreground; far off, the forms and colours of other, unsuspected hills; and, like a signal, the mountain called Tai Mo Shan.

Such a scene must hold experiences, if one had the nerve to elicit them. The island itself was less fictitious now, newly populated, as it seemed, by quilted crowds, newly smelling at dusk of charcoal and wood smoke. You were no longer out from Europe or out from anywhere, but drawn inward to a continent. You approached the immense reality, or your own acceptance of it. One January night, passing under the arcades—where, beside fine shops selling chocolate truffles and crystallised fruits, small families had set braziers on the flagstones—Peter Exley realised that there was nowhere he would prefer to be. And that fact itself was happiness. He was aware that his deeper dreams might be considered exorbitant.

The intense cold lasted little more than a month. With the Chinese New Year, which fell that year on Shrove Tuesday, the days grew longer but less revelatory. Clarity departed like hallucination. And you drew away again, from cold China, cold Russia; away from that interlude of climatic seriousness in which dailiness had seemed a spiritual condition.

Peter Exley said to Rita Xavier, "Perhaps cold places really are more self-respecting, as one is taught to believe."

"One is taught to believe that," she said, "only in cold places."

"Not in my own case. We looked to the cold north for instruction. North was the place to be." We were lolling down there at the Antipodes, hurt, hot, unresolved.

Attempts, with Rita Xavier, to deliver something of his soul always miscarried. But he returned to them—because he could not help believing in the sensibility of wounded persons. Or because he could not leave well enough alone.

From the Western world, the talk was all of war: America and Russia would grapple across the prostrate body of Europe. Meanwhile, China was poised in her own colossal concerns. Peter wrote to Aldred Leith:

You will have seen that Shamien burned, in January—the consulate, the trading houses. If it is, as said, a reprisal for imperialism at Hong Kong, surely this is anachronism? By year's end, Hong Kong will be China's only window on the world. They will turn inwards. The United States will seal them off.

He said that his war crimes cases were coming to their end, and he would soon set a date for his journey to Japan. He was writing Audrey Fellowes to the same effect. Meantime: "We've had bright winter here: *l'hiver lucide.*"

One Saturday of returning heat, Peter was walking towards Queen's Road, in the course of afternoon errands. At the corner, he ran into Rita, about to cross. She was going to the King's Theatre. After weeks of Margaret Lockwood, there was a new film—hours long, Chinese.

They stood in the shade under a scaffolding. Everything was in repair now, festooned with straw flaps, framed by bamboo rods. Grey stucco was blotched with white. The air was granulated dust, with plaster smells of some great prosperity astir.

"Would you mind if I joined you?"

She said, "It doesn't begin till three."

They stood aside from the crowd, and from all that noisy life they might have liked to join—if they could do so just occasionally and set their terms. Or, Peter thought, if there were someone to draw me in.

Rita said, "I was going to have something to eat. I've had no lunch." There was a restaurant in the theatre, one flight up.

"I'm on my way to the tailor." He pointed out the sign: OLD BOND'S TREAT. She did not smile, but agreed to meet him in the restaurant fifteen minutes later.

At the entry to a shop that sold materials, shabby stairs led to the tailor's door. This door, usually open, was today closed and locked. Exley rapped on the frosted glass. A Chinese in American clothes, coming from the floor above, smiled in passing and made a gesture to his head.

Exley asked, "What's wrong?"

The youth, surprised, replied in Cantonese, "Liu isn't working today."

"Is he there?"

The tailor lived in the shop with his wife and child. Exley had never seen the woman, although the little girl at times ran out from behind a plywood partition and could often be heard prattling or crying there. He'd been told that the wife was kept in seclusion.

The man on the stairs said, "Yes. There, but not working." Another smile, another gesture of seersucker sleeve.

"I only have to collect a package."

The man passed on down the stairs. Peter thought how puzzling they were, even such small encounters with the unfamiliar. Recalling his arrangement with Rita, he was about to leave, when there was the rasp of a bolt slowly drawn and a shadow blurred the glass. When he tried the door again, it opened.

The tailor's wife was standing immediately inside. She wore the black clothes of an amah, jacket and pantaloons. On the crown of her head, the braids were coiled and lacquered in a formal structure contrasting with a primitive commotion of expression. Exley had never seen a more afflicted face. He crossed the threshold. The windows were covered with rattan blinds, and the room smelt vilely of opium and uncleanness. Liu, lying sideways on a bench where customers usually sat, gave Exley a blinded, anaesthetised smile.

Exley said to the woman, "Is he ill?" He couldn't understand her grief—as if she wept without sound or tears. He said, "Tell me."

Behind the partition, in household clutter, a child was lying on an arrangement of clothes and rags. The bed, improvised from remnants of materials, was all plaids and florals and striped shirtings. He knew that this must be Liu's daughter, but could not recognise the sunken face, or the tiny, diminished body, perfectly still, head turned at an unlikely angle, showing a small gold hoop through the ear. Mouth slackly open, eyes closed. Exley thought, The child is dead.

Seeing his thought, the woman spoke. At the same moment, Peter saw the child draw breath. He said, "What about a doctor, what about a hospital?" and, squatting, lifted the child a little. The limbs resettled like wayward sticks, and there was an aroused stench of untended illness. He asked, "How many days?"

The woman now began to weep aloud, kneeling by the child but not touching it, rocking her own head in her hands. Exley saw that she herself was merely adolescent—a daughter, possibly, of the sampan people, traded off at puberty; so small, in her black garments, and yet with a child of her own. The human frame was often, to Peter Exley, incommensurate with all it must evince and bear.

He said, "I'll get help." Went out, ran down the stairs.

From the shop alongside there was a loud wrangle of negotiation and the dull thump of bolts of cloth. Exley crossed to the King's Theatre. The bright coloured world resumed, all animation and indifference. In the busy restaurant upstairs, Rita Xavier was delicately eating, with chopsticks, small gobbets from a bowl.

He came up to her: "Rita."

She said at once, "What's wrong?" And he saw that his tunic was marked with the child's sickness.

"Would you help?" He sat on the edge of a chair and explained: a curious moment, in which he knew all that the next few minutes would contain. Even as he was speaking, noted her relaxation of alarm, her recovery of detachment. She feels that I should not mix up in it. He said, "I can't just let the child die"—to compel her, or justify himself.

"It may die, whatever you do."

He asked, "Will the public health people come?"

"One must take the child to them, to the hospital." She then said, "Even for you, they would not come"—defining, with that imperial You, the distance between them.

It would have to be the troublesome act of humanity, or nothing. He started to ask, "Will you help me persuade the mother?" But said instead, "Will you excuse me, then?" And got up. And started then and there to forget her.

Going out, he was trapped in the exodus from the previous showing of the film. Just below him on the crowded stairs was Brenda Mills.

Peter said, "Brenda."

Brenda made a chomping motion with her jaws. "Don't speak to me."

He stared.

She said, "They stole my handbag. When I stood up for the anthem." Flushed to a colour like claret, quivering near tears. "One of these swine," she said. "During 'God Save the King.' The vileness. Don't speak to me."

He pushed his way from the theatre and crossed among the rickshaws and Studebakers without waiting for a change of light. While Brenda was saying, "Nothing of value, it's not that," and Rita was silently praying not for pardon but excuse, Exley was already on the dirty stairs that led to Liu's door. He returned to the foul-smelling room, to its certainties, with a sense of familiarity. Hardship is never quite alien. Alien was Brenda, was Rita: women who had not rallied. His mind touched, an instant, on Audrey Fellowes, who would have sprung to assist him. And he set this illumination aside for later study.

Sat again on the floor and supported the child on his knees. The head lolled as before, showing the irrelevant earring. He saw that the child's mother, even in her despair, was disturbed—like the rest—by his improbable behaviour. He understood this perfectly. He himself could be mistrustful of any sudden change for the better. He was also aware that his intervention might go wrong, and was pretty sure of being blamed somewhere along the line. All of this seemed a small price to pay for health.

It was his own health he had in mind, his dull convalescence over. While Brenda was complaining to the management, and Rita stood irresolute at the curb, Peter Exley was acknowledging a simple truth. Or so it seemed to him at the time.

He told the woman what he meant to do. She cried out to him in a dialect he couldn't understand, and he let her speak while he thought about the taxi ride and wondered if Liu's wife had ever ridden in a car. He was pretty sure the driver would take them, since he wore the masterly uniform. These moments passed, and the child lay against him, still animate, valuable, and part of prodigious being.

He thought with relief of the hospital. He had forgotten that there would be people to help him.

"All right, then," he said in English. "Time to make a move."

15

THESE WERE BRIAN TALBOT'S last days in Japan. With usual human perversity, he began to look about at the colours and outcroppings of his surroundings, and to hanker for a few more weeks to get things straight. Regretted again that he had not taken up the language, or travelled beyond his assigned district. Wished that he'd bought better binoculars or a different camera, or a flat red lacquer box timidly offered to him by an old man one afternoon in the street. He was taking a strand of cultured pearls to his mother, and had another in reserve for his girl, who had not written lately.

His immediate purpose, on return to Melbourne, was to finish with the army. Beyond that, he assumed that something would turn up. He had a decent record, Leith's recommendation, and a couple of vague possibilities at the other end. Sensations of vacancy, of going back on his tracks, were natural: he'd soon shake down again. They'd expect him to be the same as before; or to pretend to be. He hoped that he wouldn't have to pretend sameness for the rest of his life.

Anyway, it was time to go. Everything here was on the turn. They were talking of trouble with China, trouble with Korea. Of world war with Russia. He didn't care to be stuck in the East with that.

He would miss his jaunts with Aldred Leith, in whose company he had never felt the anonymity that oppressed the soldiers. Taunted by his mates, he merely said, "He's the only grown-up cove I've come across." Brian Talbot wondered more about Leith's future than about his own. Having so far distinguished himself, Leith could not stop there: he should go on to vindicate Talbot's high opinion. Somebody had to transcend sameness.

He had learned that the little girl at the compound was regarded, in the common room, as Leith's property. On this score, the hero had been labelled "The Baby Snatcher." If speculation was muted, that was due to lack of evidence, and to the girl's preoccupation with her brother, which aroused sympathy. Talbot might have said that he had seen Helen holding hands at the pictures with the American; but held his tongue. Some restraint had been absorbed from Leith. And Talbot had observed that Tad Hill stood no chance.

Her attraction was puzzling, except that she was the only girl on hand. She was the least physical woman he'd ever set eyes on. But he knew that such a girl harboured feelings, you had to stay clear. Her value in Leith's eyes influenced them all. Talbot's own leave-taking was forcing new leniency, so that in these final days he no longer held that Leith should, as the saying went, look higher; or, on return to Britain, set his sights on Princess Margaret Rose. He saw that man and girl looked to each other, and faced difficulties. He felt for the two of them in the disastrous parting that was clearly the fate of all who mixed up with this bloody Far East.

Leith, after some days at Nagasaki, came back one afternoon with his canvas bag. His trench coat, which had been cleaned, was unbuttoned over the battle dress, as it was called, that he wore in cold weather. The two men were pleased to see each other in this accustomed way, having wrested at least one habit out of discontinuity: both aware that, after these few days, they would never meet again.

Talbot had one week left. "Thought it'd never pass, in the beginning. Now it's down to six days."

"I expect to be gone myself, in a month or two. You have my address, if there's something I can do—my parents' address, in Norfolk, which will always find me."

Talbot would have liked to imagine a white-haired couple, cosy by the fire; she knitting, perhaps, he nodding off over the newspaper: proud of their boy. But had a hunch that things were different, remembering the parent's veiled ferocity on the back of the book.

"Maybe you'll make it out to Melbourne some day. Never know." He couldn't, in that instant, see himself strolling by the Yarra, let alone with Aldred Leith.

The man suddenly asked him, "What else would you like to do?"—meaning, if it weren't the army, if it weren't the Yarra.

And the youth said, "I wish I knew." Was quiet awhile, then took it up: "The choices aren't much, I have to earn a living. Part of me wants change, part of me wants to fit in. I'd like to grow up a bit before I had to choose. But they're not expecting anything like that."

"Be careful there. When we're indecisive, the wishes of others gain." What he'd refrained from saying to Peter Exley. He did not like to repeat himself, even if life appeared to demand it.

"I'd like something more, before it all closes in." He couldn't say, Adventure; having let that possibility slip during his Japanese year. "Not fun, exactly, though that would do no harm."

Leith said, "Romance."

"Yair." The boy laughed, not quite easily, giving the word a sole significance while knowing that something more was intended. "I reckon that's it."

The man said, out of private happiness, "Indefensible, indispensable things."

When they reached the gates, some arrangement was made for the following day. Brian Talbot thought he might drop in at the common room. And Leith started down the path with his bag.

He was fretted by his own assertion that he would soon be gone. For the first time in years, there was an event that he could not face, which was no longer exclusively his own. He had determined to speak with Helen that evening, and with Benedict if the boy was able. If not, he and Helen must talk in his room. He understood that here, too, the other culmination was upon them. Not that, in any of this, he was unhappy. On the contrary, he could scarcely imagine the previous life in which he had existed without such charmed excitement.

Helen was running to him. Not coming from the cottages below, but from the group of offices above. Flying down the trodden, cloddy path, loden wings spread and hair fluttering. Leith dropped his bag and went up to meet her, aware that she was fleeing, rather than arriving, from some emergency. He thought, Benedict is dead.

She came into his arms. On both sides, there was such readiness that the man realised: I'm here to do this for her.

Controlling herself: "They've taken him away."

They went to Aldred's room and sat down together. She put her green arm to her face and cried. She said, "To greet you like this." But sat up and dried her eyes, and made her gesture of touching his face, to verify existence. "Thank God you're here."

"I say the same, of you. Tell me."

Benedict had been taken, by his parents, to Tokyo. Helen, driven by Dench on a fictitious errand in the town, had come back to find him gone. This was supposed to have spared her their parting. Within days he would leave Japan for the United States, accompanied by the doctor, whose name was Thorwaldsen, who was returning to his clinic in California. It was an abduction.

Dench had told her that it was temporary: they would assess his condition and recommend treatment. He would be cared for better than before, while the parents considered an imminent departure for New Zealand. They would make a home for him there.

She was trembling. "He will never see us again, any of us. I will never see him. He'll die with none of us near him. Without me. In some unimaginable place."

Leith, who held her, could not deny.

"We couldn't say goodbye. He may think that I took part in it."

"He doesn't. He knows."

She put her arm again to her face. "I wanted to rush, to take the train. I have no money." Distraught. "I don't have a pass."

He drew her arm away. "But I do." He said, "Helen, I can't get him back, but I can see him. And you'll write him some words for me to carry." There was a late plane from Kure now, if he could reach it in time. Otherwise, the last train. "Stay here while I try to catch Talbot before he goes. Write to Ben now, the letter. I'll come back at once." At the door, he turned: "Helen, my papers?" The package stowed beneath Ben's bed.

"I have them here." She went to him, took his hand and kissed it. "How good you are. Better than anybody."

Talbot was getting into the jeep, but jumped down; reckoned that they could make it to the plane. "Better make tracks, though." He said there were messages and letters for Leith in the common room and went to get them.

Helen had his bag ready in her hand—like a wife, he thought. "My darling girl, I'll try to get back tomorrow. If not, then early on Thursday." He took the folded page from her. "I'll tell him." He said, "Helen, whatever happens, don't let . . . Be here when I get back."

"I'd have to be kidnapped." Or dead.

When he had gone, she went to the rooms she had shared with her brother. The boy Aki was there, sweeping, wiping, creating vacancy. In her own tiny room, she sat on the bed, shuddering, still wearing Tad's coat; her legs drawn up beneath her, her mind shuttling among the day's impressions, two of which dominated. What she knew now to be the last sight of her brother, watching her from his bed as she prepared to leave with Dench for their errand in the town. And her lover saying, But I can go—with his immediacy and composure.

When the young Japanese had finished his work, he came to her door, putting down his paraphernalia and bowing low, and shedding soundless, creaseless tears.

Dench came in to see her that evening. He had been to the island about some task, and brought his pursy air of having information not to be divulged. For her part she divulged nothing of Leith's visit, of which he remained ignorant. And that was her sole satisfaction. He told her that she should think of packing and sorting, as there would soon be changes. She said that she had little to pack and nothing to sort: she and her brother had only their clothes and their books; and some letters, she said, in a folder. She added this to annoy him. When he left her, she locked the door and leaned against it; and would have shot the bolt, had there been one.

IN THE ANGLE OF A CORRIDOR, against a distempered wall, there was a hard bench that made a trio with two steel chairs. No table, nothing to read. Aldred had brought a book, but was using it to balance the pad on which he was writing. A couple of envelopes and two or three written pages lay loose on the bench, at his side. No one else was waiting. The trappings of hospital passed him by: wheeled trays and wheeled chairs, gowned patients with starched attendants, hushed and incurious. And, once more, all the smells, rigorous or palliative, of such places.

Footsteps came up quietly and detached themselves from the stream. "Major Leith."

He got up, scrambling a bit with his book and the lined pad: "Miss Fellowes." Distracted, he tried to remember how she could be there. They shook hands. "Won't you sit down." He set his papers aside, plainly meaning to resume them at first opportunity.

She thought that if anyone ever looked gaunt, it was he; and so attractive. She had come in from Yokohama with her brother, who was having a new prosthesis fitted to his arm.

Leith, now recalling everything, supposed that new devices of the kind could be had from America.

"Perhaps so. But this model comes from Britain." She said, "Apparently we had a lot of practice in these matters as a result of the Great War."

There was a hiatus, in which each seemed to have something to tell.

When she began again, "Major Leith—" he said, "Please. Aldred." To which she responded, "Audrey."

"Aldred. I suppose you know what's happened to Peter." She showed some hesitant distress before saying that Peter Exley had been very ill.

"This must be recent—I had a letter last week."

"Yes, it's ten days now. He's recovering. It's been serious. He's had infantile paralysis. Poliomyelitis, they call it now. The Gladwyns—if you remember my cousins in Hong Kong—wrote to me. Both legs apparently affected, one quite badly." She said, with kindness, "I'm sorry to be giving you bad news. You may—perhaps you have anxieties of your own."

"You're very good," he said, meaning it. And told her briefly about Benedict. Now that they were engrossed, there was relief in talking. He made a gesture to the papers he had put by. "A lot is happening at once." He said, "As I was leaving Kure yesterday, I had a cable from my mother. My father has died."

"I'm extremely sorry."

"Thank you." He passed his hand through his hair. "How much can suddenly go wrong. I must get myself to England. I was going soon in any case, but it's become urgent."

"Were you close—to your father?"

"I suppose I'll find that out now. We'd seen little of one another in recent years. Lately, perhaps, some feeling deepened." He added, "And there are other things to be thought of, before I leave." Unable to forgo allusion to his love.

Yes, she thought, a fine-looking man. Eyes, mouth. And from these impressions recalled that Peter had spoken of Leith's attachment to a young girl. "I'm afraid," she said quietly, "that you're leaving someone who is dear to you."

"Yes. It's from her that I'm bringing the letter I spoke of."

Audrey saw him begin to register, now, her private existence: her pink cheeks and kind eyes; fairish hair, frilled blouse, neat little jacket. "Is there no help for it—this separation?"

"Not immediately. If she'll wait, I believe so."

"My guess is that she will."

"She's seventeen. And will be far off, and alone." He would have liked to say that he had not seduced her, but the word sounded bizarre. And, after all, he had hoped to do so.

Audrey said, "It is cruel." She gave him the account of Exley's illness, which had come not quite coherent from the Gladwyns. Peter had been saving an infected child.

Leith said, "I was supposed to be looking out for him, saving him from himself. I could have gone to see him now, had it not been for all this—my father, Benedict. Helen." Her name pierced him: the abyss opening between them; Helen alone.

"Have you eaten anything?" This was Audrey, watching over him.

"Well, yes, something. I came last night. Benedict was sleeping. This morning I saw him, but he was scarcely aware. He's been—he has been distressed and was under sedation. I'm waiting here to be called." It was noon, he had been at the hospital all morning.

"There's a minuscule cafeteria. I was on my way there."

"But they might call me, if he wakes."

"Tell me the doctor's name." He wrote it for her and she said, "Like the sculptor. Easy to remember." She told him, "I'll arrange that." Getting up. "I'm used to hospitals."

So they had coffee and glutinous cheese at a counter belowstairs, and Leith asked Audrey about her brother: these damaged brothers, and their faithful sisters. Theo, who was a scientist, had hoped to do research in Japan. "However, too many obstacles have been put in his way, and he's thought of giving up here."

She turned his book, which lay on the table: "Wouldn't you just be reading that."

When they went upstairs, he said, "Audrey, thank you for this. You have your own concerns, but you make me feel better."

"It's the cheeseburger."

"That did no harm, either. I should thank Their Excellencies in Hong Kong, who introduced us."

She said, "Send them a food parcel, by way of suggestion."

They sat again on the bench. There was no message for either of them. That morning Benedict had not been in a bed, but lying flat in a narrow cot with guardrails that emphasised his look of elderly child. The resemblance to Helen was ghastly, as if she lay there dying. Aldred had sat on a low stool by the cot, speaking to Benedict's ear, looking into his recognising eyes. He had Helen's note in his hand and showed it. The boy made some effort, but fatigue, illness, drugs overpowered him.

"They said he should revive, by afternoon or evening. I don't see how he can travel like this, even with the doctor. The parents are there, apparently, at Yokohama, making arrangements with the shipping company." Thank God they're not here.

"They don't go with him?"

"They have quite other plans. It's a pattern." The boy and girl had been left in London, with Bertram. He told Audrey, "I must be at Kure tomorrow morning, whatever happens."

Audrey said, "Look. Theo and I will be back at Yokohama tonight. Write it all down—ship, names, company—and I can go aboard and send you news, how it goes. Why not? I need to know how to reach you."

"It's too good."

"I like to do these things. What else is there for me to do? For two pins I'd fly down to Hong Kong and make calves'-foot jelly for Peter Exley, and get the Gladwyns' marriage off the Hong Kong rocks. For these things, I'm a warhorse hearing the trumpet." She told him, "I have a reason to go there, in fact. I'm trying to buy a property near Big Wave Bay. The Gladwyns are acting for me. Mark Gladwyn says there will be a great boom in the colony when China goes Red. And then I rather fancy the place. Build a house, nothing luxurious, but comfy, you know. We'll see. You and Helen can come to stay on your honeymoon." Smiling.

HELEN'S HOUSE had been emptied, except for her little room. The whole establishment would be dismantled and disbanded. Only the original house would remain, the house that Ginger called pure. The Driscolls, man and wife, would not return. As their son sailed from Yokohama with Thorwaldsen, they were back in Tokyo, their plans laid. Helen would be brought from Kure at once, by Dench. There would be a flight, by Dakota, to Manila, thence to Darwin, to Sydney;

and within days to New Zealand. Dench, though he did not know it, was to be jettisoned along the way: a good post at Brisbane.

They were pleased to thwart, also, their daughter's disturbing dreams; to settle things before they became preposterous.

At Yokohama, they learned, from Audrey Fellowes, of Leith's visit to their son. Having spared Helen the drama of Benedict's departure, they had been second-guessed. Leith's woman friend, a total stranger, appeared at the ship, prying into their affairs. They would tell Helen about the presence of Audrey Fellowes, who evidently accounted for Leith's journeys to Tokyo.

Miss Fellowes had foreseen this interpretation and mentioned it— Leith responding that for his part he would consider himself honoured by any such misconception. At which Audrey had laughed and waved his gratitude away: "See you both at Big Wave Bay. Keep in touch." And walked off to collect her brother; murmuring, of herself, "Audrey is everybody's pal." Good nature allowed an occasional irony of the kind. She also determined, now, to lose a few pounds. Perhaps as much as a stone.

WHEN LEITH REACHED THE COMPOUND, at first light, the gates were barred. Brian Talbot said, "I'll hoist you over. Easy enough, I've done it a time or two. There's no alarm, no pooch." He wondered if there was to be an elopement. He couldn't recall what had happened to Romeo and Juliet. "I can come back this arvo, in case you need something. About two, why don't I do that. After that, it's no go, I'm off duty for good. Day after tomorrow, I sail."

"I know it. Come if you can, at least we can say goodbye. Thanks for all of it, Brian, I won't forget." With the difference of a name, these were words he had used to Audrey Fellowes, hours past. What a lot of goodbyes. He said, "What a lot of kindness."

"Ar, well. Some blokes deserve a fair go, some not. I can throw your kit over to you, if nothing's breakable."

Leith caught his canvas bag, and a bundle. The deserted air of the place struck at him with a fear he would not entertain. But he found her at once, in his own room: fully dressed and wrapping a cardboard package. The package contained his papers, which slid from her hands as he entered.

He closed the door and leant against it. Helen came into his arms. He held back her head and asked, "Are these your tears or mine?"

She told him, "They will come to get me, for the morning plane." Like a prisoner. Helpless, trapped in her age and his.

"God," he said, "if I hadn't come in time."

"I told you. I wouldn't have gone."

"You're having to be so brave. We both are."

"Will it go on like that?"

"Only for a time." Which will be terrible. "I must tell you many things."

It was fully light now. They lay, dressed, on his bed, her coat over them. She asked, "Is it cold in here?"

"Not now."

"Should we lock the door?"

"I already have."

"Ben. Tell me."

Close in their clothes, as if in the one garment.

He had thought carefully of how to tell her, resolving nothing. The boy would die, remote from her. No amount of tact was going to change it.

"I saw him twice. He was well cared for. The first time, he was under some drug, but I believe that he knew me and was pleased. The following day, we were together for an hour or more. I couldn't see the doctor, who was away. They wanted me to leave, but I explained and they let me stay. I had to kneel in order to speak and hear. He held my hand."

"What did you say?"

"Mostly spoke of you. I read him your letter, my darling, and he wept." We wept. He had never in his life wanted so much to comfort anyone, as now with her. (Her letter—*How can we be separate, who will always be in one another? Who've shared our years of salvation.*) "I've left the letter with him. There is a box of his belongings, they let me add the letter, and I told him. Of course, others will read it. But its existence might serve him as proof, as comfort.

"He wanted Aki to have his coat." Tad's coat. All that Benedict had to leave. "I've brought it. I'll help Aki if I can." He said, "I must leave here, too, as soon as I can arrange it."

He told her, "There is more. And then we'll speak of ourselves. Helen, my father has died."

She lay back from him. "Dear Aldred," she said. "So you have that, too."

"I must go home. From Tokyo, I was able to telephone my mother. She was calm, it's her way. But she's guarded with me, even in this." He felt, painfully, that she was rather afraid of him, his mother.

"Are you upset about your father? Will you miss him?"

"We were never much together, even when in the same room. Not long ago he wrote me an affectionate letter. I took it for a portent, and wrote him back in the same strain. He would have had my reply. I told him about you—a line or two. He was always pleased when women entered the picture." Diabolical, too. "I also learnt that Peter Exley is in hospital in Hong Kong. Something serious."

"Such a journey, Aldred." She would have liked to repair, for his sake, all sorrows of the world. "Was there nothing comforting?"

"Yes. At the hospital I ran into Audrey Fellowes from Hong Kong. It was she who told me about Peter, they have a connection. She might visit him in Hong Kong, or so I hope. Her kindness mattered, it got me through that day." He stroked Helen's head. "She knew about you, and felt for us."

He got up and left her, and came back with the wrapped bundle and an envelope.

"Here is the coat, which you or I will give to Aki. And this is a letter of credit for a thousand pounds. Who knows what may happen, you might need to come to me in some emergency."

She said, "There will never be more emergency than today."

He put the envelope on the table. "In order to use it, you need only let me know. You can have as much more as you want."

She sat up on the bed and pulled her dress over her head. "Come back to me." She smiled. "I don't have a penny, and now I have a thousand pounds."

He had taken off his jacket. Their shoes were jumbled by the bed.

"Do you want me?" Words she'd read somewhere, with their outworn sacrificial context.

"It would not be like that, it would be shared." They lay down together, and he said, "I've wanted it so much, and dreamed it. And now there is no time. They will be here at any minute. How could I leave you, after that? We should be alone, and safe and beautiful, with time. Not hiding, which I've hated, and fearful of the minutes." She would be alone at that far place, untouchable, perhaps pregnant with his child. Afraid of himself, he got up and sat by her. "As soon as you send me their address, I will write to your parents—that we need to see and know one another, and not be parted. That you should come to Britain, where you can stay with my mother, or independently, as you choose. What I'd have asked of them had it not been for this accursed departure. Helen, we should marry at once, if it were up to me."

They had now begun on anguish.

"Write to me immediately, in England, and send me the later address. I'll be here for days only now. You'll send me news of Ben."

She said, "I will never see him again."

So they began to dress.

When they were done, and sat again on the bed in one another's arms, she burst into a flood of tears. "It's impossible."

"It's the worst thing that will ever happen to us."

"Let us not wait for them. We can walk out and see them coming down." She said, "I love you more than all the world."

When they went out on the path, they saw, almost at once, Dench and one of the drivers at some distance, not yet descending. Helen said, "My beloved. Let me go up to them alone. How can we say goodbye in that presence? When they start down the path, I'll leave you." She said again, "How can we say goodbye," and again wept.

They stared. Meeting their own eyes.

"We'll think so closely in these hours." He said, "My darling girl."

She had determined not to look back, but did so, not raising her hand but standing still under trees. He watched her turn and go up to them alone.

Brian, coming at two, was struck by the alteration. He had not expected such vulnerability from his grown-up cove. Leith, grateful for his arrival, shared a last drink with him, and was austere at his departure.

Brian told him, "Don't forget. If ever you stop off in Melbourne." Leith thought, On my way to New Zealand.

My dear, I have your little letter from Tokyo, unhoped for. It touched me so, and the thought of you going out to post it at the last hour of the day of our parting, of which I relive the moments and words, the cruel beauty. It was unbearable to see you go up like that, alone—or, I marvel more than ever at what one does manage to bear. That we can need each other as much as I do you at this moment, yet continue to go through motions of daily life. I am writing immediately to your hotel at Sydney, from which you'll send me what I shall not call your permanent address—that being in my future care. Write me now to England, where I should arrive within twelve days—the series of flights consuming most of a week. Think how I'll look for your letter.

I say your name in this flimsy room so strangely become immemorial. I love you.

16

THE ROOM WAS A SLOT, ending in a window. The foot of the bed, formed by a metal tube, was parallel to the windowsill. Outside the window, fumbling it, filling it, a mass of tropical vegetation: on which the rain, audible at times, at times soundless, was falling and falling.

Blank walls, painted grey. On the bed, a grey blanket wrapped the form of a man.

Peter Exley was waiting for the doctor. His feet were grey hillocks in the bed, the book lay like a brick by his hand. This wing of the hospital was clinically quiet—no garrulous families, querulous outbursts, rampaging children brought corridors to sporadic life. The Chinese aides and British nursing sisters passed his door with soft squeak of foot to floor. The spongy pressure, hush-hush.

The doctor entered with significant calm. Shook hands, pulled forward the only chair: "Mind if I sit down?" With the white coat, white face and hair, and the stethoscope shiny round his neck, he was a bell-wether. He was carrying a thin folder, which he placed on the bed. He was called Major Shulbred.

"This is bad luck." He reached out to switch the fan to a higher speed. Lined face, mottled hands; some thoughtfulness not merely professional.

"Yes."

"Not the most severe case we've had. Nor quite the lightest either."

"No."

"What the layman calls infantile paralysis. Medically, poliomyelitis. From the Greek—polio, grey. Grey matter of the spinal cord. You've heard all this from my colleagues."

"Yes." Exley said, "What is the plan for me?"

"Let me first explain the condition." Major Shulbred placed the dossier upside down on the bed and drew on the back of it with a pencil. "Here is the spinal cord. Here, your right leg. Here is what we call the tibial nerve. Here, the fibula. This is the femur. And here is the tendon reaching to the metatarsal bones." Politely shifting the sketch in Peter Exley's direction. "Following me?"

Exley held back mad laughter. Rysom's machine pounded in his head:

The foot bone's connected to the leg bone,
The leg bone's connected to the knee bone—

"What has happened to you, Captain Exley, is that—" Shulbred was speaking of atrophy, the body's failures. Making a second sketch, he filled it briskly with flecks of grey. "When the circulation is interrupted, these muscles can wither—"

The knee bone's connected to the thigh bone,
The thigh bone—

Fate had no sense of timing, or good taste.

The doctor went on with his flecks and swoops, his bristly picture: mounting the illusion that comprehension would alleviate fact. To understand all is to forgive all. In a few moments, however, he put his pencil aside and said, "Cruel stroke of misfortune."

"Yes."

"Europeans here aren't aware of such things. If they think of disease in this place, they think tuberculosis. Fair enough—with TB we're talking of one quarter, one third, even, of the local population. But there are serious diseases here more promptly contracted." He said, "It's not even certain that you got it from contact with that child."

He hopes to palliate the irony. Peter said, "I have no doubt, myself."

"The child died, I believe?"

"The same day." Exley said, "What is the plan for me?"

"Well now. Personally, I think you will make a good recovery. Even a very good recovery. You may eventually be able to walk without the brace, possibly with a stick. We're talking of a couple of years from now. Depending on response to the therapy. You'll always have to count on some weakness."

"Yes." Always have.

"Some effects come later, from damage to the peripheral nervous system. With age, the nerve cells diminish. For the time being, at any rate, you're not really ambulatory. We're trying to arrange direct sea passage. There's an Australian ship, the *Taiping*, returning to Sydney from here in three weeks' time, out of Kobe. Small but comfortable, I've been aboard her. I'll signal the captain myself—good chap, fine old Scot, name of Tulloch." He dropped the dossier beside his chair. "We'd arrange special care for you—may have to find someone to send along. Everything depends on the extent of their facilities on board."

The doctor placed his closed fists on his knees, preparing to rise. "In one thing, I think, we've been lucky. There's a chap going back in the same ship, says he knows you. He can help a bit."

Exley said, "Who's that?"—and at once realised: "Rysom."

"That's the name. He's leaving the army, been offered some educational post in the government, apparently. At all events, there you are."

"In the same boat."

"Yes. The appropriate medical people would be alerted at the other end. What about family?"

Exley said, "It's been played down to them. I didn't want them turning up here. I can write them now."

"Decent people?"

"They'll help, yes."

Shulbred said, "If you can't face any of this yet, we'll try something different."

Peter started to say, No point in postponing. But surprised himself: "I'd rather hang on here awhile. Get used to things, start the therapy."

Shulbred kept his fists on his knees, but smiled. "A rational response to a not necessarily rational situation."

Exley didn't mind being seen through, if it was only once in a while. He saw that Shulbred had often used these words, and with the same kindliness. He lay on his pillows, thinking how a reiterated utterance, even a valid one, mysteriously loses meaning; the repetition echoing down the words. He had noted the phenomenon in himself. He said, "The rational is still worth stating."

Shulbred inclined his head. "I remember you're a lawyer. In that connection—you'll be able to take up your profession where you left off. More fortunate than some."

"Less so than others."

"I know." The doctor got up. "I'll look in on you again." The hand on Exley's shoulder.

As soon as Shulbred went out, one of the Scots nurses came in with a note. "That Miss Xavier telephoned."

It was a message, that Rita would come after five. Exley put it aside: I can always prevent her.

"Yon fan's too draughty."

"The doctor turned it up."

"It's nae sacred for that reason." Switched it off. "I'll bring your tea." Touching his arm as the doctor had—in the same way, Peter thought, that people take liberties with the old and dying: giving endearments, elevating mere acquaintance to familiarity. Taking charge. A last chance to evince goodwill, to give the world a better name.

When the nurse came back with a tray, he asked her to ring up Rita: "Tell her, at the usual time, then." Lay there, holding a hot teacup, without appetite for the dull biscuit.

Every other day, Rita came to see him after her work. She brought what he needed—shaving cream, blades, a cashed cheque, a book from the Russian bookshop in Ice House Street; his letters. She attended to small matters with the nurses. As his concentration improved, she began to read to him. When he spoke, responded; when he fell silent, was still. She came in the late afternoons, in her green dress or a pleasing print, when the air was heaviest and the straw blind scarcely swayed against the breeze. Sat, without chatter or any arch greeting, in the single chair: never officious, never bringing bogus good cheer, never staying too long. Since she could not soothe the wound, did nothing to inflame it.

This tact, repose, helpfulness might have comprised the womanly ideal: service crowned with self-effacement. None of it could occur without a sensitivity that Exley made no effort to appreciate. His imagination was exhausted with scurrying to meet the minds of others. He held his own mind steady, like a man who carries his body carefully in pain.

In that life of few weeks past, he had held many matters simultaneously in mind—as people do. Now consciousness devolved on each event in turn, as if the episodes considered over years were being dismissed, one by one. It was enfeebling to him to think of people throughout the world reconsuming their experience, over and over: memory, regret, ideas, pleasures hurrying like caged mice. What emanates from crowds as a seething.

His own experience was not great, yet had filled up his thought at the expense of other powers. His consciousness was like half-excavated ancient cities he had seen—incapable of future, expecting only a further accretion of the past.

There was, for instance, the compulsion to return to the calamity of Liu's child—to deplore it yet again, or replay it with a happy ending. Getting away with something—the narrow squeak—is, he had always realised, a strong theme of life and art: powerful because it creates suspense. One never quite loses hope that Hamlet will discard the poisoned foil, that Juliet will awake in time, Cavaradossi rise up living, and the royal family escape from Varennes. The world loves long odds—Marathon, Lepanto, the Armada; Dunkirk. As to that, he thought, I've had my share of rescues, first by Crindle at Florence, then from Leith in the desert. And done little enough with the reprieve. Good fortune is a prodigy whose occasion one must rise to. Unpractised in such notions, I could not rescue Liu's child, or save myself.

There was a sardonic completeness to the very attempt.

These ideas came round to Rita. There is a kind of well-meaning that is doomed. It was this that Rita had a sense for, an aversion to: "You intend to be kind, but just so far"—and then her chopping gesture. Yet the intention might be better than the vigilant abstention: better than the chopping gesture and a withered heart.

To marry Rita would be to give up every illusion, on her side as well as his. And she could have no conception of the loneliness to which he would take her—the life of ostracism, household labour, suburban tedium. The White Australia Policy. Such a venture might be possible with high passion. He and Rita were dealing not in passion or dispassion but with a proposal of shared resignation. If he married her, he would perform an unresisting selfish action without pleasing himself in the least.

To offer her these excuses was unthinkable: like a private apology for a public wrong.

He remembered how Hendriks had declared, "Tolerance is still far off: too late for you and me." There was also Glazebrook telling him, "Miss Xavier is serious"; and Monica with her "tears before bedtime." Knowing all that, Rita had constructed her defences. And yet sat by him now in the late afternoons, defenceless. He should have been grateful. People expected something convenient to come of it.

I too am serious, he thought. I do not love her. I do not wish to make use of her, do not want a ministering angel who is indifferent to others. Let her be alive and demanding, and without that look she gave me when she said, "The child may die, whatever you do," on the last day of my former life. Truthfulness was his last whole good, the thing he had not sheltered or kept small for safety. He had brought it out of the fire, not intact but with appropriate scars. As an abstraction it could not help him, lying inert in the Asian afternoon. Whether it retained any private power remained to be seen.

Part Three

WHEN ALDRED LEITH AT LAST CAME HOME from war, another war was in the offing. The European peace celebrated three years earlier had loosed its rapturous hold; and London, in the cold spring of 1948, was as shabby and sombre as in wartime, and greatly scarred—deliverance being marked, by night, in the old honeycomb of lights and, by day, in a cooling of purpose as the populace awaited some suggestion of good times.

Leith arrived from Asia, making the last stage of his journey in a military plane, which accounted for his being met, once more, by an army driver—an older man who presented himself with a crashing salute ("Sir!"), relieved him of his baggage, took the trenchcoat from Leith's arm, and pointed out, in a recess of the airfield, an old Humber of metallic sheen.

The driver, having folded the legendary coat on the front seat, now stood by the Humber's rear door. Obliged to become official, Leith made no objection—only wishing to rediscover in silence the city where he was born.

"Not too fast. I want to look." He asked for a circuitous route near the river. He asked the driver's name.

"You'll hardly believe it. The name's Carr." Having made contact, and growing bored with the automaton role that—for effect, or in self-defence—he sometimes played, Carr settled in for a chat.

He had an idea that his passenger was foreign: "Ever seen London before?"

"Not for some years. I was here briefly at the time of the victory." He could have added, I was arranging a divorce.

"Those were great days."

It was past noon. Configurations of cloud and water were hatched with the roofs and rounds and angles of normal existence. The thin light proposed silence, but the driver was adrift on a stream where his wife and daughter swam companionably with recollections of the Western Desert, the fall of a doodlebug at Islington early in 1945, a fox terrier named Spiv, the sixpenny meat ration—and the inauguration, in America, of automatic transmission: "Takes the fun out of it."

For Christ's sake, shut up, thought Leith, intent on the cold, silver, shattered scene. Near the Tower, however, he gave by an exclamation further stimulus.

"Yes, yon's All Hollows, and a sorry sight."

Charred stump above smashed wall.

Childhood visits to the Tower had usually begun with All Hallows. ("All Hallows *Barking*," his grandmother made a point; and the child, knowing nothing of parent abbeys, conjured a ferocious dog.)

"December 1940, that would have been. A rare rumpus, with only the Christmas truce." The car was almost idling. "Funny, them and us, the both of us at our Christmas dinner." The prayers and hymns, the same God-Is-Love. By "funny" he meant "insane." "Well, they pounded us. And got it back with interest. When we might've all lived peaceful."

"I agree."

The next event, on its rise, was the Monument.

"And here you've got your highest point in London."

"Can it still be there?" The passenger wound down the window. He had forgotten the dimensions, or discounted boyhood memory. The plinth alone seemed vast as a building. A family was standing back to assess the height of the column, wondering whether to ascend: their loitering a signal of peace. Aldred recalled the climb, the counting of steps. ("Three hundred and ELEVEN!" his cousin had shrieked on a last gasp.) Emerging on a parapet topped by gilded flames, to the panorama of all their confident world: towers, domes, temples, and elastic river.

"Had our own Great Fire since then."

"Indeed."

They skirted, then, the plateau of grit and grasses around St. Paul's. The streets had filled, and vibrated, with buses, lorries, bicycles, and with the shifting crowds no longer dressed for battle: pale scissor legs of pale women; dark, peremptory footsteps of men keeping time to their furled umbrellas. Narrow streets once lightless at midmorning stood bare, now, from the fiery displacements. Rubble and even litter had been cleared away, leaving poignant austerity.

Leith had been booked in to a hotel in Piccadilly, towards the Park Lane end. And there, with Carr still informative and Green Park in cold glory, his luggage was unloaded.

"No one to meet you?"

"I wanted an hour to myself."

"Bit of peace and quiet, eh. We all need it."

"In any case, you've given me a thorough welcome"—entering into the fiction of his foreignness, and nearly believing himself a stranger. And handing a ten-shilling note.

Carr came to attention. "You'll find we British rather reserved at first. But once you break our ice we're a warmhearted lot."

Beyond revolving doors, the lobby opened into an atrium where Crown Derby and soft scarves were displayed, for export only, in vitrines. At the desk, he told the receptionist, "I'll go to the room before lunch."

"They've finished serving, sir."

His watch said one-forty.

"They stop serving at one-thirty." Her eye fell on the red ribbon, and she turned to a cherub in monkey jacket: "Ask whether an exception might be made."

As Leith went into the restaurant, small puddings were being distributed, and slivers of a bevelled cake. A solitary water ice, pale pink, was carried past him on a silver tray. An ice so delicately insubstantial, so smoothly chastely pink, so exactly flush with its silver rim, that he recalled it for years as an emblem of re-entry.

Two brittle chops were brought, elaborately frilled. The restaurant, lukewarm, was of good height and size. Overhead, plaster garlands converged on a chandelier. Thick blue carpet and velvet curtains contributed to a hush in which tiny collisions of spoon and china were magnified; as was, scandalously, any high voice, male or female, from the remaining diners—who wore good, serious dark clothes, and, in the case of women, hats. In general, the women were pretty. Giving up on a desiccated chop, Leith looked—his mere glance being taken, here and there, as molestation—thinking of Carr and of the pink and silver concoction. Once you break our ice.

Conduct had kept chaos at bay. He wondered if it might be abandoned now, as inconclusive.

"Unfortunately, sir, the savoury is off. Coffee is now being served in the lounge. Tea will be served between four and five, in the Brummell Room. A buffy lunch is offered on Sundays."

He collected mail from the desk. Helen not having this address, he couldn't expect the only letter greatly wanted. Yet experienced, as he was taken up in the lift, a sense of dashed hopes.

In the room, he began on his correspondence. There were two scrawled pages from Norfolk, from his mother, telling him how best to come. At the end: "That I'll see you within hours." There was a note, from Regent's Park, from Aurora, to whom he had cabled. "I'll expect you, then, about seven." There were messages and postcards and books from friends, and a pair of official envelopes concerning his work. He took up the pages in his mother's writing and put through a call to Norfolk. While he was waiting for the call, the cherub from the desk came to the door—"Flahs f'ew"—with a box of hothouse flowers packed in damp newspaper and sent that morning from the country by his godmother.

He took the flowers to the bathroom and sprinkled them. He thought he would carry them to Aurora, since they would hardly survive tomorrow's journey. When the call came from Norfolk, mother and son were both kind, composed. As right as it could be—so he, at least, thought. Spontaneity would begin, if at all, at home. Home was no longer parental: the property had been willed to him, the rooms were, on paper, his own. It would be his mother's house, of course, forever—unless Helen could, over time, make it hers. If she had managed that with a prefabricated hut in the hills of Japan, she might pull it off with a stone monument by the North Sea.

He meant to go out and walk while light lasted and, struggling into his coat, went to the window, where the world was crammed and coloured with buildings and bare branches, posted with flagstaffs and steeples, and animated to the grey horizon by an imagined milling of men, women, and machines. And by those many, like himself, drawn in again, after war and wanderings, by the magnet of a capital. The view of streets made him wish that he had not left the choice of the hotel to others. Not having cared to specify, he now found himself in this citadel—as if, at a party, he had been saddled with the bore. It was long since he'd been in such an up-holstered world, where quilted coverlets and damask hangings counted for a great deal; where cretonnes, carpets, kapok were deployed to absorb the shocks of existence—and had possibly, in recent memory, saved lives.

Leaving the hotel, he walked into the park, turning back to look at the ruins of fine houses ranked along Piccadilly. The Queen's Walk boundary was formed by a grim palisade, once the dwellings of the wealthy: wreckage on whose boarded window bays placards announced repair or demolition. In small forecourts, masonry was restrained by wire netting. In derelict gardens, green shoots, which should have been touching, were forlorn. Those ravaged houses, which had been, whenever Leith passed them in his youth, engrossed in their own charmed lives, had lost their luck.

He walked up and down the row, then turned into the arcade and headed for the Strand.

WHEN HE CAME BACK, at evening, heat was mumbling in the cold radiators. Curtains had been closed, there was the scent of flowers now arranged in vases. The coverlet had been removed from the bed, which had been turned down. As a precaution against power failure, a candle in ceramic holder was on the bureau: yellow candle of the spiralled kind, with the look of very old marzipan. Leith, who was chilled, and for the moment tired, was glad of it all, and forgot that he had disliked the room. He dropped his newspaper on a table, unlatched his luggage, and ran a grey bath. From the bathroom window, which opened with resistant scraping, there was a glimpse, and smell, of terracotta chimney pots grimed by coal fires. The glass steamed, the sill was filmed with soot. Towels were meanwhile warming on an electric rail, there was lavender soap, the tub was vast, and bright brass taps were large as his hand.

As he bathed, and dressed in civilian clothes, he was thinking of Aurora, with whom he was to dine, not seen in seven years. His father's mistress and, long ago, his own. He was glad to be going to her, rather than to anyone else on this side of the world.

He took the Tube to Baker Street, and walked. The lobby of Aurora's building was dim, frigid, shabby. Flaps of viscous paint hung loose from the ceiling. Walls signalled a historic shattering. Waiting for the same slow Edwardian lift, which worked, by pressure of water, to a clanking of chains, Leith wondered if Aurora, too, might be transfigured—fat, perhaps; slattern or crone. Which led him to ponder his own alteration—the early arrival of a few grey hairs and a general weathering. Then he was at her door, and had her in his arms, while she, in tears, laughed for joy.

"Your hands are cold," she said. "You came without gloves."

It was their code of years ago, from his first arrival at her door.

They sat in the same smaller room, by the fire: "The only room, at present. The entire place is being redone, imagine the hell." Her same low voice. The same blaze in the grate; the flowers and whisky. On the walls, blue silk had been replaced by a rippled paper. On the mantelpiece, Britannia was reinstalled, beneath the painting where girls glimmered by a stream. The theatrical brightness had departed; or had existed only in the eyes of youth.

He handed over his damp box of flowers, explaining them. A bottle of red wine was breathing near the hearth. At the opposite side of the room, a gas fire was ineffectual.

Aurora had on a dress of fine black wool, narrow-waisted and gracefully skirted in the new fashion. She was thinner, older, more delicately beautiful. The man said this last word.

"Oh . . ." She pushed back her hair, which was shorter and of a different gold. "We're all grey now, and undernourished. Or puffy, from scoffing chockies cadged from Yankees."

"I find you neither grey nor puffy. Undernourished, perhaps. Aurora, how are you managing this?" His father's death.

She looked at him quite a while, and then away. They both thought that she might cry, but she did not. "There are such fluctuations, you know. Grief, grievance, disbelief. Tenderness. Remorse."

"I think you have little reason to feel guilty in this, Aurora."

"Not guilt. Remorse. Rightful regret. Responsibility. Don't try to take that from me, Aldred—one of the ways we come to know ourselves. As I discover. People tell you that time will help—they have to say something. They don't realise that one dreads time, the diminution. One doesn't *want* to get over it." She said, "He and I— we saw each other less these last years. He didn't come to town very often, and naturally I could not go there. I resented, more than before, the marginal aspect of my life—his centre having become, more and more, the house in Norfolk, the odd bleak place, your mother."

"I don't know if you ever saw the house."

"Yes. Three times. Your mother was away. Once, in fact, and this is shameful, she was in hospital. He wanted me to see it, where he lived and wrote. And I was curious, although not happy about it. It added, obviously, to the sense of exclusion." She said, "When he came back from Greece two years ago, he was not just older, but aged. I should have been more attentive to that. I felt that he was always the difficult one, we were all anxious for him—whereas I would have liked, by now, to have his concern. The last time—it's five weeks ago—he was kinder, more loving to me. He came here as usual, and then we went out to lunch—he liked to do that, a little celebration."

Came here as usual, and then we went out. They had lain down together, unknowing, for a last time.

"I went to the train with him, I didn't usually do that. Small, silly thing to be glad about. But one doesn't always know what one will be glad about, later on. Or sorry for, or misremember." She said, "In a minute or two, I'll get dinner." Took his hand, and released it. "It seems very natural, to have you here."

He had brought a package for her, of Eastern spices and rices. "You used to like these things?"

She set them in a row, fingering their glossy reds and yellows. "Even the jars are fiery. From the warm side of the world. At the Ministry, we used to play the game of what we'd eat after the war: I said, freshly ground pepper." In an unlikely episode, Aurora had spent a year at the Ministry of Aircraft Production. "Oh, the Ministry. Oh, the deathliness, the pettiness, the squalor." She smiled, as one could now smile, at the bare idea. "Others being worse off, you weren't supposed to complain." With satisfaction, she added, "I did, though." She put the spice jars back in their wrapping and blew them a kiss. "It was in the term of Stafford Cripps, at the Ministry. Cripps had been pushed out from higher political ground and was bearing up nobly. And that set the tone of endurance." She said, "Endurance, our national god, may be running out of steam at last."

Leith had also brought her a circlet of carved jade, in the colour called kingfisher. Aurora gave him a small wrapped book. He said, "I walked to St. Paul's this afternoon." He got up and, going to the fire, looked into the lovely picture. "What happened to John Bull?"

"We forgot to pack him, and he got blitzed." Aurora said, "So you've seen the town. The clearing away has made it starker. Has put it in the past. When you were here, in '45, rubble still provided a sort of immediacy."

"Or I was too sunk in my own rubble to take things in. The churches, every one of them a ruin."

"Yes. Poor God."

From Fleet Street he had turned off into the passage for St. Bride's and sat awhile in the broken churchyard.

She said, "I suppose it means the end of monuments. Hard to imagine fresh triumphal arches, war memorials, new equestrian statues."

"For one thing, we might be backing the wrong horse."

She suddenly said, "I hated missing you, when you were here that May."

"A weird time all round."

"It was when I was at Truro, staying with poor Mummy." She said, "I never met your wife."

"Perhaps you will, one day."

She noted but did not take up the ambiguity. She was looking up at him. "You've become a bit formidable."

"Surely not." Few men would quite dislike the idea. "Just older."

"Older. I'm fifty-one, and should know." Aurora said, "Jason would be thirty-four." And: "I'll bring our dinner now, I was given some wood-cocks." Then, with hand to eyes: "Everything has such bloody sadness."

The telephone rang. Aurora signalled herself incommunicado, and Leith picked it up. A hearty voice, male, said, "Hullo hullo hullo. Rory?"

"Sorry, she's not available at the minute."

"Ah—who's this?"

"A relation."

Aurora laughed.

Hanging up, Leith said, "A sporting voice. A donor of woodcock."

He went with Aurora to fetch the dinner. The corridor was an ice-house, the light minimal, and their shoes loud on bare board. Her black dress buttoned down the back, like the frock of a child.

The kitchen itself was cheerful from the hot stove and the smell of cooked birds; and from the sight of a tray laid with silver and glasses and blue napkins, standing on a marble table. Propping his bottom against the stove, Leith could see, in the pantry, a dressing gown and bed socks arranged on a clotheshorse, and a line of small washing strung up. On counter and table, cold candles were scalloped with melted wax. All the trappings of making-do.

Aurora was dishing up new potatoes and small onions. "And a let-tuce, for your return. Did you have any lunch?"

He felt hunger, telling her about the preposterous chop.

She was pink, from steam and emotion. "At the end of the month, I'm off to Kenya, to be warm."

That she should leave, just as he returned.

"My husband that was—Jason's father—left me some money. The oddest thing."

"He died, then."

"Blown up at Mombasa, my dear, in 1946. It was one of those acci-dents left over from the war, the explosion of an arsenal." She said,

"Now I have to get to the oven." He moved aside. "Well, poor Geoff, poor chap. Then I got word that he'd left me this money. I'm advised to get it out of Kenya before some balloon goes up, or bubble bursts, or boom is lowered. On the other hand, if I bring it here, every last farthing goes in taxes. And they talk of devaluing the pound. So I decided to sail out and spend some of it there." Little upward smile, recalling smiles past: "I've never been in the wild."

At the fireside, as they ate, Aurora told him, "You'll find that they keep saying, 'Britain is finished'—and with such complacency, as if it were a solution."

"Such things are said of nations around the globe. As if countries could just sink beneath the waves like scuttled ships."

"With all of us lined up on deck, standing to attention as the waters rise. Disdaining lifeboats. I suppose we expected some prize for sticking it out, in the war. Like school. Instead, we find ourselves hungry, cold, broke, and somehow in the wrong."

Leith took the Beaujolais from the mantelpiece, where it had stood beside the surviving figurine. Britannia in trouble: poor Mummy. He filled Aurora's glass and his own. "This is awfully good, Aurora. I haven't had anything so good in years."

"Last year and this, I'm told, are fine years. For wines, anyway. I should lay up, or lay down, some cases before I sail."

He was freshly displeased by her departure. "Of course I wish you weren't going."

"Having stayed away for years, you expect to find us all in place, a regiment of Penelopes. I'm going to Africa to be free of hardship for a while." She lowered her head.

He went and squatted by her chair. As a youth, he had, on passionate occasion, knelt to her; and was now her elder, touching her without desire and saying, "Dear Aurora" as he stroked her hair, the unfamiliar gold. Kneeling as one does to comfort a child. He thought, Two weeks ago, this day, the dreadful parting from Helen. Had it been possible, he would have told Aurora then and there: I'm in love and mean to marry. And she would have had to listen and be infinitely kind. When, instead, she needed his attention.

The spell passed. He went back to his place. He and Aurora talked a little of his work and scratched the surface of his travels. She asked about his possessions, stored for years in his parents' house.

"I must arrange all that. I'll need a place in town. Tomorrow, I go to Norfolk for a few days." Imagining the bleached country of his home at that season, its web of waters. He would not allow himself to dread that renewal, or his mother's agitation.

"Another strong experience. How much high feeling you're arousing, Aldred."

"Cuts both ways." He asked Aurora to dine with him a week later. She also had tickets for a play, and wrote times and places in a little book, among other scribbles of the kind. He was reminded of Audrey Fellowes and her small green agenda; and her kindness. Pretty women, keeping track of things.

The lift was out of order. Aurora came down with him, using an electric torch on the stairs: "I have to let you out at this hour." Shivering, she looked into the silent street. The Underground had closed by now, and Leith would walk back to Piccadilly.

"Aurora, I haven't thanked you for the book." He showed it, still wrapped.

"It's a novel, I remember that you read them. You can take it on the train tomorrow." She said, "I embrace you tenderly"; and did so.

He heard the door close, and click. Under a meniscus of new moon, walked towards Baker Street in frosty dark, scarcely passing a soul. Feeling comforted; and then stricken for the familiar evening that Helen had not shared, and for the impossibility of imagining, in that moment, her obscure setting or her circumstances while he walked on through the silent wounded city, known to all the world, and thought of her eyes on the last morning, and her far desolation; and found himself near tears. Which could not be accounted for, even by his immense journey and exhausted need for sleep.

In the hotel room, he unwrapped Aurora's package. The book, a fresh work by a writer he enjoyed, was called *Back*. He finished it that night, and fell asleep near dawn.

18

HIS MOTHER had arranged for him to be brought from the station by the driver of a van whose route passed near the house. Though all happened with delays, he reached home while it was still light. The land, as yet dun-coloured, was stroked with coming life. The house, as he approached on foot over flat ground, might have been an illusion: that a fine old building should stand there in open country whose smell and story lay seaward, to the east, rather than back in busy England, was, like so many proven facts, improbable. Of light-coloured stone, and fairly tall, the house was conspicuous. After more than two centuries, structure and surroundings were unreconciled.

His mother was looking out for him, standing at the top of the few stone steps that led to the front door. Leith could not remember her having done this before—unless when he was very small, for some shade of recall did touch him, at that instant, into childhood. He was surprised, too, by his own emotion: compounded of compunction and distress.

"Dear," she said. "Dear." As if she had forgotten his name.

They embraced, and went indoors. He put his bag down in the hall.

Light from an elliptical window—set, as in a church, above the main door—showed a whiteness of walls and stairs more pure, or more austere, than he remembered. The smell of home, which is memory inhaled, was fugitive, as if less paint and wax and potpourri had lately been deployed.

They sat down together in a big room, by a fire into which his mother tipped, from a laden basket, pinecones and a few spars. A high room, with long windows and many books, a few pictures, and interesting small things on tables. He held her hand. He saw that she had feared never to see him again, not only from his travels and perils, but from his indifference. That he might have chosen never to return. Although they would resume some sociable dissembling, there would be this momentary knowledge binding them. It was mainly with women that this could occur.

In a suit of scarlet wool, his mother was, as she herself might have said, well turned out—not, like Aurora, in the new romantic fashion, but with fine conventionality. The son remembered the pin of old diamonds, and a gold bracelet like a cord. She had dressed for him as for a visitor of importance.

A young maid he'd never seen brought champagne; smiled at him. His mother told her, "You ought to set off, Dorothy, before dark." Consideration struck its own new note. As the girl opened the door again, to leave, a little dog ran in, hurried to the sofa, and made mad motions to leap aboard.

"It's never Gussie." He took the pug dog in his lap, where she squirmed with excitement, licking his wrists and fingers, raising her dark mask to see his face. "Gussie, you old smoocher," he said, as the dog trod about with ecstatic paws.

"She's fourteen. One of the cats, too, would still be from your time." His mother said, "All that fuss about the dog that knew Ulysses—when any dog in the world will know its master till the end of life." Iris condescending to Homer.

Leith put the pug beside him, and poured champagne. "This must be hard to get."

"The right kind, yes."

That was the tone of the past: a relief, in its way, since change had made a burden on the heart. Over their raised glasses, she met his eyes with enquiring love, but turned aside before this could turn awkward. In her new tact, his mother had the timidity of a person far older.

Her hair, once dark as his own, was streaked with grey. Dark eyes, like his, seemed larger now, perhaps with candour. He said, "I'm thinking that we look alike. I see myself in you."

She was pleased, but said, "You have your father's head—the form, and the brow." Intellect to which she laid no claim. She prepared herself to speak of his father. "That morning, he was quite as usual; he walked to the village after breakfast, came back with the papers. Just as always."

Here was a novelty: his mercurial father as a creature of local custom, set in his country ways, his end having come as the culmination of an ordered life. Whereas Oliver's nature had scarcely concealed a streak of contained violence. It had always been possible to imagine his sudden death—though not as the consequence of a sweet habitual rustic outing.

Iris said, "I don't know what you mean to do about the place in town." This was his father's small flat in Sydney Street, the upper part of an old house: in earlier years, no doubt, a place of rendezvous. His mother had used it on her London visits, probably with a sense of intrusion, insult, and unease.

Neither mother nor son wished to take it on. It would have to be cleared out. Leith said, "I remember books, but otherwise pretty spartan. I'll want something in London, but not there."

His mother also hoped to have a London pied-à-terre; not proposing that they share.

"You should sell it, then, Father's place."

"Aldred, it's yours now." Seeing him concerned, she said, "You'll be talking to the lawyers, there's a lot to look at, to sign. There is more money than anyone had thought. It will take a year to sort it out. Oliver was ingenious in this—in all things, I suppose. There are canny arrangements in this country and uncanny arrangements abroad. After ourselves, and Aurora, there are numerous beneficiaries. He liked to be secretive. I can do what I choose. I'd like to continue here, a headquarters. But also—to be abroad again, places one knew—if they're still there—and unknown places. To see new people." She controlled her voice. "It hasn't always been enough, presiding here on the edge of things, and with the war. And Oliver was often away."

It fell to him to say, "I too."

"You were at the war."

Then, these last three years, by choice.

So she had been bored and lonely, sometimes desperately so. Winter evenings, the dark, frigid, silent house, and lightless land. The bombers droning over. The image, at one time cultivated—of Iris queening it over her kingdom, giving orders, devoting herself, even ostentatiously, to his father; appearing peripherally in interviews as the châtelaine, the fixed point, dedicated, indispensable—had grown illusory. She had felt herself older, taken for granted, insufficiently loved.

As to a place in town, she had thought of Sloane Street, in a building where she had friends.

"Are these friends of Father's?"

"Oh no. Oliver couldn't abide them."

When Oliver couldn't abide someone, he made no secret of it.

She now asked, How did you find Aurora, with whom she spoke regularly in these days.

"I was so glad to see her." A change, also, to mention Aurora, whose existence had been long and assiduously concealed from his mother. "She's on edge, though."

"Oliver's death is peculiarly hard on her. And then, people are exhausted, in the cities. There is the anticlimax that life remains so hard."

Leith told her how he had walked through London as through Pompeii.

"You've seen so much destruction, surely, elsewhere."

"This is the demolition of my own experience."

She lit a lamp. The room was cold. "I only use this room for grand occasions. We can have dinner whenever you like. I had a present of grouse. Conserved, but good."

First woodcock, now grouse. England living off its birds.

"I'm glad," he said, "to be a grand occasion."

Standing, she said, "So you've seen Aurora, and now have come to me. I suppose that when a man returns, it is usually to women."

"Aurora said, So many Penelopes." He knew that she longed to ask, Is there someone you love? If she did, he could imagine telling her.

She said, with her newly tentative look, that she had prepared his father's room for him. This was a bedroom, adjoining a study, where Oliver Leith had slept after working, as he often did, into the night. The bedroom had a fireplace that, sharing the flue of the fire in the study itself, created a warm apartment. Both rooms had been, of all the house, least congenial to the boy Aldred, and least known.

"You can always change. The house is yours." Standing close to him, she said, "When I told you that I'd like to make it a headquarters, I understand that you might have different ideas."

"Of course not, how can you think that?"

"Things may change. You might want to remarry."

He said, "I might. Even so, some things don't change."

In the cold hall there was a large chrysanthemum in a willow-pattern cachepot: Japanese, with fringed silvery flowers like shooting stars. His mother had taken advice on it from a man at Kew.

"I'm so pleased that you like it. I thought it might remind you of Japan."

Everything reminds me of Japan.

"Because here we have nothing in the garden, what with the long winter and the terrible storm. And it's too late for my hellebores."

He smiled. "At this moment, you seem unchanged."

"I am changed, and much older." No coquettish expectation of denial. "While you, too, Aldred, are greatly altered."

"Aurora said the same."

"A man of distinction." Acknowledging, with small smile, the unknown that was his mind and life.

As they went to table, she said, "Some letters came for you. They're in your room."

IN HIS FATHER'S STUDY, the desk had been cleared of its previous life and there were letters on the blotter. The chagrin at finding nothing from Helen would have been childish had it not been so entirely adult, and he wanted to cry out to her immediately at the unreliable address a world away. He knew that she would have written, and that her letter might arrive—as it did—in the morning. Meantime, for both of them, the different, irreversible events were already crowding between.

The fire was lit in each of the two rooms. He must ask his mother about wood, which must be difficult and expensive, and of which they should lay in a store.

He turned the lamp out in the study, the room becoming kinder by firelight. In the bedroom, there were more books, there were pictures, and a crimson cushion on a seat by the window. He recalled that this segment of the house faced south. He sat on the bed, where a warm dressing gown had been put ready. His battered bag had been unpacked.

The bookcase nearest to his hand was filled with editions and translations of Oliver Leith's own works, the novels that, read by millions, had brought him fame and an aura approaching notoriety; and had made a rich man of this son—who, for ten years now, had scarcely used or needed money. Within reach, there was an early book: *A Light in Troy*, which Aldred must have read long ago. He saw that the whole shelf was given over to his father's most youthful works, some of them published before his own birth. Reading them now might arouse sympathy or propose explanations. He didn't extend his hand to those clues.

When he was ready for bed, he found that the sheets had been warmed with a hot-water bottle. He lay looking around the walls, in this room where he had seldom previously sat, let alone lain down. The two best paintings in the house hung here: a seventeenth-century Italian scene, all greens and blues, and a stark seashore of 1820 by the watercolourist of the region. There was a mirror, French, not large, in a red-gold frame. The floor was completely covered by a neutral carpet, which was overlain by two Persian rugs. The room was agreeable, and might be coaxed into intimacy.

His final sight of his father had occurred here, on the eve of his departure for the East. He was leaving before sunrise next morning, and had come to say goodbye. Oliver was lying on his bed, reading. His shins were bare and pale between slippered feet and paisley dressing gown. His son could not remember having seen his father's naked legs before, unless in childhood, at the sea, when they would have been brown, virile, unwithered.

Oliver, closing his book, had made a motion to get up, which the son prevented. Aldred sat in the chair, of a worn Siena colour, that stood now in its same place by the window. He did not draw chair to bedside, which would have created an invalid atmosphere; but for the first time was conscious of seeming to preside over his father's decline: the warrior son, back from the battle, freshly setting forth on his adventures, saluting the enfeebled parent. All such impressions being reciprocal, Oliver himself would have felt it. And was, that evening, his most astringent self, bitter about the hemisphere his son was electing to leave, sardonic about the East in tumult. Devoid of private reference. When Aldred got up to go, his father rose at once, swinging his feet down vigorously to earth and shaking hands—all the while with a hard glittering stare. Uttering dry unfeeling words: "Good luck, then . . . Look forward to hearing . . . Let us know if you need . . ." Out of the question to imagine that testy indifference as a disguise for affection or concern.

The son had gone away with a brief accustomed ache at his heart.

It came to him now that his father's legs, exposed below the knee, had been mottled with an irritation commonly called crackle—a dry peeling usual in old people in harsh winters. And that he'd averted his eyes and mind from that ordinary pathetic detail, which helplessly touched him.

Through his mother, he might gain slow knowledge of this man.

Lying back on the warm pillow, he realised that he'd never been aware of the ceiling of this room, where plaster arabesques were owed to a graceful nineteenth-century redecoration. His father's restless eyes would have travelled times without number over these leisurely loops and cursives. Aldred Leith recalled beams and bamboos under which he himself had slept, and the swollen flaps of wet canvas. There had been, often, the visible constellations; and the dangling lightbulb of some drear hotel, with aureole of insects. Years earlier, abroad, on painted vaults and cupolas, the coloured, humanistic, superhuman scenes. And the coffered rosettes, overhead, of the tiny room where John Keats died.

And, only now, a first sight of this pale paternal roof. Aurora had seen this. It was weird to wonder whether his mother had, even in earlier years, slept here. He could scarcely remember the look of his parents' room, their bed. Who could know how their love had lately appeared to them, which seemed to have languished long ago? One could be wrong about such things; about almost everything.

Helen would sleep here. He would write and tell her.

He put out the lamp. Firelight, dwindling, might have been the only light in the house. The rocking of the long plane flight, returning, did not trouble him. Outdoors, the wind was rising from the North Sea, at times with heaving force, or else with high sounds like a twanging of wires. He knew that in bitter weather men went out in punts at daybreak to gather the reeds and sedges of nearby marshes—for reeds, which could be high as a man and cut cruelly, were plucked more easily from water that was frozen ("frawn," they said in dialect). Converted to thatch, the reeds provided a living, and immemorial shelter. In youth, he had gone at times in the punts with the men, coming back blue, like them, with cold and, like them, muttering, "Oi'm frawn. Oi'm hully frawn": trying out manliness.

Because of his long flight, he perceived that marginal region now as if from a height—not a coast really, or shoreline, but a watering down of terrain, fringed and fronded with dour, inveterate growth.

These things, too, he would tell her—and was doing so as he fell asleep in his own house; back from the warm side of the world.

HIS MOTHER was answering letters of sympathy in a small, serious room called the office, which was near the front door. Having kissed her, he went to the kitchen to ask for his breakfast. In a corridor, there hung that portrait of the young geologist who had not yet become Aldred's father: a picture that had aged for the better. The kitchen itself was large and lofty, with a big strong central table. Much as remembered, but in need of painting. An elderly housekeeper was busy at the stove. Turning the heat carefully down, and wiping her hands on a white towel, she came to shake hands: "It's Mrs. Castle, sir." Her face was familiar, but unduly aged. Seeing him hesitate, she smiled: "You're perhaps mistaking me for Jessie, who was here in your time." Jessie, a much younger sister, had joined the Land Army in 1941 and married a Polish exile from the Pioneer Corps.

In my time. My mother had said it also. As if he himself were some returning aged retainer. It was as Aurora had told him, he'd expected to find them all in their places, waiting.

She said, "I'm just filling in for a while. It's good to see you, sir. Welcome back. I'm sorry about your father, a grand gentleman. Sad for your mother, after all the years. Losing your life's companion, I know what that is." She asked what he would like for breakfast, and where should she bring the tray, and he said that he would eat here, at table, unless he was in the way.

"What time does the post come?" He hadn't wanted to ask his mother.

"Round about now. The old postie's retired, it's a lad now, brings it on a bike."

She brought tea and toast, which he ate near an old coke stove that was opaquely, pinkly burning. He sat in a cane-bottomed chair that had come, he thought, from Italy. From time to time, the heavy door, which led into a grassed yard, swung back on a draught of cold, damp, delicious early air, letting in some younger person whom he did not recognise, but who nodded to him with curiosity before going about business elsewhere. There was a hiss of broth and onion from the stove, an odour of smouldering coke, and an age-old drift of humidity from worn flagstones, wrung-out dishcloths, and a rack of tea towels drying overhead. There were his mingled sensations of estrangement and belonging, which for the time being conferred exemption.

Mrs. Castle brought him a rasher of ham and an egg. He wondered what sacrifices were being incurred for his sake. Perhaps this was the last of someone's ration—last bag of coke, last onion. He had brought excellent teas with him, and other exotic supplies.

He waited for her letter. He'd shown her the ruined streets, she'd come with him to see Aurora, had been on the train, in the lorry, at his mother's side; in his bed. Would have been in this kitchen: her flushed cheeks and bright strange eyes. Ah God, how far she is, how far we inseparably are.

The yard door was flung open by a boy of about twenty, who was not the postie, but who, fair and muscular in a blue windjacket, let down from his shoulder a ragged hessian sack bulging with chopped wood. Mrs. Castle, saying, "Wait a bit," dragged out a scarred canvas sheet, which the youth took from her and spread on the flagstones.

Aldred got up and shook hands. "I know you."

"It's Dick Laister, Mr. Leith. He was a little lad when you left for the war."

Laister, unlacing the bag, began drawing out split logs. All this had happened before—yet the boy was not of an age for it.

"Your father, wasn't it?—used to bring us the wood."

"That's it, yes." The wood was being methodically brushed off, aligned. There was an enclosed room, disused pantry, where it was stacked, trimmed, made presentable for the drawing room. "Dad got a wound in the war."

Quietly, Mrs. Castle: "Dick's father lost his feet."

"Was it a mine, then?"

"No, frostbite. He joined the merchant navy. Did the convoys to Russia: Archangel, Murmansk. They were sunk in the Arctic, he was in the lifeboat. Four survivors, out of eight ships." Kneeling, glancing up from the logs. "He's at home, same place, near Norwich. But my mother died. He's got demoralised."

"Would he see me?"

"I think he'd be glad."

"I remember him as quite a young man, when I was a child. When I was grown, you'd come along with him, a little chap." Towheaded, wordless, watchful.

"When I was a nipper. For the moment, I'm just helping out."

Temporary people, visiting from their changed world. Extra help called in for his return, or for his mother's mourning: civil, easy, independent.

Mrs. Castle said, "Dick's finished his military service."

"What's next, then?"

"I got a grant, through the army, to study biology. I'm only home for a couple of weeks. Then I'll be at Aberystwyth."

"Can you make out, with the grant?"

"Just about. It's not like the old days; the government helps us, since Labour got in." Scarcely any belligerence in this: Laister knew that he was speaking to an enlisted man.

Aldred shifted his chair to look at the logs. These were among earliest memories: the heavy loads dragged in out of evening air, or out of rain, to dry in the warm kitchen. The tarpaulin spread, and the pieces brushed off roughly, one by one. Loose bark, wood dust. The kindling struck off and set aside. The child, who was himself, squatting silent on the periphery, peering into shapes, textures, colours; the mottlings and dapplings. The scrubby bark, coruscated, or the smooth angular pieces like bones. Forms arched and grooved like a lobster, or humped like a whale. Dark joints, to which foliage adhered like bay leaves in a stew. Pinecones, and a frond of pine needles still flourishing on the hacked branch. And the creatures that inched or sped or wriggled out, knowing the game was up: slugs, pale worms, tiny white grubs scurrying busily off as if to a destination. An undulant caterpillar, and an inexorable thing with pincers. Or the slow slide of an unhoused snail—the hodmedod, as they called him here—revisiting the lichens and pigmentations and fungoid flakes that had clung to his only home—freckled growths dusted, seemingly, with cocoa; red berries, globules of white wax. Wet earthy smell, forest smell. The implements set aside; the elder Laister stern with him: "Dawn't tooch the axe. I'm warning you." There had been an older man from elsewhere, who tipped him a wink: "Mind out, now, me little loover." Dick Laister's grandfather.

"Mostly pine, is it?"

"More than half. This here"—a sheer sombre block—"that's oak. Very hard, and burns a long time. But she's got to be dry. The pine burns well, but too fast. Sudden heat, and turns to ash. With time, the resin can coat a flue. This, now, that's alder."

It would have been this man's father, showing the branch of alder and telling the child:

Alder dry, or alder green,
Will make you a fire
That's fit for a queen.

Dick Laister's hands, fingers long yet thick, prominent bone at the wrist. Slight gestures, practical, responsible. He was squatting above the tarpaulin as his father had done, and caring about the wood. Continuity was delusive, however, and the youth would be a biologist. It seemed that better times were coming, at least to some, and that such a boy might choose to be his friend.

A bicycle bell rang at the door. Leith calmly asked, "Where do we get the wood these days?"

"Same timber yard, near Norwich. But it's scarce as hen's teeth, especially at winter's end. And they make you pay through the nose."

Mrs. Castle had the post in her hand and was giving a sixpence.

Leith said, "We should make the date, to visit your father. Would you let me know?"

"I'll talk to him tonight. It's a family house, a bit of a mess. He rather keeps to his room. I'll let you know tomorrow."

Mrs. Castle said, "There's letters for you, sir."

My dearest,

These days have been passed in immensities—of distance, of ocean, sky, and unending empty desert places flown over. Immensity of time, of loss and longing, helpless desolation. I would not write you this way if I didn't know that we share it all, that you imagine me as I do you, and so we live in each other's thought. And then you wouldn't believe me if I wrote otherwise.

Today, at Sydney, I had your note from Japan, so fast, as if it had come on the same plane with me. (Had I thought that, it would have given better meaning to the name Dakota, which will signify anguish forever.) My darling, I am so grateful for your words, and for the happiness renewed by them. That we were together only one week ago. Tomorrow, I think, you should arrive in London, with all that entails. You will tell me.

We reached Manila in the night, which was spent at a hotel—a good hotel that had a notice that "Firearms must be checked." My grief, numbness. Again, at morning, the interminable flight, the empty sky going on and on. Knowledge that every mile must be retraced in order to find you. Again, in darkness, reached Darwin—which, having been bombed in the war, would seem a shanty town were it not for military installations. At the airport, people were kind, seeming to understand that some terrible experience was being endured. We were given a huge meal of steak and eggs, inedible. Then began the crossing of the desert, which took many hours. One might have been crossing Mars. How to describe, except to say that an occasional sight, after endless uninhabited miles, of a solitary house there below tore more than ever at imagination. After the desert, there were more stops, more steaks, and the arrival. Today I walked out in the city, registering nothing, thinking about you. I have no tears, as if beyond them.

As yet no news of Ben, nor will there be until he reaches Honolulu. He too moves, lost, in an immensity from which I must avert my mind.

Within days we should leave for New Zealand, by a small ship that takes few days. At Wellington, a house is to be rented, but the first address is the Hotel St. George, in Willis Street. These places that neither you nor I have seen, names at the far end of earth; whereas you, at the heart of the world, walk on streets that I recognise. You have Bertram's address, if you can see him and speak of me.

I have such fear that our letters will somehow go astray. Whatever happens, you'll know that I've written. My need of your words: for such closeness, there should be a word beyond love.

He had taken the letter unopened to his rooms, where he found the bed made and the window open, and crocuses in a glass. He put the flowers on his father's blotter, remembering how he'd disbelieved in

Oliver's photographed bowl of roses, and thinking that things should now change. He sat at the desk, supposing that her writing, his name in her hand, would quicken his heart forever; since that is what happens.

When he'd read, he got up holding the two pages, and walked from one room to the other, from need of movement; unable to act on responsibilities now identical with passions. Against all reason, she must move ever farther from him, at benefit to no one and at drastic cost to them both. Her youth, which kept them apart, scarcely existed in the face of such a letter. One year ago she had been the quaint little mermaid first mentioned by Ginger, odd product of neglect and intuition: the changeling. Who now wrote from the crucible of adult suffering.

When her parents were settled in that far archipelago, he would ask them to release her. He must speak to his mother, he would write to Bertram Perowne. He would write to Helen, and sat at once to do so.

GEORGE LAISTER'S WHEELCHAIR was of poor quality and governmental issue. On one leg he had an artificial foot in a boot of unrelieved blackness. On the other leg, his trouser was turned down over the amputation. His hair was white and freshly washed, he was shaved and neatly dressed. Had been, like the room itself, put in order for the visit.

He said, "Good of you to come"—not meaning it, not meaning anything.

Leith said, "I should have come long since. I've been away, but should have known."

Dick Laister brought a chair. He left the room, closing the door and shooing away a woman who'd been standing, agog, in the hallway.

Leith said, "It was seeing Dick come in, with the wood, my first day home."

"Put you in mind? They like to say, the old days, good old days. They weren't that good. We were worked to death. There was the first war, and the Depression. Decent people begging in the streets. Then this showdown." Dismissive gesture to his feet. "Dick's not on for that, he's going away."

"He's going away to learn."

"We'll see what comes of it." He said, truculent: "I'm not much company, I know that."

"Would you come over, George, if I picked you up one day? Before Dick goes off. We could work it out."

"We've only got a Land Rover here, I can't get into it. Besides, there isn't the petrol."

"I'd fix all that. Get you out a bit when the good weather comes. Get you to the sea."

" 'Twas the sea did for me."

"Come on, George, I'm not being Lord Bountiful, I need a bit of rehabilitation myself."

"I know you got hit. You got over it, though."

Leith laughed. "What do you know, as to that? I only mean, I'll be glad of the spring." He said, "I know that your wife died."

"On top of all." Still surly: "Your father's gone. Will you take over?"

"I have to find out what that means. I've written a book and must be busy with it awhile."

"He wrote books, too, your dad. Never took much note of me."

"Or of me, I sometimes thought. That, too, I must work out."

Dick Laister came back. Leith got up.

George shook hands. "You'll be glad to go, I'm no company."

"I'll come back, if you'll let me."

"I woonder."

Dick said, "Come and have tea." They stood in the corridor. "No fun, I know."

"I think we can do something for him, change the picture a bit."

"He's hard to help. But, yes, the atmosphere's no good here."

"We can talk about it."

There was a long communal room, dated without being pictur-esque: evidence of toil, where women had aged over blackened pots and sodden laundry, setting down endless thick meals to men who struggled in from fields and animals. A place of glum silences, oc-casional harsh laughter, endurance; some brutality. On the turn for change. Two labourers, sinewed, sardonic, were warming themselves by a stove, one tall, one short. Both had clearly been soldiers. These were Dick's cousins, who grunted in Leith's direction and came to shake hands. At a long bench by the table, Laister's young brother got up, transferring his fork to his left hand; smiling. A tortoiseshell cat came curving to his ankles.

There was a girl, a child of nine or ten.

Leith sat where suggested. Dick Laister, though keeping himself in hand, was more in charge here; more familial in speech and mood. His cousins helped themselves from a tureen on the table. Places had been laid, but no woman showed herself—except for the child, who stared at Leith across the table. Lank, light hair; grey eyes, implacable. A lacklustre pinafore. A jostle of front teeth. Speechless, yet not shy. Leith asked her name, which was Edith.

There was mention of Madge: "Wait till Madge gets wind of that," "Madge won't go for it, not Madge." Leith thought of Melba Driscoll.

Another man came in, broad, heavy, in his thirties: again the evident soldierly past. Sat down, helped himself. Troubled, troubling, troublesome. Dick Laister spoke to him, and he nodded at Leith. The men talked about the government, criticising: "Better than t'oother lot, at all events"—with a glance at Leith, testing the waters. Dick said, forestalling, "Major Leith, here, was in the ranks, Tone."

The angered man said, "I saw you got the Military Medal, among the rest"—a medal given only in the ranks; but Tony could make it an accusation.

They had no time for Attlee, but liked Bevin and Bevan well enough.

Leith was eating stickily on bread and honey. The cat got up on the bench beside him, nuzzling her hard apple of a head beneath his arm. He rubbed at her with his elbow, down her arching back; said, "I can't touch her with these honey hands. She'd be washing herself for the rest of the day."

Dick's young brother remarked, "She's got no oother plans."

Edith told Leith, "I want to go to London."

"Someday you will."

"Will you be there?"

"Very likely." He said, "We'll have an outing."

"Like what?"

"You'll have to choose."

"It'd be better you choose."

"Why so?"

"If I did the choosing, you'd get fed up, and show it."

Leith said, "Edith, what a woman you're going to be."

One of the men said, "She's as good as a show, the little mawther."

Edith kept her eyes on Aldred's. "Are you married?"

The men hooted. "Wait till Madge hears." "Don't get your hopes up, Ede."

Child or not, it was the timeless challenge, and they had to put it down.

Out of her depth, the girl reddened but persisted. "Are you, then?"

"Not at the moment." Holding her gaze, he said, "Soon." The table took note.

"Is she pretty?"

"Yes. Most girls are pretty, I find. She has her own way of being."

"What's that, then?"

"She's got through a lot without much help. That's often true for girls." As you're discovering, Edith.

The men listened, uncertain whether he was making a fool of himself or not. The posh voice was always fair game, but then, all speech is an exposure. Dick Laister and his young brother were above that—though how they'd managed it, God knew. The girl was in a class of her own, like the cat.

Laister took him to the station in the Land Rover. "Thanks for this." Peered along the track. "Ah well, my cousins. Jeff blusters a bit, but he's okay. Tone's on edge. Fell in with a bad lot, he's in a spot of trouble. Got himself arrested as an accessory."

"What's his war record?"

"Record's good. A bit brutal. Not a bad bloke, really. Shows off, talks big."

"When does the case come up?"

"End of the month. At Guildford."

"If you can get the papers quickly to me, I'll do what I can."

Laister said, "Train's coming." Put out his hand. "That's good of you, really good. Everything's been good. Thanks."

Leith said, "We'll have to think about your father."

When Dick Laister got back to the farm, Tony said, "I thought your fine friend talked wet. With Ede, I mean. Giving the kid notions."

Jeff said, "Ede doesn't need anyone to give her notions."

"I thought it was okay." Laister poured himself a cup of overbrewed tea. "Tone, I need your court papers. Leith'll do what he can."

Edith said, "I think he's divine."

Aldred was home in time for dinner. His mother, who was stitching a black lace hem by the fire, looked up with pleasure. "There's hot water for your bath."

That evening, he wrote on the end of a letter to Helen: "Yes, I do tell my friends about you. Sometimes I also tell those who are not my friends—flourishing you like a safeguard, a talisman."

19

IT IS MAY, Aldred, and we've known each other for a year. And winter begins in the Antipodes, where I never could have imagined myself when I sat on your bed that morning of the terrible death, which was the start of our love, I think. And Ben and I had just come around the world, as if specifically to meet you there. A journey measured to the last inch.

My darling, we're installed now in this house. In a way, I regret the hotel—having got used to it, and having had my own isolated room there rather than being exposed to a household. I got used to its curry-coloured curtains, I suppose, and its mustard carpets, and to the kindly help who brought mutton and potatoes and blancmange, in the dining room, and extra blankets to one's bed. To the trams rattling past the central crossroad, and the total silence that fell at 6 p.m. each evening—except on Fridays, when shops are open late and I could go to bookshops—of which there are several, small and good.

The house is on a height, with mist in the mornings. I cannot say that anything is like Japan, though it may sound so. The rooms are fairly large, fairly sunless; elderly. A garden is shaded by trees, chiefly beech, and enclosed against the incessant wind by a hedge of yews. No flowerbeds, but many plants and bushes of the cool-flowering kind—fuchsia, hydrangea. Camellias have bloomed since we came, in streaks of colours such as I never saw. There are ferns, and bunchy groves where violets and lily of the valley will appear when September comes round.

Oh my dearest, will I still be here for that? How can this go on? And how can it change? Like punishment, being sent so far. Why are we punished, who have done no wrong?

On the sheltered north, where some sun arrives, a wistaria, bare except for greenery, is strangling a derelict arbor. All this gets some attention from Jimsy Frazer, from Dumfries, who does the neighbourhood gardens; and also from Miss Fry, who occasionally comes to sew for my mother and to make expert repairs to the mouldered curtains, furniture, lace mats, and even the carpets of the absent owners.

Miss Fry brings a hush. Swift at her work, infinitely polite, she no doubt observes us; but of herself tells nothing. A dozen ready sources inform us, however, that her name is Elinor, that she speaks French (which makes her a prodigy in this land), and that she lost her fiancé late in 1914. Near sixty, she lives with widowed mum in Kelburn, a suburb adjoining ours. Miss Fry has such a good face— handsome yet somehow bare, perhaps from giving so much unreciprocated attention. Spare, also, in build, and well dressed always, in one or other of two "costumes," as they're called: jacket, skirt, and blouse of subdued and Fry-like tones.

What she brings is not "hush" but calm. She's the best thing that happens. Also—forgive vanity—she notices me, and looks up from her work when I appear. No one else does that, here.

At evening in her room, writing her letter, Helen Driscoll was repossessed of her powers. It was the sole occasion of her exile: the hour preserved from, and for, another life. Distilled in that exercise, existence was emblematic in its materials: a pad of blue imported paper, a good black fountain pen, the envelopes marked AIR, for freedom, on which she wrote his name; and the tiny Florentine leather box with its flutter of New Zealand stamps. If the incidents of her days were weighed for possible recounting in the letter, that was less for their interest than as an opportunity for expression, even for artistry. A girl transported to the last curve of the globe might write what a great man would read at the self-sufficient northern heart of the world. The love that moved her then was nearly joyful, no longer victimised by distance.

Miss Fry's time was afternoon. It was Helen who prepared the tea tray and carried it to where Miss Fry, in an overall of ochre linen, sat at her work: always the small circular black tin tray, the white-and-gold Rockingham cup, and two ginger snaps poised like coins on the saucer. Miss Fry—who said, "Thank you, how kind," as the tray arrived, and "Thank you, delicious," when it was removed—one day looked up over a porcelain rim with delicate receptivity. Additional words came to be exchanged—though never, as days wore on, many words at a time; for Elinor Fry dealt with friendship as with some quick creature, lizard or leveret, that might dart from an obtrusive hand.

Miss Fry has invited me. Next Sunday at four, I make my way to Nightingale Road. Her mother is said to be a personality, though that, at Wellington, might signify the least quiver of animation. Did I tell you that I wore my green coat in the town and was stared at? In these islands, virtue begins with self-effacement, and any sign of life is flashy. Decent persons are home by six, when they too, perhaps, like the streets of their capital, fall silent. Despite this, there is, maddeningly, enough genuine decency to make dislike impossible.

I hear from Tad Hill, whose green coat draws such disapproval. He's back in America, and leaving the army. He means to study Japanese in California—he says, "At Berkeley." When he goes there to be interviewed, he'll visit Ben, of whom I have otherwise only clinical news. I write, but never learn whether the letters are read to him. Tad will carry a letter to him from me. Remembrance of that day when he was taken away, and of my last sight of him, has grown bearable because of what you did—for him and for me. Your impulse to rescue, that is the more beautiful, yes, for being part of your reserve.

ON THE SUNDAY, Helen set out in small rain, wearing a mackintosh and stout shoes that could draw no glance. Devoid of glances, suburban streets rose and fell over Jurassic slopes. No car or person passed. There was the indoor bark of a bored dog and a shake of drops from low cold branches. Weatherboard houses stood back from footpaths, insubstantial. Roofs of corrugated iron had been painted dark red. Behind low palings or a hedge of box, gardens laid out like military grids were unlikely to grow riotous with the seasons. Air of an uninhabited freshness rushed at crescents and inclines with its southern chill. There was, too, a southward vision of grey sea, and of the distant gorse-grown hills that shaped the bay. Across the strait, and beyond the flung skein of farther land, the matter of consequence was the South Pole, to whose white magnet the nation was irresistibly drawn, even while directing its yearnings elsewhere.

In the large setting, the city was small, rickety, irrelevant: unresponsive to destiny. And Helen saw herself creeping, Lilliputian, over that disregarded topography, walking to Kelburn without expectation of change.

Dreaming, once more, the only possible dream.

Near Nightingale Road, a cyclist saluted her. This waterproofed boy—who steadied a basket between handlebars—was Sid Briggs, whose parents helped with dinners. Cooking and serving, the Briggses also rented out for an evening not only tableware but, for a set fee, a centrepiece of hothouse fruit that could be returned next day with additional payments for items consumed by any inconsiderate or defiant guest. (The grapes, snipped and dusted, might do another round or two; while a softening of pears or peaches could be disguised by greenery.) As to parties, the father—in youth a boxer, and known yet as Tiger Briggs—would arrive early to set up drinks, while Sid, in the kitchen, deftly chopped and spread. However, it was Mrs. Briggs who ran the show, gave tongue, and cultivated her legend. Of short, pouting build, her liveliness ever within bounds, she had sized up the situation and was content to be a character—who knew, at the grander gatherings, what the Prime Minister would drink, and was mindful of the ulcer of the High Commissioner; who rallied to the greetings of Sir Keith or Sir Patrick, but never quite took a liberty—liberty being, to her, of small importance. A measure of power, benign yet attestable, was what she was after, in her black rayon dress, apron scalloped in organdie, and cuffs white as the paws of an immaculate pet. At home she recounted to her men what she had heard and overheard, and reigned in consequence.

Helen had observed Mrs. Briggs, as she was beginning to notice others who had exempted themselves from the national desire to belong elsewhere, even if this meant that they would never leave these shores. No one quite belonged here, not even the indigenous people, who were themselves invaders. The British experience was tentative, almost apologetic: successive generations remained, but as settlers. While Mrs. Briggs had settled conclusively. *Fatalité des lieux.* Her example aroused respect; and filled the girl with terror.

At No. 12, Helen pushed a solid gate. Chimneys were visible above old trees. Shrubs, still sporadically in bloom, gave place to autumnal flowers. The roof was slate blue, and otherwise distinctive—being large and high with fretted woodwork about the eaves. Upstairs and down, bay windows shone like mirrors, displaying curtains of white gauze. Not gaiety, but airiness.

And Miss Fry was in the doorway, mildly smiling and extending her mild hand.

Helen gave up coat and umbrella. She had not opened the umbrella, and her hair hung flat and darker. She had no sense, these days, of her appearance. At such a moment, could forsake her adult life, and was shy. Miss Fry, however, would not take up the slack of authority—as people are apt to do on their own ground. And they were thus briefly immobilised.

The living room was warm and waxed, and reflected the care of Elinor Fry. Charcoal briquettes the size of duck eggs were burning in the grate. There was expansiveness, a simplicity quite free of that cut crystal and walnut veneer on which the neighbourhood liked to insist. Chairs, a desk, a sofa, aged and admirable, came, clearly, from the great elsewhere beyond the seas. There was a large rug from the Indies. Glazed cases held the leather colours of old books. In a farther room, on open shelves, books lined a wall. Everything appeared to be in an agreeable state of use. On a table, a lamp was lit against the dark day. Overhead, a glass disc hung from three bright chains.

"You found Nightingale Road." Mrs. Fry had come, startling, out of a chair.

Her daughter explained: "Mother tends to materialise."

"So you've come to enliven us."

Helen said, "That wasn't made a condition of acceptance."

"It is understood." Mrs. Fry was a straight stem, flowering into a nimbus of white hair. When she sat, her dark dress spread on sofa cushions that were the texture of fine sand. Beauty, long since drained of erotic appeal, had remained a habit. "Whoever comes here from the outer world brings novelty. Above all, a young person and pretty."

"Mother, you're perhaps too personal." Miss Fry had taken a workbasket on her lap. In becoming a daughter, she had not relinquished character. And began, herself, to be beautiful now—the grey hair in its coil, the thoughtful brow and pliant wrist.

"You have unusual eyes, which is lucky, because the eyes last." Mrs. Fry's own dark eyes, now soft, now bright, had lasted. "I have my father's eyes. He was Bishop of Wellington, my parents came out by reason of his appointment. It was four months then, from Britain, on the sea. Whoever comes to these islands, even now, feels that it is forever. The distance is fateful."

"Mother, you will frighten our guest."

"I am frightened, yes."

"Like your own parents, mine came for a fixed term. But life will not always abide by such arrangements."

Both women had low, clear speech, unhesitating.

"My father had this house built to his taste—taste not being otherwise procurable. There were woods here then, we were in countryside.

I recall, on our land, a great stand of kauri that was felled, when I was seven, to make houses. Buildings were all of wood at that time, even in the town, for fear of the earthquakes. Strangely, it was only after the great earthquake, at Napier not twenty years ago, that they started in earnest with their concrete and bricks. Men," she said, "feel compelled to test their fate: to learn, once and for all, who is master. The lesson is not always to their liking."

"Where we are," said the girl, "it's mainly beech."

"Native birch, as they call it. I don't know why."

"*Nothofagus.*" Miss Fry was stitching a geometrical design, blood red, into a fold of canvas.

"The road itself was made after we came. And named, of course, for the heroine rather than the bird. Miss Nightingale was then still living; but died, mercifully, just before the Great War. Elinor is named for her—Elinor Florence."

Miss Fry observed that the name had been current in past ages but had lapsed for a time. "It was revived in the last century by English travellers to Italy. Such gestures were in fashion. Shelley himself gave the name of Florence to a son born there." She drew, with such elegance, new silk from a crimson twist.

"I was born upstairs," said Mrs. Fry, taking up her own thread. "In the room over this. The house had been intended as a second residence for the bishop; but my father loved it, and when his term was out, he arranged to buy. We stayed on. My poor mother was dying of tuberculosis and could not undertake the journey home. After her death, my father and I set sail, and this house was rented for many years." She said, "Elinor's impatient, having heard it all."

"She doesn't look impatient."

"And am not," said Miss Fry. "But will bring the tea."

"Sometimes she says, 'Mother, don't start on the memories.'"

"Only when the theme is painful." The daughter laid down her work. "There's Indian, of course, but we have excellent China."

"Thank you, China."

When Miss Fry had gone, her mother remarked, "Why not tell one's story? There are so few stories here, or perhaps a fear of telling:

the mere suggestion that one matters. I myself forget much of the forty years I spent in England after my marriage. In all that time I came here only twice. The voyage was so long, whether by the Red Sea or the Cape route. As it is still."

Helen knew precisely: six weeks, or seven, depending on the ship, the route.

On the waterfront there was the office of the Shaw Savill line. In a window on the street, black hull and red funnels made their stately getaway. People went in to get brochures, to enquire, to embellish the fantasy. Durban, Cape Town, Las Palmas—the pilgrimage known by heart to all the nation. So long, so far. Young people set their hopes on it, then began the slow retreat into impossibility.

Had it not been Sunday, had she not been visiting—in the house of these sybils—another century, she might have leapt up then and there, in her panic to sail.

Mrs. Fry said, "Don't grieve. You will change it all. Luck is always welcome, but you won't find it here. This is not a venturesome society. In any case, one must make the great changes for oneself or it doesn't amount to destiny." On this word, the house fell profoundly silent, as it would one day without her. In the distant kitchen, Elinor Fry made no sign. The old woman said, "Possibilities are open to you. What is terrible is to be entirely helpless under events, as in those wars."

To be trapped, a world away from him, by war. The press spoke, now, of war as if it provided continuity.

Over the mantel, there was a tall seascape, mostly sky. Helen looked up at this with eyes that, at the sound of private kindness, gleamed with private tears.

"I made the trip here alone, my dear, soon after I was widowed. That was early in 1914. The year having become an epoch, and dreadful, one forgets that it was largely passed in peace. Elinor was in the south of France. She had fallen in love with a Frenchman, a landowner from the Var, and his parents said, 'Stay.' So she remained. The idea was that they should come to know one another. The delay, in which I myself was instrumental, proved fatal. A decrepit old house they had: the *mas*, as they call it—handsome but not comfortable, like the man himself. Who was killed that October, at the Ypres salient. And Elinor stayed on in the Var."

Elinor Fry came back, impassive, with a large teak tray.

"How good, Elinor, the smell of that tea. It must be a new caddy."

Miss Fry, seated, told Helen, "There's an importer—"

"The only one," put in her mother.

"—on Customhouse Quay, upstairs, in a room without windows."

"He is quite concealed. Elinor found him through those people who rent out the fruit and flowers."

"The Briggses."

They all smiled.

"This man has paté and interesting preserves. Such small pleasures must diffuse themselves by stealth at Wellington. The Scots heritage is strong: mortification of flesh and spirit."

"Mother, surely an exaggeration."

"I am half Scots myself, and may say so. My mother was a MacPherson, from Fife. How good these patties are, Elinor."

Helen said, "Everything's good—a feast. High tea."

"My dear, not quite. High tea, to be correct, must include meat—pressed tongue, at the very least, or smoked fish. It should include, we used to say, that which has drawn breath. A piquant expression. Ham sandwiches can scarcely qualify, still less sardines. Our present cakes, too, are of a somewhat frivolous kind for a genuine high tea. All are made by Elinor, with the exception of the frothy one, concocted by our Italian maid and called *zuppa inglese*. Said to be modelled on trifle—if one blob may serve as model for another. Elinor, now we need hot water."

When her daughter had departed, Mrs. Fry resumed, "To have been on earth, merely, during the First World War is to have experienced Hades. Afterwards, everywhere, the climate of mourning. In France, where I would visit Elinor in her slavery down in the Var, it was a world in tears. It was that, I daresay, set me to thinking of coming home—not to this country, which was itself grieving, but to this house, which in memory had remained a shelter. I am saying, Elinor, that I put it to you, in 1927, would you come with me?"

"It was a venture," said Elinor, returning. "I was ready for something of the kind."

"Of the kind! A removal to New Zealand has no kindred." She said, "Elinor, however, had nothing to lose but the drudgery of staying where she was."

"I had learned to be of use." Elinor, in her composure. Not difficult, however, in her case, to imagine youth and wild weeping. Or her condition of having nothing to lose, in which the mother had been instrumental.

"She had remade that house in France: rugs, furniture, the very pictures, retrieved from ancient neglect. Garden, orchard—even pigpen—became beautiful. There was an *allée*, of indescribable romance, where peacocks walked at evening, going up at dusk to roost in the cedars."

"I had nothing to do with that. There were peacocks long before my time." The daughter reached again for her work, extending the smooth arm that had carried swill to pigs. "I never changed the growth of that path, which was sublime. As to the rest, the work was a satisfaction."

"She had learned to care for things." Some emphasis on the word.

"For their own sake," said Elinor. "Not from acquisitiveness."

The mother gestured grandly, in the first such movement of her hands. "Everything here is of her creation. Repair especially is her genius."

"I enjoy, simply, what is well made."

The mother said, "It is the need to love. Balked of love, women will turn to religion, to nursing, to pets and plants, to things inanimate. My daughter's generation was cut off from loving by the Great War. 'Thy sword hath made women childless,' says the Bible."

Miss Fry had the sewing box on her lap.

"In the dreadful aftermath, one found those women teaching in the schools, working in the hospital wards. For some, perhaps, life even gained in meaning, they were spared certain other cruelties. But that is hypothesis, whereas the denial of love is fact."

"But the men," said Helen. "It was the men who died." Her man, who might have died.

"They were deluded," said Elinor Fry, "by the craving for action. These outermost lands, in particular, promised no other experience, offered no other escape. They did not call it death, they called it action. Killed in action. Killed escaping."

The girl put her cup down, with trembling hand. "In Thucydides, the young men longed to see far places and couldn't believe that they might die." Helen, who had been indistinct, was recovering line and colour; her hair, having dried, fell loose and fair. She looked herself— the self that had been, and was yet to be. "All the youth of Athens was drawing the map of Sicily on the ground. In imagination, they were already conquerors."

And Mrs. Fry, but languidly: "In their thoughts, most men are conquerors."

Mother and daughter were thinking, with quiet sighs, The Sicilian expedition, the Dardanelles, the Ypres salient, the Somme. While the girl wondered, When shall I sail?—and in her mind sketched the map of the world.

The mother, with a second gesture, appeared to indicate the heavens.

Elinor Fry said, "A tremor."

Overhead, the lamp swung lightly on its three brass chains. In the grate, the white-hot eggs collapsed in ash.

The vibration, infinitesimal but absolute, passed through the room, and on, on through all the decorous suburbs: shivering some plaster, fracturing an ornament or two; and bringing down, in a parlour in Thompson Street, a dim painting of Mount Egmont.

"I should like something more," said Mrs. Fry, "but cannot think what it might be." As dishes were assembled, she went on, "We might read the passage this evening, Elinor, in Thucydides." Having closed her eyes as if to doze, suddenly said, "They are more frequent this year," in reference to the earthquake.

Walking home in rain, Helen Driscoll thought, I didn't enliven them: it was all the other way. Their world of women, the pure room, and how the calm daughter held her own with the swift mother. Although the bishop had been commended, husband and father had gone undescribed. Women's lives, suspended in the monstrous summer of 1914. But Mrs. Fry had laughed with the laugh of a merry girl, and Elinor had used the word "sublime." And the earthquake had been discounted.

She would write of it to him, that same evening. There was also something of her own: she had not expected to become curious at the end of the world, within her own suspension. She wished there were somewhere else to go instead of home.

She would be questioned as to the event, the house, the eccentric mother. To all of which she would reply, "Beautiful"—or with some other such evasion.

WHEN ELINOR FRY PUT AWAY THE DISHES, she sat again in her chair. She knew—Mrs. Driscoll being vocal on the subject—of the girl's infatuation with some public man on the far side of the world. She had spent some time considering what small alleviation might be made. The two women agreed that Helen, who had glimmered into life at the last, should come again, preferably on another Sunday—"A day," in Mrs. Fry's view, "when all need rescue."

If her daughter felt that rescue might be welcome on any day of the week, such concepts had long since become impersonal, unless in the case of others. When her mother said, "Let us not read tonight, after all, about the Sicilian expedition," she agreed, and took up her crimson work again from habit. Later, however, she sat with idle hands and thought of matters, noble or terrible, that were known to her alone. And of how, at evening, the peacocks parading in the *allée* were led by the eldest, the doyen, who would one day be supplanted, by a young challenger, in a ritual duel to the death.

When they roused themselves to go upstairs, as they had done at that hour for more than twenty years, Mrs. Fry remarked, "Perhaps, at this moment, little Helen is writing her love letter."

"I do hope so," said Elinor Fry.

20

AURORA had a close-fitting black hat with a turned-back veil that cleared her brow and touched the nape of her neck. She was squinting at the menu, not having liked to put on glasses.

Aldred said, "So pretty, Aurora. The men of Kenya will run wild."

"I'll report." She said, "On that subject, and since we won't see each other for three months, I might ask you—" But she faltered.

"Whether there is a woman in my life?"

"Just that."

"There is, yes."

"Will the wedding keep till I get back?"

"It must. There are difficulties. I've wanted to tell you."

"She's either married or very young."

"She's not quite eighteen. And lives, for the moment, in New Zealand."

"No one lives in New Zealand for a moment. Parents averse?"

"Very."

"Do you have a photo?"

Leith, bringing out his wallet, handed a small picture taken by Tad Hill.

Aurora said, "No one has a right to look like that."

They smiled, touched hands. Ordered food and wine. He put the picture away.

She said, "Will you go and get her?"

"I think of it every day. Time is supposed to pass, then she should come here." He said, "I also seem to have developed a conscience."

"You always had that."

For a while they spoke of her own departure. Her flat would be fixed while she was gone: a friend would camp there to oversee things.

She said, "Look, Aldred, I was seventeen when I married. It's true that Jason was on the way, but we'd have married anyway, Geoffrey and I. Also true that it didn't work, and that Geoff was a drunk. However that may be, one is surrounded by unhappy couples—divorced, separated, shackled together by children—who had the appropriate ages and were sober as judges. Brides who were photographed in *Country Life* flashing their radiance and their rings, and in their right minds. There is no greater lottery."

Other than war.

She said, "I can't urge anything, what do I know. Only that you'll regret it always if you don't, and that she'll have to die and reinvent her existence. How long since you last saw her?"

"Two months. She left Japan just as I did. We were together on her last day."

Aurora asked, "Will she have a baby?"

"No. We haven't done that."

"My God." Then: "It might have been a solution."

"I told you I'd developed a conscience. Aurora, she'd have been alone with that, ten thousand miles away."

He was extremely glad of her company. They were so kind with one another. He was remembering what he had never, of course, forgotten: that during their months as lovers they had spoken of having a child. He would have fathered Jason's successor. Aurora would not consider marrying: "Derail your life," she'd said. She was past forty, it was held to be dangerous.

She too, as he knew, was recalling these things. Which led her to say, "Oliver would not hear of having a child."

Oliver's son experienced, from labyrinthine love, indignation at the selfish father.

"It makes me feel old," Aurora said, "that we can talk this way. As if historic."

"No. Right and good. No one else can shed this light on us." He could not bear it that her hand trembled as she stirred her coffee, and he took the spoon from her. "Can I ask you this—if my father ever knew that you and I had been together?"

"No. You came with impeccable credentials, as Jason's friend." She said, "I remember, that day at lunch, when I met Oliver the first time, how you sat back a bit, realising. That was our real parting, yours and mine. I thought I would let you keep—" Hesitated.

"That advantage?" The only one I ever had over him, but mighty.

When they left, he put her in a taxi. They would speak by phone, she was sailing in two days' time. They kissed, and she waved to him, smiling through tears. He was going in the same direction; but, had he got into the taxi, would have gone back with her. There would have been finality—the ritual consummation, as with Moira. Aurora, too, had known this.

When he called her that evening, she said, "You didn't tell me her name."

He said, "Helen."

Helen. The pleasure of writing this name—and how glad I'll be when I can write it less and say it often. That's the most important of several things I have to tell you. The second is that I've finished my work on China and am busy with the section on Japan. All this will soon be sent for typing, and subsequently to the publisher— the whole being blessed by having ripened under Benedict's bed. The large part, on China, is as good, I think, as I can make it; but seems to have happened in another life—an effect due to your appearance on my scene, and to the terminal stage, which the world now witnesses, of the Chinese war.

I've been with any number of people, some of them lawyers. Dined with Aurora Searle, who has left for Kenya. When I showed her your photograph (by Tad Hill, near the stone garden), she said that no one had the right to be so beautiful. My fear is that others must see your silver eyes and hair, and interfere with my chances. I've discovered something about myself that disturbs me: that I worry a hell of a lot about things that don't happen. Was I like that in Japan, or is it the result of our separation?—that I cannot comfort you or know your days completely.

I beg you to send me other photographs. I'm relieved that they won't be taken by Tad, whose proximity to you, from California, seems on the map to be closer than my own by several thousand miles.

Berkeley is a university, highly regarded, where they have a school of Japanese studies.

Since you and I will probably spend time in Norfolk, I think of incorporating another room into "my" section of the house there—where at present I occupy what was my father's study, bedroom, bath. I would not bother you with these prosaic matters, except for the happiness it gives to envisage your arrival in a place where I already imagine you, at times, in the next room.

Bertram Perowne has replied, a fine letter from Yorkshire, saying that he'll be in town next month, when we'll meet. This is mildly complicated by the recent irruption of Hugh Calder, the Renaissance scholar whom you'll remember from Japan. (Ben gave him a lecture on Erasmus, on the day of our first meeting, yours and mine.) Calder asked me for a drink at the Ritz. We sat on a recessed platform screened by potted palms—where, by way of swank, I used sometimes to invite a girl in my hot youth, if I was in funds. Calder had his own proposition to make, which I declined.

It emerges that Calder, when not a don, is a government

agent—to put it plainly, a spy. He began this in the war, but has continued, less commendably, in peacetime. He offered to enlist me in the same business. Out of the question. This all has to do with my competence in the Wu dialects and with the Allies' desire, after Mao comes to full power, to track China's relations with the Soviets. It would have involved a period of "briefing," as they call it, at some clandestine centre in western Canada. I don't intend to live, or die, by such means. The near-assumption, as it's becoming, of a new world war is hideous to me.

His second, and harmless, suggestion was that I should shortly go to Germany for three weeks or so to cast an eye on our High Commission there, which is considered ineffectual. There would be nothing surreptitious about this, but it is again the context of Occupation, from which you and I have just been extracted. I don't know what I can contribute to such a survey, but agreed to discuss it. Nothing imminent, and you should continue to address letters to Norfolk. If I do go, the first proofs of my book should be ready for my return.

I told Calder that I intend to leave the army very soon, and that I hope to be married. He congratulated me on both counts, and guessed correctly.

If I make the trip to Germany, I'll speak to my mother about our plans before I go. She has shown me such affection since my return here and will be glad that I shan't now waste my life.

It's been suggested to me that I stand for Parliament. This idea arises from the everlasting medal, as do similar fantasies that I should join boards or sit on committees. All this strikes me as an attempt to lure me back to a future that I long ago discarded. A better use of the medal is that I can make small interventions on behalf of war casualties. An amputee who used to work part-time on our property should get proper attention and a better pension. His nephew, meanwhile, will be given an implausible last chance to go straight.

I fear I make it sound like a little kingdom here—distributing alms, dispensing justice, carving up supposedly ancestral rooms. It's new to me to find a home—or to find myself attached to it, even while I need my absences in London. Perhaps the same will be true for you, Helen, who've also led a wandering life. Not that we regret, how could we, our *années de pèlerinage*.

I'm glad to learn of your times with the ladies Fry: secluded authenticity of which you'll tell more. Your brother said that you need affinity. The Frys go deeper, endorsing love. It's good that you have such conversations, as long as they're with elderly ladies.

As Leith finished his letter, Dick Laister rang up to suggest Thursday for the drive with his father. Arranging it, Leith asked, "Would Edith like to come?"

"She'd be over the moon. We can pick her up as she leaves school."

Minutes later, Laister called back: "Madge says she'll come, too."

"No. Not Madge. Madge can come another time." Leith said, "Tell Madge that my mother will act as chaperone."

Laister laughed. "Good for you. I'll tell her it's not Bluebeard's castle."

AS THEY SAT DOWN, Bertram asked, "What do we call each other?"

"I only know you as Bertram."

"Better make it Bertie. We could spend a year or two being Leith and Perowne, but circumstances are against."

They were sitting by a tall window. Cars were passing. Bertram had suggested dinner at his club. Bertram was well but plainly dressed: lean, not tall; fair hair balding. Fine-tuned, fine-featured. All to scale except for his ears, which were large and arched rather high. As expected, his face was compassionate, and had not got that way without suffering for it.

He said, "Our trouble is, we only know of one another as paragons."

"In your case," Leith said, "I accept the evidence. Benedict said that you were Adam, naming the world."

"They would have named it without me. At ten, Benedict was a literary man. He was a beautiful boy then, when I first knew him, like some Dickensian angel-child headed for extinction. Fragile, but not yet stricken. His colouring—one sees it in Helen."

"One does."

"She too, they read together when she was a tiny tinsel thing. At kindergarten she was taken out of the classroom to read aloud to the upper forms, to show what could be done. Later, she used to laugh about it, to say, 'How they must have hated me.' I think not, however. She wasn't a competitor or a contemporary. In that country, then, she was a thing apart."

"A changeling."

"Yes, like Ben." Bertram said, "The older sister had started out clever, too. Got disconnected, turned on herself. A caricature of the mother. Married, by all accounts, an oaf. One can say, obviously—the parents. But they, too, had started vulnerable. Well, so it goes, and one can't keep on tracing it back to, let's say, Adam. There is that sorting out that happens in adolescence—some save themselves, some settle for less, others throw it away. Process as mysterious as art."

"I'm watching it myself, postwar, the unaccountable exceptions."

Bertie said, "Ben. They will never bring him back from California. They've been detaching him for years. His infirmity appals them. Driscoll himself wanted to be a champion, an athlete. His own father had been thwarted of a medical career, in a family without means, and was set on his son becoming a doctor. Driscoll qualified but never practised. The son, Benedict, was appointed to reverse the balance. You see how it was; everything went wrong except that the boy understood it all, and could live in his mind, and had someone to love and comfort him, who was his sister."

"And they had you."

"I had to play it very carefully, you know. I was there on sufferance, I'd come out to Australia under a cloud, we won't go into it, a question of preferences. When the war went into high gear, I still had connections, I pulled strings and went back. All that took time. However, they were looking out for me, I'd got a prize in mathematics before my fall from grace, and they had my name to go into the decoding business.

When I was on the high seas, dodging torpedoes, the Driscolls got themselves to Bengal. I was determined to keep in touch, and then, last year, they came here."

"Again, they had you, you did everything. I know the mother left them on your hands."

"It was a beautiful time for me. They were so excited, so responsive. My circumstances had improved, and I could be helpful. I knew I wouldn't see Benedict again."

"Nor I, now."

"I did the medical rounds with him. He was well enough, still, to go about quite normally; and we could travel. He knew what was happening to him, and Helen knew it as well. The parting, when I put them on the ship, that was a drastic day." Bertie said, "Ships have been prime centres of everything extreme. I daresay that all will be speeded up now, grief and joy included. The world accelerates. Takes the meaning out of it, rather. Which brings us to Helen, whose circumstances might be speeded up with no loss of meaning."

Leith said, "I've had a reply from the parents, to my letter asking that she be allowed to come here in the care of my mother, or by whatever arrangement they agree to. Absolute refusal, even faintly threatening."

"To put the law on you, I suppose—alienation, abduction, something of that sort. I know something of the law in these matters, and I can tell you that they won't and can't. They have some hold over her until she's twenty-one, but little that can be exercised in this context. They could make a public rumpus, your name being known—what one would do anything to avoid, for her sake and yours. However, that can be forestalled."

Bertie, dreamily, to the window: "Does the name of Lillian Geary mean anything to you?"

"Nothing whatever."

"She's a nice, plain, placid woman who has been the mistress of Brigadier Driscoll for the past twelve years, having travelled from Sydney separately to their various ports of call, Bengal or Kure, and being currently installed in a suburb of Wellington, New Zealand. Driscoll, on whom she oddly dotes, lives in terror of discovery—so far averted, though some hint was the cause of Melba's scuttling back to Bengal from London last year. In the straitlaced society to which he adheres, such a revelation would put an end to Driscoll's expanding career. I think that Helen knows nothing of this. Ben, I'm pretty sure, had twigged it. So there you have it, my dear chap. Middling situation, but not desperate."

Tad would have known of it: had kept silent from scruples of his own, or to spare Helen. Or not to pave the way entirely for the fellow contender. Or all of those reasons. Leith said, "I can't think of anything I'd less like to do than challenge Driscoll—blackmail him, in fact—and on such a matter."

"Naturally. However, I've been, in the past, called upon by Driscoll to get him out of tight corners on this theme. Lillian continues to be in touch with me. It will do no harm for him to learn that you are aware. Lillian is a dear, affectionate, deluded woman, much put upon, who would speak up for Helen. She's seen you in Japan."

"Not that I know of."

"Yes, a driver of yours used to bring Driscoll to see her. He didn't visit her in the official car. Then she'd spot you once in a while in Kure with the same driver."

Brian Talbot. Another one who knew how to hold his tongue.

Bertie said, "Helen should be sprung from all that. Young people like to be rescued. When she comes here, she can stay with me if she likes. I'm fixing up an old family place in Philbeach Gardens that got shaken by the buzz bombs. Plenty of room. I've also got this place in Yorkshire that needs a new roof." Bertie was pleased with his evening. He said, "The thing is, I've succeeded."

Driscoll had once said of him, A pervert and a failure.

"I had two older brothers, not that we were close. One died in the war, unmarried. The other, who had four daughters, has now also died. As a result of these matters, I've become the successor."

"Is a title involved in this?"

"Oh yes. I could have refused it, but my sister is keen that I keep it. Succession matters to her. My sister stood by me when I was shipped out to Australia, smuggled funds to me when she could. It was her money, and mine, but her husband was a brute and I was in no position to complain. If you're concerned about the family you're marrying into, think of mine. However, I'd like you to know my sister."

When they parted, Bertie told him, "You know, they're making Helen take a typing course. That's a life sentence. Perhaps you can put a stop to it. I don't see her in an office."

Leith thought of Aurora at the Ministry. It had not occurred to him, as they had so much before them, that Helen might need more from the world than their shared habitation of it. She might learn as she had already done. He could not envisage her intent on biology at Aberystwyth. But he said, simply, "She will choose, when she comes. For now, she only told me that she was seeing a French teacher."

"I rather think that's to counter the blacking factory. Her French is good, I taught it to her. She needs to keep it up. One of those old pussycats she sees, the one who does needlework, found her a teacher. She's made a friend there, in the French class."

"A girl called Barbara. The new friends all seem to be women, for which I'm grateful."

"She'll still need rescuing." Then, harshly: "The separation is fierce, at that distance. A death. I can testify."

"I'll see to that. My great preoccupation." His mother had said, Obsession—not unkindly, unless such a word is always unkind. Had said, indulgently, that she would write to Helen. Said also, "When you are forty-two, Aldred, she will be only twenty-eight." As if he himself could not have made the calculation; and meaning, The romance of it will wear away, she may look for it elsewhere.

He told Bertie, "I'm going to Germany for a couple of weeks, as part of a survey. I seem to be getting a name for looking things over. When I get back, let's see each other." As they waited to cross St. James's Street, he said, "As to rescue, I need not tell you that Helen has already rescued me."

"From what, precisely?"

"From becoming formidable."

"As yet, not entirely."

21

THE GALE HAD BLOWN ALL WEEK from the Pole, raising foam on the sea and grit in the city. On Friday it faltered. And the town, which had been obscured by dust and by the visible force with which dust was driven, reassembled itself into roofs of red iron and walls of buff weatherboard, and concrete buildings, called modern, from before the war. By Saturday morning, the south wind was felt only in salt gusts at the corners and crossroads of the town, where it was usual.

Helen, invited to Lowry Bay by the friend from her French class, crossed the town on an early tram to take the bus for the bays, which left from a shed near the station. Shops and offices were open until lunchtime, and the tram rocked behind a flock of Morris Minors and bicycles, striking, with ancient bell, its note of the past as it listed into the main street of the capital, where it passed the shops close to their tin awnings propped on dented poles; close enough to see stained linoleum in the tearoom and glazed buns beneath a celluloid dome, and to read the titles of books in South's windows.

It was radiant morning in the potholed streets. From intersections, you could see, beyond the quays, the blue harbour and white mountains, whose incommunicable grandeur might, for all the town seemed to care, have hung there on a calendar. Remoteness had generated a fear of occasion, and the populace clung to the safety of its small concerns, just as their forebears had clung to these islands, greeting them as rafts and spars in the wild ocean, rather than as destination. They had left their destination behind them, and could only re-create, here, its lesser emblems. Audacity had been exhausted in arriving at the uttermost point of earth. They wished above all to pretend that nothing had happened.

Aboard the bus, there was the Noah's ark of caps and cardigans, skirts and shirts. The mixture of sandy and saturnine, and a stalwart couple with Maori blood. And the fat child content, as yet, to be smothered in Mum's embrace, while the baby lay awhimper in Granny's arms. A man of thirty-odd had lost a hand in the war and held his newspaper with a device of metal and black leather. In the national hush, the rustle could be heard whenever, with a glint of steel, he turned a page.

Weatherboard straggled, fence rails suggested countryside. They were near the sea, and the bus trundled into gravelled depressions and swept, with its petrol breath, the encroaching scrub. Like pupils in a class, the passengers wished for unseemly diversion, if someone else would provide it.

So it seemed to her, parted from her best thoughts.

The hills, approaching, were bristled with thick gorse, with which the founders had reconjured Scotland: introduced for sentiment, it had come to dominate, ineradicable. Someone said as much, to the bus in general, for the gorse supplied a topic irreproachable as weather. And the public words stood in air, like skywriting, as if no one would exorcise them with reply.

Until a man with plentiful white hair half-turned his body in the metal seat and said, quite loudly, "It was the longing." A jacket of gingered tweed was buttoned to creaking point. "They were longing for their home."

All high-flown utterance was to be deplored, alarming as nakedness. As to the speaker, it was unclear whether he had distinguished or disgraced himself, nor did he appear to care—smiling with rather fleshy lips and with eyes of a clear blue unsuited to his age. Something carnal was not incompatible with sensibility.

He got off at a country crossroad. Helen, at her bleared window, watched him walk away on a dirt track, smiling abstractedly and slightly swinging a string bag of small packages wrapped in newsprint. Even so, there was the antipodean touch of desolation: the path indistinguishable from all others, the wayside leaves flannelled with dust, the net bag. The walking into oblivion.

At a tin shelter that served as terminus, Barbara was waiting. When she stepped out into sunlight, tall, smiling, and dressed in blue, people could not help admiring; and thought, She should be meeting a lover.

The two young women touched hands. They walked off on the earthy path, laughing not quite naturally, for they could hardly help being pleased by the momentary attention of descending passengers and by their own almost meritorious youth. In this place, too, the scrub closed in, but they were near a rise of handsome firs; and, nearer still, on their right, to the sandy shore.

"A man on the bus spoke about longing."

"No, really? Out loud?"

"Well, audibly—obviously." Helen added, "Only a few words." Meaning, This man was not a maniac.

"They must have had a fit."

"They went rigid." Recalling the man's pink sensual face, the white excessive hair and brows, the incommensurate eyes. Elsewhere, he might have been a danger to young girls. But here the Bush had swallowed him.

By now there was no one to see how pleasant these two looked in their coloured clothes, or how, in passing there, they enhanced the scene. They felt it themselves: the waste.

The Baillie house was backed by trees and faced a short pale beach. At the far end of the cove there was one other house, smaller but similar; and that, too, was painted "cream." Both built by the Baillie grandfather, architect also of a family house in the town and whiskered subject of an incompetent portrait in a civic hall in Tinakori Road. The

profession lingered in Barbara's father, who was a building contractor—
an easy-natured, ruddy-faced chap who drank a bit, made good money,
and was proud of, if baffled by, his three slim, articulate daughters.
Bruce Baillie would have been, elsewhere, a plain good sort; but the
great south wound was on him, as it was on many men of the hemisphere: the sense that something more was required of, and by, them.
His eyes, when he laughed, remained dark and glassy like those of a
Teddy bear.

Barbara's mother, born in Timaru, was distantly if emphatically connected to a signatory of the Treaty of Waitangi. Pale and heavy-lidded,
with a grooved almond of mouth, she sloped into sad shoulders and at-
tenuated limbs, and wore discreet clothes that appeared faded even
when new. Some youthful glow had been consumed in the obsessive
gentility that, without blazing, shrivels all. Though dissimilar, husband
and wife were never quite distinct: the shared error of their marriage
had grown to be a bond.

Too cautious to detest, Mrs. Baillie did, with some regularity, not
quite like. Mrs. Baillie did not quite like Barbara's connection with the
Driscoll girl—who had lived overseas but not in quite the right places;
and was said, by her assertive mother, to be enamoured of a grown man
met in India or Japan. To be in love was itself not quite desirable, was
not at all the same as announcing the engagement and having one's
photograph—demure, pensive, and misted by tulle—in *The Dominion*.
In Featherston Street, behind the Government Life Insurance Building,
there was a nice shop displaying fruit plates in Crown Worcester, and a
tea service with roses; and table mats, backed with cork, reproducing
English county scenes by Rowland Hilder. Standing one day with
Helen before this shrine, Mrs. Baillie had said, "I do feel that Barbara
should begin to gather a few things together." And the girl's silence had
displeased. Sharpening her argument, the mother had remarked that
French was all very well, but would do nothing for Barbara in the life
to come—an observation that referred neither to love nor to religion,
but to domesticity.

By now, the two girls had crossed the wooden verandah at the bay
and were entering a grotto of limp cretonne, rugs of grey peonies, and

rose-painted tin trays. Fronds of real Dorothy Perkins, intruding through north windows, partook of indoor dust. A reproduction of *The Laughing Cavalier* called for alignment. For entertainment, an old wireless teetered on cabriole legs, and folders of sallow songs were stacked on an upright piano. Books, in their single mesh-fronted case, came from the lachrymose or costumed past: *Anthony Adverse*, *Lorna Doone*, *The Prisoner of Zenda*. Outdoor smells of shrubbery and shore were no match for humid linen in warped cupboards, pipe tobacco, camphor, mildewed bread, and a slight leak of gas.

Only the presence of the three pretty sisters, all together, might have let in light.

In the kitchen, Barbara put milk in an enamel saucepan and spooned coffee from a canister. They took turns to watch and stir. Drops from the spoon fell on linoleum. A window above the sink overlooked a fenced clearing between house and woods, where spring planting was even now coming through. The yard ended in tangled shrubberies, and in the twin peaks of a compost heap and kitchen midden.

When the milk puckered, Barbara took a sieve, poured the mixture into mugs, and turned out the grounds in the sink. Helen had the better mug—uncracked, and marked CORONATION DAY, August 9, 1902— showing the royal pair in red and yellow: Queen Alexandra in pearl collar and satin bodice; King Edward incorrigible in ermine.

There they stood: sipping, munching. As far as the world was concerned, they might stand thus forever, in this or similar kitchens. Of that menace, both were mortally aware.

In the living room, light entered through diamond panes. They would read their French lesson. Each had a book in hand and was turning pages. Barbara Baillie, extending her legs on a sofa and imagining herself some third party, wondered whether she or Helen might be considered the more attractive. Decency did not permit an immediate decision in her own favour. Helen's case was curious: so small as to be insignificant, yet sweetly made, and with strokes of undeniable interest—and having, as to wrists and ankles, what the French called *les attaches fines*. Some broad clumsy man might take her smallness under protection, for men were, and wished to be, disarmed by mere evidence.

It could not be said that Helen's reputed condition of love conferred luminosity. Such passionate absorption inspired pity, or some fearfulness. It was only when seeming to forget her far predicament that she appeared original, vivid, and destined indeed for other lands and lovely times. Meantime, the months were passing, and the southern spring.

They began to read aloud what Barbara called "the famous passage," because their teacher thus referred to it: "The celebrated passage of the thrush." They opened their books laughing, but were soon decently engrossed.

Hier au soir, je me promenais seul; le ciel ressemblait à un ciel d'automne; un vent froid soufflait par intervalles.

Yearnings that were in themselves a consummation.

Transporté subitement dans le passé—

Declaiming such phrases in so remote a place, these women became not provincials but exiles.

They continued to read, by turns, for that magic—which, on Barbara Baillie, worked less consistently. She was aware of the discrepancy, but did not repress—even while raising her voice to crystal words—some thoughts about love, clothes, and a possible trip to the Bay of Islands when summer came round. For her, for her contemporaries, love was above all a release of tenderness—of which they had far more than almost any man could stand. Of transgression, such a girl had no conception; and Wellington was no place to throw over the traces.

For three years now, her father had annually promised to set his work aside and take the family to Britain: three months on the sea for the round trip, and three months to make sense of the blinking place. He did not expect to enjoy himself, but knew what was due to his position and, more obscurely, to existence itself: they'd have achieved that much, at any rate, and could queen it when they came back.

Again and again, disinclination prevailed. And when, in the third year, he renewed excuses, Barbara had asked—not, in that moment, a daughter, but speaking levelly as one person to another—"Won't we go then, ever?" he'd shifted, shuffled, and mumbled, "Course we'll go. Yair." Had stood looking at nearby air, and from time to time taking a palmful of dried fruit—raisins and scraps of apricot—from a bowl on the sideboard. The girl was sorry for him, knew he would be concerned for expense and ill at ease abroad; even that he dreaded the entire enterprise. But she'd said, "I'd like to have the chance," without comprehending all that this implied. Still examining vacancy, the father had replied, "Ar well. Next year she'll be right." Could not stave off a pang as he focussed on his girl at last and met her pleading, penetrating eyes.

He thought, The trip, that's one thing. But in the end she'll have to knuckle under. His wife herself, however she queened it, had knuckled under along with the rest, raising the kids and pitching into the ironing and baking and mending, the lot. For her, too, he feared the great round trip, among glacial persons with whom Waitangi and Timaru and the whole bloody Canterbury Bight might cut no ice. He said to himself, Poor old lass, fading a bit, and never any capacity for a laugh; but still with some fancies tucked away, mulled over in silence with moist eyes.

With women, disappointment could take the place of experience.

With this never out of mind, his daughter lolled among dank cushions at the world's end; swung a foot, twirled a lock of hair. On a low table, the mugs looked derelict, their stains and leavings. Putting Chateaubriand aside, Barbara observed, "No man here would stand for it"—meaning, Such ponderings, such poetry.

"They couldn't bear it." That vulnerability should make a man strong. That there could be thought without helplessness; without that very helplessness in which their women were marooned, as if, by existing at all, one had become a victim.

She would have said, I've known a full-grown man. But dreaded these death sentences that came to her as if from the perspective of future years: the antipodean consolation of having once touched infinity.

As if, in age, she looked back to the exotic evenings when she had bowled along in a chariot, singing about the Foggy Dew.

So they read from an anthology of wartime verse on wartime paper, lines from unhappy France that passed like spasms over the inert and wilted room. This in turn was put aside, and Barbara swung down her legs, of which she was proud, and proposed that they walk on the beach. The morning had passed, as mornings did pass there, with this and that. Later, there would be sandwiches and ginger beer.

At the shore, the gale was returning in grainy gusts that hurt the eyes and throat and set hair flying at one moment forward and then streaming behind. Speech being swept away, they could not use expendable words about the strong sea and the rough passage of the Picton ferry; each thinking, rather, of what had been read and said, and recalling the rhymes of impassioned love. When, in a lull of the wind, they lingered under trees, Barbara asked, "But have you known— abroad, that is—a man who might really talk that way?—'*toi seule existes*,' all that."

"Yes." And then: "Yes, yes, yes."

"I thought it might be only in books." Barbara put both her hands to her hair. "Oh, I would like to find out."

The sea had risen so high on the horizon that those watching it might imagine themselves prostrate on the shore. In an intolerable instant of life, Helen wondered in what fine street on the other, centuried side of earth, the passersby glanced at him, who was more present to her than this sand and harbour, and more to her than all the beautiful splayed islands of the Great South Land.

They walked on to the end of the cove, staying aloof from the smaller house there.

"That place belongs to us, but it's rented. I don't want them to think, you know, that we're hanging around." Barbara said, "My grandfather built it for his children, so he'd always have them within cooee. A good idea, or maybe not. But the eldest son was killed at the first war, and Grandpa died early, and the house has drifted."

"It looks closed up."

The house needed painting, there was a break in the verandah railing, and a front plot of garden was untended. You could feel the splinters in the wooden steps.

"Still, someone might be there." Barbara turned away, scrunching over a glittering rubbish of weed, shell, and tiny carapace, and chips of coloured glass. Walking back, she said, "We've let it for the spring and summer to those Fairfax boys. They come out from the town from time to time."

Two British brothers were at Wellington awaiting the return of their father from the Antarctic. Explorer-father had set out months previously, from the South Island leading an expedition, and would resurface at summer's end. The sons, meantime, were to experience the Antipodes. The elder was of an age, barely, to have served in the war; the younger might have been twenty. Here they would linger, figures in some legend, until the ice, melting, released their father. That was their nearly primaeval condition. The elder was writing a dissertation, of which no one had discovered the theme. It was not known how the younger passed his time. Rarely apart, they made a fine pair on the uneven pavements of the capital: well formed and well turned out, light-eyed and fair. Barbara's mother had declared, Two princelings. The ladies of the town openly doted; their menfolk, resentful, were cowed by a quiet show of self-possession, which they mocked in surly asides; and by the reality of the icebound father, whose polar tradition had been sanctified, at Lyttelton in 1910 by the fateful departure, to his death, of Captain Scott.

Helen might have liked to know what books the explorer-father had taken with him to the ice floes, and by what light they were read; to smell the reek of whale oil, and to learn whether, in winter, the sun rose at all. She had seen the two brothers one evening at the Majestic, where dances were held in a big blank room, darkly red, that also served as a cinema. The young men had been pointed out to her, and she had tried to understand whether, in their own land, they would have appeared as princelings or merely as a pair of pale-headed and impassive youths. With these matters in mind and her elbow on the viscous tablecloth, she'd watched them refuse dry sandwiches and swallow thin coffee in heavy cups; and rise civilly, to dance well, with each of the women in their small party. Meanwhile, her own coffee was cooling. And when her partner for the evening asked her to dance the hokey-kokey he placed her white saucer over the cup, to keep it warm.

Barbara said, "It's obvious. They made a vow, coming here, not to saddle themselves with local girls, not to risk life sentences to colonial connections." She picked up a pebble, as if to throw, and instead examined its markings. "What I mind is their imagining we don't see it." She laughed then, rolling the stone in her hand. "If one of them did ask me out, I'd probably go. Wouldn't you?"

"I might." From curiosity, or boredom.

"How funny you are. So indifferent. Anyway, when they came to see the house, my mother had them to tea. It was only polite, but did look pointed. Janet wouldn't show herself, Flora and I sat and smiled. Afterwards, the sides of our faces ached from the smiling. And Mummy actually wore a hat, the big white hat she got at Kirk's. In her own house, as if it were Windsor Castle."

The white hat from Kirkaldie's, flat and circular: a saucer placed to impede further cooling.

"They haven't asked us back. They've been lent a flat in town and are mostly there."

"Whose flat?"

"I don't know. I daresay, someone with daughters. It's in Buckle Street, near the museum." Barbara disclosed the stone in her palm, then dropped it. "Out of exclusivity, they've become mysterious and desirable. As women are supposed to be."

If Barbara were to wed a Fairfax, she would supply the spontaneity and candour. Realising this, why would some Fairfax not go on his knees to her? Such was the thought of both young women; so clear to them, it went unspoken.

Reaching home, returning to the sink, they spread mustard and hacked at corned beef. Barbara had brought, from town, a dod of cabinet pudding, and they ate in the living room on a seat by the leaded windows. They did not go back to their books: that aspect of their day had run its course.

Barbara carried the dishes back to the kitchen and splashed water in the slate sink, into the Coronation mug: ENTHRONED IN THE HEARTS OF THEIR PEOPLE. It was said that Queen Alexandra always wore that collar, of pearl or diamonds, because she had once tried to cut her throat. Probably untrue, the legend gave the private measure of such a marriage.

She looked from the window at the tumbled yard, which had been this way, with seasonal variations, ever since she could remember. She would have liked to rush, like the girl in a poem they had read that morning who ran to meet her lover in the street, under the rain.

She could not remember whether, for his part, the lover ran to her also; or just stood waiting.

When it was time to take Helen to the bus, Barbara closed the house against the wind. Along the shore, the sea rose, and combed, and fell heavily; and rose again, thundering, and again fell. The gale was bedevilling the furze, and the small house of the princelings was preparing to yield more of its matchstick decoration. Solitary, irrelevant, it did suggest the last obscure retreat of some monarch no longer enthroned: one could envisage the historic photograph. Unlikely places of the kind lay in wait for the deposed.

Barbara was recalling, not happily, how her father's brother, staying there with his family on a visit from Auckland, had broken the verandah rail during a balancing act. The girl liked her Uncle Doug, who was funny and kind. There had been other damage, including a broken toaster, and the holiday had ended badly. When they had all gone, her mother had sat in a chair and said, "That's Auckland for you."

The bus was there, taking on passengers. Helen found a seat to the rear. She and Barbara mouthed farewells through the glass, and raised their hands in a show of good cheer. When Helen looked round from the bend of the road, Barbara was still there, not watching the bus, but lowering her head submissively against the gale and holding down her clothes.

From the day's sensations, Helen could retrieve the solitude that never now completely left her. And was able to think of how they had read about the past, which was full of desires and dreams and delusions, so that the planet seemed entirely charged with human wishes, existing for the most part silently and in vain. She thought about her brother, to whom Thaddeus Hill had read her letters, and who would die without her. And of Miss Fry, whose talent had been spent in repairs. And of the mother who had been instrumental.

There was the climate of resignation, which had opened to admit her and closed behind her, and from which she must get up and go. Mrs. Fry had said, You must save yourself. She would write and tell him, I am coming.

She remembered the drive out in the bright morning, and how the white-haired man had spoken up for longing, and had gone away exulting for himself alone. It wasn't enough.

Among the passengers, she recognised the elder of the Fairfax brothers, alone and reading. The back of his head, and of his neck in particular, did not seem invulnerable. He might have been misjudged. He would sometimes raise his eyes to the window, to be reminded of his surroundings or his existence. By the roadside, lone figures walked bravely against the wind; and, within the bus, the same baffled acceptance of obscurity.

She would write and say, I am coming.

IN THE TEA SHOP ALONGSIDE South's, Helen sits alone with Sidney Fairfax. The hour, near closing-time, is not propitious for lingering, and the shop itself—its very walls, counter, and coat-stand—grows restive. The bookseller next door has already locked up and left. Due to the licensing laws, there is, in the town, no bar where they can sit and talk.

The spring continues blustery, reluctant. Far to the south, the polar ice is, to the souls grappled there, adamantine.

Helen and Sidney have come away from a film called *The Blue Lagoon*, about a boy and girl shipwrecked on a tropical island, who grow up in a state of nature. At the outset, these two are helped along by a third castaway, a kindly elder who, having taught them the rudiments of survival and served his cinematic turn, conveniently dies. Boy and girl, attaining adolescence, become lovers in all innocence, and produce a child. At the end, they are rescued and borne away to the clamorous, censorious, contentious world.

Sidney Fairfax says that there have been books and other films on the theme; that it is the old story—Garden of Eden, Adam and Eve, the Expulsion. The old mentor was God the Father, revealing the world and leaving them to it. Sidney is aware that Helen considers him over-ready with the obvious, and that the formula is his nutshell of safety and authority. He himself is inclined to agree, having always found his thoughts more original than his utterance.

"An open-and-shut case," he says, smiling. Tolerant of a common-place world that refuses to give up on sentiment. Sidney is becoming, literally, a philosopher: that will be his profession. While waiting at Wellington for his snowbound father, he will complete a doctoral the-sis: here is another man carrying pages around the world. He, the older of two reticent brothers, is agreeable. The younger, Gerald, is terse, reclusive, sometimes surly. That, at least, is the judgement of the capital.

Of the movie, Helen says, "The first part was a bit like my brother and me with our teacher." She has not previously mentioned the absent brother, but the background is known in the omniscient town. In the picture-house, she has blinked away tears.

She says, "I suppose that there will be no more desert islands. Only castaways."

He has met her just twice before, but believes that he sees deterio-ration: among them all, they will wear her down. (It wasn't in his na-ture to say "break her.") He knows, who doesn't, that she has been separated from an older man: that is no concern of his. He has heard the mother say, "We nipped that in the bud." Mrs. Capulet.

Helen says, "They'll poison us here if we don't go."

"I feel they already did that." They have shared one of the glazed buns. "There must be somewhere we can talk for half an hour. If we were to loll in the lounge of the Hotel St. George, would you be fatally compromised in local society?"

"It will be noted. But they do know me there, at the desk." Not that blame would attach to the gallant Fairfax; only to the forward girl.

They get up and Sidney says, "What a fine green coat." He himself is coatless, but wears a long striped scarf furled like an undergraduate's. Ruddy-cheeked, blue-eyed, longish-haired, shortish-limbed, and compact in body, he looks the student. But Sidney, who is twenty-four, has been a soldier in the Ardennes.

Under frugal street-lighting, they walk the chilly block to the hotel, where Helen is soberly greeted at the desk: "Miss Driscoll." It is agreed that they may sit awhile in the lounge, where all is brown, and where commercial travellers from Invercargill and Wanganui very quietly pass through, and toll calls are announced over a loudspeaker.

Sidney remarks, "They might have been less repressive. It's not as if we were asking for a room."

Helen laughs out loud, they both do, at the very idea, and they sit down companionably. Sidney says, "I was never so consistently aware of my position on the face of the earth, were you? Sea-girt, southerly, sundered. And my father so much more so, near the Pole."

Helen thinks "face of the earth" a fine phrase. Then, "Yes, the islands seem adrift on the atlas. There is our helplessness, even to register. I suppose it could be seen as floating free."

"My father isn't helpless. He has chosen. His entombment down there haunts one, but it's voluntary."

Helen says that Sidney and his brother have also chosen to pass, here, these months of waiting.

Sidney Fairfax says, "Not quite."

She asks how his brother spends his days.

Sidney doesn't look at his watch, but says, "At this moment he is waiting for me. At other times, he also is writing." Sidney now genuinely turns to Helen for the first time, seeing her not exactly as herself, or as a woman, but as the responsive being with whom he can share, in this brown place, a fragment of self: appreciating her. "My brother Gerald," he says, "is writing the story of his life. As he is a literate man, it has been proposed that this may help him recover from a breakdown of two years past, which is a factor in our presence at Wellington. His collapse had some origins in early bullying endured at school, but came on during his months of national service, in which he was utterly at odds with his surroundings and assigned to specific hardship tasks intended to make a man of him. When he foundered, in an episode that it would be hard for me to speak of, a medical discharge was procured for him, partly through my father's influence. For, yes, there is influence, and thank God for it.

"This achieved, Gerald disappeared for a time, having gone to live with an unscrupulous woman, the first woman in his life, with whom he fathered a child that did not live. He then attempted suicide, and has since been in a series of treatments, the latest of which intermittently continues here. All is precarious. My mother, who will come out, now, for my father's return, has been magnificent throughout and is now exhausted. It was felt that each should have a respite from the other. A curious outcome of all this is that my mother has taken up the study of Law. I had not realised that there are women lawyers—who are, as yet, few.

"My father, meanwhile, departed for his white entombment. It must be said that he could hardly do otherwise. Plans for such a gruelling expedition are begun far in advance—in this case, before the war was over. My father's withdrawal would have dismantled all. He suffered over this. He is kind, and was tender to Gerald in his trouble. However, in best and worst senses, it was in his character to go into hibernation at such a time. All one can begrudge him, perhaps, is the huge relief with which he must have greeted the first ice floes as he steamed south from Lyttelton.

"For my brother and me, Wellington has been our ice floe. I had my own reason to come away. When a life goes off the rails, the casualties are many. One grows by turns patient, even saintly, and furiously resentful. These fluctuations occur in rapid succession or simultaneously, and the habit of abnegation loses its interest. Like others, I turn to my work, which occasionally palls. I resent my broken engagement—with life, as well as to a girl. But this limbo is now best for us both, making no demands. It's right for my brother to go about a bit, to rehearse being normal. I have friends at the University, nothing exciting. We're giving up the house at the bay. Even in fine weather, it was melancholy."

"I remember." The sad, splintered place, the place of exile. She says, "What a cruel story. Does everyone have a cruel story?"

"I begin to think so. If one's lucky, the cruel part occurs within a better context."

"Do people call on you, at home?"

"Yes. Would you come, Helen?"

"Certainly."

"He needs company that isn't knowing or solicitous. Someone a bit odd is good, provided they're sane."

"I hope to qualify." Miss Fry would be just the thing. Helen says, "My own brother, who is ill, has been a strength to me."

"Next time, you'll tell me."

They go out through the lobby, Helen nodding, queenly, to the desk.

Sidney Fairfax strolls with her to the tram, puts her on board. Walking home uphill, he feels with certainty that it will not happen: the far man will not come for her: too long, too distant, too much discouraged. Those two, having had their dream, will never meet again. It is in her face, her fate. Everyone has a cruel story.

At home, Gerald has left the porch light on for him, and lit the fire. Such offerings can be deceptive, but are welcome. Gerald is reading *The Dominion*, but puts the newspaper down as Sidney comes in, and says, "For the first time, this evening, I miss my home. Is that insane?"

22

"Aurora, let me get you another one of those."

"No, truly. I just want to sit and look."

"That's what we do best here, spend time looking."

"It gives a different sense of the globe." She said, "I'm loving idleness. Sitting in the sun, which hasn't yet reached the marrow of my bones."

"I was the same when I first came out. Haven't thawed even yet, and it's been two years. Enjoy yourself."

She was enjoying it, the heat, hills, and colours; the flowered terrace, and the party. "Everyone's so kind to me."

"That's because you're a poppet, Aurora. Isn't Aurora a poppet?"

"Stay on. Stay forever."

"I'll think about it." Laughed. Thought, No.

"What was it, Pimms? I'm going to get you another."

"Aurora, there's someone who wants to meet you. Ray Harkness."

"I don't think I know him."

"It's not him, it's her. Mrs. Harkness. Another poppet. She lives near here, fine property, husband, two kids. She asked to meet you, she's here indoors. There's some connection."

Aurora got up. "I can go and find her."

"I'll take you, she's in the far room. Young and beautiful, like you."

In the far room, Mrs. Harkness turned her head. She was over thirty, perhaps; and beautiful, certainly. Someone said, "Husband's a cad. She bears up bravely."

"Ray, this is Aurora Searle, who's dying to meet you."

Peach-pale face, huge dark eyes.

"I am so glad." Slight accent. Some shyness. She did not so much shake as briefly hold Aurora's hand. "If we could have a moment together."

Someone said, "Secrets. There's a cosy corner in there, past the curtains. Look, I'll show you. Nobody'll bother you."

They sat on a sofa. Mrs. Harkness was simply dressed, in a pale perfect creation. She said, "I think that you knew the writer Oliver Leith."

"We were very close." Oh, Oliver, what scrape did you get into with this beauty?

"I saw that he died."

"It's the reason I'm out here. Trying to get used to that."

"I'm very sorry. These are the great sorrows: *i grossi dispiaceri*." Voice soft and truthful. "I knew his son, before the war."

So that's it. "Aldred."

"We called him Dino—first, Aldredino, then Dredino, then Dino." Smiled. "He used to come to my family's house at Florence. He knew me as Raimonda Mancini."

"I do remember. I knew him during that time. He'd gone to school with my son."

"Is your son here?"

"My son died."

"Was it the war?"

"Yes." And what if I were to cry now, what if we both cried? Why not? She too, I've forgotten it, went through some ultimate experience of war. "You'd like news, then, of Aldred?—and I can give you good news of him."

"I saw in the paper that he survived the war, and was brave."

"Braver than anyone."

"He was good to us in our first trouble, more than good, an angel. His father also, who sent us money when we needed it, although he never knew us. Does Aldred live in England?"

"I saw him in London a month ago. He went to China after the war, to write a book, and came back. Was wounded in the war, but is over it now, and things go well for him. He remains what he was, admired and loved."

"Did he ever marry?"

"He was married during the war, but they were parted and agreed to divorce. Nothing very unhappy, I think. He means to remarry. There's a young girl he met in the East, a romance. He was always a Romantic." You'll remember, as I do.

Raimonda said, "We used to tease him when he was stern. When he would conceal his kind heart. My family, we all admired him, he wasn't much more then than a boy, but already a man, the very best man." She said, "He was a bit in love, at that time, with my sister."

And what about you, Raimonda?—who ask about him with tears.

"And what about you, Raimonda, how did you weather the war?"

"I have two brothers living, otherwise all are dead. Gigliola died in the war, my father before it, and my mother just afterwards. We mustn't make each other sad. One of my brothers lives in the house at Florence with his wife and children, and is repairing it. The other is in New York, but will soon come and see me here. I have two little boys, and hope to show them Italy one day."

"I'll write Aldred's address for you." They scrounged around for pen and paper. "He's in Germany just now, but soon goes home."

"Will you see him?"

"Of course."

"Ask him if he remembers Raimonda Mancini."

My dearest,

I am in a small town in Germany. The town is the seat of the British Command and entourage. It is ringed by a barbed-wire fence, nine-tenths of the houses are occupied by our army, and the only Germans to be seen in the town are those employed by us. The surrounding countryside is pleasant and unharmed, but not exciting. What matters is the extreme futility of our existence. The only solid thing, which is the Soviet menace, makes us afraid and impotent. We talk of a western union, to give ourselves hope. Much else could be done, but will not happen. Possibly some crisis will occur, short of war, to galvanise the West. I wish I could think so.

I find myself again in an army of Occupation, and with less appetite than ever for the role of victor. Out of regard for your tender years, I shan't describe the forms taken by victory in the ruined cities I've so far seen. How, with the evidence before them, men can contemplate more war is incomprehensible and terrifying. It is also completely beyond the ability of people like ourselves to influence. I at last come to believe that, in man, the primitive prevails. My consuming anxiety is that war may seal you up in New Zealand. If war should come before I can reach you, I beg you to do all you can to get over here, where in spite of added dangers we will be together. My attitude to the war is puzzling even to myself: I believe I have become a pacifist, without any doctrinaire approach. Having had one go at setting the world right, I decline a second opportunity.

Forgive me if I frighten you. The better aspect of this is that we must begin our adventure without delay. My set task here has been extended, but within the month I return to England, where I'll immediately put things in motion to leave the army conclusively. I must tell you that I spent a very good evening with Bertram— Bertie, as he invites me to call him—the chief joy of which was talking of you to someone who knows and loves you. We are both anxious for news of Benedict. If I don't hear from Tad on my return to England, I'll cable him. Meanwhile, Bertie has been helpful in other and critical ways.

Although I made careful arrangements to have correspondence forwarded, it has been misdirected from Norfolk to London. Thus I am eating bitterness waiting for your letter. Helen darling, how I want and need and love you at this moment. How happy if you were here, how happy we will be.

The news from Peter Exley isn't good. He sends short letters at long intervals, and my main news of him comes from Audrey Fellowes, who is still in Japan. This, too, I'll try to look into.

Infinite thanks for the photographs, which are so fine that I assume the hand of Miss Fry, who does everything well. As they are clearly taken with affection, I don't want to think that anyone else was involved.

Dear Aldred,

Helen tells me that this will reach you as you return to Britain from Germany. I was in Germany on my trip back to the States: a grim scene. Less of a clean sweep than Hiroshima. I always felt, at Hiroshima, that the crust of the earth had been lifted off only to reveal more man-made horrors beneath. Even in California, I still hear the slurping sound that is a world licking its wounds.

My studies force the pace here, which is good for me and enjoyable. I've made some friends. I survey the post-war USA and wonder if I need new eyeglasses. I peer, also, at Japan from this side of the Pacific, no longer Tad Pinkerton who set sail one year ago. New powers are seeking new worlds to clobber: I might just opt out of that.

You won't, I think, expect any great news about Ben. I soft-pedal a bit to Helen, but to you I can say that the end may come at any moment. Everything is giving in, respiration included. His heart is laboring. He knows me when he is awake. Between weakness and sedation, that is not much of the time. Thorwaldsen does pay attention, but is full of jargon and furthermore lacking in some critical element of self-doubt. Or maybe all that's needed is a course in basic English. I'll cable you if there is drastic change, Helen also. The Parents will hear from Thorwaldsen, in such case. The time for reserving a phone call to New Zealand is, as you no doubt know, twenty hours in advance, with some abbreviation for emergencies. Long distance indeed.

I read Helen's letters to Ben. Even when he can't take it in, he gets the message: I know that it's so. You'll understand me when I say that I enjoy my times with him. I've been glad to be on hand. I love the little guy, and won't forget him.

Same goes for Helen, and—again, you'll believe me—for yourself.

Dear Aldred,

As you see, I write this from Hong Kong, where I'm back at the Gloucester. My brother is with me and a great help, although he must return to Yokohama in a week or so. News is not good, but could—as you'll see—be worse. Ten days ago, Peter tried to take his own life—a very ingenious attempt, involving pills, which was aborted by the Portuguese lady who visits him at Queen Mary Hospital and who alerted the staff in time. Morale not good, as one might imagine, and I thought it better to come here and lend a hand. Peter's parents have arrived from Sydney—perfectly nice people, who are naturally beside themselves and with whom my brother has been nothing less than angelic. The doctor, a trump, has also pitched in a bit with the parents, as have my cousins the Gladwyns—whom you may recall from that day when we all shared hard tack at the Governor's table.

The flurry of attention—the narrow squeak, even the materialising of parents—have possibly been good for him, if it doesn't all go on too long. I regard Peter as a casualty of war. Persons of sensibility have enough trouble finding their bearings without being plunged into fires not of their making. These observations are, in your case, *les véritables charbons à Newcastle*. He worries about his obligations towards the helpful Miss Xavier from his office, who has now heroically compounded things by saving his life. It seems that you had let slip to Peter some Chinese maxim whereby one becomes permanently responsible for the life one saves. When you're next in touch (and you'll doubtless want to send him word), you might let him know that you got that all wrong.

He's pleased, I feel, to have me here. This is a long haul. I'll stay around for a while to see how he goes on. Meantime, I should tell you that foundations have been laid for my putative house at

Big Wave Bay. It won't be ready for a year, which will be late for your wedding journey with Helen, but in time for the first anniversary.

I'd say—

Attend to your own life at this decisive and exciting stage of it. When I next report, we will all, here, have passed into some other phase—Peter, parents, and Miss Xavier included.

Do let me hear from you. I value our connection. With love, if I may send it—

Audrey

He wrote out two telegrams for Hong Kong. The text to Peter was longer than that to Audrey. Neither was extensive, both were plain and heartfelt. As was his own sense of emancipation.

He might have suspended his life and flown out to see about Peter, who had tried to die. That was the pattern of their long solidarity, their male comradeship in shared enormities of war. But Peter had been confided, for a time, to the care of women. Peter's emergency heightened the sense of Helen's. Leith felt, as if it were his own, her precarious hold, now, on the rim of the world.

Everything, other than his imagination, trailed in slow motion around the globe. It had been that way throughout their separation, the shared consciousness converging at some scarcely geographical midpoint of the known world. Leith was in London, and left a message for his mother in Norfolk. He reserved the call to New Zealand, which would be hours coming through; and made enquiries about the sequence of flights that would take him to Auckland. Having made these preparations, he slept.

The call woke him: "You have precisely five minutes." There came a woman's voice, neither Melba's nor Helen's. It was the housekeeper at Wellington, who said they'd had a number of calls but this was the first from Britain. Not understanding, he asked for Helen, who wasn't there.

"You heard what's happened?"

In great dread: "No."

"Their little lad in America. He died."

"I'm terribly sorry. When was this?"

"They had the news last night."

It was tomorrow, in New Zealand. "Is no one there?"

"They went to Auckland. They're going to America to bury him."

"Has Helen gone with them?"

"They went to Auckland, the lass along with them, to take the *Mariposa*."

"*Mariposa*."

"The ship." Surprised at ignorance. "The boat that goes to America. There's a sailing. The other daughter joins the ship at Hawaii."

Leith telephoned Bertie, who said, "I don't say, Poor Ben. It's dear Ben, extraordinary Ben."

Bertie knew of the *Mariposa*. His shipping friends might get him news of sailings.

Leith requested a call to Elinor Florence Fry, as she was listed. He explained that there had been a death, and received a priority of some hours. The operator, in her humanity, did not ask for proof. He thought of Ben's tender ironies at such affairs. He thought that Thaddeus Hill would meet the *Mariposa* at San Francisco.

Before Miss Fry could come through, there was a telegram from Helen:

Ben died this morning. Please ring me. My love.

And from Tad:

Will call you. Benedict has died. Love.

Miss Fry came on the line, composure itself: "How do you do, we only have five minutes. How did you find our number? I did not know there was such a service. Yes, in Auckland for the sailing of the *Mariposa*. But Helen will not sail, by her wish. Did you hear me? Helen does not go with them. Helen returns to Wellington on Thursday."

"I will have left by then, for New Zealand. It takes some days."

"Do bear in mind the Date Line. You will be very welcome here, Mr. Leith. We had asked her to stay with us, since she shouldn't be alone. But as you are coming we will not press her . . . We will tell her. You will be very tired after such a journey. If I may say so, very glad also. And she—" There was an interruption, then her voice returned, languishing. "Happy . . . if I may say so."

People unknown to him were favouring his cause, and hers; as if he had tapped into some undepleted vein of the world's goodwill.

IT WAS NOT YET QUITE LIGHT, as on the morning of their parting: the earth as yet uncoloured. There was no bus, no taxi, and he begged a lift from the one motorist at large in the city. He had never seen a serious town so still. Learning of the long journey, the driver said that he would take him to the door: "Nothing's all that far, in Wellington." Yet all was far. What she had told him: a hemisphere of skies and seas, a world of that, with the land a mere crumpled interruption. At the close, the clustered fragile wooden city, just as she described it, clinging to its improvised moorings.

An orange sun was rising in fresh and blue Pacific air, on the mountains and gorsy hills. He thanked the motorist, who said, "Any time." There would never be any other such time.

Leith unlatched the scraping gate and walked the mossy path. In this oblivion, the sounds rang out, clanging and scrunching; and subsided in eternity. But the place itself, the enclosure, was poised, attentive; and the man, trembling with such a delight in living as he had never known.

She was not—as his mother had been—standing on the steps; but asleep, awaiting him, in a swing-seat on the verandah. Dressed, with a rug about her. And he remembered how he had once seen her in her bed, and had imagined the putative lover who was now himself.

He said, "Helen," and bent over her and wept.

The moment came naturally to her. She had often lived it, after all, and sat up into his arms. They were nearly speechless, nearly asexual, not to disturb their great good fortune, while the rusted swing-seat gave out a series of iron-clad screeches and drooped beneath them.

She said, "Such happiness."

"You didn't sail."

"I felt that you might come." And if not, then never. "All this long way," she said, and cried for the risk they had run.

"I was preparing it, before I knew of Ben. Let me look at you. You didn't leave."

She said, "The *Mariposa*."

"Ben would say, Another Marseilles. You rescued us, Helen." There is no arguing with exultation. "We can go together, now, to Aix-en-Provence. Ben should have come with us." He stroked her hair. "You spent the night out here."

"I was afraid I'd sleep, and not hear the bell."

"And that I'd turn round and go back without finding you." He said, "Miss Fry was lovely."

"We can telephone her."

Leith said, "Later."

"Yes. She's so glad for us."

"We'll telegraph your parents." The *Mariposa* would not turn round and come back.

"You arrived in the dark. How did you come up here? The town must have been deserted."

"The capital was silent and submissive. One celestial chap with a car brought me all the way."

She said, "Oh, it's thrilling," and held him as she had once clasped her brother, to verify life. "That morning at Kure, you said, 'Are these your tears or mine?' " The sun was up, and she said, "Let's go in. You'll be exhausted. Do you want to eat something?"

"No."

She got up, trailing her blanket and setting up an exhausted croaking in the swing. There was a screen-door, creaking, and a wooden one, warped. They stood in the musty hallway, and she put her hands to his face, saying, "We are older."

"We began to age, that morning in Japan. The worst day." And you've grown up, Helen, in all the hours between. He laughed. "Yet we would know each other anywhere." He said, "Helen, how we need each other."

She said his name. "Now it will be complete. It will come true." She asked, "Do you want to sleep?"

"No. I want to live these hours to the full. Will you lie down with me?"

"Yes. That day, you said that we should be alone and safe and beautiful, and with time."

"And how I've regretted them since, my lofty words. Regretted them in that hour. Are you afraid?"

"No." She said, "My bed would be best, where I've so much imagined you."

Tracing his face with eyes and fingers. "We will know each other differently now." So this itself is a farewell. "What are you thinking?"

"Of how easily I might have died, while this was forming, waiting, all unknown."

Even to her, he would not say outright that he was thinking of death: of the many who had died in their youth, under his eyes; of those he had killed, of whom he'd known nothing. On the red battle-field, where I'll never go again; in the inextinguishable conflagration.

These hours would be lived to the full. Years of hours would follow, but not this. He had felt their chance passing; she too, in fear. For this he had travelled to the airy, empty harbour where, like a legend, she lay in a mildewed swing-seat, waiting. As surely as if she had leapt from a planked deck into the ocean and swum ashore, she had jumped ship for him. Ten thousand miles had been retraced, down to the final fleshly inch where he could wake and touch her, and say her name.

Many had died. But not she, not he; not yet.